Love for

Optioned for film!

***Love & Lobsters* is a love letter to the people
who raise us, to the land that shapes us,
to the community that saves us,** and of course,
to those brave enough to fall in love, and to be loved."
~ Rebecca Podos, award-winning author of *Like Water*

"Wow! **Incredible!**"
~ Shannon's mom

"A beautiful, big-hearted tribute to love in all its
forms—I can't stop thinking about this book.
Wonderful, swoony, and sweet in all the right ways,
you'll be smitten with Christmas Cove!"
~ Amber Smith, *New York Times* bestselling author of
The Way I Used to Be and *The Way I Am Now*

"A generous, charming, and moving story of love, land (and sea),
and leaping into the unknown. **Readers will savor Charlie's
honest, brave (and sexy!) journey!**"
~ Kathleen Glasgow, #1 *New York Times*
bestselling author of *Girl in Pieces* and *The Glass Girl*

"**A heart-skipping small-town love story** with tight
pacing, captivating prose, and memorable characters."
~ Kirkus Reviews

First Riveter paperback edition October 2024
Text copyright ©2024 by Shannon M. Parker
Cover illustration copyright ©2024 Shannon M. Parker
Cover design by Alexandra Norman

Created in the United States of America

Names: Parker, Shannon M., author
Title: Love & Lobsters / by Shannon M. Parker
Library of Congress Control Number: 2024916491

Description: First paperback edition | Riveter, 2024 |Damariscotta, Maine
Summary: "Female lobsterman Charlie Pinkham has always been more comfortable braving the bold Atlantic rather than diving into the messy business of romance. When she writes a post for her bestie's Happily Ever Holidays blog, Charlie's decidedly unromantic piece goes viral, and Charlie must determine if plunging into uncharted waters is worth the risk."

Identifiers: LCCN 2024916491 | ISBN: 979-8-991-3069-04 (ppbk)
Also available in ebook!

Also by Shannon M. Parker

The Girl Who Fell

"An invaluable addition to
any collection." ★
~*School Library Journal*,
starred review

"WOW!"
~*The Guardian*

The Rattled Bones

"The feminist ghost story
you've been waiting for."
~*Bustle*

"Wondrously compelling."
~*Portland Press Herald*

for my mom, for everything

The Cove

For most people, Christmas is a day. For me, it's a place. The only home I've ever known.

The tranquil, coastal village of Christmas Cove, Maine is a well-kept secret. To be fair, I'm playing fast and loose with the term *village* as I free my limp braid from under my wool beanie and throttle my lobster boat through the waves and toward home. In truth, Christmas Cove doesn't have shops, a Main Street or…well, village amenities of any kind, really. Here, life exists at the end of a twelve-mile peninsula, where a perfectly round harbor is perched at the edge of the world. Beyond the harbor, a salt river meets the sea and the sea meets the sky like poured eternity. Not a bad place to call home if sleepy hamlets are your jam. And a sleepy hamlet that needs to be combined with two adjacent sleepy hamlets to constitute an actual town for census purposes? Well, that's my Happy Place, population 1,267.

Just one peninsula to the east of Christmas Cove is Boothbay Harbor with its internationally famous ice cream shops, boardwalks, ocean view restaurants, and whale watching tours. But that bustling metropolis is a whole seven miles away by boat—thirty by car. Boothbay's seasonal bloat of visitors jams up summers with long lines, rushing tourists—and worse, slow tourists—parking so scarce it's an endangered species, crammed restaurants, and a swell of pretentious attitudes. In winter, the town is practically boarded up, shop owners migrating alongside 75% of Maine's bird population as they head south toward a milder climate.

For residents of Christmas Cove, our sensibilities lean toward the self-contained. Inherently, we're a practical people, and we stay close to home, and close to big nature. Trees far outnumber people on this peninsula where I was born and raised. Tall, old growth spruces stand like guardians, buffering the harbor and our homes with an evergreen curtain that inspires fancy travel magazines to refer to Christmas Cove as a "hidden gem," which is a much nicer term than the names locals call tourists.

Today, my boat's battling December wind as gulls glide above, squawking over my catch as I round Little Heron Island and steer toward Christmas Cove where my family's stout and sturdy sparkplug lighthouse comes into full view. Decommissioned in the eighties because its lens needed repair—and technology had made its guiding light obsolete—I've never seen the beacon shine during my twenty-nine years. Still, every time I pass Cove Light, I swear it flickers for me. Just a wink—the sun catching the glass in the round lantern room even on late winter afternoons like today when the sun is low and slow in its retreat to the other side of the world. I like to think the sparkle bouncing off the glass is a hardy hello from the Pinkham women who came before me, like Memma's mother (my great grandmother), and her mother's mother, the original station keepers of Cove Light. Built by the state upon a long stretch of dark granite that spreads into the sea and beneath a thin blanket of waves, the lighthouse is now a rental cottage. You know, for tourists.

At the helm, I lean forward, my sharp hip pressing against the wheel like I'll get to Memma and home faster if I push my whole body toward my destination. I realize this small, impatient action doesn't actually increase my speed, just as I'm aware that sucking in my breath when passing under a tight bridge doesn't make my boat any narrower. Still. There's no one out here to tell me I'm ridiculous, which, factually speaking, makes me slightly less ridiculous.

I shove my glove-fattened fingers into the front pocket of my rubber overalls to free my flip phone and let Memma know I've returned from fishing just as static wakes my dash-mounted VHF radio.

"*MerSea* to *BlueBug*," Maia broadcasts through the two-way transceiver, her voice threaded with a low hum. "Find me on eleven."

I smile at Maia's signature best friend assertiveness and slow my speed before making the familiar switch to the private radio channel. The round harbor grows wider before me. Its water is nestled within the horseshoe bend of the coastline where a few brave boats nod in the cold, slack current, their pointed white hulls huddled as close as old men in a coffee shop exchanging gossip. Though my windshield's caked with icy spray from the open ocean, a porthole of defrosted glass allows me to take quick inventory of the cottage I share with Mem. Directly across the harbor is Maia's little pink house that appears to be perched in the trees from this angle. The oversized picture window in her living room shows me Maia's nervous energy pacing her back-and-forth, as if she's forced to report ten thousand steps to her bossy watch in the next seven seconds.

"How was the trip?" Maia asks, sounding winded. "Wet and smelly?"

I depress the button on my transmitter mic. "Basically."

Maia isn't wired to care about the lobsters I haul or how many miles offshore I need to travel to trap them this time of year; she's more concerned with my safe return, even though it's a worry she won't discuss out loud, particularly on the VHF. Fishermen are a superstitious bunch. Maia is next level.

"Did you check on Memma?" I thrust my engine to neutral and my boat bobs in the swells, the wind turning me toward Maia, my true north.

"She's at the diner playing Scrabble. She's *fine*, Charlie."

But is she?

Because how would we even know?

Memma had been doing *just fine* before she fell on our gravel path during an otherwise completely forgettable Tuesday nearly one year ago, mere moments after beginning her day with a polar plunge, that same vigorous morning dip she'd used to start her days for more than sixty years. The stumble sent us to the emergency room where the doctor explored the wounds to Memma's hands and wrists after they broke her fall. He studied the contusion in the center of her forehead and maybe it was the bright examination lights of the hospital room, but I finally saw the other bruises, too. Discoloration marred Memma's forearms, thighs, her calves and ankles. The short hospital gown exposed so much of her I hadn't noticed. How hadn't I noticed?

When the second doctor arrived, I was in full battle mode, ready to take on the person who'd been hurting my grandmother. But nothing would have prepared me for the real culprit. Acute Myeloid Leukemia. The diagnosis was so impossible, so far-fetched, so absolutely not the way things were supposed to go that I knew the doctor was wrong. She had the wrong chart. The wrong patient. The wrong next of kin.

But, no.

Mem's blood had turned on her. That was the *Diagnosis for Dummies* abbreviation I still have a hard time wrapping my head around. Dad had raised me to honor the ocean that ran through our Pinkham blood, but somehow, in the pockets of life where I wasn't paying attention, Mem's blood had drained enough of the sea to make room for leukemic cells. And at seventy-three she had a two percent chance of survival with treatment. For four weeks, the doctors pumped poison through her veins and she shrank into a skeleton as I sat and slept and lived in the chair next to her hospital bed.

On her twenty-eighth day of care, my mem woke clear-eyed and quick-witted. Her smile was easy, her laughter full. She fussed with her feeding tube. Asked if we could watch *Jeopardy*, and when I'd be springing her from the prison of her room and tubes and illness. When the overnight nurse began her shift, she warned me to be careful with my joy, and my expectations. It was common for patients to display a surge of wellness before they passed. This was often the pattern of death, she'd said. One final gift of life before it ended.

She was wrong. She had to be.

I returned to Memma's bedside, her closed eyelids twitching, the skin there fragile and thin and blue as she slept.

"You can beat this," I told my grandmother with the simple, straightforward Yankee pragmatism she'd raised me on. Like when my dad didn't return home from fishing when I was nine, and Mem promised me I could weather any storm, no matter how terrible.

She stood behind me then, gripping my young shoulders during Warren Sproul's late night visit all those years ago, his wool hat at his chest as he stood in our kitchen, telling us he'd rescued my father's boat and body. How he'd discovered him in calm seas, my dad on his back on the deck, his face to the sun, his arms and legs spread wide, as if his body's last act on earth had been to remain open to the possibilities of the vast elsewhere beyond.

Mem kept me safe then. And after, when the entire village mourned my father, every home forgoing the use of electricity to drape the cove in darkness. Boats were silenced, too.

Maybe it was superstition, but no one wanted our earthly light to obstruct the soul of the deceased on its journey away from life.

There was too much we didn't know about the ocean and the afterlife so our village treated them both kindly, treading lightly, showing stewardship and love. In the darkness people made space for grief, all of us living close with death as we lived by the deep.

Mem had been the one to break the news of how my mother had returned to her people in Tucson, before Dad's funeral, before saying good-bye. My mother couldn't stay near the salt and the sea and the sadness anymore, and Mem promised me she'd be my mother, father and memma all at once. And she was.

So, at her bedside with all the life-monitoring machines beeping and watching, I asked Mem to pull up her inner grit the way she'd taught me.

She did.

Somehow, miraculously, Memma survived the tubes and transfusions and toxic treatment. Two percent can look like the smallest number in the world until someone you love lives inside that statistic, and then it is a figure filled with hope and wonder and infinity.

It's been months since she returned home to the cove, post recovery, post physical therapy. She's thinner but just as spry. Like cancer was a hiccup, a blip, something that happened before breakfast. For me, the threat of her illness returning lurks like a hazard just beneath the surface of the sea, a catastrophic peril my internal radar can't stop scanning for.

"Hello?" Maia pulls my attention back to the VHF and the inky harbor where fog gathers a handful of harbor seals to the cold, granite ledge at the base of the lighthouse.

"So, tonight?" Maia says.

"Fine, yes."

"Do not *fine, yes,* me, Charlie Pinkham. Are you even listening?"

"Not entirely." Not even remotely.

"Grr," Maia growls—an actual, legit growl that snarls over the surge and static. "I'm freaking out about the missing post, remember? For December's blog feature."

"Of course I remember." I was hoping she'd forget.

Maia is the proud owner of *Mer*/Sea, a fabulous lifestyle company with a blog devoted to trends inspired by the Atlantic. In all honesty, I'm not entirely sure what a blog is or even why a blog is. For a hot second a decade ago, when we were young and trying on freedom and college for size, I attempted to decipher Maia's dialect of *driving traffic* and *content marketing* and *social media shares,* but quickly zoned out, my brain limited to understanding concepts my hands can touch, feel, manipulate. Now, my participation in Maia's lifestyle brand generally consists of affirming head nods, redirects, and lots of praise. Mostly because, at my core, I'm ill-equipped to comprehend what a lifestyle is, seeing as I barely have a life.

Yesterday, Maia was panicked about an ocean kayaking guide who immerses participants in forest bathing on remote Maine islands. The guide had bailed, leaving Maia one contributor short for her annual *Happily Ever Holidays* blog—a series that features a Maine entrepreneur's festive, romance-y post about their artisan industry.

"Have you given any more thought to writing a piece for me?"

"I have."

"And?"

"And I'm convinced your interest is misguided. I know as much about happily ever afters as I do about blogs."

"You know the sea and you know me—I'm your happily ever bestie. Come on, Charlie."

"You really cannot find anyone else? Martha Stewart? Erin French?" Maia had Oprah contribute to one of her themed series two years ago. Seriously, Oprah.

"Martha and Erin are already contributing."

I bark out a laugh that's disturbingly similar to a seal yelp, harsh enough to bruise the air and verify I'm hardly a dignified *content provider.*

"Come on, Charlie. You were a mad talented writer in college."

"Ha! For two seconds before we bailed on our first and only semester."

"Whatever. You loved writing."

"I loved writing in my journal about how much I hated being away from the peninsula."

"Fair, but I wouldn't ask if I didn't believe in you. And I need you."

I depress the transmission button. "If you need me, I'm in."

She revels in my acquiescence even though we both knew it was coming considering how Maia's been my ride-or-die since kindergarten when I peed in my school-new pants while all the other kids were busy being normal and dry on the red, alphabet circle rug.

Maia held my hand as she led me to the in-classroom bathroom, offering me my choice of the three pairs of clean leggings she'd packed. Then she took me to her cubby stocked with a second pair of shoes, one shirt, a sweater, a baggie of spare hair ties, a granola bar, and two different colors of nail polish. Yep, two. (For art projects and in case her nails got bored, naturally.) When Billy Williams poked fun at me and the wet pants Maia rolled into her repurposed hair tie baggie, she walked right up to him and had words. Billy Williams was a mountain of a kid, twice her size at least, and looked as if he'd already failed a few grades, but Maia shut him up without even raising her voice. To this day, I still don't know what she said to our classroom bully, but it's never mattered. I learned a lesson in fierce loyalty that day, and it's a gift I've never taken for granted.

"I did have an idea for a post," I admit.

"Yes! This pleases me."

"It shouldn't. My topic quickly descended into cannibalism."

"Cannibalism for Christmas? I *am* a fan of alliteration."

"Everyone's a fan of alliteration, but that isn't my working title."

Maia's prolonged silence sounds as if her busy life as a mom of two is pulling her interest somewhere other than our conversation.

The current pushes me toward the strip of land that separates the harbor from the ocean, where my family's cottage and lighthouse are perched. The cottage is small and shingled, largely unremarkable amidst the tall, lodgepole pines. It's our family's lighthouse that gets all the attention. Only fifty feet from the cottage, Cove Light sits at the outermost point of Christmas Cove. It stands at attention along a sheer spread of rock that spills into the ocean, the granite's end arched in a permanent dive, looking like a humpback returning to the deep. Directly across from my family's side of the cove is the village, complete with a town common and local shops and a one-lane paved road that leads to larger towns and bigger cities. A car turns off that road now, heading down our private drive.

"I say run with your idea." Maia's voice sounds distant with distraction. "I'm sure it will be amazing."

"You know what's weird?"

"In general? Or right now?"

"It's weird you're not disturbed by the fact that the subject of my article shifted so quickly to cannibalism."

"Let's be real." Maia's tone is easy over the wire now, like she trusts that I've got this.

I definitely do not got this.

"Isn't every conversation one comment away from being about cannibalism?" she says.

And that, right there, is why Maia is my forever favorite person.

"Oh, and Charlie? It's not an article; it's a blog post. Get over yourself."

I laugh.

"By tonight," she adds. "I'll give it a quick read and edit before posting, okay?"

"It's okay adjacent."

"Excellent!" She pauses. "Hey, I think you've got a visitor." I can practically hear the squeak of her hand as she cups it against her window.

"Maybe my rental guest?"

"Which is great since you love when people arrive early. I forget. Is it your *favorite thing* for people to be pre-punctual or your second favorite thing?"

"You're hylarical." I duck my head beyond the pilothouse to see a man exiting his car, stretching his arms high above his head and shifting one knee into tree pose. In this part of the world, women and men work eighteen hours on the sea and barely give their shoulders a stretch, but this guy's feeling tight after a little drive north from—I squint to read the license plate—Rhode Island? Perfect.

"My, my," Maia says. "He's sporting quite the puffy puffer jacket."

"Ga-reat." My eyeroll is nearly audible.

"Oh, right! Pre-punctual dudes who do yoga in puffy jackets are your favorite thing." She laughs. I do not. "Don't forget: tourists think cranky Mainers are kitschy and cute until they have to deal with one in the wild so be nice."

"Reminding me to be nice? Nice."

"Ha! Well, you can be scary to the unacclimated. Hey…" Her voice lowers toward conspiracy. "Is it me, or might your renter be cute under all that pufferwear?"

Legally, Maia shouldn't be using a land-based VHF unless she's checking in on the business needs of my vessel. The two-way radio license is granted to her husband's volunteer work as the controller of the harbor. "Don't make me report you for illegal radio use."

"Oh, that's good!" she says. "You should write your post about how much you love rules and regulations and maritime law. My readers will love that!"

"Is that a dare?"

"No! It is definitely not a dare. Do not take that as a dare, Charlotte Pinkham."

Driving Maia to the point where she feels compelled to use my full, legal name gives me a secret thrill. Every time. Clinical therapy would likely reveal how this odd excitement is rooted in my motherlessness, but it makes me smile all the same. "I need to go."

"Tell me if he's cute."

"Will do. Right after I give you the full report on his stunning wife."

2

The Cordiality

After signing off with Maia, I hang up the mouthpiece, dock my boat and shut down my electronics. December air bites at my wet hands, my fingers sore from bullying hard, frozen rope to set traps since before dawn. I blow into the pocket of my palms as I disembark, my body turning inward against the blistering wind as I make my way along the dock, up past my house to the lighthouse where Pufferfish Man stops circumnavigating Cove Light to wave at me with too much enthusiasm. I return a short wave, clocking his leather dress shoes, blazing red earlobes, and general overeagerness.

I give him a week. Two, tops. Confined spaces and winter-induced cabin fever have a way of turning people into a version of themselves that makes Stephen King movies look like cartoons. There's no way he'll last the month he and his wife rented the lighthouse for. A not small part of me expects the wife to exit the car in stilettos.

"Logan?" I call over the wind.

"That's me."

I approach, extend my hand, noticing how the car is empty, the seats spotless. "Charlie. Charlie Pinkham."

His head tilts sideways. "You're Charlie?"

"I am."

"I guess I was expecting a man."

"An overrated expectation in my experience."

His mouth turns up at the side in a smile and he meets my outstretched hand, shakes it. His grip is firm, but not tight, and he lets go first—a sign of good character, according to my dad.

Maia would want me to notice how he's easily got a few inches on me, which isn't typical since I'm five foot nine. He's probably in his early thirties. Wisps of blonde hair peek out from under the lip of his slouchy hat, and is there gray in his facial scruff? Maia will definitely want the details about how his fair skin comes as a package deal with apple red cheeks that look sweet enough to bite. I'm nothing if not thorough when it comes to Maia's curiosity.

He throws a look toward my boat bobbing at the dock. "You fish?"

"Lobster."

"You like it?" he asks.

"More than the lobsters do, I suppose."

His half smirk deepens along with the soft lines around his blue eyes, and I hear Maia coaching me against being a crotchety human.

"It's honest work," I tell him.

"Tricking lobsters into a cage with bait is honest?"

My back teeth clench. I want to tell him he has no right to comment on an age-old vocation he knows nothing about. I want to tell him I've met him before—or at least guys like him—all arriving from away and having plenty to say about fisheries and regulations and what fishermen should and shouldn't be allowed to do—at least until they're at their country club, setting aside all their judgment to make room for a bright red lobster served up on a platter surrounded by sunshine and privilege.

I don't say anything of the sort, of course. I fumble the keys from my overalls, even though I don't need them to open the door to the perennially unlocked lighthouse. I mean, who's going to steal a lighthouse? December gusts whip the primitive wooden door inward, pushing us inside. I set the keys on the shelf, confident this is what a good rental host does. I know. I watched a video.

"This is her," I tell him. "Cove Light." I extend a nod toward the small interior. "A fire in the hearth will warm this place up quickly, and I'll keep your wood stacked outside. My number is on the fridge and you can find me just there." I point to the small cottage I share with Memma, the one with a low roof courtesy of its 1760 construction. "You can't throw a pebble around here without hitting someone who'll know how to reach me if you need anything."

He sets a small duffle to the floor and takes in the stone fireplace, the tiny bedroom, the bookshelf of games and books. "I don't think I'll need anything."

He's wrong. Being on the edge of the world is isolating, and being in isolation with a partner is the fastest way for a relationship to go beyond horribly wrong. I'd seen it before. Couples honeymooning here after their simple, expensive Maine weddings. Couples arriving to rekindle their love or passion or whatever. Almost all of them left early because they couldn't hack the quiet. The hermit in me can't understand how a person can ever get tired of serenity, but the spotty WiFi and relentless sea force visitors to sit up close and personal with their thoughts, and that's not always the relationship they're looking to deepen.

Pufferfish Man moves beyond the small kitchen to peer up the tight, spiral stairs to the beacon of the lighthouse while I wait for him to mansplain about the lens in the tower, how fractured glass and one tiny bulb can cast its light far enough to warn ships on the horizon. *That's how the lights in lighthouses work, don't I know?* In the summer, I use the lecture time constructively, thinking up nicknames for men like him: Big Important Man Dude. Starched Pop-up Collar Bro. Pink Shorts What Was He Thinking. And worse. But not this guy. He doesn't mention the light. Maybe he doesn't know anything about Fresnel lenses.

"There are fresh linens on the bed, and towels for you and Hannah next to the tub."

"Great, thank you. She'll appreciate that." He watches the view from the portal window over the short sink as I provide the welcome-to-Christmas-Cove-run-down in a customer service voice that would make Maia proud.

"There's only one restaurant on the cove: Earl's Eats. Opens at five a.m. every day, closes at four, but not really. If the cook's there, he'll feed you. We have a small market at the Harbor Store, and a bigger grocery shop is three miles from town. Supermarket is twelve miles away."

"I clocked the amenities on my way in," he says, without breaking his view of the ocean that's dark now, the light faded from the day. His arms are set to the counter in a wide arc, his eager puffy jacket expanding into the space between his torso and elbows.

I knock on the panel near the door and he turns around, resting his back against the counter so he's as far from me as possible. It's a courtesy that doesn't go unnoticed in this tight space. "These are your lights here. This one is for outside. Might be safest to keep it on if Hannah arrives in the dark."

"Ah, good tip." His look is warm and grateful, his concern for Hannah jolting my spine with an unwelcome shiver.

"The rock can be slippery." I drop a look to his shoes.

"Gotcha." The upper lids of his obnoxious wingtips shift like he's wiggling his toes.

We say our goodbyes and I close the plank door behind me, leaving the forged iron hinges to rattle in the wind as if someone were trying to get in. Or out.

I board my boat to deliver my catch to the co-op at Earl's Eats and hurry home to the restorative smell of Memma and warmth when I see her note on the table, its corner tucked under a jar of bread-and-butter pickles we'd canned in late summer: *Out with the ladies.* My heart hammers with jealousy for her book group because Mem should be here, next to me on the deep couch watching our taped *Jeopardy* reruns, taking things easy as her body recovers.

But my need for companionship is selfish, for sure. Because lately being alone on land is wholly different than being alone at sea. No matter what I do, when Mem's not here to distract me, I can't shut off my mind when my body stops moving. The silence makes room for me to stress about Mem's medical bills that refuse to stop arriving, even multiplying. Doesn't the hospital's billing department know she's in remission? That the worst is over? I can't even fathom how other people overcome medical debt. I wouldn't have been able to afford keeping my boat or our house if Maia hadn't run the lighthouse rental and organized neighbors to pitch in and cover our household bills. All so I could stay by Mem's side through her illness. Peninsula families showed up for me, no different than when Dad died, taking his income with him.

When I sit down at my desk, the bills feel too big, like a mountain I can never summit. I'm underwater in a new and terrifying way. And alone. Really alone. Because I can't tell anyone about the debt, especially Mem. She's already been through too much. My finger punches at the calculator, adding the off-season rental income from Cove Light and what I can make fishing in winter. It doesn't feel like I can make enough in a year. Or even three. Because it's not just medical bills; it's debt to friends and neighbors that I need to pay back, even though no one will hear of it, our Yankee stubbornness as strong as a rip current.

And maybe it's my own stubbornness that makes Memma's late night outing more unsettling than I'm comfortable admitting. Because she could still fall, get dizzy, need me and I'll be too far away. I strip off my clothes and step into a hot shower trying to wash worry from my mind, which is wholly unsuccessful. When I get out, the house is so still all I can hear are the crashing waves along the breakers and a strange *wah wah* thrum in my ears, which is definitely not in my ears when Memma is here to laugh, bake, plan, and joke with me.

Unmoored in my solitude, I pull on an emotional support sweater and do a thing for Maia. For love.

~ Post I'm Unqualified to Write ~

After typing the title for my post, the blinking cursor taunts me for what feels like hours, as if it knows I'm an imposter. But, seriously? How do authors create columns and essays and entire books starting with nothing but a blank page? It feels like an impossible feat, as insurmountable as writing about happily ever afters when I'm a recluse who loves weird sea insects and has zero capacity to trust after losing my dad and being ditched by the mother who was never a mom.

You know the best part about lobsters?

Ugh, no. Delete. Delete. Delete.

What if you don't believe in love?

Um, no. Maia would take out an ad for a new me. Delete. Delete. Delete. I stand and do jumping jacks until my arms hate me. When my brain and body are limp with exhaustion, I let my fingers have their way with the keyboard.

I love exactly two people. My mem (rhymes with gem) who has shown up for me as father, mother, grandparent, and guide all at once, all my life. And my bestie, our destinies aligning in a kindergarten classroom. If you knew me, you'd already know I'm the least likely person to write a romance-inspired *Happily Ever Holidays* column. You'd also know the disappointing news doesn't stop there. See, unlike other—far more appropriate— contributors to this annual series, I am not famous. And I'm not fabulous. I'm barely even interesting on a good day. I'm a female lobster fisherman, and my *Happily Ever After* comes in the shape of the two previously-mentioned humans. Two people who feel fully, wholly, superbly mine. And this makes me lucky enough.

I've never felt the need for more. No partner. No "better" half. No soulmate. I'm already buoyed by my grandmother who has lived a selfless life endlessly assisting the families of fishermen who are hurt or lost at sea, like my dad, her son. And, then there's my bestie. My most perfect human who never fails to radio me every time my boat returns from sea, her voice a safe harbor and beacon all at once. She's the reason my words are interrupting your life right now. She is your fearless editor. Blame her. Because I won't be writing about love.

Not the romantic kind.

Not the happy, head-over-heels, squee-filled kind.

Or even the human kind, really.

I can't. I'm not even sure I believe in dreamy love or Happily Ever Afters. (See? Worst holiday romance column ever.) But if you're still reading this terrible holiday essay on not-love, consider this: I'm writing this terrible essay on not-love from Christmas Cove, Maine, a place where a river meets the sea, and the sea greets the horizon. It is a place of eternal blue, where time and tides are fearless. And here, in this frothing world of life and light, I have unending freedom. Most days I work my boat alone in the slip of space between sky and sea. I take my time. Or rush. Haul or don't haul. Stay close to shore or travel to the deep. I'm good at my job, efficient at my tasks.

And I don't just catch lobsters; I study their behaviors, paying attention to their habits, how they survive, and how they thrive. Because being a successful lobsterman depends on keeping the oceans healthy for generations to come. And for future generations of lobsters to arrive, they need to mate first.

This is (maybe) where it gets interesting. Or (maybe) even romantic. Because underneath the slate sea, lobsters are resourceful and enduring, and spend a lot of energy on the sexy time. The American lobster engages in complex mating rituals involving seduction, arguments, and total trust. On any given day, lobsters know way more about romantic love than I do.

If I haven't disappointed you enough, let me share this final, fun fact: lobsters don't mate for life. Nope. Not a thing. I know. I know. Nineties kids' hearts are breaking all over the place, but it's true. Even though tourist spots throughout Maine will sell you cards with "You're My Lobster!" in cutesy font, or wedding cake toppers with two lobsters attached at the claw, the reality is much less adorable, far less marketable: if two lobsters are trapped together long enough, the large lobster will eat the smaller one. Every time.

My goal is never to be the smaller lobster. Or the bigger one for that matter.

It feels important to share that lobsters don't lean cannibalistic in the wild. That said, the scent of blood can inspire eating a friend. (Note to reader: choose friends carefully). But here's the thing: lobsters don't bleed often because they're biologically designed to self-amputate seriously-injured sections of their bodies, shedding the wounded part of their frames to save their whole being. That's some serious commitment to self-preservation.

In the very depths of their DNA, lobsters are hardwired to protect themselves from their own species—and this has always made sense to me.

Because love hurts.

Crushes, too.

And in the human world, I've never had to look far to catch sight of a relationship where one person was being consumed by the other.

Despite all this, we're fed a steady diet of starry-eyed stories about romantic love. Particularly now, when the holidays sweep under us, strong as a current. We decorate with white lights in an attempt to dazzle the long darkness out of shortened days. Marketing firms, books, and entire television networks try to sell us the idea that Happily Ever After can only be achieved by finding a perfect mate.

My simple life at sea reminds me to pay attention to the Happily Ever Now so many of us have with people we hold dear. Sisters. Friends. Neighbors. Mentors. They love us *now*. They already know we're enough. More than enough.

And isn't that enough?

Because if the glorious people around us can love us as fiercely as they do, then we must be great. And maybe it's a nice twist on Happily Ever Afters to indulge in a little self-love. Because self-love has never made me feel trapped.

Self-love doesn't ask me to shed or sacrifice parts of myself. Self-love endures. It's here now and forever, and all the days in between.

3

The Quiet

After writing, I only reword and rework my post seven hundred and eleven times. Roughly. When I reach the point of hating all words, communication on a global scale, and alphabets specifically, I heat the kettle for elderberry tea and email the passage to Maia. On the plush chair in the corner of my room—the one next to the oversized window that affords me a clean view of Maia's house—I sit cross-legged and...alone. Beyond the glass, the harbor waves crash against the breakwater rocks as they do, breathing in and out, steady and dependable. With my laptop open on my pretzeled legs, I do the Instagram to put my attention anywhere but my financial stress.

Maia insists I'm the only person on the planet who doesn't check their social media on a phone, but my phone is just a phone and I don't need it to be smarter than that. All my advanced technology can be found in my boat's radar, depth finder, compass, GPS, and two mounted VHF radios connecting me to the Coast Guard and safety.

The last thing I need while at sea is distraction, which is why my Instagram page is anemic and private.

I've posted exactly zero pictures. My avatar is of me on my dad's shoulders over two decades ago. I follow only two accounts: Michelle Obama and Maine's Midcoast Lobstermen Association. By nature, I'm not a joiner, but Michelle Obama's optimism helped me through Memma's sickness and Maine's Midcoast Lobstermen Association kept me connected to the ocean while I shared Mem's hospital room. Michelle's posts have remained reliably magnificent, but the posts by Maine's Midcoast Lobstermen Association have changed in recent weeks. A couple of months ago, the Association revealed a new logo—a graphic of a bearded older lobster fisherman flanked by a younger male fisherman on one side and a female fisherman on the other.

I liked the inclusive representation, but it was the new vibe to the posts that had me visiting more than normal. The posted pictures were no longer a barrage of merch in the form of shirts, hats, and lobster embossed mugs. The captions had recently become reflective, even insightful, with actual personality pulsing through the short narratives. And something more. The account paid loving tribute in sepia-toned *In Memoriams* every few weeks to honor a special someone we'd lost from the working waterfront in decades past. Maine is a small town, so chances were good I knew the person responsible for this shift, but I liked the online anonymity, the privacy to reflect on the tributes to those who came before. Working at sea might not be as dangerous as it was for previous generations, but Mother Nature is fierce, and accidents happen.

The poetic posts reliably bring me to tears, even when I didn't know the deceased. It isn't always grief that makes me cry, exactly; the posts make me sad I *hadn't* known the person. The men and women in these black-and-white tributes remind me of my dad and my youth, which feels heavy, for sure, but in a good way. Like I'm seen. Connected to those who came before me. Like my life out here matters.

The rhythm of the posts feels familiar too, so similar to the way my brain processes grief. Loss doesn't occupy my every thought, though when a memory arrives—my dad's silvery laughter, one of his silly sayings, or the way he'd always leave the last sip in his coffee cup to feed good luck—it pushes against my everyday life in stark relief, obscuring my senses for the duration of its visit. But now, twenty years after his passing, my grief is balanced by levity, an equilibrium the Instagram page has achieved effortlessly in recent months. Because beyond the heavier emotion-laden *In Memoriams*, the daily posts take on the perspective of life under the sea. It isn't a surprise to see a graphic of a barnacle or bluefish, their inner thoughts conveyed with unexpected insight and hilarity. Today, two sharks sit at an underwater diner calculating their protein intake if they split a vegetarian meal in their ongoing effort to rebrand after decades of bad publicity.

I catch up on the recent handful of posts and lean back in my chair feeling...joy. Or satisfaction. I can't decide. Either way, it lands like a salve, a respite from the hardness of the past year. Like I've been introduced to someone who is brilliant and hilarious yet anonymous in this interface and needs nothing from me, which is exactly what I'm willing to give.

A normal person—a person who clearly isn't me—might feel comfortable heading to the account's DMs, but boating twenty miles offshore in rough seas today caused me less anxiety. Maybe it's my anonymity that makes me brave. Or maybe it's the high I'm riding from writing a bunch of words telling romantic love to suck it.

> @BirdieBlueBug:
> These posts feel new.
> Like spring. Keep it up.

The words are way too corny for Normal Me but tonight I'm Anonymous Me. I press send.

> @MidcoastMaineLobsterAssoc:
> Thank you!

I'm immediately notified that @toothpicks3478 is requesting to follow me. Zero people follow me. Not even Maia follows me, mostly because I refuse to give her my username and made her promise not to fish for my online presence.

I cruise over to @toothpicks3478's page like I'm cool and this is normal. The bio informs me that @toothpicks3478 writes for the @MidcoastMaineLobsterAssoc, and I'm greeted by a fluffy red dog with a show tail as thick as a skunk's. The dog—without any sign of a human—is on the bow of a small wooden runabout boat, in thirty or so pictures, fur in the breeze, wind pushing its floppy black lips into a smile that makes me smile back.

Until my phone rings and I jump.

"Hey," Maia says. "I saw your light on."

I go to the window, press my nose to the glass so my breath makes a foggy, fleeting mask.

"Captivating as always," she tells me. "So, did you give up on getting dressed halfway through the ordeal?"

"Creeper." I cross my bare legs, pulling my sweater over my underwear. "Though your eyesight never fails to impress."

"Binoculars."

"Unsettling." I move to my bed, build a backrest of pillows.

"What's unsettling is your email. I'm kinda at a loss for words." Maia is never at a loss for words.

"That feels ominous."

"No. It's the opposite. I admit I harbored slight doubt over your commitment to cannibalism, but you leaned in and it's good. Really good."

"I'm glad it met with your high standards, now never ask me to do anything like that ever again. And feel free to edit or change or make it better or whatever. It's not precious."

"Can't," Maia says. "It's already posted."

It takes me longer than it should to pull up Maia's *Mer*/Sea site considering my best friend status but when I arrive, my words are there. "Damn. Okay."

"What do you think?"

Maia elevated the article—ahem, *blog post*—with a new title that is, well…perfect: *Love & Lobsters*. Under it, my words are formatted with fancy font and flair and all the general high-end internet coif that makes regular words look professional. My post follows one titled "Real Life Instalove" by Maine's queen of metal jewelry (hammered with pre-Colonial tools, of course) and, unbelievably, the first feature of the series, which was written by Martha herself.

"Wow. My heart's a little racy." My post is attributed to my initials only and I can practically hear the collective eyeroll of Maia's two million followers as they read my contribution before a new one replaces it. But here, right now, seeing my thoughts in the wild feels fairly amazing.

My computer dings with a follow request from the Association.

"What was that?" Maia asks.

"I did my first DM."

She inhales sharply. "You did not!" She yells it like an accusation. I'm certain it's an accusation.

"I did. I feel like I should get a T-shirt."

"You should get all the T-shirts. Holy crap, lady. Tell me who! What? When? Tell me all the things! Was it Michelle? Are you hearing back from The Obama Mama herself right now?"

I laugh. "Slightly less riveting."

"No. That cannot be a thing. You DMing on the InstaSphere is major. Tell me who."

"The lobstermen's association."

"Ugh. *Really?*"

"Ha!" I bark. "I can literally feel your disappointment."

"No! I mean, yeah. Okay. I definitely wanted to show up for you in this huge moment, but this account belongs to fishermen. Snore."

"Offense taken." I walk back to the window and make a face I hope she can see. "I do have a request from a new follower. Does that make me cool?"

Her living room lights flash with Y.E.S. in Morse Code we learned as kids thinking we were sending discrete messages across the harbor.

"I'm rightfully devastated I was not your first, but I'm pulling up my big girl panties to instruct you to stalk your new follower's page and follow back if appropriate. It's Insta 101."

I pop back over to the pictures of the dog wearing a bright red doggie life vest in his travels and search for familiar harbors and ports, waterways and landings, but it's almost as if the photos are purposefully generic. And then I see it, the artistry of the page. The way each photo captures a dog at the center, but also a seal sunning on a rock in the distance, an osprey curling in a high hunt, a cormorant diving, a bald eagle gliding, all with Maine's wild blue as the backdrop.

"What's their grid like?" Maia asks.

I squint toward the screen. "Is that code for six-pack abs or something?"

"Oy. Their Insta grid," she says with that familiar tone of being equally intrigued and horrified by me wandering around the internet. "Who is this human? Girl or boy? Old or young? Married or single? Or, you know, any of the places in between any of those identifiers."

"Don't know."

"What's their handle?"

"Not happening."

"Oh my god, come on! We don't keep secrets."

"It's not a secret. I just don't want you invading my Insta because then you'll inspire a bunch of people to follow me and I'll feel guilted into following them back and then I'll get updates from rando strangers and I'll lose my intimacy with Michelle—and, yes, my lobstermen peeps—and I'll feel overwhelmed and underworthy and then never log on to the Instagram again."

"That is a horrifyingly astute prediction." She pulls in a breath, restraint being a perpetual struggle for Maia. "Okay, so tell me about the account at least."

"It's basically a page about a dog." I give some details, but not all. Maia has a history of getting bored quickly with nature. And while she'd love to know the user's tiny avatar is a silhouette of a man, I keep this detail close and lean in, unsuccessfully trying to recognize him.

"Okay, this is good. I can work with that," she says.

"Why must everything be worked with?"

"I don't tell you how to fish; you don't tell me how to Insta."

"Totally fair."

"Okay, I've decided generic is probably good."

"Why am I curious about your logic here?"

"Think about it. This person isn't a girl who is so girlie she has to take selfies of her perfect make-up and blowout to be the center of her world and your Insta world. Nor is this person a boy who needs all of social media to know he has huge wood or big, veiny arms."

"Stereotype much?"

"Maybe they're a hybrid like you," she says, ignoring me.

"Hybrid does not sound like a compliment."

"Really? It's high praise. You're tough as nails yet goddess like with all your skinny height and killer green eyes. Basically, the perfect human."

"Says you." I curl onto my side, tuck my legs under the covers.

"Literally no one else matters. Remember that as you venture into a relationship with InstaHuman. I have zero tolerance for you finding a new bestie."

I laugh. "I'm aware."

"Wait. What happened with lighthouse couple?"

"Lighthouse man. No wife yet."

"Do you think she's in his trunk and he's just renting your place to stage a tourism wife murder? OH MY GOD! You'll be interviewed on one of those primetime investigative shows! I *cannot* wait. I mean, I'll feel terrible about her death, of course, but seeing you on camera would be a thrill I never knew I needed until now."

"I'm hanging up."

"How dare you! At least tell me if he's cute."

"He's a man. Married, like you. He's from away. Seems quiet enough."

"It's always the quiet ones."

"Still hanging up," I say, and do. Maia's living room lights flicker in protest before giving up and going dark.

Walking through the house, I fixate on Mem's absence. It's past nine and her car's still gone. She hasn't called. I shake my arms in an attempt to release nervous energy through my fingertips as my mind jumps to all the worst-case scenarios before reeling itself back, again and again. Memma has told me there's no place for my anxiety in her new lease on life so I try to shelve it. I do.

I slip on my boots and step outside. The winter wind cuts at my bare legs and exposed neck with its razor-sharp breath as I stand at the edge of our property before braving a quick trip to the renter's car. The lighthouse is pitch black as I approach, the horizon haunting as I give the sedan's trunk a slight knock. I listen for an answer that doesn't come. I knock again, harder this time, and am grateful it's just me out here with the breaking sea.

Pulling my sweater tight at my middle, I walk past the darkened lighthouse to the tip of the breakwater where the ocean hums slate blue, hung tonight with the lacework of low, frothing waves. Under the crescent moon, I stand strong against the winter squall in my drydock version of a polar plunge. Immersed and exposed in the cold, my senses heighten, my skin wakes, my nerve endings fire bright and bold. My body and mind push past the temperature to revisit a place where I feel my most powerful, most confident, most alive, and closest to my father.

In a city or in a crowd, I become insignificant. Out here I'm tied to something greater. My bones are sturdy enough to stand at the sea, with the sea, against the sea—a strength that's harder to take for granted after watching life drain from Memma. So, I stand strong. For her. For us. Because if I could give Memma half my strength, I would. More, if she'd let me.

When I can't bear the icy sting any longer, I blow Dad a kiss that gets carried by the wind. Inside my room, my fingertips grow colder as they thaw. I pop on my Walkman and pull Dad around me with one of his mixed tapes. Meatloaf's "Paradise by the Dashboard Light" blares in my headphones and I dance in my room until I'm warmed by movement, surrounded by love—invincible and glowing bright as a knife's edge.

Maybe it's this courage that makes me follow back @toothpicks3478, this feeling of anything being possible, of being infinite. When a sway of headlights comb across my window, I slap my laptop shut, change into pajama bottoms and a tee and head to the room beside mine, the only other bedroom in our home. I knock on Memma's door just before turning the handle that's oddly locked.

"Mem, you okay?"

"I'm perfect, Charlie girl. I'm off to bed now. See you in the morning."

"Okay. Good night." My sad palm flattens against the door and I really do try my hardest to trust Mem knows what's best for her, for us.

In the silence, it occurs to me I might be lonely, which feels entirely different than being alone.

4

The Kitchen

Hermon Benner is sitting at my kitchen table the next morning. Not working the grill at Earl's Eats with his back to customers the way he's done since he was a teenager. He's here. In the heart of the house I share with Memma. At 5:30 a.m.

"Um, good morning." I head to the kettle to get my daily hot chocolate on.

Hermon Benner grunts his hello as he reads the folded paper he's using as a coaster, his coffee mug showcasing an interrupting lobster raising his claw asking, *"Excuse me, what's the butter for?"*

I've known Hermon Benner since I was knee-high to a grasshopper (Dad's saying) so I'm well aware of the way he navigates life in unhurried, two-syllable bursts: *Ayuh. Can't says. Grub's up. You bet.* Then, once in a supermoon, Hermon Benner will drop a multisyllabic response like: *There's no tell'n 'bout tomorrah.* He might even belt out a chatterbox rendition of: *I'm not the one who should be sayin'.* Lots of men who fish like to shove their masculinity around by aggressively mansplaining hard work and naming their boats *MASTER BAITER* or *THE CODFATHER* so no one forgets the captain comes equipped with a phallus. But Hermon Benner manages a fine life by saying very little—a trait I admire on a cellular level.

While watching water refusing to boil, I stand at the stove and consider how Hermon Benner's wearing his wool scarf but no jacket. This scenario is the result of one of two realities. One, he made his way here at the start of his day, though I don't see his coat or smell winter on him. Two, he started his day here. *Shudder.* My body twitches with a leftover shake from two seconds ago when I considered Memma and Hermon Benner and a Maybe Sleepover. There's no time of day when I want to think about Memma and S.E.X., but pre-six a.m. is officially too early. A third shudder ripples up my spine.

Memma bursts in through the side door, fluid as a gust of wind carrying the sharp cold.

"Ya slept late," she says to the room so I can't say if she's talking to me or Hermon or both of us.

She shoves a canvas bag to the deep shelf of the tall jelly cupboard by the door, and plants a chilled kiss on my cheek as her gnarled hand curls around my shoulder in an efficient hug that no one outside our family would identify as a hug. In what looks like one liquid motion, she shrugs off her coat and hurries eggs from her bag to a bowl before chopping scallions on the long, hand-crafted table we use to prep, eat, puzzle, and gather around, the room feeling even smaller with three people occupying its air. It strikes me how I don't remember moments with Dad in this part of the house. In my memory, my father is always outside, the sea around him. Or he's at the side of my bed in the evenings, telling tales of the sea and the sun.

I bring Memma a cup of hot coffee, which she accepts with a quick, shallow sip. Memma isn't a slow woman, and since her recovery she's been on overdrive, an accelerated variation of natural vigor that makes me uneasy. I sit across from Hermon after Memma declines my offer to help. She folds eggs in the skillet as she gives me the rundown for her day.

"Gotta get those pots over to the green, Charlie girl. Folks'll be stringing up lights tomorrow—buoys, too."

"Lights and buoys?" I ask absentmindedly.

Mem magicians a tray of biscuits from the oven and turns on me with an accusing stare, one which barely stings because her biscuits are pure flaky, buttermilk perfection, able to distract the mind and befuddle the senses with one whiff.

Memma snaps for my full attention. "We're setting up the holiday tree in town. We got to collecting boxes of lights last night. Everyone's pitching in."

"Oh, right. The tree." I'd almost forgotten Mem's request to make a small holiday tree for the common, one fashioned from the new lobster traps I'd purchased last month. It had hurt to spend money I didn't have, but in the balance of risk and reward, I'll be able to increase my yield next season. And it feels right that Mem will put the pristine traps to good use before they meet the water in the spring. She deserves all the joy after such a hard year.

"Not one of us will miss Cove Light if we have a tree lighting on the common," Mem says.

"*Ayuh,*" Hermon Benner agrees.

Memma scrapes eggs onto three small plates, sprinkles them with scallion and flakes of cheese, serving the dishes along with a basket of biscuits I grab for with a graceless movement that lands somewhere between a dive and a lunge. She stirs a dollop of vanilla ice cream into my hot chocolate and serves me like I'm still nine. I don't complain. I eat, unable to find the right words to actually ask how Hermon Benner got to our kitchen table.

Then he lifts his chin to me as his signature conversation starter. "Haulin'?"

"Not today. Just dropped a hundred pots for a soak yesterday."

"*Ayuh.*"

"Good!" Memma slaps her palm to her corner of the table, waking the utensils. "Then you've got time to get those new traps across the harbor. We'll meet you there."

Mem's all business, built of fire, quickly settling her dishes to the sink, filling her to-go coffee flask, heaving on her heavy coat, and swiping her thumb across the framed photo of my dad that hangs above the light switch, as if she's giving him a kiss or soothing an ache. And then she's outside, like walking toward town, in step with Hermon Benner, first thing in the morning, isn't something she needs to explain.

I dress, pull my hair into a knot and splash cold water to my eyes when aloneness-that-feels-more-like-loneliness settles into the house again, creeping in like low rolling sea smoke. I suddenly feel restless, reminding me of when Memma was first diagnosed—before she'd started her chemo—and I'd paced the length of our tiny cottage like it was an Olympic sport, wearing grooves into the old pine floorboards as if my traction would cure her blood, quiet my mind, bring her home. Stillness haunts me as it presses into every corner of the house so I shiver and do what any normal insane person does when feeling creeped out by loneliness: I creep on someone else. I slink to the northeast window to spy for signs of life at the lighthouse but am quickly disappointed. Pufferfish Man must not be an early riser, and there's still no second car in the driveway. Beyond the lighthouse, a wink of gold sunrise sits like a promise on the horizon, which is pretty, to be sure, but not exactly the distraction I need.

I make a predawn pivot to revisit my blog post before it's replaced, but see a notification waiting: a DM from half an hour ago.

@toothpicks3478
Why "BlueBug?"

The question pushes away the uneasy stillness that's forced its way into my at-home solitude. My fingers hover over the keys and then:

@BirdieBlueBug
I caught a blue lobster when fishing
with my dad when I was a kid.

What I don't write is that I'm still a fisherman. Or how my blue lobster found its way into the first solo trap I ever baited and released to the deep. After a three-day soak, Dad helped me haul the pot onto the deck of the boat, old-school style, our grips moving hand-over-hand up the sea-slicked line until the trap surfaced above seawater, swinging over our deck to meet us. I was six. My catch was pure chance—a one in two million catch. As the trap lifted and water and seaweed slipped away, one cobalt blue lobster stared back at me, looking like she'd traveled from the distant Mediterranean Sea carrying its exotic color on her shell, all to show me that one in two million was possible. That even in the course of everyday life, there was always an opportunity for the extraordinary to arrive. For me, she was something entirely different than a lobster, more like a jewel, a lost treasure pulled from the unknowable fathoms of the ocean.

"Blues carry the color of the deep sea, open sky, and chance," Dad had said. *"They're rare. Just like you, baby girl, my blue bug."* He let me pet her abdomen, the bouquet of her tail. I studied her blue shell under the sun for so long I still remember every line of her, the hard ridges of her body where the blue deepened toward black. How her antennae had flinched, trying to understand the new world she'd been pulled to. She was the most beautiful creature the sea had ever made. In time, Dad and I tossed her back to the water together, watching her sapphire shell disappear below the waves. I'd wanted to keep her as a pet and Dad was proud I'd been strong enough to let her go then, but I didn't. Not really. She's still with me every day. Same as him.

I'd been too young to know that while I was catching my blue, my mother was slinking home to her beloved southern desert, tired of Dad and the sea and (presumably) me. Later, when I found the love letters, I learned Mom wasn't just running from her life and me and Dad during her repeated trips, but to another man.

My parents were a lot like the variations found in lobsters. My mother common, my father rare and extraordinary. He never chose to leave me; his body gave out. But my mother made a choice. More than once. And that kind of betrayal breeds a different kind of grief, one I've never been strong enough to forgive. There's more, of course, though none of it belongs in a DM.

> @toothpicks3478
> Lucky!

I'm surprised by the almost immediate response, and how good it feels communicating with someone who knows my industry, and how lobsters are called bugs. Because catching a blue lobster is lucky, even if luck wasn't what followed me in the subsequent years.

> @BirdieBlueBug
> Why toothpicks3478?

@toothpicks3478
Maine has 3,478 miles of
coastline. Nearly four times
as much as California if
you're a stats nerd like me.

> @BirdieBlueBug
> And 'toothpicks'?

@toothpicks3478
Longer story. Slightly more
personal. Maybe another
time.

> @BirdieBlueBug
> Totally fair. I'm a big fan of
> leaving personal details with
> the person they belong to.

@toothpicks3478
Ha! Same. It seems like
gossip is all people have to
talk about sometimes so it's
a pleasant relief to meet a
fellow private person.

> @BirdieBlueBug
> Private is an understatement.

@toothpicks3478
We could start a club.

> @BirdieBlueBug
> I'm not really a joiner either.
> And I have to head to work now.

@toothpicks3478
Then I'll wish you a good
day, and not ask what kind
of work you do.

I'm about to close my laptop when another notification dings:

@toothpicks3478
Great dads are hard to
come by. Hold on tight.

> @BirdieBlueBug
> Every day.

As a rule, I never use the past tense if I'm talking about Dad to someone who wasn't lucky enough to know him. It's my way of keeping my father alive, keeping him close. It's not a lie, exactly; more like a shift in perspective.

The advice to hold my dad close feels intimate yet distant, like it's coming from a friend and stranger all at once. The words buoy me as I head to Dad's barn and begin to shuttle my new lobster traps to the bed of my truck. By this time next year, the traps will be marred with seaweed and dents like my six hundred working traps. For now, these beauties will serve as the building blocks for the holiday tree Mem wants to gift the village. I stack the pots into my truck one-by-one and the familiar movement warms me, my heart rate quickening, my neck heating enough to make me nudge my coat zipper lower.

"Can I give you a hand?" Pufferfish Man approaches as if from town. He stands well beyond the barn door, giving me space. He's sporting his puffy puffer jacket again, but changed into a decent set of muck boots for his earlier-than-early jaunt.

"I'm set." I give him a short nod as he takes a step back.

He looks toward the truck bed. "Are those for the trap tree?"

Surprise throws me. "How'd you know about the tree?"

"It's why I'm renting here."

"Really?" It's impossible not to sound skeptical.

"No." Pufferfish Man cocks his head, the barn's lantern light revealing the rise of his strong jaw, a smile he might be trying to suppress.

It unsettles me how much I want to ask him why he's here. I mean, who vacations on the coast of Maine in the belly of our winter? For a month? I'm also more than a little curious about where his wife is, when she'll arrive, if she'll arrive. Why is he out so early, before the air's warmed enough to burn the sea smoke from the harbor? Is he thinking through the last-minute logistics of an elaborate vacation murder, or is its execution already underway? Or, is he honeymooning without his honey? Maybe they're on a break. Maybe he isn't waiting for his wife at all, but makes a reservation as a married man only to meet up with a lover at the same time every year, like that old movie Mem loves.

I shove my shoulders together, stretching my back with a sudden exhaustion that has nothing to do with moving gear. I'm fatigued just *imagining* all the possible iterations of another person's love life. I couldn't fathom dealing with the complete and total chaos of being in a relationship. Being responsible for another person and their feelings and their baggage and their needs? Oof. How do people do it? *Why* do people do it?

He waves to the stack of traps still inside. "I'd be happy to lend a hand."

There it is again, an offer. Not a man-demand like "Let me help you" or the ever-condescending: "Here, I got this." His offer feels like kindness extended. I consider his unassuming approach even as I yank down both sides of my hat with a firm "I'm set" on my lips. But then he squats to pluck a blanched Hershey's candy bar wrapper from a winter-yellowed Rosa Rugosa's outer branches, tucking the rogue trash to his pocket with a quick, instinctive stewardship that changes my mind.

"Have at it." I jump into the back of my truck as he shuffles traps my way with an efficiency I appreciate on a physical and moral level. I might even notice how he handles the trap's considerable bulk and weight with ease. "You fish?"

"Never." He stops, balancing the rectangle of wire across the spread of his hips, his arms strong, his face flirting with a satisfied smile. "This is the closest I've ever come to lobster fishing and I'm kind of digging it."

"Well, I won't complain about the free labor," I tell him, as I hear Maia in my head, coaching me to ask about the comfort of his stay and the softness of the sheets—or if the hot water is hot enough for him, even as I barely consider these luxuries for myself. "You settling in okay?"

"Great, yeah." His smile breaks then, rising quick and wild along with a short, surprised bolt of laughter. "Perfect, actually." He passes a trap my way, mindful I have a firm grip on it before letting go.

"Do you usually rent lighthouses in winter?" I try not to notice the crisp lines that appear in the corners of his eyes as his smile tightens.

"Not in winter, no."

"It's a bold choice." I tie down the growing stacks and climb to the side of the truck bed to start a final row with the pot he passes my way. "And not for everyone. Abby Burgess is legend in these parts for her dedication to light-keeping in the worst weather. She manned— or wo-manned, rather—a lighthouse in Maine for thirty-eight years back in the mid-eighteen hundreds."

"I'll definitely check out before then," he says with a chuckle. "Four decades would be a hard stretch."

"Right?" I grab the next pot. "She was only fifteen and had no access to the mainland, no amenities. Each winter must have felt like years."

"Brutal. But maybe beautiful, too."

A flicker of something stirs in me. "She was built of grit and resilience, that's for sure."

He throws a short exhale. "In fairness, aren't all women built of grit and resilience?"

My full attention darts to his comment, but he's disappeared to the barn where he efficiently fishes out the remaining traps. I'd been filling the silence with facts from this part of Maine, my classic approach to bridging awkward up-close-and-personal encounters with tourists, but he'd been listening. Really listening. When he offloads the final trap to me, I make the mistake of watching the way he lifts his gaze upward, his eyes squinting against the sun behind me, his pupils a wash of blue so uncommon it's as if the bright sea and clear winter sky were mixed into a new color created for his face alone.

He raises a hand to shield his stare, which he casts well past me to watch the apricot haze waking the skyline. For a long time, we're quiet together, arrested by the rising sun bleeding light into the sky—deep orange melting up from the horizon as if stretching, bending, yawning alive.

"Maine sits on the traditional land of the Wabanaki, and their name means 'People of the First Light,'" I whisper, all awe.

"I can see why."

Together, we watch the sun fatten over the lip of the ocean, rapt at the beauty of this daily repeating miracle.

"Is it possible to spot whales from here?" he asks, reminding me how close he is, how comfortable I feel even though he's a total stranger. "I had my binoculars out at the breakwater last night but of course it was too dark."

"I saw a Fin whale once," I tell him, my focus on the sun waking the sea. "A long time ago."

Our small runabout had been just off the rock at Cove Light when Dad and I saw the long, broad back of a Fin whale surfacing mere feet beyond our bow. She was solid and unwavering, parting the ocean with her sleek, curled rise. She was beautiful and unexpected and so close to our boat—a sign of good luck Dad said, though Mem's later panic about our encounter disagreed.

I feel the wet ocean spray of the Fin's exhale on me now, the way its memory raises gooseflesh over my neck and arms. Or maybe the chill on my skin is for the unexpected ease I feel with Pufferman in this moment. "Whales don't usually come close to the harbor."

"I suppose this place would be too perfect if they did."

Too perfect. Such simple words to describe this sacred place. My home. The cold rises on my neck and back now that we've stopped moving and I feel its arctic breath spreading through the tender tissue in my lungs, the sting of salt and winter on my cheeks. I steal a look in Pufferman's direction. His stare is cast so firmly to the horizon it allows me to sneak a solid peak at the color in his cheeks and the hints of gray lurking in the short stubble along his jaw. It might be concentration that makes him bite on his bottom lip, but whatever the reason, I look away, suddenly hot.

Against the unbroken sky, the tip of a tall spruce shakes to regain its balance, evidence an eagle or osprey has returned from a hunt, settling into a camouflaged nest high above. We fall silent again to appreciate the seabirds cawing, the waves crashing then receding down the granite to rejoin the ocean as the wind rattles through the branches of spruce limbs. The rhythms of the cold coast wash over us, uninterested in our presence as we stand in witness to this pulsing seascape, and it never occurs to me to feel uncomfortable in our shared silence.

Pufferman inhales a long breath. "That was the last of the traps. Would it be okay if I grabbed a ride into town?" He cocks his head, as if trying to ask me another question entirely with his stupid blue eyes, all deliberate and intense. He looks away.

"On one condition." There's a part of me that doesn't recognize my own voice, like I'm flustered despite a lifetime spent purposefully avoiding the state of being flustered.

"Name it."

I jump down and shove at the tailgate of my truck so it closes with the hard slap of old steel. "Tell me how you knew about the tree."

He laughs. "I saw your grandmother out on my walk this morning."

"Ah. Say no more." Mem is the opposite of me when it comes to privacy. She'll talk to anyone about anything. *Meeting a new person is always a good thing,* she'd tell me growing up. *Even when you meet a bad apple,* she'd say, *that sour fruit will be best reminder of how not to treat others.*

When he gets in the truck, I kick myself for not asking when he saw Mem exactly. On a walk with Hermon Benner earlier, or just before she returned home with eggs and scallions? It seems unlikely she'd take two morning walks, a thought that reminds my body to shudder, except it doesn't. Because Pufferman feels too close across the bench seat. The poof of his ridiculous jacket is so thick it nearly encroaches on my strict boundaries of personal space. So why is my elbow curious about what it would feel like to touch his elbow?

I crank the key and the reliable engine turns over just as the smell of him hits me, all crisp evergreens, newness, and impossibility.

5

The Karma

We drive along the curve of the harbor toward the common where the village green is more yellow than green, all bright color surrendered to the unrelenting brutality of Maine's harshest season. The sky isn't cooperating either. The sun decided to rise in a pout, gathering clouds to settle their gray over the common like a mood. Even the ocean looks pallid. Despite Mem's breakfast, stacking traps has made me hungry again so I pluck a banana from my bag on the seat, offering one to Pufferman, which he accepts.

He strips the skin. "I've never been able to say no to a banana. They might be the perfect food."

I take a bite of the sweet fruit, and am surprised to see so many people already on the village green as we approach. "Not on a boat. Bananas are bad luck."

"Good to know."

"Especially if you're a fisherman." I navigate around a large pothole hiding under thin layer of ice.

"Are you a fisherman? Or a fisherwoman? I feel like that's something I don't want to get wrong."

"Female lobsterman," I say, nodding my appreciation. "Most people get it wrong."

"I try hard not to be most people."

I dart a quick look in his direction, but his attention is turned toward his side window.

"Does the whole town come out for the making of the tree?"

"Looks like it, but this is the first time we've made one so I can't say what the plan is. I'm generally partial to solo work."

"Why do I feel like that's a requirement for a fisherman?"

"Female lobsterman."

"Exactly." I hear his smile deepen. "Just making sure you were paying attention."

The thing is, I am.

I drive beyond the parking spaces to the center of the common, a large parcel of land in the middle of our community that was donated by the Chapman family a hundred and fifty years ago for communal conservation and recreation. I've long suspected Old Lady Chapman loathed tourists and crowded living as much as I do, and she was wealthy enough to keep the threats of overdevelopment at bay. Whatever her motivations, I'm never not grateful for the wild heart at the center of our village.

I'm unprepared for the synchronized interest of the crowd. At the outskirts of the common, the two youngest McFarland boys have strayed from the gathered herd like they're young rivals on a nature documentary, readying to challenge elders for dominance. Jimmy McFarland, only fourteen but taller than his dad by at least a foot, runs to meet me as I climb out of my truck, Jace behind him a step, and younger by two years. Being kid-less and marriage-less at twenty-nine—and homeless except for the cottage I share with my grandmother—local teens see me as something of an interloper on the adult scene and generally trust me with their youthy angst and bad ideas. They'll at least deign to talk to me.

"Jimmy, Jace, this is Logan. He's staying at the light." My voice hitches in a way I don't approve of. "Logan, this is Jimmy and Jace McFarland, tolerable troublemakers."

They shake hands and I'm lifted into the air, pulled up from behind by the strong arms of Haggard Goodwin as he calls, "Hey gorgeous!"

Being scooped from the earth might feel unsettling to the unsuspecting, but this has been Haggard's standard operating procedure since high school when his growth spurt made him big enough to scoop up other humans. One August during our junior year in high school, he'd been perfecting this unique social custom and snuck up on me while I was chewing ice, trying to cool down after a grueling field hockey double practice. He tossed me into the air so fast the flip sent an ice cube down my throat to lodge sideways while I choked for the eternity of seconds it took my trachea to melt it.

Since that near-fatal toss, Haggard's grown into a bear of a man with full shoulders and thick arms, his face covered with a long, bushy beard that's won actual contests, and he's gotten a lot better about announcing himself before pitching people skyward. He presses a sound into the crook of my neck now that's a mix between bird call and *zerbert*. The noise is singularly ridiculous and tickles even over my jacket—or maybe that's the beard. Anyway, I tolerate all of this nonsense because it arrives courtesy of Haggard Goodwin, the backbone of our small village, the boys' soccer coach, girls' ice hockey coach, the first to volunteer, the chief of the fire brigade, road mender, and general problem solver.

"Get a room!" Jimmy calls, carrying a stack of two pots from my truck. Jace laughs, but tags behind him, balancing one.

Pufferman gives me and Haggard a quick look, but returns his attention to unloading traps.

"Where are these headed?" Jimmy asks.

"Better ask Mem," Maia says, joining us. "She's in charge." Maia rolls her eyes at Haggard. "Down boy." Haggard shakes me twice like he's trying to empty my pockets before setting me back to the hard earth. Maia links her arm in mine.

Mem joins us to instruct Haggard, Pufferman, and the McFarland boys to ferry the lobster traps to a spot of her choosing. Then she turns to me and Maia. "It's a big turnout for a little tree."

"I think everyone is here for you, Mem," Maia says.

Mem dismisses Maia with a short wave and gets busy organizing before Maia leads me toward a fancy new bench in front of Earl's Eats.

It's not even an hour past sunrise on a Saturday and Maia's hair waterfalls down her back and shoulders in thick, brown waves like she's just returned from getting a full blowout. Her eyes are painted with an understated effect that would take me a decade to master.

And, of course, her fabulous Frye's are boot shaming my sensible black rubber, fleece-lined waders. Across her middle, Lillie—her seventeen-month-old daughter—is wrapped with such complicated swaths of material I grow legitimately concerned she won't be unwrapped in time for Maia to give birth in three months to her third child. Maia appears undeterred by this impending complication. Lillie, too. She's passed out in a blissful sleep, her head against her mama's heart, her legs splaying out in a fat V on either side of Maia's pregnant belly.

"Parenting is exhausting." Maia maneuvers onto the mystery bench without a hint of fatigue.

Beneath me, the wooden slats feel warm enough to risk removing my gloves on a ten-degree morning. "How is this seat heated?" I sit on my fingers, smashing warmth over my skin and into my tired joints.

Maia gives me a sly smile. "Mama needs luxury."

"You are literally amazing."

"Obviously."

I can't calculate the time and energy it would take me to dream up a heated bench of all things. Then locate one, buy it, transport it, plug it in or charge it, and move it into place in front of Earl's. Maia on the other hand makes things happen as if from a swipe of a magic wand. I've spent more than three quarters of my life being in literal awe of her.

She pours me a cup of tea from a thin, steel canteen she produces from beneath the cradled baby. Seriously, in awe. I nurse the hot mug in my hands. In the near distance directly across the harbor, the two large front windows of our cottage watch us, the door a proud nose. Cove Light stands sentry.

"Hermon Benner was in my kitchen this morning. At 5:30."

"Dressed?" Maia asks.

I gag, the hot tea missing my lip and hiccupping down my jacket. "Don't be gross."

"I'm fact gathering."

"Yes, dressed. But how and when Hermon Benner arrived at the table is the mystery I'm not sure I want to solve."

She laughs. "Why are you using his full name?"

"I'm trying to psychologically distance myself from senior sex."

Maia adjusts Lillie. "If they're doing it, you'll have to call him HerMan Benner." She purses her lips in an exaggerated smooch. "Or Mr. Ben Dover."

"How are you the owner of a posh company when you're basically a caricature of a twelve-year-old boy?"

"You love it."

I do. "I will call him Hermon Benner until I feel safe calling him by one singular name again."

She pushes her side into mine, the warmth and weight of her both pleasure and ballast. "They're definitely together, or want to be. Look at them. They're adorable."

In the middle of the town common crammed with kids and energy, Hermon Benner and Memma stand close enough that she appears like a woman to me for the first time. Not a grandmother but a person independent of me. She is gorgeous, her smile full, her small but sturdy frame capable and steady in the sea of men and darting youth. She puts her hand to Hermon Benner's arm as he holds it straight for her, Mem's face trained on his like a summer sunflower turning to the sun. They exchange a look and while his back is to me, I see her smile light in a way that makes my heart skip.

"Le sigh," Maia says. "I want romance."

"You're fine. There is zero chance you're making babies without the romance."

I've long suspected Maia doesn't gush over Sam to me because she doesn't want me to feel like an outsider to their partnership considering I was born without the romance gene. Back in school, lots of girls tried to muscle in on our friendship and we'd nickname them "Three," as in Third Wheel, because we knew their alliance didn't have staying power. Our boyfriends, too. Anyone I dated was named Three until we broke up. Anyone Maia dated was dubbed Three. Until Sam.

"Um, hello. Delicious new guy alert." Maia sits up, her eyes trained in Logan's—Pufferman's—direction.

"My renter."

"Your hot renter." She leans forward despite the bulk of two kids at her core. "Does he have a nickname yet?"

"Pufferman."

"*Mmm*, right. The jacket." She tracks him through the crowd that doesn't seem to be making any progress on the lobster trap tree. "Have you met the wife yet?"

"No wife yet."

She places a mitten over Lillie's hat at her ears. "Have you checked his trunk?"

I laugh. "I actually did. I knocked on it. Twice."

"You're a good woman, Charlie Pinkham. And?"

"And she knocked back and I freed her and now we're besties."

Maia face turns, grows long. "Are you trying to hurt me?"

"Sorry. Sorry. Bad joke."

"Delicate pregnant lady here with all the hormones," she pouts.

I grab for her hand. "You are still my best everything."

"Better be." She leans into me and I put my arm across her shoulders to pull her close.

"Mama!" The call comes from the wind, as if Maia is Earth Mother herself. But it's three-year-old Casey, Maia's oldest, in full sprint, Sam in tow.

"Hi, baby girl!" Maia calls, wriggling free from my feeble apology hold.

Sam trains his careful watch over Casey as her mini-person body crashes into Maia's middle with a targeted efficiency that barely disturbs Lillie. This family is basically a batch of kittens, purring and smooshing into each other constantly for warmth, sustenance, reassurance, safety, and everything else a human could ever want from their people.

Sam kisses me on the cheek before stepping back, reminding me of Pufferman. "Whatdaya think? Cool bench, eh?"

I give him the thumbs up. I'm fully aware Sam is the steam engine behind all Maia's magic wand wishes. "Did you dream this up?"

"Nope. That's all Maia," he says.

"It's a new Maine start-up that's connecting with our *Mer/Sea* brand." She pats the seat. "I feel like their company really understands people like me."

"People who only participate in winter if they can sit in heated luxury?" I say.

"Exactly."

Sam unwraps Lillie from Maia and ties the baby to his middle in a feat of Olympic-worthy fabric weaving. He's the most calm, steadfast man who has ever been fashioned of flesh and DNA, devoting all his time to caring for the kids and smoothing the world for Maia so she can be fabulous, something that might sound like an easy gig to an outsider, but I'd rather brave the temperamental ocean any day. He bends to Casey, whispers: "Wanna go see a man about a unicorn?" Casey tugs him across the grass and I crush on their family as I do.

"Wait!" Maia calls. "How much longer until I get my phone back?"

"You can have it for an hour in an hour."

Maia pouts, but her eyes shine in Sam's direction so she's swooning on him and I'm swooning on them.

I drop my head to rest on her shoulder. "What would your followers think if they knew your husband limited your screen time because you're kind of shit at adulting?"

"Dad!" yells two-year-old Casey, tugging at Sam's jacket hem and twisting to point at me with an accusing mitten. "Auntie Chawlie said *shit!*"

He rolls his eyes. "Yes, well, Auntie Charlie's a potty mouth."

"She teaches Mommy all the bad words!" Maia calls.

"Nice. Way to throw me under the bus."

"Listen, parenting's a jungle. I'll throw anyone under the bus if it helps me cling to the shred of power I've deluded myself into thinking I have over those little minions. Honestly, having kids isn't for the meek. Anyone who acts like they're some kind of rockstar for having three kids under three isn't paying attention."

"Oh my god!" I snark. "You do that! *You* brag about having three kids under three. It's literally the cornerstone of your *I'm killing it* lifestyle brand thing."

"So articulate."

"And true."

"Listen, no one's interested in hearing another person's actual truths. Not really. If I can't be my real self around you, what's it all for?"

"I love that you're a hot mess deep down."

"You would."

"Full offense taken." I snuggle deeper into Maia's side. "You need to get Casey checked for bionic hearing, though. That's a next-level superpower."

"I have maybe ten minutes until a small person requests my involvement in a vital need so can we please not spend this precious window of time talking about my small persons and their spooky abilities? I want to know more about Pufferman. How's he here for a month?"

"He never said and I didn't ask."

"You need to ask these things."

"I will never ask these things."

"Then do it for me. Knowing people's business is my literal business. It's my life blood. You wouldn't deny me that, would you?" She doesn't leave room for me to answer. "Hang on. Do you think Pufferman's a politician? They seem to be on vacation a lot."

"Doubtful. He's not a hundred and four."

"Excellent point."

I take a sip of the homegrown tea. Mint and lavender hit my tongue, spiking my memory of Maia's mom, how she'd brew harvested herbs from her garden, and serve them in hot water with honey for whatever ailed us, even when our pains were emotional bruises or the general agony of coming of age in a world crippled by decades of poor adult decisions.

"A spy?" she guesses.

I watch Pufferman on the green, like I'm a predatorial bird stalking the movements of unsuspecting prey in the wild. But, you know, nicer. Less deadly.

I lean forward in my seat. "Maybe he's just a man."

"Umm. What is happening?" Maia turns to face me. "What are you not telling me, Charlotte Pinkham?"

"Nothing."

"Liar. You are lying right now. To me." She crosses her arms over her baby bump and glares.

"He just...." I hesitate. "He plucked a piece of litter from a rose bush out at the light this morning."

"Oh my god!" She shoves at my arm with two open palms. "That's like, what? A full-on mating ritual for you! Like a tropical bird's horny, bright red feather dance in the heat of the rainforest."

"Calm down. It's more like a moderately excitable shuffle. It just made me see him as different than other tourists."

"This is karma for Christmas! *Ohh!* That's a great title for a holiday movie. Girl writes a blog post about telling love to get bent and then falls in love."

"The title's solid alliteration would sell the project."

"This movie premise has legs. Trust me."

"Good thing I don't watch those movies."

"Everyone watches those movies. Like it or not, happily ever after is part of our biological imperative."

"Okay, Jane Goodall."

Maia snuggles her hands into her coat pockets and draws up her shoulders. "I'm loving this crush for you."

"No. And double no."

"Why?"

"Um, because he's married and we're not in junior high."

"You're sure? About the marriage bit?"

"Totally sure. I took the booking in summer—this may surprise you but I was super cranky after a long day on the Gulf—and I was annoyed when the woman wanted to spell her first name for me so I could run her credit card. I mean, how many different ways are there to spell Hannah?"

"At least four."

"For real?"

"For real."

"Oops." I laugh.

"Did she use the actual word husband?"

"I'm sure. I remember she said Hannah and Logan West because I liked the way she put her name first. Most hetero couples don't do that and it really bugs me. The woman's name should always come first. Besides. This is an unnecessary conversation. I can tell from his body language—he's not available. Also, let's not forget the lighthouse keeper's cottage is the size of a shoebox with exactly one bed that barely fits one person. So, yeah. As intimate as you can get. Whoever she is to him, they're close. Besides, this speculation is beyond my scope of interest. Have you not read my recent fancy blog post about self-love?"

"Is it weird you saying *self-love* sounds pervy?"

"Says the twelve-year-old boy masquerading as an adult woman." I lean back in the seat. "I feel the important takeaway here is that I'm the last person who's interested in the complications of another person, unless that other person is you, of course." I raise my face to the sun that sneaks out from behind a thick cloud. My passing interest in Pufferman is nothing. A wisp of a hint of a crush.

"Fine, you win. No Hallmark happily ever after plotline for you. But what about a fling? What's up with your Instahuman?"

"You're relentless."

"I'm aware."

"It is literally nothing. We exchanged messages this morning about literally nothing."

"How?"

I cock my head. "What do you mean how?"

"*How,* Charlie? Did this person call you, send smoke signals, deliver a telegram?"

"We direct messaged."

"Ha! I knew it! Look at you all city girl, letting rando follower slide into your DMs. You know that means sex, right? You're basically working the same angle as a hook-up app."

"Don't make this weird. I don't know anything about this person and prefer it that way."

"Okay. You do you." She rubs her hands over her belly and I sink deeper into the radiating heat of the seat as Maia tells me some story about a lifestyle brand rival I only half listen to because Maia's movie idea might have legs.

Not the film itself—but her penchant for making small things bigger than they are. Like, much, much bigger.

I lean forward, studying my neighbors gathered to support Mem. "Hey," I interrupt. "What do you think about this tree made of lobster traps?"

"I think no one's making much progress, but I like the idea. It's cute."

"What if it could be more than cute? What if we made it big? Really big. We could double or even triple the traps so the three could be tall enough to really wow, you know?"

"I think you're speaking Mama's love language."

"I might just be. I mean, if this little tree idea can gather so much local interest, what if a giant tree on the coast of Christmas Cove could draw actual visitors *at Christmas*? For an event of some kind."

"Charlie Pinkham, professional recluse, are you talking about attracting strangers to our humble cove for a festival?"

"I think I am. And what if we did it annually?" My brain races. "And raised a ton of money. Or a little money. The amount doesn't matter, really. But what if every dollar raised went into a fund for families who need it. Like me and Mem last year, and when I was a kid. A fund that could pay for losses when a fisherman gets hurt or sick or...lost at sea."

"Oh my god, stop. My brain is in party planning overdrive."

"Yeah?"

"Hell yeah."

I smile, feeling full. "Good. Because I have no idea how to pull off a festival."

"It should start on the Solstice, obviously. Run for three days. Anything longer than that is just a bore. That will leave Christmas Eve quiet for us locals." She pats my thigh. "Which gives us just under three weeks. I'll get planning and you start with a big tree. Big, big."

"On it," I say as Sam returns with his daughters and Maia's allotted screen time.

Honestly, between her kids, husband, and phone, it's a toss-up over which one she's happier to have returned to her. She powers up her phone and pets its screen. "I must do what I do now."

"Use your powers for good!" I whisper-shout as she accepts Casey's grip while Sam stays latched to Casey's opposite hand. They walk home as a perfectly balanced trio, Casey getting lifted up and through the air every five steps with such harmonized precision Haggard should be taking notes.

6

The Collaboration

After Maia leaves, I take a beat to watch my village. The McFarland boys faux spar as a way to channel their unrelenting energy. Mem and Hermon stand next to each other, so close their hips brush. Tommy Palmer claps Pufferman on the back, and Haggard calls Pufferman close in conversation. Mainers so easily accepting an outsider is about as rare as the use of the hard R in these *pahts*, but this morning shows me how exceptions can be made.

Memma waves me to join her at the tiny, makeshift coffee table where she pours me hot water and dumps in a packet of hot cocoa since I'm only mostly a grown-up.

"It's a good day, Charlie." Memma's glowing, a smile in her eyes. I can't say if her joy springs from the crisp winter air, the invigoration of our village, the anticipation of the holidays or Hermon Benner so close. Maybe after last year, it's all these things.

"You're happy?" I inquire about hot drink stirrers by miming a stirring motion.

Mem hands me a metal spoon from a small condiment bucket labeled **CLEAN**. "There's no plastic, Charlie. Hermon insisted."

"No tops," Hermon says with a wink.

I give him a grateful nod. Every time I get a to-go tea or hot chocolate at Earl's Eats—or anywhere else—I forego the plastic lid. I only want the warm beverage and a paper cup that will biodegrade. I don't need the plastic and neither does the ocean. Seeing the way Hermon respects what's important to me tells me there might just be a man of mystery underneath all those two-syllable exchanges. I sip my cocoa and place my dirty spoon in the receptacle Hermon's labeled: **USED**.

"I'm happy, Charlie." Mem looks toward the center of the green, the base row of traps set out in a small circle.

"Then it's a good day." I give Mem one of her hugs and join the men as I dodge kids jumping over the strewn traps.

Pufferman kneels on the hard ground, rubbing the outside corner of a trap while talking about concentric circles and weight distribution and physics in a way that makes actual sense. Everyone's nodding head says so. He answers questions with a quiet confidence, stepping out of the circle to join onlookers beyond the ring, like he doesn't want to be the center of attention even when he's exactly that.

"What if we add more traps?" I ask. "To make the tree really, really big. Other coastal communities have done it."

"How tall are you thinking?" Pufferman asks.

"Fifty feet?" I say.

His eyes widen. "We'll need wires. Ropes. And sturdy stakes." Pufferman nods almost imperceptibly as he bites his lip. His focus turns inward toward what I can only imagine is problem-solving and math and calculating load and mass, and I'm not thrilled with the way it's hard to watch the sheer art of him compute. "It'll take about two hundred and fifty traps," he says. "If my rough calculations are right."

"I've got two hundred new," I offer. "Happy to donate all to the cause. What do you think, Haggard?"

"Whatever your memma wants, Charles."

"Actually, Maia and I were thinking the tree could be a centerpiece of a festival. For the holidays. People could come and do all the festival things, and proceeds can be for the village, a fund for when a local family needs helping out."

Haggard settles a full mischievous smile on me. "Careful, Charles. Your idea almost sounds like holiday spirit." To the crowd, he rallies: "Whose got new traps to donate to the cause? Let's build a trap tree the size of Cove Light!"

Murmurs and excitement rise quickly, the crowd tightening.

"I got twenty-five new," Clyde Winchenbach offers.

"My barn's got at least that many," Nathaniel Hilton adds, the two men putting away a century-old family fishing feud, demonstrating how life on a seafaring peninsula is always a delicate balance of competition and cooperation.

"We're gonna need a much wider base," Pufferman says, rubbing at the stubble on his chin, letting me know the project is in good—if not unexpected—hands.

By the time I return with my next truckload of traps, neighbors have stacked the pots in a base circle, three traps high, each layer tighter than the one before it by about six inches. The overlap's a rough guess for me, but Pufferman measures each connection as our community gathers ladders and cooperation to spiral the rows higher. Hermon's setting out lunch and snacks to keep energy and spirits high. We're well beyond midday when I deliver my last load of traps, just as Kermit Hodge pulls his long-reach excavator into place, its front bucket affixed with a hook. I join Kermit in the warm cab since it's officially not a good idea for me to watch Pufferman do the math.

Kermit works the hydraulics to place pot after pot onto the high stack and I watch a tree grow into shape, Haggard waving down the traps and Pufferman easing each one into place as Jimmy and his dad secure the tension lines. Pufferman gives me a wave when he's ready for a new pot. Not a wave *to me*, exactly. He doesn't see me. He's invested in the work. Careful. Calculating. A thousand percent present in the moment. Like me when I haul traps from the deep. As the last pot is set into place as the topper, the crowd has seemingly doubled and people let go of a collective cheer. I admit, it's satisfying.

Among the celebrating, Haggard yells to Jimmy McFarland to fetch his truck since Jimmy's fourteen and been driving boats in and out of the harbor for a couple of years now. The thing is, Haggard's truck is a big one and the tree is a perfect target for a kid with too much bravado. Yet, Jimmy's careful and conscientious with his maneuvering, like responsibility and respect might just grow into the next generation.

Haggard talks to Kermit with smooth, confident hand signals, as if he's a symphony conductor helping the large steel star get lifted out of the bed of Haggard's truck and set onto the tree's top.

"Well, I'll be," Kermit says. "Haggard's gone and made a star."

"Haggard's always the star," I say.

"*Ayuh*," Kermit says.

A familiar ache of grief rushes through me for Dad not being here, not having the chance to see his village raise a piece of hand-crafted art that's part tree and part lighthouse and all human heart. Little kids race to the base of the tree, ferrying new, freshly-painted crimson red buoys into piles for the adults to hang before the ladders return home. In this part of the world, every fisherman has buoys with a different color combination. Law mandates a fisherman's unique colors appear on their boat and their buoys. The colors, shades, and tones—even the thickness of the stripes—connect a vessel to a person, no different than a family crest.

The deep crimson is a new color here. No one on this peninsula fishes with solid red buoys. Maybe it was Haggard—or even Hermon—who coordinated the painting of solid, mono-colored buoys while it took an entire day to raise the tree. The color of the buoys signals to everyone the buoys don't belong to anyone. Instead, they belong to all of us. It'd be hard to understand the scope of this communal gesture if I were a person who hadn't grown up around the language of buoys. But I have, and I like what these were saying about the way people could come together.

Hard work and strong backs have never been in short supply on the cove, and by the time the sky has given up its light, many of us are ready to thaw out in the vintage red dinette booths at Earl's Eats. As a general rule, Mainers are about fifty years behind the rest of America, and maybe more so here at the edge of the continent. Ours is a place where traditions get preserved; we don't live in a state people drive through to get somewhere else, so change doesn't arrive on the heels of outsiders. That's fine by me, and—by the looks of it—everyone else here. As trays of pulled pork, biscuits, and corn are opened self-serve style, it's an unspoken courtesy to help the old and young fill their plates first. So, I lean against the back wall, giving elders their elbow room and kids the space to crash to the floor in exhaustion, their legs jutting out from under tables and chairs in spent surrender. Together, we're a wriggling, animated mass that's almost enough to distract me from Maia making her way through the diner, parting the sea of people with her pregnancy as she aims straight for me.

"Are you sitting down?" she asks.

I laugh. "You are literally standing right next to me standing."

"Charlie, I'm doing my best not to cause a scene but your post"— she looks around as if to ensure the people surrounding us are sufficiently engaged in their own dinner and drama before shoving her phone in my face—"it's on Reddit with more than a hundred thousand upvotes already."

"You're saying words I mostly don't understand."

"I have never loved you and your crustaceans as much as I do in this moment."

"Still lost."

"Charlie. Your post." She flicks at her screen with her thumb. "How are you not getting this?"

"Probably because you're not communicating in a way that actual humans can comprehend."

"Okay." She inhales a deep breath and pats her belly as if to say, *not now.* "The piece you wrote on not-love is a big, fat, delicious hit. You wouldn't believe the comments. So many people connected with your call for self-love over romance. It's..." she lets out an enormous breath. "It's huge, Charlie. Beyond huge."

"That's great. I'm happy for you."

"Be happy for *us.*" Her eyes lift, wide with an impending request.

"*Uh-uh.*" I shake my head. "Do not ask me for another."

"I am your best person. I shouldn't have to ask."

"I'm not doing it. I've got a festival to whip together, remember?"

"I'll take the lead on the festival if you write another post."

"I can't. I gave you my one idea."

"Okay, but when can you have the next one written, really?"

"Never."

"Monday is great. Then maybe one or two a week?"

"No."

"It's only for the month."

"Still no."

"Perfect. I can't wait to read your next piece!"

"You're relentless." I let go of an exasperated huff that is half laugh, half protest.

"How can you deny my readers their love of your lobstering life? They're obsessed with your independence and creepy bottom-dwellers. Look!"

She positions her phone in front of my face, scrolling through the blurred remarks with a quick flick of her thumb. But I'm not looking at her screen and when she notices, she presses the side of her head to mine and parallels her gaze to watch Pufferman slipping off his jacket just inside the entrance.

The in-swinging door has cleared a half-moon of space, essentially carving out a private island for Pufferman to exist within a sea of bodies. He tucks his jacket between his elbow and hip, the movement easy and fluid under the crisp span of his strong shoulders I try hard not to notice. His long fingers slide the cap from his head so his thick blonde strands fall over his forehead in every direction. He rakes his hand through his hair, his silver band catching the light of the diner's hanging glass globes.

Pufferman's smile jumps as he spots me at the opposite end of the diner, his full bottom lip curling. Worse, the fine lines camped at the edges of his eyes deepen as he waves at me, making warmth pool in my belly, my entire body tipping toward the source.

"Pufferman's gonna need a new nickname," Maia whispers.

"Yeah," I breathe. I shake him and his beauty from my sightline and turn to Maia. "I'll do it. Tonight. I'll write you another column or post or whatever you call it."

Anything to keep my mind off this man walking toward me.

~ Love & Lobsters ~

I'm an expert on exactly two things: lobsters, and caring for the people I love.

I've never considered these commitments to be mutually exclusive because I make my living off the land—or the sea as it were—and out here, on a wide finger of rocky peninsula that meets the ocean in three directions, survival depends on balance and respect. When I respect the magnitude of the sea, she will tolerate me. If I think I'm stronger than a storm, I've already lost. Balance is reciprocity, a loving give-and-take.

It's why catching lobsters makes me humble, fierce, tireless, and exhausted, sometimes all in the same breath. Braving the sea also makes me clear-headed. To survive, I have to know where I'm going and when to pull back. I put myself at risk if I'm not constantly aware of my boundaries, my territory, and my limits.

Lobsters are no different when it comes to carving out strict boundaries.

The American lobster is a fiercely independent and territorial creature, and their desire to dwell solo is a personality trait I understand. If a smaller predator threatens their chill space, a lobster will wave one long antennae over their eyes like a windshield wiper. This micromovement serves as a warning: a polite, gentle request for the intruder to step back. If the trespasser persists, the lobster will go to the mattresses. Equipped to fight with a "crusher" claw and smaller "ripper" claw—also known as the cutter, seizer or pincer claw—lobsters are built for battle. The very names for a lobster's front claws are fighting words, and adversaries should take them seriously.

What does all this aggression have to do with love?

Literally everything. Or nothing, you decide.

See, I'm not the only boundary-protecting lobster fisherman. We're a territorial bunch, and we protect what we love. Our long-standing, unspoken rule is simple: Never fish in another person's territory.

It's a good rule.

There are consequences for not obeying this basic norm. Traps intruding on my territory get a zip tie fixed to their buoy handles, my micromovement serving as a warning that quietly and kindly conveys: *this seat's taken.* My zip tie is long and thin and not unlike a lobster's antennae and the warning it carries. If the trap remains or more appear, I'll haul the offender's traps and open their doors to set free any catch before returning the traps to the ocean floor. On the sea bottom, door open, lobsters will dine buffet-style on the bait before moving on with their bottom-dwelling business. The trespassing fisherman will pull up an empty trap, unable to misinterpret the clear message of the open door. This is a bit like me using my "pincer claw," squeezing the profit from a lobsterman who isn't respecting boundaries. I've known lobstermen who reinforce the longstanding rules of territory by flashing "a cutter" claw by severing the offending trap lines from the buoys altogether so the traps are lost to the deep forever. Some flex their "crusher claw" and pull the traps, capturing them as spoils of war.

The habits of the lobster and the lobsterman are as linked as our destinies.

To the unsuspecting reader, this might feel very distant from love or happily ever afters, but my perspective is different. The simple, age-old rules lobstermen (and lobsters) live by can—and should—be observed by humans in their quest for balance and love.

If you're a person who's looking for love, don't fish in someone else's territory.

Taken means taken.

It's that simple.

If you're a romantic and your radar is permanently dialed toward love, there might be times when a shiny new person will cross your path. Maybe you'll think this new person could be *your* shiny new person. Just make sure they aren't already the center of another's orbit. Because if they are, it doesn't matter if they seem perfect for you.

They are with someone else.

You need to move on.

After all, the planet is mostly ocean and oceans are mostly undiscovered worlds—you can fish somewhere else. There are, as the old adage goes, plenty of fish in the sea. Do you really want to start your great love adventure by wading into someone else's territory, your tender story beginning with verbs like *crush* and *seize* and *rip*?

Because whether its self-love or a Happily Ever After you fish for and wish for, it's always better to cast your line in a way that doesn't crush someone else.

7

The Conversation

I don't love my second piece of writing, but I send it to Maia because now that I'm away from the common and the energy of the crowd, I can't stop the deluge of self-doubt that threatens to drown me. Who am I to be writing for an audience? Or brainstorming a festival? What if no one shows up? What if the entire peninsula chips in to create a party that nobody attends and I cost them twice? First for supporting me and Mem, then for supporting a festival that could very well strain their wallets, time, and energy.

I need distraction. Lots of distraction. I go looking for it on Instagram where there's a message waiting.

> @toothpicks3478
> I thought of you today in
> a non-gossip kind of way.
> Isn't that strange? I mean,
> considering I don't know
> the most basic things about
> you. Like, if you like chocolate.
> Or have a favorite color, or
> feel strongly about condiments.

> > @BirdieBlueBug
> > Not strange, but definitely a sneaky
> > way to get intel. Though I won't bite.
> > Unless it's chocolate. Duh.

I settle onto my bed, propping a throw pillow across my legs. Apparently, the fingers belonging to Anonymous Me are extroverts:

> > @BirdieBlueBug
> > I did a thing today. Not a good thing
> > or bad thing, but a thing. It's just...I
> > don't think it was my best work and I

pride myself on having a lot of pride.
When I do something, I do it right.
Or try my hardest.

@toothpicks3478
Your work ethic and love of
chocolate are admirable.
Have you done this thing
before? Asking for a fellow
perfectionist.

@BirdieBlueBug
Just once.

@toothpicks3478
Ah, classic sophomore slump.

@BirdieBlueBug
Is it that obvious?

@toothpicks3478
You've got One Hit Wonder
written all over you.

@BirdieBlueBug
How do I break the curse?

@toothpicks3478
Do you need to break the
curse? Doing one thing brilliantly
one time is a major success.
Repeatability is overrated.

@BirdieBlueBug
What makes you think I did
something brilliant once?

@toothpicks3478
Because you set a high bar
with the work ethic you describe.
First time brilliance isn't a fluke.

I allow the compliment to wash over me.

@BirdieBlueBug
What made you think of
not-gossip today?

@toothpicks3478
I pondered whether or not
I could truly get to know a
person without exchanging
personal details. And if
they could get to know me.

@BirdieBlueBug
Do you often ponder?

@toothpicks3478
I devote an inordinate
portion of each day to
pondering. It's a problem.

@BirdieBlueBug
This tells me so much about you.

@toothpicks3478
Does it?

@BirdieBlueBug
Yes. You'd be crap at Jeopardy.
Taking too long to think through
your answers and all.

It's only when I try for a sip of tea that I realize I'm smiling,
which makes me think of the sweet swell of Logan's—I mean,
Pufferman's—bottom lip, which I definitely do not want to be
thinking about.

@toothpicks3478
Ha! You're not wrong.
I do tend to overthink.
And undersay.

@BirdieBlueBug
Undersay? Does that
mean you're quiet?

@toothpicks3478
To a fault, I've been told.

@BirdieBlueBug
Ouch?

@toothpicks3478
Life altering ouch.

@BirdieBlueBug
Would it help to know
you don't seem shy?

@toothpicks3478
Yes.

@toothpicks3478
Would it help to know I
believe there's high statistical
likelihood that whatever you

did today for the second time
was executed brilliantly?

@BirdieBlueBug
To be determined.

@toothpicks3478
I look forward to the update.

I'm slow and careful about closing my laptop because I don't want the conversation to end. I'm not quite ready to nickname this person Internet Three, though it feels good to have a light conversation with another human, a luxury this past year hasn't often afforded. While I'm waiting, a reply email arrives from Maia about my post. It's only one word: THIS!!! I refuse to read into its meaning because what could she be saying? That she's happy I wrote another post? Or I missed the mark, going in a direction she doesn't like? Or, that the post meets with her high standards? See. Not reading into it.

A Barred Owl calls *who-cooks-for-you* over the slapping waves of the harbor and I imagine the bird's full feathers fattening around her neck as she perches in her protected roost behind our barn, her head tilted and waiting for a singularly special member of her species to answer her call. I snuggle deeper into my nest of comforters and turn out the light, wishing my father a goodnight as instinctually as I close my eyes.

8

The Commute

I wake in a fog, and tiptoe to the kitchen where Mem's already busy at a saucepan, whipping cocoa for my morning hot chocolate.

"How are you up right now?" I scan the room for Hermon Benner's coat, hat, boots—relieved to find no sign of him other than the happy tune Memma hums. I grab my hoodie from the side of the jelly cabinet and kiss her on the cheek, her fingers squeezing my shoulder in that way she has of giving me a hug, encouragement, and love all in one practiced movement. Starving but distracted, I bury my nose inside the fridge for a long string of minutes before Mem shoos me to the table and sets out hot cocoa to cool in my favorite yellow mug.

Mem holds the back of my wooden chair at its upper rail. "Feels like change is visiting the cove, and I know new things aren't always your favorite."

I scoff. "I'm fine." They're the same words I said to her when my world broke open from her diagnosis. She was the one who got sick, and I hid behind the lie that I'd be strong enough to accept it, absorb it, continue on.

She pats my shoulders. "I've got your lunch made, all ready to go." She nods to the deep metal lunchbox Dad used for his peanut-butter-and-strawberry-rhubarb-jam-sandwich, small bag of Cheetos, and an apple or orange—never a banana.

I run my thumb across the hollow dents in the lunchbox and pop the rusted latches to peek inside at two apples, a bulging chicken salad sandwich wrapped in parchment, and a thick brownie folded into a paper towel, its hard edges still frozen from Memma's homemade stash in the freezer.

"How long have you been awake?" I ask.

"Restless mind. Couldn't sleep past two so I gave in and got up."

"You need rest, Mem."

"There's lots to do now there's a full-blown festival afoot, Charlie girl. I owe this town my life."

Sadness catches in me, rising through the crevice in my heart that split open when she got sick. Because of course Mem would fully dive into prepping for a holiday fair, never a woman to do anything half-mast.

"Don't push yourself too hard. I don't have to pull pots today. I can go tomorrow…stay here, help out."

She dismisses my concern with a *tsk* and pours the remaining hot chocolate into my thermos. I grab the vanilla ice cream from the freezer and she adds a dollop. It was the way Dad took his coffee: black except for a scoop of ice cream. He claimed his technique was more efficient than adding milk and sugar separately, which still feels like solid logic.

Together, we eat flax cereal dotted with the blueberries that grow wild in Maine's barrens. The tart berries break open in my mouth, soft and intoxicating as summer.

"Promise me you'll take it easy today."

"Not in my nature." Mem's already clearing her dish with hummingbird energy. "You can do one thing for me, though."

"Anything." I lean back, and can't recall the last time Mem asked me for help. Even when she was at her worst, I was the one leaning on her for support.

"Never make a promise you can't honor," she reminds me.

I lift my elbows to the table, lean in. "Mem, I'd do anything for you. Just ask already."

She gets extra interested in folding a nubby orange dish towel. "I don't like you boating so far offshore alone this time of year."

"Mem—"

She raises a hand and places the towel next to the sink with too much precision. "I know you'll tell me you'll be fine and I'm not saying you're not right; I'm saying I don't like it."

"Okay." I want to defend my independence, remind her I've been fishing solo most of my life, but literally everything is different now—not just the way I view Mem after her illness, but the way she sees me, the way we're each mindful of mortality and careful with our time together, and our time apart.

"I asked the McFarland boys to serve as your sternman."

"Great, done." While I don't need the help, the McFarland boys are good hands to have on any boat, and if their company sets Mem at ease well, that's a bonus. "Which one's joining me?"

"Well, they're already working for their dad so I asked Logan if he was free."

"You didn't." I stand, moving to the back of the chair, holding onto its high finials with tightening fists. A person who doesn't know the sea can easily be a bigger liability than me fishing alone any day, a concern I won't say out loud for fear of ratcheting up Mem's worry.

"He's been on the dock waiting for you and the poor man's probably near frozen about now."

I pull in a deep breath, knowing that arguing with Mem isn't the way I want to spend a moment of our time together. "Okay." My exhale comes quiet and low. "I'll be offshore by twenty miles or so, long past the isles." I twist my grip over the turned wood. "Maia can raise me on the radio if you need me, but don't need me, okay? Just have an easy day of being easy with yourself." I gather my raincoat and slip on my boots at the door where Mem hands me my lunch. She tugs the sides of my hat lower over my ears.

"Be back by five."

"I'll be here." Probably before. While Pufferman might be nice to look at, the chances he'll be able to persist fourteen hours at sea are not good. Being near the sea and on the sea are different things entirely.

Outside, the harbor steams. Coils of drifting mist climb from the water into the air. The cold hits my lungs with a punch so fierce I tuck my chin behind the high collar of my foul weather jacket and spy Pufferman seated cross-legged on the rocky breakwater like cold yoga is a thing. I'll have to ask Maia if cold yoga is a thing.

"Mornin'," I call, keeping my head down as Pufferman follows me to the boat while I decide I absolutely do not need to ask Maia if cold yoga is a thing because I shall not be remotely intrigued by Pufferman or his behaviors for the next three weeks, four days, and six-and-a-half hours.

Stepping onto the boat, then into the protection of the pilothouse, I say, "Heard you were coming with." I turn over the engine and its low hum rumbles into the sea, waking the water. At my console, I light up my dash and flick on my running lights.

In the low glow, Pufferman watches me, his head tilted. "Your grandmother said you invited me aboard. Did I get this wrong?"

Memma's watching us from the kitchen glass while trying hard not to look like she's watching us from the kitchen glass. "Not at all. I give all our guests a day at sea."

This is a lie.

I'd just planned to wait for Hann—" his wife's name dies on my lips as I turn because he's not wearing his puffy jacket. Instead, he's sporting a cable knit wool sweater like an old-school fisherman. The fabric stretches close to his skin, and when he raises his arms to the roof-rail to board, he's all strong torso and wool sweater and ...married. Married. Married.

I break my stare but not before noticing his orange rubber overalls and how good he makes them look. "Where'd you get the fishing attire?"

"Jimmy loaned me a few things."

I make a mental note to knuckle punch Jimmy McFarland square on the upper arm next time our paths cross. Hard.

"Where should I stow this?" Pufferman lifts his tightly-packed backpack and it's unfair how even his hands look good in the thick, blue insulated gloves that are industry standard against cuts and cold, and which have never looked good on a human before. Ever. Not even once. I nod to the cabinet under the dash and when he bends to stow his bag, the flexing muscles of his back make my breath skip.

"You been on a boat before?"

"A few times." He returns to the deck. "Most of what I know I learned from *Deadliest Catch*."

Oh, boy.

He at least knows enough to untie us from the dock without me asking and kick us off so I can turn in the harbor and set out to sea. "We'll steam offshore for an hour or so to reach my traps." Thankfully, the churning rumble of the engine doesn't encourage small talk. "You good?"

"Never better." He gives me a blue-thumbed thumbs-up, raised with that same measured confidence I watched him carry on the common yesterday. The wind twists inside the pilothouse, racing up my neck.

"Give that winterback a close, yeah?" I gesture toward the pocket door behind me and he latches it shut, locking us inside with the heat and each other. My boat is sixty feet in length, and I've never considered her small before, but a lobster boat is mostly deck and the enclosed wheelhouse feels tight with him next to me. The windows steam.

We stand through the highest swells and I'm overly aware of the black rubber tip of my boot and how close it is to Pufferman's boot, and how one strong wave could choreograph our boots into touching. Our boots! Black rubber footwear has topped the Least Sexy charts since they debuted on the scene, yet still my toes curl under, as if shyly anticipating a chance encounter with this man who smells of evergreens and early mornings and line-dried wool. Dad liked to say that any day spent fishing was a good day, but my toes disagree. Today's going to be a long day.

As we jockey to the deep ocean and approach my fishing grounds, we have a front row seat to the sunrise, its yellow yolk breaking open along the horizon.

"Is that fog?" Logan asks.

Strands of silver float up from the twilight sea, churning pink as they reach for the sun before fading to white, then disappearing all together.

"Sea smoke. Maine's way of telling us it's cold. Really cold."

"I've never seen anything like it."

"It's rare." As precious as finding someone who's as awed by the language of Maine's waters as I am—a fact I try to ignore as I slow to my first buoy, cobalt blue with a wide white stripe across its middle. His focus is fixed on me as I demonstrate how to fetch the line with the gaffer pole to pull the rope and trap onboard. Pufferman is a fast learner. He gets the braided line on the second try, but the waves are confused, and they shift with force so we're tossed against each other at the rail so many times I look around for a hidden camera planted by Maia to capture footage for a scene in Karma for Christmas, where the strangers-to-lovers begin to fall for each other as they literally fall into each other. I shake away my suspicions and cast off my imagination. Luckily, he keeps his attention on the work and I feel Dad's wordless nod of approval for my sternman's acute focus and attention to safety.

Working solo by the fifth pot, Logan—Pufferman—effortlessly threads the line into the pulley and re-baits. It's not an easy job and no lobsterman worth their salt would want their sternman to fail at it—except me. Within me there pulses a chemical, cellular need for Logan to fail at something. Anything. Because even though I need every dollar I earn from fishing, I'd have an excuse to turn homeward and call it a day. The image of his shoulders straining with each hauled trap would be lost to distant memory along with any knowledge of his long, solid legs holding a determined stance at the wet rail.

"I haven't seen any other boats," he yells as we make our way to the next buoy, his arms raised to the hardtop of the pilot house so the length of him is behind me as I steer, his words meeting my ear in a hot rush despite the negative temperatures.

"Less than half of us fish this late in the year," I call. "You have a better chance of seeing a whale than another boat."

He pops into the pilothouse, his smile wide and youthful, filled with wonder. "Do you think?"

"Maybe." His enthusiasm is contagious, even as he tries to reign it in.

He plants his arms wide across the dash for balance, and spreads his legs wider so that he's essentially a human starfish. The posture should be ridiculous. Instead, I want him featured in all twelve months of the World's Sexiest Lobstermen calendar. The cover, too.

The sea hits the starboard side of my bow with a slap, her salt spray reminding me to keep my head in the game. I give the ocean a side eye, never quite unconvinced Dad isn't out here with me somehow. Today, it's possible he's using nature to reprimand me for my straying thoughts.

"Lobsters move offshore when the water grows colder so I need to go farther to find them in winter. Not everyone thinks the journey is worth the cost of fuel." For me, the solitude, purpose, and peace are always worth it, no matter what the season, even if this year I'm fishing to relieve debt. "I usually don't fish past October when the lobsters are closer." I share a bunch of boring facts about my seasonal work while my imagination fixates on the month of July. It's a hot mid-summer's day and he's wearing his orange fishing overalls but no shirt. Plus, he's managed an excellent tan and the summer sun is a big fan of his hair, painting light streaks into his already golden....

Oof.

I cannot jog to the next buoy fast enough.

Except on my way there, I let my Maine pragmatism take over. Because today is one day. Logan is married and I'm his temporary neighbor and friendly local female lobsterman (okay, grumpy local female lobsterman. Fair). Still, whatever happens in my head out here, stays in my head out here.

"I'm grateful you're still fishing," he tells me. "Gives me a chance to get on the water. Lobster fishing is a bucket list accomplishment for me."

"I'm glad." It's the truth. Smoothing a path for someone else to be happy is never a bad thing. I slow, round to the next buoy, which Logan hooks, pulling the line on board with his bare back glistening below his wide, tanned shoulders, his summer skin slick and....

"Can I measure?" he interrupts, drawing me back to the fine reality of his absurdly well-fitted sweater.

I hand him the brass gauge, practically having to wipe sweat from my brow as I demonstrate how to measure the mottled brown lobster along its length from eye socket to tail.

"Anything too small gets thrown back. This one's a *short*, probably doesn't weigh more than a pound." I pluck a small perch from the bait bin and offer it to the lobster's crusher claw, a gift the juvenile lobster accepts quickly and instinctually before I toss him and his meal overboard.

Logan watches me with a cocked head and squinted stare. "Did you just give the lobster a snack?"

"I did."

He nods, grinning. "Kinda like an oceanside take on a drive-through window."

"Never thought about it like that before, but yeah. They feed us, so I feed them." I can't remember a time when anyone helped me see my customs in an unexpected light.

He shifts his attention to the lobster he frees from the trap, careful about his fingers' proximity to its front claws as he measures up the length of its body. "Good, right?" His smile widens, the wind reddening his upper cheeks, turning them into taut, tiny apples just like in his October calendar photo when he's wearing a Henley thin enough for me to see the chiseled outline of his chest and arms as he reaches to pluck a high McIntosh from a branch while wearing only his boxers. On a ladder. In unlaced work boots. His thighs—

"Charlie?"

I twist the lobster upside down as I return to the present. "So, if they're big enough"— I clear my throat, trying to clear my head— "the next step is to check for eggs or a V-notch. Either indicator means she's an egg-bearing female and we throw her back with a snack."

"What's a V-notch?"

"A mark on the tail made by another lobsterman, telling us she was found with eggs at one time."

"Smart."

"Conservation. Keeping her in the ocean means we ensure future generations of lobsters and lobstermen." I eyeball her, keeping an acceptable distance from Logan. "She's a keeper."

"Really?"

His smile is pure joy, and I see Young Me, the way Dad must have seen me that day I pulled my first pot, found my blue. Delight strips twenty years from Logan's face and he's a kid again, treasure hunting, pulling secrets from the sea. I think Young Me would have liked adventuring with Young Logan.

Dad definitely would not approve of any aspect of my inappropriate daydreaming so I concentrate on fishing hard until midday when I call: "You hungry?"

"Starved," he flashes a devastating smile.

"Let's head inside!" I yell over the wind that arrives from the west, tossing the boat, and making the enclosure feel even smaller than before. I gesture toward rest and just as he moves to take a seat, a surge broadsides my boat and heaves us together. We scramble for balance, and it isn't until we're steady again that I realize we're holding each other's arms. I drop my grip like he's contagious. He steps back in that way of his, grabbing for his chair and steadying himself onto it.

"Sorry," he says.

"Never apologize for staying safe at sea." I try to appear sage and unaffected by the way his touch lingers.

I extract the sandwich Memma made for me, unwrapping the parchment and offer him half.

"No, thank you." He collects his backpack from storage. "I made my own."

I take an enormous bite and am grateful I don't have to play nice and share, even if Logan is a world-famous Maine lobsterman calendar model. My eyes close to the perfection of Memma's culinary creation where I can literally taste the care she invests in my meals. The fresh cubed chicken, the hint of homemade egg mayonnaise, lettuce that's julienned into fine strips then finely chopped into squares so it's mixed with the chicken and mayo and miniature chunks of celery for democratic distribution of all ingredients in all bites. My sandwich is so much more than a sandwich. It is home and inspiration and motivation. When I open my eyes, though, I see it has competition.

From an organized box (balanced on his muscled thighs, if one cared to notice), Logan extracts a roll of rice that he dips into an open tin of miraculously unspilled sauce.

"Is that actual sushi?" An enormous bite of sandwich is shoved to the inside of my cheek so my mumbled words can confirm my destiny never to appear in Logan's calendar fantasies.

He laughs and raises his rice roll in a kind of food toast. "In my defense, I made it before I knew I'd be on a boat for lunch."

"You *made* your sushi?"

Of course he made his sushi.

"Seriously? In that tiny lighthouse kitchen?" The back of my hand covers my lips to keep my lunch from spilling out—my version of high etiquette.

He offers me the roll along with a wide-eyed smile that lifts his wool cap higher on the ridge of his soft, clear forehead. "What, you don't make sushi?"

I wave off his offering. "I can barely make toast. The kitchen is not my preferred ecosystem."

He leans forward, resting his elbows on his knees. His hair is slicked with sea spray and salt, his face burned red from the cold. He looks toward the back of the boat, toward the water. "I'd say you're doing all right for yourself in this life." He pulls in a deep breath, as if he's inhaling the sea, even if we're in the pilothouse and the heat is on, the fresh air locked outside. The way he gives over to the ocean around us, coupled with the intimacy of floating together makes me relax into the moment.

"I'd never want to be anywhere else," I tell him. After an entire life feeling anxious with new people, I'm oddly comfortable with Logan and how he gives me the gift of seeing my vocation with a new lens.

The sea reprimands me by heaving us in a rolled pitch that sends the cup of my thermos tumbling his way. He steadies and plucks the mug from the well-worn deck. When he passes it to me, our fingers graze. Electric. Unnerving. The smallest touch that makes my mouth go dry. He recovers and slips the offending hand under his thigh.

Lucky hand.

No. Not a lucky hand. Just a hand. A hand that has no relevance in my universe.

"You know you don't have a typical commute, right?" he asks, like I'm not still inappropriately reeling.

My seal bark laugh jumps in its wild way, making the corner of his mouth twitch upward at my lack of grace.

"I couldn't imagine another life. Hours wasted to traffic or watching the clock to see when my shift is done. I know that's life for a lot of people—and those people are lucky, having jobs they can depend on—but for me, the freedom and expanse of the sea is everything, even if the work is hard."

"I get that. I don't think I've ever felt less lonely and there's literally no one else around." His face lifts to the spray of the sun, no different than a trusting seal on a trusted rock.

"Exactly."

My entire life, newcomers to the cove have asked some variation of: *Don't you get lonely out there?* or *How can you stand it with just you and the sea?"*

Not Logan.

I mean, Pufferman.

Ugh, Logan.

He gets it.

This outdoor expanse is the exact opposite of the loneliest place on earth.

And it makes me wonder if I've been wrong about my independence all this time, because sharing this freedom with Logan isn't horrible.

"You still with me?" Logan's head ducks, searching for my attention and drawing it up. "I asked if you're Charlie of *CHARLOTTE ANNE* fame." He gestures to the backside of my boat, where my first and middle names are decaled, the letters forming a subtle arch across the stern. Dad would pat the name each time he boarded and docked his boat, no different than Mem swiping her thumb over his photo when she leaves the house.

"Yes and no. Anne is my middle name but also, I'm named after my dad's grandmother so I think my dad named the boat for me and her. It's considered bad luck by some fishermen to name boats after wives since wives can come and go. It's the daughters who stay."

He lets go of an easy laugh. "And what does your mom think of this?"

Something in me hardens, straightening my spine. "She lives in the southern desert. It's unlikely she's had a boat named after her."

"Does your dad still fish?"

I put down the second half of my sandwich, rewrap it in parchment. "My dad passed when I was a kid." My movements are restless and clumsy as I restore the messy sandwich to its rightful place in the lunchbox. When I glance up, he's looking at me. Seeing me.

"I'm sorry," he says.

His words ground me, the way so many hands fell to my shoulders when Dad was first found at sea. Logan doesn't break his stare and I meet his gaze. His blue eyes are like chameleons, shifting almost imperceptibly from sky blue to deep ocean blue. If I weren't paying close attention, I might not notice the flickering of his lids, the way his look tightens and expands, his eyes searching mine and finding something there.

But I am paying attention.

"I lost my mom last summer," he tells me. "It's why Hannah and I rented your place. My mom had read about your lighthouse becoming a guest cottage a few years back and wanted to visit but...didn't have the strength. Hannah and I promised we'd come here and a few other places my mom had wanted to see. I'm excited for Hannah to be here. We'll explore for my mom, keep her close when we do."

"That's really lovely."

Suddenly, I'm aware that *this* is why people put up with romantic love, and carry the weight of someone else's baggage—their promises, concessions, grief, laughter, decisions, and dreams. Because the Perfect Someone will rally behind you and intentionally, carefully, lovingly shift your world from hard to soft. The way Hannah's name, their join intention, and the memory of his mother slip so effortlessly from his lips, I feel joy and jealousy for what he has. So much like Maia and Sam, a one in a million connection. Maia claimed no one outside a person's inner circle was interested in hearing another person's actual truths, but Logan makes me see how the right person will always be interested. Because those truths are the exact reasons they love their person.

"What was your mother's name?"

His smile curls. "Gertrude. She *hated* that name. Everyone called her Dolly." His short laugh is sad or unsure, something I can't quite read as he sinks deeper in his seat. "Gertrude was my secret weapon when I was a horrible teenager and wanted to be cruel to her. I'd spit that name at her like it was a curse." He looks to the horizon, the wash of light there. "Now, I can't think of one thing my mom ever did that would deserve cruelty." He pushes at a tear forming.

"I know what you mean." We are surrounded by water, around us, within us, a current connecting us. "My dad became a saint the day he died. I've never been able to remember a thing he did wrong."

"Maybe that's the measure of a well-lived life, when the people you leave behind only remember your good bits." We sit with the warmth of that sentiment for a long while until he rummages in his pack and offers a container my way. "Want a slice?"

My curiosity leans in. "Is that pineapple?" But even as I say it, I know it's something more. It's an exotic fruit, appearing in winter. A snack that can't be obtained in any hyper-local way.

"It's good luck on a boat, right?"

I smile. "Yes." I pluck one of the two fat slices and let the cold juice slip down my throat, tasting of summer and ease. And something more? Like intention, maybe?

Before we turn for home, I stand at the wet rail and invite him to join me and the wind and the rolling water. He keeps a respectable distance as he does. I take the longest inhale I've had all day, my spirit buoyed by Maine's wild blue.

"Why the deep breath?" he asks.

"Habit. I always offer appreciation to the ocean before I return home," I tell him, confiding this truth that I've never shared with Mem or Maia, a ritual I brought to the sea when it was just me out here, alone with my thoughts and the imprint Dad left on my heart. I loosen my grip on the rail. "I take a quiet moment to ask the sea to be kind to me in the same way the water is kind. It follows the moon's instructions, swallows rain, and hosts life. As much as the sea feels like my home, I'm a stranger here. So, I pass with caution and respect, and I ask the ocean to care for me and spare me. I have no other gifts to bring our planet but kindness and a soft footprint."

"That might be the most beautiful thing I've ever heard another person say." His compliment sounds as if it startled him, but strengthens my nerve, shoring up my willingness to be this exposed in front of a stranger.

"Just before I start for home, I say goodbye to my dad. Or sometimes it's hello or thank you." I give a small laugh. "Most days it's everything in between." I hear the lift of Logan's light, knowing chuckle, but don't look his way. "I thought, if you want...," I offer. "We could send a wish to your mom, too. Or I can leave you to do it alone."

"Together," he says, the word a whisper.

I turn up my palms at the rail, letting go of control. "I miss you, Dad. May the wind be forever at your back." My gaze falls to Logan who fixes his stare on the horizon. I join him. "And, Dolly," I say. "I wish you fair winds and following seas."

"Love you, Mom." Logan's words are choked with sadness and we don't say anything for a long time because sometimes in the face of grief and in the midst of all the universal unknowns, there are no words to say.

When Logan reaches his hand to mine on the rail, he squeezes my fingers in that efficient way Memma hugs at my shoulders. His glove links with mine for the time it takes a second to blink and then we are two people with two stories looking out in one direction before we haul and rebait the remaining traps to fill my tanks, our backs warmed and worn with hard work as we speed toward the distant shore, conversation flowing easily between us even as we say nothing at all.

9

The Crisis

I'm fully aware that saying any variation of *it's a great day* while on a boat will turn a good day into a bad one, sure as the sea has salt. Still, I've always been able to think it in my mind, know it in my heart. It feels a lot like tempting superstition the way I want time to bend and slow, to stretch far enough outside of its comfort zone to grant me a few more hours with a person I can't be with after we disembark. But today has made me greedy. On the journey home to Christmas Cove, light drains from the sky, shifting from daylight to dusk blue as we coast through the path of the setting sun, the glow of its aftermath a reminder that time moves on without our consent.

Still, as I pass the rugged, rocky swell of uninhabited Damariscove Island, I slow more than normal, justifying my reduced speed as a measure of safety, even as the low twist in my belly reminds me I'm trying to protect my time with a new passenger. But there's something else. Something wholly unexpected. And not okay.

My inner compass struggles to make sense of the blackness around and beyond Cove Light. Christmas Cove sits as a gateway between land and sea, perched as a harbor, a safe haven. And yet.

The harbor is dark.

I squint, then check my gauges and GPS, wildly searching for any way to make sense of how my distractions could have rerouted me, pushed me off course when I've never needed instruments to find Christmas Cove.

I know these waters and the channels.

The current leading me home.

But tonight, there's nothing but shadows.

Panic rises, its hand clutching my throat because I know what it means when our harbor goes dark. I lean forward on the wheel, even as I want to turn back.

"Everything okay?" Logan asks.

"Yeah." My whisper is a dismissal, and a lie.

Because the last time the harbor was draped in darkness, my father had died.

My heart races. My brain spirals with thoughts of Mem. Her illness. Because that's what this is, right? Cancer returning as a thief to steal both life and light.

I try to breathe. I do. But I can't pull in enough air. I step back from the wheel, dropping my arms to my sides, my fingers failing to shake off my growing anxiety. I throw open the pilot house door and the cold wind scolds me for not being home with my mem, tucked into her side so close there'd be no room for tragedy to slip between us. Why wasn't I home with Mem, savoring my time with her, our cottage, our life together? She was stretching herself thin and I knew it. And I left for the water anyway.

I'm only faintly aware Logan cuts the engine with a turn of the key as I crouch, pulling my knees to my heart. My head's light enough to faint yet heavy with dread. "My grandmother." My words are barely a squeak. "I...I need...the...oh, god...Mem..."

Logan bends to me, holds me at the shoulders. "Charlie, you're okay. Everything is okay."

"No." I shake him off and stand too quickly, immediately feeling unsteady. The waves threaten to knock me to the icy water where I'll be too burdened to swim because a person can only bear so much tragedy before loss becomes too big, too heavy to carry, an anchor and an end.

Logan grabs me harder now, his grip firm at my elbows. "Charlie."

"I can't breathe."

"You need to breathe."

I try to shake him off again but I'm too weak, clumsy in my mortal body. I'll faint here, die here. My heart thunders too fast. My mind empties of everything but death and loss and my ribs turn sharp and jagged, slicing me from the inside. "Mem!" I try to scream, but her name comes out as a whisper. "She's my whole world."

"Look at me." Logan bears down on his hold, even as I don't try to wriggle free. Because what's the point? There's nothing left to fight for. He tries to catch my eyes, but I'm only half here. "You are not alone, Charlie. I'm here. Can you hear me? You are not alone. I'm here."

"I need…to get home."

He pulls me to him, holds me up, and I'm a ragged thing, hollowed out, all shell. "Then let me get you home."

I nod, and reach for the VHF to call Maia so I can hear the truth in her words, in her voice, all of me needing her as a compass. And just as I engage the radio, I catch a wisp of light out of the corner of my eye. It's a small glint from across the harbor. Not the dulled light hiding behind curtains in a home. Not the blue light of a television. Not the yellow haze of a modern lantern. It is a small, crisp flicker in the darkness.

My hands claw at Logan's chest as I straighten toward the signal that must be Dad joining me or Mem saying goodbye. Logan holds me tight, upright. "Did you see that?" I ask. It flickers again. "There!" The light is faint and wobbly. I can't hone in on it. Can't read it closely. Still, it feels like hope. Or home.

I keep my eye trained on the place where I saw the wisp of light as I fumble in the pilothouse for binoculars, Logan's hand at the small of my back to keep me steady. I search through magnified glass but there's nothing beyond blackness. Desperate, I flick on my search beam. Then off. On, and off again: a signal. In response, the small, faint flicker returns, weak and fleeting as a lightning bug caught out of season. My hands blindly search for Logan, the heartbeat of him behind me.

"I see it," he says.

I want to turn to him, turn the boat, turn this day around, but I can't stop searching for the flash that's disappeared. Darkness stretches for miles. No matter how much I search and wish and want light into existence, my eyes meet only murky dusk and I'm sure I dreamed the glint of light except...Logan. He saw it.

And then.

The harbor glows quick and fast as a match sparking, the surprise of it shoving me back against Logan who lets go of a sound that feels like pained relief.

Brightness showers onto the common from the tower of the fifty-foot trap tree. Lines of soft white lights coil around the human-made tree from base to top, ending with Haggard's lit star. The brilliant glow stretches, reaching over the water where it doubles in its own reflection, throwing pinpricks of light to the waves, its luminescence like glowing drops of rain. Across the harbor, joy explode. Cheers. Clapping, too. There's laughter and children screaming, and the sound of my own heartbeat settling back into place.

The holiday trap tree is a beacon. A homecoming. The exact opposite of what I'd feared, what I'd remembered.

"Charlie." My name is a push of breath across Logan's lips, but I don't turn to him. Not yet. I let his hands stay on my shoulders, allow my body to lean on his.

My phone rings, startling me in a new way.

"Welcome home!" Maia yells over the crowd. "I wasn't sure if you could see my weak Morse Code signal." I press the phone so close to my ear it hurts. "I don't want to break our forever ritual so pretend I'm barking at you to turn to Channel 11."

"Done. I've never been more grateful for your welcome home." I try to sound normal, to hide the shake in my voice.

"How does it look from your view?"

"It's stunning. My mind might actually be blown."

"Right? Any doubt I had about a lobster trap tree being amazing because—well, lobster trap tree—is totally gone. This bad boy has forced me to shut my pie hole."

"An epic accomplishment." My heart leaps in my chest, my body finding the captain's chair and collapsing into its curves. "Is Mem with you?"

"She's here, practically glowing from the success of this day. She orchestrated the entire lobster trap tree debut. Want to talk to her?"

"No." Mem's radiance from yesterday is with me again, her joy entwined with Hermon. She couldn't have known I'd return before the harbor was lit, or which dark memories would surface. And maybe this isn't about me at all. Maybe it's Mem choosing to live in the light, ready to move past her own losses, her own darkness. "Don't disturb her."

"Done. Hey, listen. My minions were promised push pops after the tree lighting and they're currently climbing on me like I'm an event ride at an amusement park."

"Weirdos."

"I know, right? Who wants push pops in winter? So, can I call when I get home??"

"Sounds perfect." I don't flip my phone shut. I don't do anything as the call disconnects. Instead, Logan and I wordlessly watch the night, and somewhere in the distance between dark and light my breath settles.

Like life, returning.

Logan passes me a cup of hot chocolate from my thermos, still warm, his eyes staying on mine as if gauging my wellness. At some point, he returns his hand to the small of my back and ushers me to the deck where we sit in the open air upon the bait table where he's spread spare life vests like couch cushions.

He doesn't ask me if I'm okay, which I'm grateful for as it feels like an absurd question, one I wouldn't know how to answer truthfully or coherently because sometimes you can be okay without being fully okay.

10

The Crush

Because the bait table is short, Logan and I sit close enough to lock in our body heat as the night wind curls around us. Across the harbor, a bolt of laughter lifts from the common and kids scream with all the inflections of a game of tag.

Logan pinches my pinky with a tenderness so light I barely feel it over my gloves. "I can take you to the shore," he offers.

I should take him to the mainland. I should be on solid ground. But that's not what I want.

"Or we can stay here in the harbor," he says.

"I'd like that." I feel the red rising on my face, up my neck. Of all the truths I've shared with Logan today, this one feels most revealing. Once we disembark, my time with Logan will be over, not just for the day but for the length of his stay. I won't allow myself another outing with him because I can't deny my attraction and that's not fair to either of us, or Hannah. For now, right here, under the forgiving night and so close to my community gathered in joy, this moment seems like a Happily Ever Now, something that's at once fleeting and forever. I drop anchor and return to our makeshift seat.

"Is it okay to ask what happened?" he says.

My worry. My panic. My mem. I give him the cliff notes version of our peninsula's grief customs, and why my dread spiked.

"You're sure you're doing all right now?"

"I am. I just let my worst fears win, but my mem's safe and happy and that's all that matters."

"Then I hope it doesn't sound callous to say I'm glad we were out here to see the tree light. I mean, I definitely wouldn't wish that kind of scare on you again…but there was something magical about that surprise of light."

"Yeah," I say, and it's strange to agree, but he's right. Of all the places my brain spiraled, it never spun toward joy or Mem getting her dream. "I think my grandmother wanted the lights on the trap tree to beam like the lighthouse, and our community gave her that. So, yeah, fairly amazing." My hands warm around my cup as I stare to the near distance, my mind recovering, resetting. Do I remember Mem saying something about the tree lighting ceremony? No. Maybe? Time blurs and my thoughts slow as I relax.

"The trap tree *is* very cool."

"It's the coolest," I say, my voice far off, all my defenses down. "I sometimes think it's easy for people to take the majesty of real trees for granted because nature makes them all the time, and in every ecosystem. But this tree? The way an entire village had to come together to make it into existence? It somehow manages to feel wild with humanity."

He shakes his head and looks away from me, a shiver twitching his shoulders. "The way you string words together sometimes sounds like poetry."

"I'm not a poet."

"That's the thing, you're not. You're this incredibly resourceful person. Like a spider."

An uncertain laugh skitters free. "Thanks?"

"Hear me out. The spider is nature's engineer. It only takes a passing glance at a spider web to see the geometrical lines, the precision math and craftsmanship that gets spun into a home that's equal parts art and a trap and a safe place for eggs. A spider makes art look effortless all while it's killing it being practical and hard at work. That's what it's like watching you work. Like your skill has no choice but to be its own beautiful art in the world. And then…."

"Then what?"

"Nothing. I should stop."

"Stopping in the middle of a compliment is against local customs. If, you know, you *were* stopping in the middle of a compliment."

He laughs. "Your connection to the work you do, and nature all around you...it's moving. Really and truly."

"Huh." I smile at him and he looks away. "That's a really nice thing to say."

"Yeah, well. Spiders deserve way more praise than they get."

"I'll pay more attention in the future."

"You won't be disappointed." He raises his mug and we toast the night, today's experiences forging us into something other than strangers.

He leans closer, his head so near to mine as he looks past me and I smell the ocean on him. Evergreens, too. "Look at the way the tree brightens the white paint of Cove Light. See there, it even ricochets off the high windows." He takes a deep, admiring breath.

"Imagine how beautiful the harbor would look if the tree and Cove Light were lit in parallel."

"You need to do that. Turn on the beacon."

"The light hasn't functioned since before I was born. The lens needs an expert and...we never prioritized its repair. I can't say why. Cost, probably. Time. My dad was busy raising me, practically solo. Then Mem taking over. You know what's funny, though?"

"Tell me."

"I miss it. I didn't think it was possible to miss something I'd never known."

"I think I've missed fishing all my life and didn't realize it until today."

"Really?"

"One thousand percent." He heads into the pilot house for his bag, and when he reappears, he asks, "You still doing all right?"

I let out a long, full exhale, my breath a push of vapor against the night. "I'm perfect."

"So, you're not hungry?"

"Oh my god, starving!"

He shakes his bag. "Leftovers."

"My favorite." I dig deep into the hold in the pilot house to gather the emergency thermal blankets Dad and Mem always insisted stay on the boat. They're in dry bags, one for each of us and we lay them over our legs, warmed by the weight of the wool.

Logan unearths stone wheat crackers and a block of cheese from his lunch and a half chicken sandwich from mine. I break Mem's brownie in two, contemplating if Dad's apple is safe to eat in the harbor since technically it's returned from travel, but I tuck it back to my lunch pail, unwilling to tempt superstition.

"Is it dangerous? Not having the light work in a lighthouse?" His gaze is cast to the dark sea and its roiling waves.

"It's officially a decommissioned light. Redundant now that we have GPS and depth finders and maps. Besides, it's not like Christmas Cove is a bustling port." I take an enormous bite of my half of the half-sandwich, chewing, happy to return to discussing things I know for certain, a metaphorical solid ground. "I should find a way for one of Maia's clients to sponsor its repair. Or maybe if the festival can become a real opportunity to make money, we can devote funds to fixing the beacon to attract more visitors in future years, if that's what the village wants."

"Those seem like solid plans."

"More like wishes, but I would like to see the lighthouse work again one day, for Mem, seeing how her grandmother built it."

"Your grandmother's grandmother built a lighthouse?" He leans in, inviting the story, his closeness a comfort I'll allow myself just this once because we are both calming, resetting. Returning in more ways than one after the scare. That's all. Tomorrow he'll be in the lighthouse and I'll be at sea. As distant as two people can be.

"She had help from other women on the peninsula, and Edwin Fernald, an engineer, army trained."

"Edwin Fernald is a man with a story," he says with a quirked smile.

"How could you know that?" I set a cracker and square of cheese onto my tongue, and doubt there's enough food anywhere to satisfy my hunger.

"Because Edwin Fernald has a cool name and people with cool names have cool stories. It's a fact. You can look it up."

"I just might." My smile crooks. "But you'll be disappointed by how little I know about the mysterious Edwin Fernald."

"Tell me?" He breaks off a square of cheese and marries it to a cracker with slow precision.

The boat sways, and sounds from the village rise to meet us as joy is carried on the cold wind. "Edwin served in the first world war. He was only nineteen when he got sent home. Family legend says he was a kid who was too afraid to die and even more afraid to live."

"Shell shock?"

I nod. "Likely. Mem says Edwin came to Maine because he was trying to walk off the edge of the continent, but the women and beauty of Christmas Cove changed his mind. He was one of the only men here, and all the women fished then." I let out a small laugh. "People are always surprised when they hear I'm a female lobster fisherman, but only because they forget how women have always done all the things men do, all while giving birth and caring for the weak, and generally plugging up the holes men make with their wars." Silence sits between us for a beat as I take my last bite and chew. "The state sent up some ragged equipment in 1917 and enough funds to cover the cost of materials. The women put Edwin up, kept him fed, got him good boots. In return, he showed a team of women how to build a spark plug light, and they did."

"Damn."

"Right? Not only can you rent a lighthouse for a December getaway, but your stay comes with a historical yarn, no extra cost."

Logan smiles. "What happened to Edwin?"

I give a small shrug. "Dunno. Not for sure. Plenty think he's my great-great-grand-dad, though no one will say for sure. He went away when the men came back. Walked off looking for a quieter home in a quieter place."

"A quieter place than Christmas Cove a hundred years ago?"

"I hope he found it."

"You know all this about him, but don't know if he's related?"

"It's sort of a Pinkham women tradition not to keep husbands around. Their stories have a way of disappearing to the background."

"Unless you design a lighthouse."

"Exactly." I finish the final, syrupy sip of my cocoa and Logan offers me the last crackers in the sleeve, which I don't refuse. "All I know is that Mem's grandmum was unmarried and had a baby and no one asked questions. Then or now." I imagined Memma's grandmother to be fierce, like Maia in kindergarten, forged of conviction stern enough to silence haters.

Across the way, the weak, flashing light appears again, this time from inside the window frame that's served as a compass nearly my whole life. Maia's signal sparks in quick bursts, three longer lights broken by two longer flickers and a final quick glow. I'd know the word anywhere: HOME.

Logan tracks my attention. "Is that for you?"

"Yeah. Morse code." I return Maia's light language, spelling the word LOVE with my search beam. "My friend, telling me she's left the common and arrived home."

"Morse code. Lighthouse builders. Forbidden love. You don't do things half-mast around here, do you?"

"Ha! Nope. And you haven't even heard about my family being rumrunners during prohibition."

"Let me guess, the women."

"Subversive, ingenious women."

Logan smiles and clears the waste from our snacks, folding the parchment together into a tight square and zipping it into the outer pouch of his pack. "I think I need to head inside if there's any chance of avoiding frostbite on my toes, but I'd like to hear the rumrunner story sometime."

"Definitely." I stand, ushering the blankets and life vests back into place.

"Can we wait for Hannah, though? She'll be here in a few days and I want her to hear all your stories first-hand."

I look away for the briefest second. "That sounds perfect." A part of me means it.

I pull anchor and with the crank of the key, the engine turns over faithfully. We putter the short distance to the dock where we say goodnight and I head to town to unload my catch to Earl's Eats co-op tanks. On my way back across the harbor, the innkeeper's cottage at Cove Light glows with faint yellow light from the kitchen window and I wonder if Logan's inside making sushi, or on the phone with Hannah, my story becoming his story as he shares it with her. And I think of how different the lighthouse will look when he leaves, already knowing the void he'll leave, no different than the beacon light I've missed in my bones my entire life but have never seen.

~ Love & Lobsters ~

A Maine lobsterman will never pull an empty pot. It literally cannot happen. In fact, we harvest all sorts of life from the deep. The unpleasant surprise of a monkfish is common enough, a creature that's nicknamed the *Sea Devil* for its vicious bite and matching attitude. I've hauled up horseshoe crabs, those living fossils that have existed for four-hundred-and-forty-five million years, scurrying along the ocean's floor long before dinosaurs existed on land. And I've always felt a little lucky to pull up a Sea Raven, a fish named for its enormous pectoral fins that were once wings before the critter settled into its resolute existence as a bottom dweller. Once, I caught a boot. A prank, for sure. But a boot nonetheless.

Still, a trap pulled from the deep won't be empty. It's impossible.

Even if some contain no sea life at all, every trap carries water to the surface. The ocean itself is dragged up from the bottom, only to reach the side of the boat where it spills back into the waves, churning brine into the great tide. Lobstermen have a term for this type of haul: *changing the water.*

I've changed my fair share of water. All lobstermen have.

But we never pull empty traps.

See, as a species, Maine lobstermen are an optimistic bunch. *Changing the water* isn't a euphemism for defeat. It's an opportunity. And I think this says something about our integrity, our grit, our determination. Nothing worth pursuing is easy.

Nothing.

So, what do unexpected hauls have to do with love?

Clearly, I'm no expert.

But I have had days when I accomplished more than changing the water. Like the first time I fished, when I hauled one cobalt blue lobster over the edge of my father's boat, my young mind seeing the creature as a jewel, the reigning benevolent queen of All The Lobsters with her fancy royal blue blood and matching regal shell. She wasn't a queen among her rusty brown species. She was just...different.

An exception.

Exceptional.

There's a complicated scientific reason why her unique mix of chemicals and proteins made her different, but that never mattered. She was blue and she was mine. I named her Birdie Blue because she was the same color as the bluebirds that visit our peninsula all year, out of season. By the time I tossed her back to the sea with a snack, she was forged in my memory. And my heart. To me, she was remarkable because she was rare. The chances of catching a blue lobster are one in two million. Fishing is a gamble, for sure, and no one would bet on odds like those.

Still, she was my first.

My blue.

A nearly impossible occurrence turned possible.

Years later, when I was a teenager, a bright orange lobster watched me as she was tugged up from the sea, as if I were the one surfacing in her world. She wore such a vivid, carroty hue, I'd been convinced I'd hauled a cooked lobster to the sunlight. But when she arrived on deck, she was alive, clawing and curious, her antennae investigating me as I studied the wonder of her. Her bright shell glistened in the bright sun and I named her Clementine before gifting her a herring inserted into her crusher claw and sending her on her journey to continue life as a lobster. The chances of us meeting were 1 in 30 million.

Other Maine lobster fishermen have caught split-colored lobsters, crustaceans who sport a shell that can be blue on one side, and orange or brown on the other—the divided color occurring in a straight line, completely symmetrical, as if the sides of two creatures were fused together to make one. Typically, the blue side is female, the other male—the blend marking it as a true natural wonder. A gem. My best friend, your fearless editor, calls these Gemini lobsters, and the chances of catching a two-sided Gemini is 1 in 50 million.

And somewhere out there is the cotton candy lobster, a find so singularly scarce that she exists in rarefied air—or seawater as it were—with a shell that shines like the pearlescent interior of an oyster, shifting and sparkling though a range of colors like pink, baby blue, aqua and pearl. If you see her, you'll know she's 1 in 100 million.

All this is to illustrate how fishing is filled with chance and awe. Some days I spend a lot of time changing water. Other days, I marvel over the unexpected treasures of the deep.

It makes me think the chances of meeting a person who gets you, sees you, accepts you, and inspires you aren't so different from my chances of pulling marvels from the sea. For those of you fishing for love—in a friend or spouse or partner—wait for the 1 in 2 million. Or better yet, hold out for the 1 in 100 million—a wonder that's pearlescent and glowing, every side of them a discovery of art and beauty and exceptionality. Because the wait will be worth it, the search a beautiful journey.

The sea is filled with average, everyday lobsters who stay close to home and remain easy to catch. But I keep fishing for the cotton candy lobster, or a chance to see my Birdie Blue again. Or for anything unexpected. Because a once-in-a-lifetime catch is intoxicating, maybe even as potent and memorable as finding a once-in-a-lifetime love.

I send the post to Maia with the message: *In case you need a reminder you're my 1 in 100 million.*

11

The Confession

The next morning, I call Maia over a late breakfast. "I need an Adventure Day."

"Me likey, but only if I drive."

"As far away from the cove as possible," I tell her.

"Intrigued. I'll have Sam wrangle the girls and see you in twenty."

Adventure Days are a long-standing tradition involving me and Maia getting lost, a journey when we abandon day-to-day demands and cast ourselves into the unexpected. There are two rules for our expeditions: pack enough snacks to masquerade as lunch and dinner, and fill a go-bag with clothing brave enough to contend with New England's temperamental, ever-changing weather.

Outside, as I wait for Maia to pick me up, I give the lighthouse a side glance, wishing Hannah would show up already so she can hurry up and get creeped out by a ragged, remote existence at an end-of-the-world lighthouse. Then she can drag Logan to a happy spa for the next three weeks to recuperate from the trauma of isolated living.

With my luck, though, she'll probably love solitary life in a wind-beaten light so much they'll return home to their perfect friend group with stories about their time roughing it on the cold Atlantic. While I stay here with the persistent sea, replaying how Logan steadied me when I drifted so far off course, my heart farther from okay than it had been in a dozen months. I shift from one foot to the other, trying to warm myself as I remember how Logan's palm spread across the small of my back, the way I'd instinctively reached for him when I felt alone, and at my most fragile.

Maia's car approaches, beeping just as my hand reaches the door handle, the noise making me jump in tandem with Maia's grin.

"Hilarious," I tell her, climbing inside.

"I'm aware." She spies the lighthouse. "Has the investigative crew arrived yet? Have they found the body?"

I give her an eyeroll that doesn't fail to notice how inappropriately glamorous Maia appears. Frye boots. Argyle wool socks pulled over her knees like gravity suspends its rigid rules for Maia's fashion. Her gray flannel skirt clings to her thighs as if its afraid to get too close to me and my well-worn jeans.

"I like the commitment to the cape." I flick at the swinging sleeve—hem?—of her coat. "Or is this a cloak? Hold on. Is our first destination an impromptu Sherlock Holmes-themed house party?"

"How amazing would that be? We should plan that."

"We'd be the only two who'd attend."

"Then we should definitely do it. I only pretend to like everyone else." She pulls out of the driveway, her attention lingering on the rearview mirror and the lighthouse I'm happy to leave behind.

"How are you this fabulous looking? I called you a half hour ago."

"I'm never not fabulous."

"Even your scarf is beyond. If scarves were sold in that perfect shape, mine would collapse by the time it got to my neck."

"I've seen the one nubby gray scarf you own. It surrendered any mission to be fashionable somewhere around 1972."

"Hurtful and unfair."

"Unfair or all flair?"

"Flair? Is that what we're calling that little beret? It's so entitled it's not even pretending to keep out the cold."

She pats the indulgent, berry topper. "Don't hate the hat."

"That is not a hat." I pop open the glove compartment and fish out an ancient paper map of Maine, the creases worn thin and white as thread. "Where are we off to?"

"I'm driving so you pick." Maia pulls over, I close my eyes. "Go."

My finger toggles above the map then drops at our first destination: the Atlantic Ocean.

No way," Maia protests. "I am not fishing. Or going on a boat. Or swimming."

I drag my finger in a straight line, due west until my path arrives at Camden, a coastal town with an enormous ego, located halfway between Portland and Acadia National Park. Technically, Camden is a town in Maine, though it's more like a Hollywood version of Maine, with its fancy mansions, quaint collections of brick boutique shops, and a golf course at the edge of the sea. But Camden doesn't stop its bragging there. The town is practically built of summer schooner races, an internationally-renowned Toboggan festival, and the 1957 movie setting for *Peyton's Place*, which was shot primarily in the buildings of the abutting town of Rockland, but Camden isn't the kind of place to let a neighbor hog the spotlight.

"Camden it is!" Maia says.

"Am I even allowed in Camden without a passport?"

"Stop it. Camden will be lucky to have you, Charlie Pinkham!"

"At the very least we'll get intel on the activities planned for their annual *Dancing Ice Crystals and Shaming the Rest of Maine Festival*." I make air quotes that lift Maia's smile. "We'll take their best ideas and make them better for our festivus."

Maia throws me a happy side-eye. "Do not ever let anyone tell you that you aren't a renegade. Always living on the edge."

"Listen, you're not exactly dressed for spelunking or army crawling along a trail in a fairy garden." Both things we've done on past Adventure Days, thank you very much.

"How dare you! Any fairy garden would be thrilled to have me and my boots. I'd slay that all day."

She's not wrong. Maia is the equivalent of a coydog, able to adapt in nearly every environment, slinking effortlessly into social ecosystems with hair that collects compliments.

We drive north and traffic is non-existent; it's Maine in winter, after all. Still the slick roads make us cautious and it takes us over an hour to reach the seaside town where we obey the slow, lazy speed limit of Main Street to gawk through shop windows. In the spaces between high-end brick buildings, the massive luxury harbor winks at our approach, its waters no longer jammed with tall ships, summer sailboats and visiting yachts. The moorings are pulled now, the boats in dry dock, most of the vessels in heated storage, being pampered and prepped for their rigorous use for a full two weeks next summer. In this part of Maine people don't catch lobster, they eat it.

Maybe it's my discomfort with snooty towns that makes my spine itch, or maybe it's the truth that bubbles up so close to the surface now that it's just me and Maia and our unbreakable trust. Either way, I let go of this thought that won't leave my brain. "I might have a problem."

"You're gonna need to be way more specific."

"Hylarical. It's Logan. I might have the teeniest crush on him."

"Ah." Her tone lilts. "He's Logan now, is he?"

"Nickname status no longer applies to him, sadly."

"Don't be too hard on yourself for crushing. Everyone's smitten with Logan. Mem's definitely given him the once-over more than once. God, even Sam said he was jealous of Logan's non-dad bod."

"Sam does not have dad bod."

Maia slows to a stop in the middle of near-empty Main Street to throw me the death stare. "Do not ever say Sam doesn't have a dad bod. Then Sam will start to believe he's good looking and has options, and that's the last thing Mama needs."

"Your reasoning feels problematic." I brush the air in front of me, urging her to go before we're rearended by a holiday tourist in hot pursuit of wild Maine blueberry jam plucked from an overpriced window display.

"We're talking about you now, Charlie, and having a crush on a married person is harmless. I love Sam more than I love myself most days, but I still want people crushing on him. Crushes are innocent. You're good."

"Wait. You just said no one can think Sam is hot. I'm confused."

"Welcome to pregnancy. I might be Aphrodite-like in my fertility, but I'm also evolved enough to disclose that carrying a growing human makes me fragile." She fans back tears. "I've evolved into one giant mood swing, and talking about Sam and crushes in the same conversation makes me all insecure because I just love him so much."

"Oh my god. I cannot with you two."

"I know." Maia's voice breaks. "We're gross."

"Beyond."

She sniffs, reigning in her distress. "I'd only worry if a crush grew to something more, you know. That's when things get dangerous, and you'd never let that happen."

"I don't know. It's not exactly in my DNA to respect the sanctitude of marriage."

"Charlie." Maia parks on Main Street. "You are not your mother."

"No? It's not like I've had a relationship long enough to put your theory to the test."

"You know my policy for refusing to dignify absurd logic with a response so use this time to elaborate on Logan. Why the pivot? What makes him worthy of graduating beyond nickname status?"

"We fished together yesterday."

"Oh, yeah. I heard." Boredom drags her voice low. "Sam ran into Hermon who told him everything."

"*Hermon* told him everything?"

"How are you still so gullible after all our time together?" Her face is all joy. "Tell me everything."

I do. She hurries me through the details of fishing with perfected detachment, until I hook her with my wildly inappropriate calendar fantasies.

"How naked are we talking?"

"Shirtless, mostly."

"And wearing orange overalls?"

"In the bright, summer sun."

"This is dork porn, but continue."

I don't. Just the mention of thinking about Logan shirtless has me thinking about Logan shirtless—except this time it's August and so hot the plum red juice of his popsicle has dripped into the valley between his pecs, finding its way down to his hard, hairless abdomen before collecting in a tiny pool at his navel.

Maia snaps her fingers in my face.

"Right." I shake off the tremble in my lip and tell her how Logan and I talked about love and loss. My fear in the harbor, his arms on me, his strength collecting me. When I finish it's so eerily quiet, I realize Camden is too fancy even for seagulls. "Tell me it's fine. It's fine, right? I just need to stay away from him."

"'Course, yeah. That's a super easy, chill solution. I mean, he's only living...what? A hundred feet from your door?"

"Fifty, but who's counting."

"I know just the cure." She points beyond my window to a café storefront with painted glass announcing ping-pong! pinball! espresso! "Bespoke ping-pong fixes everything."

"I understand ping-pong, but add bespoke and I'm lost."

"It's bougie. But it's also a fun, sport-adjacent adventure my preggers belly can handle, and it will get you out of your head. Promise."

"How do you even know about this place?"

"Finger on the pulse." She taps the underside of her opposite wrist. "You in?"

"Okay." Maia parks and I unclick my seatbelt. "But now you're gonna have to define bougie and bespoke."

"Few things would bring me greater joy," she says, popping off her seatbelt before we head into Paddle Palace where I don't think of Logan once.

Okay, once. Maybe even once and a half.

It isn't until we leave for Ragged Mountain with its ski resort overlooking the sea—a particularly unique social-geographical phenomenon Camdenites like to think they're personally responsible for—that Logan's July-tanned torso becomes all I can think of.

We take a short hike then settle onto the tailgate of Maia's SUV to gawk like tourists at the smooth curve of Camden Harbor, a protected cove of Penobscot Bay that's lined with the stark beauty of winter's sparse landscape. It pains me to admit how pretty it is here.

"I have a thought," Maia says, raising her legs to my thighs. "What if your crush problem isn't really a problem?"

"Yes, good. Say more things like that."

"Well, what if he's not actually married? Or going through a divorce. Let me sleuth for you. I'm very sleuthy."

I raise an eyebrow. "Sleuthy?"

"It's a word. Remember when you were in love with Jamie Senechal in eighth grade and I walked by his locker a hundred times a week so I could listen in on him and his friends, getting intel on what music he liked, where he hung out—all so you could have solid starter conversation material when you got up the nerve to talk to him?"

"That was me." I bark out a laugh. "*I* walked by Jamie Senechal's locker between classes for *two* years. We called those scouting missions *jolts*, remember? I nearly failed science his locker was so far from the labs—all because you were too chicken shit to talk to him. So, yeah. Not to get too bogged down in the details here, but it was *you* with the crush, *me* doing the spying."

"Huh. Yeah, that does sound more familiar. I wonder where Jamie Senechal ended up?" She brushes off her misremembering. "Anyway, I can sleuth. Let me sleuth."

"I'm good. Logan mentioned his wife several comfortable times and there's no way they're not happily coupled if they're planning vacation getaways to honor his mom's memory because Logan and Hannah and Mom were so perfectly perfect in their supportive relationship that Logan and Hannah have made it their mission to live for Logan's mom's bucket list now that she's gone and Logan is a man who is in my life because he's my renter and nothing more because he has a life and it's not with me and that's okay because he will check out in January and I will forget him just as easily as you forgot Jamie Senechal and his disturbing dedication to Uno and overusing eighties' movie quotes because he didn't have an actual personality of his own."

"Processing much?"

I let out a huge, desperate breath. "Obviously I have some unresolved feelings regarding my overexposure to Jamie Senechal during his years of pubescent onset."

"Gross." She snaps her fingers. "Can we be here, please? Let me investigate."

"No thank you."

"Good. I'm glad we're agreed." She bites back on a smile and nods toward the serene harbor. "We need to focus on making our town believe it's this town for a week so we can attract all the money."

Cold swims around us, making me tuck deeper into my jacket, while Maia looks as if she's kicking back in a sauna.

"What about a festival polar dip?" I say. "People love that stuff."

"You're a polar dip." Maia's self-satisfied grin widens.

"Sadly, I think that might be an accurate description of my current role as a human."

"This cannot be true. What's happening in your seedy DM boudoir?"

"Nothing worth telling."

"What details do we know?" She spins on the tailgate like she's a journalist readying for a lead story.

"I literally know nothing about this person. Except they handle the Instagram account for lobstermen."

"Well, maybe get your flirt on for a bit, take your mind off Pufferman."

"Logan."

"Shit."

"Yeah."

"Well, if it helps any, your post on territorial love gutted me. I was hunched over my screen like my spine had never met a yoga class. I was all in on your bizarre fishing journey. You're pretty talented, girl— and that's saying a lot since I have a strict policy against learning facts without my full consent, but you manage to sneak data and statistics into your writing in a way that doesn't make me hate data and statistics."

"It makes me happy you're happy."

"That is exactly the right sentiment, Charlie Pinkham. A statement so versatile it can do the heavy lifting in all situations that involve me, really." Maia heads to a nearby evergreen and hikes up her skirt, inviting me to look away as she christens the mountain by peeing at the outskirts of a pine glen.

"I forget," I call, louder than necessary as she holds a low branch to balance in a full squat. "Do Camden residents love public urination or am I remembering that wrong?"

She straightens and smooths her skirt. "Please. If men had to carry babies there would be pee stations every ten feet for their precious man bladders."

She's not wrong.

As we snake our way down the reel of mountain road, we're openly mourning how our Adventure Days have become slightly less adventurous since their inception.

"It's an off year," Maia says. "When we're old our Adventure Days will make Thelma and Louise look like homebodies."

This thought warms me all the way to Christmas Cove when we brainstorm about everything needed for the festival, Maia impressing the hell out of me with her marketing ideas that are so fluid it's as if she speaks an entire second language I didn't know existed. I'm inspired and relieved, because for the first time in too many months, I have hope that medical debt won't drown me.

When she stops at Earl's Eats, she tells me she needs to pee. Again. Hermon appears at the window, his brow furrowing against the glare of her headlights. Then he waves us in because the door is never locked, even as we arrive past closing. Maia scoots to the bathroom, shouting: "Hermon, if you would cook me a greasy, dripping hamburger with more cheese than burger you will make a starving baby so very happy!"

I close the door behind me as Hermon fires up the grill and drops a small round of beef to wait for heat. Then, he invites me to a booth. I slide along the bench seat and he sits across from me, his back and shoulders coat-hanger straight as he leans forward, his elbows on the table, his Snoopy apron still tied high at his chest, Woodstock flitting toward his neck.

"Ya good?" he asks.

"I'm good." I decide Adventure Day will end with restraining myself to two-syllable responses with Hermon Benner.

"I've been needing to talk to ya, Charlie."

I don't know if it's all the words spilling from Hermon's mouth or the sincerity in his stare that has my interest suddenly sitting at full attention. "Okay."

Maia returns, her nose leading her to the grill where she flips her burger, the meat throwing up a long, committed sizzle as she flattens the patty. "What's up?" she asks when she slides into the booth, her shoulder colliding with mine as I hide a smile, wondering if she's secretly playing the two-syllable game, too.

"I've a question to ask ya, Charlie, and I hope it's a question ya want to hear," Hermon says.

Maia sucks in a breath. "Oh! I want to be asked a question." She leans forward, elbows propped, chin nestled into the cradle of her hands.

"Shoot," I say.

Hermon drums his fingers so that his thumb beats at the chrome ledge of the table, where our classmate Alex Simmons carved his initials into the Formica, basically tempting every kid ever to add another S. For his crime, A.S. spent an entire summer serving comfort food during breakfast and lunch shifts to pay back his debt, a sentence handed down from Alex Simmons senior, not Hermon. As a habit, Hermon tended to forgive the sins of the young, knowing how most kids had more energy than their bodies could hold responsibly.

Hermon clears his throat. "I'd like yer permission to court yer grandmother."

"Court my grandmother?" It's a phrase that bears repeating.

Maia elbows me. "Hermon Benner wants to court your memma, Charlie. And he wants your permission," she says, as if I'm not quick to comprehend big ideas and bigger unions.

But it's the opposite. Mem is the biggest part of my universe, stepping in as my stars and moon, sea and sky. Staying strong for me as I grieved, even while she was grieving. One person, my whole orbit. Tolerating me through middle school, supporting my desire to fish because college didn't fit, staying stronger than me when she was sick. A lifetime flashes before me. No, not a lifetime. My lifetime. My life of just the two of us with our *Jeopardy* nights. Our silly superstitions. Synchronized cleaning. Early bedtimes. Our bodies moving through our shared space, fluid as water.

Hermon waits for my answer in the diner that was founded by his own grandfather during the pause between world wars, an establishment which has provided nourishment and community for generations. I physically don't know how to say no, and I'm not sure I want to.

"Yes. Certainly." I shift in my seat. "You're both adults. You don't need my permission."

Hermon shakes his head with a deliberate cough. "Charlotte, what ya think matters to me." He sits up straighter. "Now, I'm gonna love yer grandmother and that's not something ya have a decision in. But I want to spend every one of my remaining days with yer grandmother and I won't do that unless ya say it's something yer okay with."

My chest cramps with emotion, tears pooling in my eyes. Maia holds my hand under the table like this is my proposal, my Happily Ever After.

"Yes," I tell the quietest man Maine has ever grown. "Yes. You have my permission. It would be an honor to have you as family."

Hermon Benner leans back with a smile, his face belonging to a younger boy with a tender crush.

"Hot damn," Maia says on our way to the car.

"Hot damn," I say. Because there are no more words to say. Hermon Benner has said them all.

12

The Cooks

Maia's insisted I drive her car so she can devour the burger that's making my mouth water. The engine regains its warmth as the holiday tree glows just beyond the windshield while we ready to leave Earl's.

I hug the wheel. "I want to make this festival the best festival that's ever been festivaled," I tell Maia. "Our peninsula deserves it."

"We're short on time, but fear not." She sinks an enormous bite into her burger and lets out a satisfied groan.

"We need to attract and welcome everyone, from people who ice fish to visitors who want fanciness. It can't be just another holiday festival, it has to be a party Christmas Cove style, complete with curmudgeons and…"

"Caviar."

"Curmudgeons and Caviar. Yes!"

"Solid alliteration." She nods approvingly.

"Curmudgeons and Caviar festival at Christmas Cove."

"It's a fundraiser, Charlie, not a tongue twister."

"Too far?"

"The art of alliteration is a delicate balance."

"Okay, but we're keeping Curmudgeons and Caviar, even though we won't serve actual caviar, right?" I pull my focus from the tree and turn to Maia.

"We're serving up an idea, Charlie. Just twelve miles downriver, Damariscotta has its annual Pumpkinfest and in one weekend they attract nearly fifteen thousand tourists to a village that's home to just over a thousand people. And you know why they're successful?"

"Because farmers grow thousand-pound pumpkins, hollow them out, and attach boat motors so they can race in the river?"

"Yes, exactly. The pumpkin regatta is epic. And the yellow ducky race, bouncy house, pirate ships, street art in the form of painted gigantic pumpkins allows something for everyone. People travel hundreds of miles when Maine towns serve up mystique on a platter, and we can do that. Easily. We're Christmas Cove. Who wouldn't want to come here?"

"For curmudgeons and caviar."

"And all the cravings in between," she says.

"Okay, now you've got me excited."

"Yep. We've got this. Seriously, leave the marketing to me. We'll unleash Haggard for sporty, outside events. You catch all the lobster you can. The diner can feed people. Our common can be the park grounds."

"I can give boat rides. Putter around the harbor, or maybe loop around Damariscove Island?"

"Love it. Authentic local charm is what tourists will come for, and we've got that without trying. You'll see. Quaint Maine is the most marketable destination there is. Throw in a peninsula and a holiday trap tree and our biggest problem will be parking."

"You make it sound so easy."

"Organizing is my superpower. Though I reserve the right to stick you in a kissing booth and hope you find your lobster."

"Lobsters don't—"

"I know. I know. Lobsters had one redeeming quality, but you've made it clear they don't actually mate for life." She knocks on the dash. "Now let's boogey home. I miss my babies."

We drive past the lit tree, around the bend of the cove and head down the long road that doubles as my driveway, the cottage ahead radiant with amber light winking out of every window, as if the entire house is alert and watching for our return.

"You think your mem's having a rager?"

"No way. She definitely would have invited us. Right?"

"No idea, but I'm coming in to find out. And to use your bathroom." Maia practically pushes past me before stopping so abruptly in our kitchen I crash into her.

"Ah, Maia!" Mem stands, wrapping Maia with a hug as I squeeze into the space—where I find Logan at the table.

Logan.

And is he helping Mem cook? The two of them prepping the mounds of potatoes that cover the table? For a quick second, I question the powers of the wide-wood plank table and try to fathom the reason it's become so attractive to men in recent days.

"So good to see you, my darling." Mem gushes over Maia as her hand reaches to my shoulder to set love down into my bones. "Have you met Logan? He's renting out at the light."

It's always been my favorite trick of Mem's storytelling, how even though the lighthouse lives steps from our door, she can make it sound like it's a day's journey away in a carriage, belonging to another time entirely.

Maia gives Logan a polite wave as Mem holds my hand, squeezing it twice with all the efficiency of her love. "I've heard so much about you," Maia says, her slyness slipping through in a way maybe only I can hear.

Logan stands. "It's a pleasure to meet you." The combination of his height, shoulders, voice, presence—right here in my house—extracts all the air from my lungs. I step back.

"Maia is famous," Mem says. "She's a homegrown star."

"Hardly," Maia downplays. "More like a big fish in a small pond. How are you liking the lighthouse? Cozy, isn't it? Are you finding there's enough room over there for you and...Hannah, is it?" She barely takes a breath between rapid-fire inquiries as she rounds the table. "I need to pee real quick, but I can't wait to hear all about it. And you."

When she dashes beyond the kitchen, Logan lets out a small laugh. "Does everyone know I'm here?"

"Small pond," Mem says, but his attention lands on me.

"How are you, Charlie?" My name is butterscotch smooth over Logan's lips.

"Good. I'm good." What could be wrong?

"I was just filling Logan in on how you said he was a big help on the boat," Mem tells me.

"That feels like too high praise," Logan downplays.

"I was happy to have the company." I am fully and completely overcome with a need for generic conversation: "Whatcha making?" I tuck my interest over Mem's shoulder.

"Potatoes for chowder." Logan holds up his hands that are milk white with starch.

"Chowdah," Mem corrects. "Tourists like to hear us drop the r. Makes them feel frisky." She returns to her seat, peeling a potato lodged in her tight grip. "Hermon asked me for help fixing up enough chowdah to sell and serve at the festival, and I went to the lighthouse asking Logan for help."

"Huh." I toggle a look between the two of them, working in tandem, a steady, easy rhythm that reminds me of working with Logan on the boat. "Anyone want tea?"

"Always," Mem says.

"That would be grand," Logan says.

Grand?

Who says grand on this side of the pond? It's almost too adorable.

I smile with my back turned to Mem and Logan, until I see his wedding ring on a folded napkin just off the rim of the sink. The band is thick, solid. A wide ring of water echoes around the silver in a circle, as if one ring isn't enough.

"When is Hannah coming exactly?" Maia asks when she returns.

The kettle screams beside me.

"Next week," Logan says. "She—"

"Hush now, you two," Memma says. "Logan needs his focus on that sharp knife and his work. Your generation is so fixated with being distracted. You can interrogate Hannah about Hannah when Hannah arrives."

Hannah cannot arrive quickly enough.

Because Logan is inches from me now, our shoulders nearly touching as he turns on the faucet to wash his hands, and even though I'm pouring tea I can't miss how his long fingers lather soap into bubbles as they slip in and out and around each other, gliding over the spread of his palms, my whole body remembering the grip he had on my elbows as he balanced me, heat rising though my arms and neck and face like a hunger.

"How ya doin' over there, Charlie?" Maia says, her words winking.

Logan disappears his hands into the folds of a towel, and Maia's smile couldn't be bigger as she sniffs out the full-on inappropriate jealousy I'm feeling for a dishrag.

"It's time to get these next batches of potatoes boiling," Mem says. "Charlie, help Logan take them to the lighthouse to cook. We've got to have both the stovetops working overtime."

"I'll help," Maia says quickly, knowing how my moral compass won't let me journey into the lighthouse with Logan alone.

"Wouldn't hear of it." Logan lifts the deep pot with two hands, forcing his muscles to flex. "You're already doing the unparalleled hard work of growing an actual human."

Maia's shoulders fall alongside mine in a double swoon I shake off before grabbing Maia's hand. "I'll walk you out."

On the other side of the door, I draw cold air into my body as I walk her to her car. Out here, I have clarity. There are no calendars or beautiful married boys, only sea and salt and sanity.

"You're in trouble, girl," Maia tells me. "That boy is treacherous waters."

"I know," I whisper. "I don't want this."

She grabs my hands, and holds them like she does with little Casey in the moments before daycare when reminding her daughter of the rules of the classroom and how to give and receive kindness in her preschool universe. I'm all ears for her guidance.

"Just fish, Charlie. It's what you love, and you're damn great at it. You've got a reason to extend your season, and it's a good reason. It speaks to the solid, dependable person you are. Keep your energy focused on what you do best, and I'll get Sam to wrangle Logan into some of the festival preparations. It won't keep Logan from the peninsula, but it will draw him away from your side of it."

Gratitude jams in my heart. "You'll do that for me?"

"I would literally do anything for you. Except fish. Even friendship has its limits."

I throw my arms around her neck to protect the baby bump.

"This will all be over soon. Do whatever you can to keep your mind off—"

Logan appears at the entrance, warm inside air following him—because, of course. Mem props the door wide and he carries out our largest boiling pot stuffed with cubed potatoes. "Have a great evening," he says, the three of us returning the pleasantry.

But it's only me and Maia watching as he walks toward Cove Light, his silhouette chiseled into bold relief by the tree lights reaching from across the harbor because they're crushing on him, too, apparently.

I wrestle up a hardy goodnight for Maia and Mem and disappear to my room where I pace for distractions until the chrome of my computer winks at me, its message as clear as the meaning behind the green paint on a channel marker in the ocean: pass here to stay safe, it tells me. I follow its guide to a dazzling distraction waiting in my DMs from early this morning.

> @toothpicks3478
> Have you ever had a perfect day?
> So perfect it was like it was made
> just for you and no matter how much
> your face hurts you can't stop smiling?
>
> > @BirdieBlueBug
> > I have.

Normally, my mind would jump to one of my days with Dad, but today, my thoughts go to my day at sea with Logan, our comfortable work at the rail, our shared lunch, the wishes we sent to the horizon for those we loved and lost, and the lights of the harbor wiping away worry after our return, his presence reassuring me that all was okay, even better than okay. A response pops up immediately, and I'm thrilled and relieved to chat with distraction in real time.

@toothpicks3478
I won't ask details, but
I'm glad you've had that
experience. Hopefully
more than once. Is that
greedy? Have I jinxed it for
both of us now?

@BirdieBlueBug
I'm a big fan of people who
respect the superstition.

@toothpicks3478
I'm a little superstitious
chatting about superstition.

@BirdieBlueBug
Honestly? Same.

@BirdieBlueBug
Hey, I need to ask you something
but it will violate our democratically-
elected rules of honoring privacy.

@toothpicks3478
Ask and I'll let you know if
I'm comfortable. Sound
democratic enough?

@BirdieBlueBug
Yes! Okay, so. I don't know you and
I don't need to know you, but I do
need to know if you and me messaging
in this space would cause anyone else
pain or confusion or even a hiccup of
sadness. I guess I'm asking if you're single,
but more than that: I'm asking if you're
really single. As in, no one can get hurt if
you know me here and I know you here.

@toothpicks3478
When we agreed not to
exchange personal details,
I didn't realize how holding
back specifics could actually
reveal so much.

@BirdieBlueBug
Meaning?

@toothpicks3478
You're thoughtful. About
yourself and others.

@toothpicks3478
And, no. I'm not attached to
another person in any way
that our DM exchanges would
cause harm. If you knew me,
you'd know that's the last
thing I would do.

Relief washes through me, a current of permission and freedom
all at once. But then:

@BirdieBlueBug
And you're an adult? Over 18?

@toothpicks3478
I'm an adult male who
celebrated my 18th
birthday more than a decade
ago. I have the passport,
birth certificate, license, and
wrinkles as proof. You?

@BirdieBlueBug
Same. Except I'm an adult female
with fewer wrinkles and no passport.
I've never left the country. I'm not
sure where I'd even go.

@toothpicks3478
Australia.

@BirdieBlueBug
Why Australia?

@toothpicks3478
Petting a saltwater crocodile,
maybe? If you have a thing
for large reptiles that specialize
in drowning and devouring
earthly species.

@BirdieBlueBug
I do not. Next country?

@toothpicks3478
I'm not leaving the topic of
Australia, home to the two
most deadly jellyfish on the
planet.

> @BirdieBlueBug
> You're not selling me on Australia.

@toothpicks3478
What if I threw in a cone snail?
It has teeth sharp as harpoons
and is one of the most venomous
of all animals.

> @BirdieBlueBug
> I'd say I'm growing concerned about
> your fascination with deadly wildlife.

@toothpicks3478
Ah! But that's just it. Australia is
a country and an island and nearly
an entire continent in the Pacific.
Wouldn't you want a deadly
species or two protecting you if
you were that exposed?

I bite my lip, reminded of my first blog post for Maia and all the ways I see nature protecting itself as something to be admired, even replicated when it comes to protecting my own heart.

@toothpicks3478
AND! While these species technically
exist in Australia, they hardly ever
come in contact with humans
because there's so much wide-open
space and clear ocean and nearly
endless reefs. That's what I loved
most. The balanced wild.

Balanced Wild would be the name of my memoir if there were a person other than Mem interested in reading my life story. Still, I hold the phrase tight to my chest like a gift.

> @BirdieBlueBug
> What's the fascination with Australia?
> Are you Australian?

@toothpicks3478
Not Australian. I think it's
illegal for an introvert to
claim Australian citizenship.

@toothpicks3478
I lived in Melbourne for a year.

> @BirdieBlueBug
> Okay, I'll google "how to get a passport"
> in the morning.

> @BirdieBlueBug
> Actually, that's not a truth. I'm crap at
> googling and internet technology in
> general. It's why I'm rarely online.

@toothpicks3478
Can you be online more?
If I'm here?

> @BirdieBlueBug
> Yes.

The promise of meeting again is a thrill. Relationships in the real world with new people are terrifying, but this space is free of worry. In the Insta world I can't be trapped or consumed by another person because I'll never truly know the other person.

Even if chatting online is a thrill I never knew I wanted until now.

13

The Contempt

I wake at 2:30am, my body restless to fish. Instead, I head to the shelter of Dad's barn where I hang two hundred new wooden buoys from their break-away swivel hooks to paint and prep for the summer season next year. On the table, I line up any damaged or faded buoys from the past year. I fish with floats made of Eastern White Cedar, which doesn't make me popular with other boats considering the damage a wood buoy can do to a propellor. Still, the alternative is styrofoam, which might be better for fishing, but not for the ocean.

My family buoy colors are cerulean blue on top, a bold white band in the middle, with goldfish yellow on the bottom—as if each float were dipped in sunshine. After the buoys are fully repaired and painted for another year, I'll retrace my permit numbers on the top of each blue collar with glossy black paint, my numbers synonymous with my name, my family, and my heritage.

The chemical smell wakes my senses while I paint. As an homage to my father and lobstering tradition, I'm careful with my strokes, etching a straight line of color with the side bristles of my brush, always trying to make Dad proud even on this side of lobstering, the season no one thinks about: the off-season, the quiet periods when we repair and restore. Both our bodies and our tools.

By late morning, my stomach turns on itself, insisting I'll need more sustenance than hot chocolate. I close up the paint, grab a bucket from a high shelf to soak my brush and The Box catches my eye just enough to remind me it exists.

The Box is metal and holds all the terrible secrets Mom chased to Arizona to Maine and west again. I hate how it's impossible not to thumb through the familiar blue envelopes in The Box, correspondences that reek of metal and dust and desertion, my mother's name penned above the cottage's address. My chest tightens with shame for not throwing the cards and letters out years ago, searing them in a blazing bonfire the way Teenage Me wanted so many times, particularly when she'd dare call on my birthday or at Christmas, as if there could be anything to talk about after she'd left.

I try to shake off betrayal from my childhood, but need a break.

When I head inside, the warm kitchen welcomes me, the local newspaper folded on the jelly cupboard, the weekly photo winner announced on the front page. In this edition, it's a picture of the festival tree, taken from above, credit going to Kermit Hodge. I look closer, not even realizing I'm searching for Logan's silhouette among the grainy crowd until I don't find him. Hermon and Mem are in the front corner of the shot, their backs to the camera, their shoulders close, their attention intrigued by something in the middle distance.

Mem joins me, surprise on her face. "Didn't know you were still home."

"I was in the barn, repairing." Okay, more like hiding.

She nods, asks me if I've eaten and settles cornbread between us that's too hot to butter so I make the morning awkward. "How come you haven't talked to me about you and Hermon Benner? Are things getting serious between you two?"

"Oh hush." There's no mistaking the blush on her cheeks.

"Do you love him?"

"That's a mighty big question for an early morning, but yes. I do love him. Think I always have."

"But, Mem. You're still healing. Don't you think this is all a lot?"

"Sit down," she tells me, joining me at the kitchen table. She spreads her palms to the wood, her fingers extended and smoothing circles across the surface, as if she's spreading flour across rolled dough.

"Lemme tell you something, Charlie girl. I'm an old woman and there's something special about getting old that no one told me about until I arrived here myself. You see"—she sits back, meets my eyes—

"there isn't a thing another person could do to hurt me now. I've lived a good life. Only thing that could break me is losing you. So, if you're asking after Hermon Benner because you feel like me and him going out to a movie once in a while or staying late at the diner or even showing up early at the diner is gonna put any kind of wedge between you and me, well that's no bargain. I'll choose you any day and all day, just like always. You're my Charlie girl, Charlie girl."

The letters pulse from the barn, taunting me with reminders of the damage love can do. "You're not worried about being betrayed, or getting your heart broken like Dad did? Or about how Pinkham women aren't exactly known for our ability to make room for love?"

"Well, I think I've failed you there." She straightens her forearms on the table. "It might be true how Pinkham women have endured enough bad husbands to make them a footnote in our stories, but that doesn't mean we don't make room for love. We've managed to make a lot of love, despite our men. There were decades when I knew I couldn't love your father more." Her eyes lift to his picture by the door.

"Sometimes I felt guilty for all the pride I felt for him, knowing how other mothers had it different with their sons. Then he gave me you and I felt I'd never truly known what love was until I held you as a newborn. Having you and your father made my heart fuller than any person's heart had a right. Most days I see you walk into a room and think I'll split open with pride. If that's not love, well, it's something bigger and I'll take that any day."

I reach across the table for Mem's hand, my eyes filling.

"There's always gonna be disappointment, but the world is swelling with love, fit to burst most days. There isn't a woman alive with a stronger heart than mine with you at its center, Charlie girl. You've made my heart so big it has room for Hermon, too. You've been my luck and my love and my life, and that's a hard thing to say out loud because you know how superstition works."

"I do."

"I know." She gives me a small smile and my hand a quick pat, even as tears swell between us.

~ ~ ~

When I head to my room, I'm still trying to process Memma being so at ease as she breaks the unwritten rule of Pinkham women, all because love expanded her heart. My father and mother must have loved each other wildly once too, right? They built trust together. Built a life together. Made a home. Made me. So why did my mother have to fill that life with lies and enough hurt that I feel pain like a sharpness in my chest as I pop open my computer?

> @BirdieBlueBug
> Sometimes I don't
> understand humans.

@toothpicks3478
Me. Always.

> @BirdieBlueBug
> Really?

@toothpicks3478
Really.

I'm relieved he replies right away and settle into my oversized chair at the window.

> @BirdieBlueBug
> I mean, *really* really? Or are you
> being amenable because you want
> to appear as if you agree with me
> in order to lure me into a false sense of
> safety in our weird online chat space?

@toothpicks3478
I'm generally amenable.

@toothpicks3478
Crippling shyness and all.

@toothpicks3478
So, no. Not lying.

@toothpicks3478
And baffled by humans
on the regular.

@BirdieBlueBug
Okay. I'm new to this DM stuff and
trust doesn't come easy for me.

@toothpicks3478
I'm new here, too. Also,
not so good with the trust.

@BirdieBlueBug
Why do I feel like everyone
DMing a new person is writing
these exact same words?

@toothpicks3478
You're likely not wrong.

@toothpicks3478
What specifically about
humans is baffling you today?

@BirdieBlueBug
Lies.

@BirdieBlueBug
And how they last.

@BirdieBlueBug
Like a sickness.

@toothpicks3478
I feel like someone hurt you
and I'm sorry for that. No one
deserves to be hurt, and maybe
it's true that hurt people hurt
people, though I like to think
most people are good.

@toothpicks3478
And good people are good to
people.

@toothpicks3478
No. I don't write tea bag
affirmations for a living.

@BirdieBlueBug
Phew.

@toothpicks3478
My platitudes are all framed,
sold to hang in sterile, lifeless
office buildings.

@BirdieBlueBug
Another reason to avoid
soulless offices.

@toothpicks3478
It's my greatest achievement
in life, leaving my 9-5 gig where
I spent seven hours of every
eight staring at a clock.

@BirdieBlueBug
Same! I want to ask what you
do for work, though maybe it's
better to keep it mysterious. Then
I can imagine you milk cows or glue
those spear things onto the tops of
skyscrapers or you're a pediatrician,
bouncing a hard rubber Elmo head off
of kids' knees to check their reflexes.

@toothpicks3478
I would enjoy all of these things.

@BirdieBlueBug
Does that mean my guesses are wrong?

@toothpicks3478
I think imagination is always
more important than being
right. Hang on while I jot that
down for a coaster set I'm
working on.

I laugh out loud with my seal bark I'm grateful Instagram can't hear, and bite on a smile as we chat about nothing at all.

@toothpicks3478
Favorite ice cream:

@BirdieBlueBug
Mint chocolate chip.

@BirdieBlueBug
No. Maple Walnut.

@BirdieBlueBug
Grr, it's neck and neck. Impossible
to decide. Favorite fruit?

@toothpicks3478
Red Delicious. The best apple,
obviously. Its superiority is in
its name.

@BirdieBlueBug
Never in history has one person been
so wrong. Just ask Golden Delicious.

My time online restores me. It's the silence outside of my room that's less welcome when I finally shut down my computer to rejoin the day. I can't decide if the house is quieter without Mem since she's been seeing more of Hermon Benner or if it feels quieter because she's choosing someone—not necessarily *over* me—but other than me.

At the window, the harbor is calm. Maia isn't in her living room. Logan's car isn't parked in front of the light. Everyone has somewhere to be but me. And I'm certain Logan is getting groceries for his wife's arrival because he'll be whipping up chicken *cordon blue*, an assortment of *soufflés*, and cheesecake for their snacks and lunches. I see their running grocery list at their tiny, architecturally bold house nestled in a woodland setting with just the right amount of open, wildflower field, their needed items written in cursive pastel chalk on a blackboard kitchen cabinet between their fridge and pantry because they are *those* people. I rub at my arms, my mouth remembering the slick of cold pineapple juice at sea.

Some trigger of appetite starts me thinking all the things I shouldn't be thinking—like how I like being near him and his delicious December pose as he wears a Santa hat and nothing else. I shake the thought free. I mean, not right away because…well Santa hat and only a Santa hat. But when I eventually become clearheaded enough to check my files, I confirm Logan's booking. His name and her name. Together. One address.

I keep searching for any loophole, any crack where my interest in him might be allowed to live inside and thrive. But I can't find any way in, and I need to stop looking. Because holes, like love, are places where people fall.

When my phone rings, I answer to Maia asking, "Any run-ins with the Hottie Who Shall Not Be Named?"

"Nope. I'm basically a hermit working in the barn."

"Good. Stay inside always and blog for me. Your last piece on waiting for the 1 in 100 million? Totally brilliant. I'm posting it tomorrow so your fans will stop begging for deets about my mystery lady lobsterman."

"No personal details, right?"

"Never, but I'll need two posts a week like we decided."

"I feel like *decided* is a stretch."

"Okay, so when?"

"When I feel inspired."

"Stop it with yourself! You cannot be a tortured artist already."

"I can be whatever I want when I grow up."

"Please do not grow up," she says.

"Working on it. Hey, I found out a thing about InstaHuman. He's a man, over 18 and single and funny."

"Those are four things. Four glorious things. I love this for you and InstaMan and need all the details." The high-pitched screech of a child drowns out her garbled excuse to leave our conversation.

"Go. Be with your family."

"Okay, I'm admittedly not being the most present friend in this exact moment, but never forget I'm your biggest fan, Charlotte Pinkham."

"Never forgotten."

For the next few hours, I return to painting. When I'm exhausted, I make popcorn and plop onto the couch where Mem joins me. We eat diner fare and watch Alex Trebek on reruns, all while failing epically at guessing answers despite seeing the episodes at least once before—though that's never really been the point.

Sitting beside her, I wonder if she can feel Hermon here, too, the idea of him wedging a beat of change between us.

~ Love & Lobsters ~

The Maine lobster trap has remained essentially unchanged for the last 200 years. It's a simple contraption with four interconnected sections: an entrance, a kitchen, a parlor, and an escape vent. The kitchen is located just off the entrance, not unlike the kitchens in most homes. The kitchen is the area where a lobster will be tempted to indulge in salted herring tied into a netted bag and set out as...well, bait. This treat feeds an estimated 20 lobsters for every 1 that's caught. It's an inefficient system for the fisherman, but best for the lobster.

If the lobster is small and nimble enough to make it to the escape hatch, they can enjoy a free meal and depart. Traveling to the parlor to get to freedom is something a lobster does hundreds of times throughout their lifetime spent roaming the sea bottom. They feast on the convenient buffets lobstermen lower to the seabed. When the lobsters grow, their size makes escaping the parlor more difficult. The typical result is a trapped lobster.

This might seem like mundane technical information about a deceptively non-mundane piece of equipment, but I think the trap's design says more about love than engineering.

Stay with me.

See, Maine lobstermen don't always fish close to home. In the summer, our coastal waters teem with lobsters, the crustaceans making their way toward the shoreline as the ocean warms. In winter, they retreat to deeper waters, moving closer to the continental shelf. When freezing temperatures recede, they migrate close again.

As lobstermen, we move with them. We push our boats and our wills toward the deepest ocean to search for the species that sustains us. And we are careful with our catches. Not every lobster that arrives in a trap's kitchen is a keeper. Size, timing, and circumstances matter.

By nature, American lobsters are independent, solitary creatures, and lobstermen honor this sensibility. We even lean on it to ensure sustainability. Lobstermen treat every lobster singularly. Each lobster is measured. Studied. Its underside considered. If the lobster is a female with eggs, she cannot be harvested. She receives a V notch to her tail and is returned to the deep to ensure future generations of lobsters and future fishing for families. Lobstermen don't keep lobsters that exceed five inches. Those lobsters are the elders, the survivors. They've earned the right to live out a long retirement during their projected hundred-year lifespan. Above all, we protect the young. If a lobster's midsection is less than 3 ¼ inches, they haven't matured enough to breed and they are also returned to the sea.

I'm not sure I know of any act more loving than protecting our young. Our elders. Females who bring life.

Which is why the window for a harvestable lobster—"a keeper"—is small. Fixed. It is as much a regulation as it is an honor code. A partnership with the sea. Because these rules didn't begin their lives as industry-imposed standards. No. Ideas for supporting a healthy ocean came from lobstermen. They knew they had to take care of the young, the females, and the hardy elderly that had survived a hardscrabble life. When industry regulators saw how lobster populations thrived because of the care, attention and, yes...love Maine lobstermen had shown the species, these sustainable practices became law.

This is all to say a lobster trap kitchen is a key component in my daily work, though recently I've been thinking more about kitchens in a home. My kitchen, probably much like yours, is the place where I'm nourished by food and family. My coastal Maine kitchen is the same one I was raised in, built by my family nearly three hundred years ago when living at the edge of the world was hard and harsh and windswept. Like today, minus central heating and WiFi. The thing is, I've had some new guests to the space lately. While neither are strangers exactly, they are both new to my kitchen, brought to the heart of my house by the hearts of those I love.

One of my recent kitchen guests will stay, one will not.

I realize this makes the core of my home sound like ground zero for a twisted reality TV show where we make visitors enter through a lobster trap. The truth is far simpler, though. Not everyone who arrives in our kitchens will remain. Some will run for the escape hatch. Some will appear for the food, their visit purposeful and brief before they continue on. And some will be keepers, fitting into our lives with such perfect shape and size and ideals that we'll move the furniture in our rooms to accommodate their addition.

It seems to me like the success of a loving relationship—just like the success of a lobsterman—depends not solely on an ability to commit, but on our willingness to let go.

Not every lobster is a keeper.

Not every person a good fit.

Timing and care matter.

14

The Cards

After spending three days arranging festival details, making a day's run to the continental shelf to set new traps I'm piloting, and doing enough soul searching to dredge up heavy emotion, I ache to be at sea, and at peace with my past. I tuck The Box under my arm and my slice of unbuttered toast cools quickly when I step outside and make my way to the dock in near darkness. The wind is irritable, like me without my morning cocoa. Its wrath rustles the stand of spruce trees at their tips, and wakes high waves in our protected water. Its bite lashes at my eyes, warning me to pay attention. I give the wind and waves my respect as I untie my dock lines and journey beyond the cove, where the squalls whip harder, pushing my bow slightly off course until I throttle up—only to cut the engine when a figure appears on the craggy breakwater rocks at Cove Light. My boat jerks to a stop, forcing my hips forward against the wheel. The figure is haunting and shadowed in the pre-dawn. At first. I think it's my father the way the person's arms are stretched wide at each side, the body perched and still as a heron hunting.

As the current pushes my boat closer, I recognize Logan and his lean legs, tall stance, and overly ambitious puffer jacket. A protective feeling rushes under my skin when I see him challenging today's wind that's too headstrong to trust, and the open mouth of the sea that's too hungry to tempt.

I slide open my side window to yell: "ARE YOU OKAY?" Waiting for any answer won't satisfy me because Logan needs to be on dry land, safe. My boat tosses in the waves, a mere toy in the mean current as he yells back, the gusts snatching his response.

My worry for Logan makes me change course to meet him at the dock.

"Good morning!" he says like it's perfectly normal to stand on wet ledge at the edge of an unforgiving sea.

I throw my inflated fenders over the side and let the waves push me to the dock. "What were you doing?" My question has the bark of a reprimand. It *is* a reprimand.

"Couldn't sleep!" he calls. I can barely hear him so I throttle down and cut my engine. "Thought some fresh air would help."

"Fresh air? More like a gale storm! You shouldn't be out here!" Waves slap at the side of my boat, forcing my portside against the dock. Icy wind cuts at my eyes.

"Need a sternman?" he calls.

"No!" I've never needed a sternman. I do need to see Logan safe. "But I'll take one." The words are out of my mouth before I can reel them back in.

A smile fills his face. "I'll grab my gear."

Waiting on someone to fish is something I've done exactly three times, and each time was for Maia in high school. For anyone but her, my rules are rigid. Show up on time or spend the day docked on land. Yet as I tie up, I find myself leaning toward Cove Light, waiting for Logan to reappear. When he does, a surge of relief washes through me even as I pretend to be reading my instruments.

When he steadies to climb aboard, he reaches both arms to the upper rail of the pilothouse so that his sweater rises above the waist of his jeans, flashing a slip of skin that pulses taught with muscle. My insides flutter. Then he's in the boat, beside me in the wheelhouse, stowing his pack to safety with fluid confidence. When he secures the door closed behind us, he somehow smells like cold and warmth all at once, like both storm and safety.

"Thanks for the invite." He's tucked his orange bottoms under his arm, and unravels the foul-weather overalls with all the precision and respect of handling a flag. He steadies enough to step one leg in, then the other. When they're on, he flicks the straps so they slap against his chest. The windows fog.

I try not to watch. I do. But his presence is arresting. And my body is too close. The nearness of him makes me feel as if my flesh isn't mine anymore, and isn't that the thing about crushes? They hijack you, mind and body. As I steer past the lighthouse, I'm no longer worried about Logan's safety. Now, I've returned to my significant, legitimate concerns about how delicious he looks in a cable knit sweater.

Maia's words are in my ears, strong and true enough to meet me over the wind: *Girl, you're in trouble.*

I don't argue.

I can't.

"And here I thought today was going to be boring." His smile tugs up one side of his face the way it does.

I bite my lip.

"I've never hitched a ride on a lobster boat before." There's a hint of wonder in his voice.

"Is that what you'd call what you did?" I dare a quick look in his direction.

By the dashboard light, his face beams into a deep smile. "Kind of. At least, that's the way I'll replay it when this becomes one of my favorite stories."

I want to tell him he shouldn't have been out on the rocks. Wind can't be trusted. I want to tell him he's out of his element and the elements are unforgiving. But I'm the one who's unmoored.

"I made the mistake of leaving the peninsula yesterday, spent the day in Augusta."

My mouth curls into a smirk.

"What?" Curiosity lifts his question.

"We call the capital Disgusta."

He nods. "I hear only true Mainers are allowed to call it that. The ones with the most maturity." His self-satisfied smile is on full display, even as his side is turned to me, his gaze locked on the hinting horizon, his bottom lip set like a challenge I can't accept.

"Why Dis—? Augusta?"

"Business," he says in that vague way television actors do when they don't trust the characters they're with.

My grip tightens at the wheel because that's fine. If he doesn't want to share, that's perfectly okay, better really, because we shouldn't even be on a boat together again and—

"There are legal things, you know. For my mom. I'd put them off as long as I could." His quick reflexes catch the VHF radio receiver that pops from its perch on my dash when we're hit by a high swell. He hooks the handset into place, with quick, unflinching accuracy, as if he knows the intimate anatomy of my boat, its weak points, and how to fix them. My insides coil.

"I'm sorry," I say, collecting myself. "I mean it. I feel like *I'm sorry* can sound so recycled sometimes. Like just by saying these two words people think they can actually make your grief more—I don't know, palatable. Easier to swallow."

"For them, not us."

I dart him a look he catches. "Exactly."

"Thank you," he says. "Loss and love and logistics are…a lot."

His alliteration flirts with my brain, a thing I didn't even know could happen.

"My grandmother likes to say: 'Big love, big loss,'" I tell him.

"I like that."

"Me, too." It's simple, straightforward, and grounded in honesty. Like fishing.

We boat offshore for a long while when Logan points to the water up ahead. "Is that one of yours?"

It's a buoy, just off starboard. Banana yellow body with three thin vertical stripes of emerald green. "That's Bobby Pelletier's run. Nice to see he's out here, too."

Logan searches out through his side glass. "You mean his buoys, right? Nice to see his buoys out here?"

I give a half shrug. "Same thing." I check my coordinates. "Today we're not pulling buoys, though. You up for something new?"

"I'm up for anything. I'm just now convinced that the best adventures start with, *I hitched a ride on a lobster boat and then…* so, yeah, just tell me what to do."

I get extra interested in the new radar screen on my dash, which should be the center of all my attention instead of the grin refusing to leave my face. Traitor. It's impossible to stop picturing how his eyes will light up when he tells this adventure to his wife and friends gathered at his rugged, repurposed dining table at their quaint beach house they visit on sunny weekends. Surrounded by wine and music and ambiance, naturally.

Thankfully, the new screen emits a series of quick beeps and I put the boat in neutral. "There. That's one of my pots on the seafloor. You want to call it up?"

"Like, sing to it?"

I try to hide my smile. "Sure. Or you could press here." I point to the bright yellow button on the prototype screen that says Recover.

"Right." He steadies his stance against the waves, moving closer as he hovers at the gauge. "Just push it?"

I nod encouragement. "Press and wait. This is my first ropeless trap. It has inflatable bags attached." I double check the blinking yellow lights on the radar screen. "When you press the button, air releases into the bags to make the trap rise. We'll grab it when it surfaces."

"No way."

"Way. At least in theory. The gear's still being piloted."

"This is very exciting, and I can say that because I'm a dork engineer and can get very, very excited about emerging technology." Logan depresses the button with military precision, all his attention concentrated on the task. Then, he scrambles out to the deck to watch for his reward. The cold whips inside, a reminder I need to be careful.

"The bags are orange and they'll carry up the top of the first cage," I call. "Once you see them rise, I can activate the rest of the line and the whole string will be waiting for us, popping up one by one."

"Can I grab the first pot?" he says, exhilaration in his raised eyebrows. "I mean, if you don't want to."

"Have at it. It'll give me the chance to scout for the rest of the surfacing bags."

"Best. Day. Ever!" He heads to the back of the boat, his assured steps light and joy-filled.

I clock the trap's serial number, release date, and exact longitude and latitude from an inset screen. I document all this data in my logbook. Then, the first pot rises with the help of her inflated orange buoy bags, it's wire structure popping above the ocean's surface. I run to the deck to join Logan, one or both of us initiating a sloppy high five courtesy of our rubber gloves.

Logan snags the first floating bag with the gaff hook and pulls the line through my hauler like he's an expert. He fist-bumps the first three lobsters he unloads.

"I'm testing these first new traps out here, where whales run."

"Why the new gear?"

"Traditional lobstering sets long vertical lines into the deep and sea mammals get tangled in lines."

He inhales sharply, his face wincing.

"Exactly. No Maine lobsterman I know wants to see a sea mammal suffer, and even though entanglements are typically from heavy trawlers and bigger operations, this alternative reduces any chance of whale injury if they meet my lines unexpectedly. There's a bunch of us beta testing. My thinking is, what harm can it do to try another way?"

"I get it." He pulls the first pot in our string. "Care is a verb, an action. Something we have to actually do, and not just talk about. This new technology is a good thing, Charlie. A really good thing. Plus, it's cool as hell."

Excitement tenses my body as innovation changes the way I work. The lobsters come and we sort them, giving the young and the elderly and the egg-bearing populations a herring snack before setting them back below the waves.

We talk hungrily about invention and pioneering and how change is hard and intoxicating in equal measure.

I tell him the new gear is still too expensive for a large-scale roll-out, but didn't even exist ten years ago, proving a rigid industry can bend, adapt, lean in.

He tells me there will always be people resistant to change. And how there are people like me, willing to voyage toward new frontiers.

His stare locks on mine, challenging my equilibrium. "And the vast majority of us are somewhere in between, happy enough just to be fascinated with all the possibilities that can be reality because someone dared to dream them up."

Logan rebaits our last trap, his fascination fixed on the mechanics of the release box now, the technology embedded within the trap. "I've been making things and remaking things since I was three but I don't ever think I've seen a contraption this cool."

"What kinds of things do you make?" I ask, even as I shouldn't. There are reasons why I don't ask Logan direct questions about himself, his life. I think I shouldn't know them. Or knowing them would make me like him more, and that's not something I need.

He laughs. "More like, what kinds of things *don't* I create?"

I'm glad for his levity. "Mad scientist?"

"Something like that."

When we reach the end of the third line, I fall back hard into my captain's chair, my body fatigued with the excitement of the morning and the restrained thrill of Logan so close. When I suggest lunch, Logan collects our bags from the hatch.

When we eat, Logan shares my chicken sandwich and divvies up his cold noodles before I offer him an apple, which he takes to shine along the wool surface of his long arm. I'm still hungry, but return Dad's apple back to my lunch bag.

"Wait. You're not eating one?"

"Not that one. It's kind of a rule."

"A rule or a thing that can't be talked about like the things people can't say on a boat?" he whispers.

I smile. "Just a thing. From way back. My dad would take a piece of fruit with him when he fished but never ate it. He'd bring it home, telling me his fruit liked adventures—how they craved opportunities to see what the world looked like outside a kitchen—so I have a thing about making sure one gets back to the mainland."

"That is a very cool tradition."

"I think so." I roll up the bag, tuck it and the apple to my lap. "When I was a kid, I'd imagine their escapades while sitting at my assigned desk in class, my teacher reading us books that didn't contain nearly enough epic fruit explorers."

Logan laughs, then hands me his apple, our knuckles brushing. "I'm not eating your one apple."

"I'm not taking it back."

"Fine." Logan stands, turning his apple over in his palm. He takes a bite. Deep and crisp. He watches me watch him. Then, he holds the fruit in front of my mouth like an invitation, or challenge. His quiet stare is dark, unreadable. He nudges the apple closer to my mouth, its skin only inches from my lips. Then, closer still.

I lean in. He holds the fruit firm as I take a bite. As I chew—slowly, our eyes trained on each other—he takes another bite. Moments stretch into what feels like days as we ceremonially share one single, solitary fruit, it's sweetness bursting across my lips, the juice slipping down my throat and satiating something deep within me.

I'm so unsettled by the unexpected intimacy of sharing food in this way that I'm speechless, and when the apple is finished, Logan holds the core and my stare for so long it feels as if time stops altogether. My heartbeat finds its way to my ears, my entire body electric with want and intrigue, fear and a new kind of hunger. When he opens the hatch to store our lunch waste, I study his every fluid move until the tinny crash of The Box clatters onto the pilothouse floor between us.

The one working latch pops open, spilling dozens of blue envelopes onto the wet deck. The scattered papers wick up water quickly, sending Logan to his knees. He tries to make sense of the chaos, placing sopping envelopes on the seat, as if trying to line dry them one-by-one, but the paper is already soddened with sea water, the ocean dripping from their edges.

"Shit! Shit! I'm sorry, so sorry. I didn't even see it."

"Stop. Please." I put my hand to his shoulder before stepping back, waving him up. I scoop up the envelopes from the floor, most of them tearing or buckling. I pluck the ones from his seat, stuff them all back inside The Box before snapping the lid firmly shut. I band The Box with a bungee cord and tuck it under my arm where it's an anchor.

"I must have bumped it," Logan says, so close to me, the two of us sandwiched within the space between the captain chairs. "I'm so sorry, Charlie."

I want to ask him to stop saying my name just like I want to stop watching his lips when he says my name but neither of these things happen. "It's nothing. Really, it's actually less than nothing."

"That might be impossible." He gestures to The Box. "I mean as far as physics goes. I'm pretty sure a thing by its very nature of mass and existence can't be less than something." He looks at me for a long time, reaching out his hand, and dropping it right before it touches my sleeve. "Hey, where'd you go? You look like you're spinning."

"Accurate." I drop into my seat, The Box clanking on my lap. I give its lid a hard tap with my thumb and check out his butt as he turns to his seat, because stuck to his slick, wet rubber overalls is one blue envelope.

"Umm...." I point in the direction of his bottom that manages to look perfect in unflattering fishing gear.

He turns quickly so my finger now points to his front...place. Great. Heat rushes up my neck, spilling across the backs of my ears.

"What?" he asks.

"You have a...." I snatch my finger back and want to say envelope. I want to say letter. I want to say words that are words that make sense, but I can only gesture at the general vicinity of his hip and look and sound as completely incompetent as I do, all while I scold myself to *get it together, Charlie.*

Logan twists to get a view of his backside, grabbing his hip for purchase.

"It's a…." Words refuse to cooperate.

He plucks the soggy, rumpled blue envelope from the underside of his rubber overalls and outstretches his palm like a serving tray. "I want to say I'm sorry a hundred times because I really am."

"Don't be."

"I've ruined the letters, haven't I? They're obviously important to you."

"Not exactly." I draw in a breath and lean on the trust that seems to come so easily between us on the boat. "These are letters to my mother—"

"Oh, god, Charlie—"

"No. Stop." I hold up my hand. "The letters aren't precious. They're from the guy she left my dad for. I just…kept them for years without any real reason."

"Maybe you didn't need a reason."

"Maybe." I run my hand over the metal as if to forgive the container for what its carried. "Or maybe I needed to keep them as a reminder of her betrayal, so I'd never forget."

He watches me with a sympathetic stare that threatens to draw out all my secrets.

"Last night, I'd made what had seemed like a foolproof plan to toss them overboard but then you were here and I forgot about them, and now they're on my lap and somehow I still can't throw them off the deck because I can't bring myself to put trash in the ocean."

"What can I do?" he asks.

I can't say what makes me take out the first letter, the words illegible now as the ink bleeds. Still, I remember the sting of everything that was written. How even filler words like *and* and *but* and *if* printed in a stranger's neat handwriting felt like a tiny, little cut, a place for salt to find its way inside my younger skin. And heart. The letters are no longer in order the way I'd arranged them a dozen years ago: by date, first until last, a twisted kind of storybook tale from my childhood.

And now, I don't think of my mother when I hold the letters, I think of Dad, the way he must have read all the notes to her, too. Before she left or after she bailed, I can't say. He'd have held them in his hands, felt their bite attach itself to his heart. His heart that wasn't strong enough to survive this kind of treachery.

And I blame my mother all over again, for all she stole from Dad and me as I think of her slinking to the mailbox to send letters. Then, intercepting these mailings, squirrelling them to some private place away from her family, just like the secret life and love she built on the other side of the continent.

"I want the words to her to be gone, for her to be really gone, but I don't want to throw paper in the ocean because the ocean is too good for her letters. But I'll also feel like a complete failure if I don't get rid of them because I've held onto them for too long and being a lobsterman is synonymous with letting things go, you know? Like, we can never keep everything we catch and we shouldn't keep everything. Maybe I'm not making sense."

"You want the correspondences gone but you don't want to pollute."

"Yes!" The word is a soft push of relief, for someone seeing me, understanding me, even at my most inarticulate.

He stands, looks out at the sea. "What if...?"

"What if what?"

"How would you feel about dumping the letters into a trap and then submerging the trap? Then we could pull it up again—I mean, you could pull it up again—you know, whatever feels right for you, and the paper will be recoverable but the salt and water will have washed all the ink away, or at least blurred it beyond recognition. Then it's just paper, no power."

"Just paper. No power." I swallow the emotion rising in my throat. "I like that."

We peel the letters from the envelopes, inadvertently tearing them as we do, which feels on point. We stuff the collection of paper trash to the netted bait bag and plunge the trap to the waves as we count to sixty-three because Logan says it's a random number and randomness is a necessary component in emotionally complicated situations like this one.

We observe each other as we count.

He watches my relief build, my stress ebb, all of me a wave.

I watch the numbers form on his lips. His face shifting, rounding over syllables, his bold bottom lip firm and concentrated. On me. For me.

When we haul the trap back up together, I'm satisfied with the missing ink, the messy ink, the ink washed to nothing but smeared lines, tie dye, and cloudburst. With the protection provided by our blue rubber gloves, we gather the detritus to a gummy ball and exhilaration swells in me for letting go in this way, my heart and mind surfacing from under the weight of someone else's mistakes.

Dad joins me, too—from a time when there was no betrayal, only betrothal. A time when he and my mother must have been happy, choosing each other as wife and husband, the other person's forever person. I become hyperaware of the softness of the wet mound of paper, the significance of the pastel blue, the lightness in my heart, the borrowed lineless trap—all things old yet entirely new.

My smile surprises me. "Is it weird this reminds me of wedding tradition? The bit about something old and something new, something borrowed, something blue?"

Logan lets go of a long, shallow sigh. "I mean, I guess." His face twists up with that apple cheeked innocence I've come to adore. "But I'm the wrong guy to ask about weddings. That's definitely not my field."

~ Love & Lobsters ~

Lobsters communicate by peeing in each other's faces.
We need to do better.

15

The Confusion

"Not my field?" Maia repeats for the fifth time. Possibly sixth. Precision is an impossibility at a time like this.

"Those words exactly. Don't forget about the *I'm the wrong guy to ask about weddings* bit."

"I literally cannot forget any of these words ever."

If birds people-watched, Maia and I would be spotted on our respective sides of the cove, our attention pressed to our windows with all our interest aimed directly at Cove Light, as if the lighthouse were true north and we were the shivering compass needles magnetically compelled toward its pull. But unlike the north star or a ship's guide, the soft yellow glow bleeding out from the kitchen windows tells us exactly nothing, except that a lighthouse, not unlike the sea it perches near, rarely gives up its secrets.

"I don't get it." Maia's voice is sharp, pointed. "Why don't you know what he meant? I mean, why didn't you *ask* him what he meant?"

"Don't yell at me."

"I'm hardly yelling. I'm accusing. There's a difference. Isn't it standard practice to ask a person what they're talking about when you have no idea what they're saying?"

"I don't know what to tell you. There was a lot going on. I'd been pretty occupied with freeing myself of my mother and all her bad karma when he said what he said and I was speechless and dealing with more than a bit of shock, if I'm honest. And he just moved on from the comment like it was nothing. He was more interested in these new traps and—"

"Gah! Fishing! Why must it always be such a buzzkill?"

"Not a buzzkill. It's my actual job. And your specialty is human relationships and reading people so if anything, this is on you."

"Me?" She scoffs.

"Yes, exactly. I function in a world of rules and regulations where I can literally measure every decision. You're the one with the people skills."

"Okay, fair. In theory I'd be your go-to advisor for enigmatic communications, but this is unprecedented territory. No nice guy has ever been this mysterious."

"You're not helping."

"In fairness, he's not giving me a lot to go on," Maia says. "But there is an upside if you're in a place to see it."

"Yes, good. Show me what that looks like."

"Men of mystery are a sought-after breed."

"Please do not slap a PR spin on this absurd situation. My head hurts." And while my brain does feel waterlogged, it's the ache in my chest that bruises more. A rope-coil twist that wraps around my heart, which refuses to act like all my other, normal organs that have never burdened me with emotional drama and trauma.

"And...," Maia says. "Doesn't this open things up for you to make a move?"

"Hello? Have we just met? I don't make moves."

"Well, maybe you need to. Ask him outright. Or don't. The point is you get to decide what you want to do next. If you're interested in this person as more than a crush than you have to woman-up and get in there."

I pull in a cleansing breath. Okay, yes. I feel at home with Logan when we're talking. I trust him at sea. And I'd like to apply for the job of dressing him for calendar shoots. So why is my stomach tightening? Reminding me that every story ever told—real or imagined—meets the same fate in two reliable words: *The End.* And Logan's story—like his time on the peninsula—has a fixed expiration date. In January, he'll return home to his real life like all tourists.

"I've always been a trainwreck in a relationship, and the same would be true if I were with Logan, a man who is so bad at communication we're not sure if he's married or not." I wince as I blame him because I'm not sure if this is on him or me.

"Correction. You've been highly successful at attracting dudes who dig you, but you always bail before it gets serious."

My genetic flaw, flexing its muscle. "Exactly. I'm more comfortable crushing on Logan until he leaves and then I'll thank him for his stay, clean the towels and the bedding, restock the wood and it will be like he was never here at all. Emotionally simple. Clean. Just the way I like things."

"You mean emotionally sanitized."

"Ha! See? The word 'sane' anchors the word *sanitized*, and if I knew any Latin, I'd feel more confident in defending its root word status. Because sanitized crushes are sane. Simple. Safe. I think I've proved they're about all I can handle. I'm just not wired to be the kind of human who needs a happily ever after."

"Everyone needs a happily ever after."

"Okay, what if I already have that? What if life on this peninsula with you and Mem and your minions is my happily ever forever? I don't need more, Maia. I really don't."

"I hear you and I love this for you. Also, what if your happily ever forever on the peninsula includes a boy and you have babies who marry my babies like we talked about when we were kids? Or don't have babies, you know, whatever you choose. But what if we've been wrong about his sitch the whole time? Hannah isn't Logan's wife; maybe she's his sister." Optimism elevates the end of her question, her synapses snapping along with her fingers. "Think about it. Same last name, neither married."

"Gross, no. That's an immediate crush killer for sure. No grown brother and sister are vacationing together in a space that's barely more than a room. I'm sorry, but this is the real world. Join me here when you're ready."

"His mom then? Good sons can vacation with their moms in tight quarters." Maia's ideas dart wildly, looking for a place to land.

"I told you. They booked this trip to honor his mother's passing."

"That does complicate the mom theory."

"What if there are no theories? What if he doesn't have a sister? Or an explanation other than the one staring us in the face?"

"Hannah is his stepsister!"

"Or…maybe none of this has anything to do with Logan's family tree. Maybe we just need to accept that marriage and weddings are different things entirely. You don't have to know anything about weddings to have a courthouse ceremony, right? I mean, not everyone wants to have a lavish party and kiss on command in front of a hundred of their closest friends and family."

I pin my phone between my chin and shoulder to pluck Dad's Walkman headphones from my desk and twist their cord around my middle finger until blood pools in the tip, fattening and reddening the skin before I let it release, the way I used to in high school when situations felt beyond my control and I needed a way to ground my thoughts back in my body—or reality—again.

"I'm not built for romance or eloping or fancy champagne flutes. Even if Logan were single, I could never be his happily ever after."

"You're being ridiculous."

"The only ridiculous thing is this conversation—and my hot calendar dude fantasies—because forevers and commitment don't exactly dominate my lineage."

"Heart of the matter? You are not your mother, Charlie."

"Well, see. You're wrong. I'm half my mother."

"Yeah, and you're half fierce Pinkham. You descend from a line of seriously badass broads and you can't let your poor excuse for a mother mess with your future. She had her chance in the past and blew it. Her huge loss, obviously. And now your future is yours. I don't want you choosing to be alone because you think you're predestined to hurt yourself or someone else—"

"Or a lot of someones—"

"*She* did that. Not you." Maia inhales deeply. "I hate this line of thinking for you, Charlie."

I'm eager to move the conversation away from my hereditary faults.

"You sound like me preaching to Mem about taking it easy, and honestly it's really condescending now that I hear it."

"How dare you! Do you have any idea how many people would feel honored if I loved them as much as I love you?" Her tone is light, breezy and demanding in an emotional trifecta Maia's mastered early.

The start of a smile slips across my face, and through our conversation. "No, but I'm sure you'll tell me."

"The list is long." Maia hesitates, the line going silent between us for a moment as I let my mind float free of questions and confusion and everything except the mesmerizing lights of the lobster trap tree across the harbor, how water can effortlessly transform beads of light into a fitful sea of stars. "Your mem's headed home," Maia tells me. "She's turning down the drive now."

"Excellent. I need food. Hermon doesn't let her leave the diner empty-handed, which, now that say it, has likely been his way of placating me so I didn't rebel against their union. Sneaky bugger."

"I see we're on first name terms with Hermon again."

"Duh. He feeds me."

I head to the kitchen to triple check the floodlight is on for Mem and peek out the door window, just as the approaching car's headlights lurch through the glass, the car wobbling its way over the frost heave-rutted driveway, the driver flicking on the high beams as they slowly pass the cottage, heading to Cove Light.

"That's not Mem," I say, and run to her room at the rear of the cottage. I peel back her curtain just enough to see brake lights flare red against the night. Then, the plank door to the lighthouse flies open, the wind driving it inward to slam against the stone entry.

"*Shiiiiiiit,*" Maia says. "Pufferman has a guest."

"Logan," I whisper, just as his perfect shape appears in the wash of light between the car's headlights and the kitchen's warm glow. The fat moon conspires to make sure I don't miss the T-shirt he's wearing or the way he ignores the risk of death-by-rocky-ledge to run to the woman exiting her car, scooping her from the ground the way Haggard has pulled me to him countless times. Except. They face each other, their bodies meeting so their hearts press together.

Two cores, connecting.

His arms catch her in an elevated hold that makes her legs dangle, all her trust given over to his strength as her nose and eyes and chin rediscover the nook of his neck, her parts burrowing into the familiar space there, as if his hollows had been waiting for her, made for her.

"Charlie?"

"I'm here."

"Should I come over?"

"No. I'm good." If Maia hears the crack in my voice, or how the lie springs from its ragged crevice, she doesn't say. "I need a shower and food. You know, essentials."

"Call if you need emotional support wine."

"'Course." I hang up and immediately need Maia and Dad and Mem and even Hermon here with me, filling the house with Scrabble challenges and backgammon tournaments and pie. I'm certain I can feel my heart harden, lodging so high in my chest it's hard to breathe.

I swallow down the stone before showering and scrubbing the residue from the tile walls and floor while I'm at it, ever-efficient as I scour soapy circle on top of soapy circle so the disinfecting rings fan out across the wall, overlapping and connecting so it's impossible to know where the pattern originated.

When I'm exhausted, I succumb, letting my back find the shower wall, the weight of me slipping down into a seat so the hot water sprays over my flesh as I will the steam to clear my head, wash away my obsessing thoughts about Logan on the boat, at the rail, sharing an apple in a way that felt like something much more, helping me with my mother's letters, and running to his forever person who isn't me.

Closing my eyes to the pulsing spray only creates a black backdrop onto which the movie of Logan on the breakwater replays, his body braiding into hers with an intimacy that haunts me, even as I towel off and make my way to the fridge, where I stare at its blurred contents long enough for the light to turn off, as if too has no interest in me.

When I realize I have no actual appetite and am no longer willing to continue being an adult with complicated emotional feelings, I open my computer for a distraction DM. But like my love life, my DMs are a deep, vacuous nothingness. I troll @toothpicks3478's page but there aren't even recent dog posts for me to settle displaced emotions upon.

Perfect.

I owe Maia a decent post, so I open a file only to stare at the black flashing line appropriately named the *cursor*. Well, I have a few choice names for the marker as it blinks at me, all attitude and accusation.

I need control. That's all. Control has served me well for twenty-nine years and it will be triumphant again. Right now. I only need to type. One word, then two. They don't even have to be good words. The delete feature is a perennial favorite.

I piano-hover my hands over the keys and wait for inspiration to travel to my fingers because there are ideas in my head, for sure. Like about how a lobster molts roughly twenty-five times before it reaches approximately six years old. At six, they've grown to weigh roughly one pound. Each time a lobster molts, it looks for a place to hide in rocks, grassy areas, and nooks until their hard shell makes them adventurous once again, their thick skin a layer of defense against threats that dwell in the deep. Or in lighthouses. Because we all need a thick skin to survive, right? And the odds are against us. I mean, against lobsters. For every 50,000 eggs, an average of two lobsters will survive long enough to grow into a pound. Very few will ever get the full life they want. Or deserve. All because nature has a plan for them and they have no control and we have no control even when we want all the control and we act all bossy about having control, but really all we're doing is hiding our soft shell because we molt every day, sometimes multiple times a day, becoming vulnerable to our surroundings and looking for a place to hide, recover, and renew.

Ugh.

Okay. Toothpicks.
You're up.

@BirdieBlueBug
You around?

@toothpicks3478
Right here.

@BirdieBlueBug
Why are we so bad at
communication?

@toothpicks3478
Instagram is a clunky
technology.

I smile, an involuntary act that supports my choice to hide in the
craggy rock hollow of social media.

@BirdieBlueBug
Humans in general. Not us.
We're perfect.

@toothpicks3478
You make it very easy to
agree with you. Anyone
ever tell you that?

@BirdieBlueBug
Literally no one.

@toothpicks3478
whistles

@toothpicks3478
Okay. Communication. It's
our biggest human failure.

@BirdieBlueBug
Say more.

@toothpicks3478
It's documented fact. Perhaps
not *scientifically* documented,
but we all know it, right? No
one in our species could think
we're crushing it on the
communication front.

@BirdieBlueBug
Yes, this. Also, WHY?!!! We
should do better. Right?

I mean lobsters pee in each
other's faces to say all sorts
of things other lobsters understand
fully and yet we have All The Words
and still fail.

@toothpicks3478
Putting aside my smirk to agree.
And also...humans are wired for
intricate, complex communication.
We have vocal cords, range, the art
of inflection and tone, the gift of
vocabulary and an incredible flair
for introducing words into the
vernacular that literally never
existed before we say them—and yet
our very process of saying new words,
and bringing them forth, gives them
meaning and brings meaning to the
rest of us dumb talkers. But I haven't
given this much thought. You?

@BirdieBlueBug
Your off-the-cuff throwdown
on communication pleases me.
At least makes me feel less alone.

@toothpicks3478
This pleases me.

I settle onto my bed with my laptop across my knees, my pillows
and toothpicks3478 providing the perfect cushion for tonight's
blow.

@toothpicks3478
Oh! I forgot hand gestures:
the great communicators.
And still, we're all only barely
articulate most of the time.

@BirdieBlueBug
Yes, this.

@toothpicks3478
We're so afraid of saying our
truth to others, particularly those
we love or maybe love. Or could
love. We're afraid of saying the

wrong thing, we're afraid of trust
itself because giving over to
someone else first feels like the
most dangerous risk.

> @BirdieBlueBug
> Using actual words to tell
> another person about the
> messy bits crowding my heart?
> My survival instincts refuse.
> I mean, it's impossible. And
> awkward. And probably why
> sixth graders everywhere rely
> on the Do you Like Me? Check
> box YES or NO system.

@toothpicks3478
It's a solid system.

> @BirdieBlueBug
> Simple and effective.

@toothpicks3478
Way better than face pee.

@toothpicks3478
Too soon?

> @BirdieBlueBug
> Too hilarious.

@toothpicks3478
Phew. It's a risky maneuver
to mention face pee in a new
DM relationship.

> @BirdieBlueBug
> So awkward, right?
> It's a struggle!

@toothpicks3478
EVERY TIME!

@toothpicks3478
I mean, this is a first for
me, as I've said.

> @BirdieBlueBug
> I needed this laugh.
> Thank you.

@toothpicks3478
Thank you for your
thank you.

@BirdieBlueBug
You got me thinking about how risk
and danger is something I slay every
day. It's in my job description. But
you reframed all that for me, made my
shortcomings shorter somehow—or
less short. I don't know. How do you
say your shortcomings get smaller?

@toothpicks3478
I think it's called maturity,
but I'll have to look it up.

@toothpicks3478
Also, now I think you're a
dragon tamer. Or at least
you have the coolest job ever.

@BirdieBlueBug
Not saying one way or the other on
the dragon tamer front, but my job is
definitely the coolest.

@BirdieBlueBug
Though my close work with dragons
does leave me defunct in the
communicating with human people
arena.

@toothpicks3478
Not a thing. I'm a human
person and I'd say you're
slaying the person-to-person
thing.

@BirdieBlueBug
Sure. But you have the protective
shell of the internet.

@toothpicks3478
As do you.

@BirdieBlueBug
Exactly.

16

The Colors

While spending the morning in the barn repairing trap nets and painting an assembly line of buoys in my family's fishing colors, I'm fully aware of how my shoulders have taken up almost permanent residence in the space just below my ears, creeping up so high my back is hunched, as if curling into myself will provide some kind of escape from the agonizing proximity of Logan in the lighthouse with his wife.

So far, there's been no sign of him—not that I'm looking, of course. My brain's been entirely occupied with obsessing over how he's likely still in his boxers, his fingers tracing the lines of his wife's curves as their easy banter moves between them, conversations continuing from where they left off in the middle of their shared life.

Or, in Terrible Scenario #2, their two heads are pressed together as they search real estate listings for lighthouses because they are so blissfully happy in the bed with the four-million thread count sheets Maia made me buy.

In More Terrible *Terrible* Scenario #3, their bodies are tangled within the four-million thread count sheets Maia made me buy, all their reunion sex making their breath short and fast.

In Endlessly More Terrible Scenario #4, she's sarong-wrapped in the four-million thread count sheets Maia made me buy while Logan models several dozen delicious poses for next year's lobstermen calendar.

I toss my paintbrush to the bucket and cannot with myself. Inside, I change and splash water on my face and definitely do not look toward the lighthouse to spy on activity as I pin my hair to a twist that fails to commit and ends up looking more like a question mark. Because, of course.

As a reward for all the Not Looking I accomplish, I pull up my Instagram account and there's a DM from after I fell asleep last night:

> @toothpicks3478
> Luckily, even with all of
> our linguistic failings, we
> do find ways to communicate
> all the messy stuff in the end.
> At least I hope so.

The message is evidence of a conversation that could have extended longer than I'd allowed it to, and I find myself leaning in, reading back over our easy exchanges, lulled by the vulnerability and sage advice coming from @toothpicks3478. Even still, I can't message back now, can I? The etiquette of DMing is uncharted territory. What if the same social expectations apply to DMs as alcohol consumption and it's not acceptable to DM a semi-stranger before five o'clock? And if I do imbibe in a little pre-five-o'clock DMing, what will such reckless behavior say about my loose morals? I let out a long exhale, because, really. Who makes up these rules, anyway? And why isn't the handbook for adulting on bookshelves yet?

When I've sufficiently sacrificed most of my thumbnail to my incessant obsessing, I pay brief homage to Obama Mama's feed before I pop over to the Maine's Midcoast Lobstermen Association grid where there's a new *In Memoriam*. This latest tribute is for Seamus Kinneally, my father's dear friend who passed the year after I lost Dad.

The black-and-white photo pulls my childhood to the surface so I'm barefoot on that long, sun-bleached dock again, the summer heat radiating up from the weathered planks and challenging the soles of my feet to a game of hopscotch to stay cool. Nearby, my father lent a hand loading wooden lobster pots onto the stern of the EMERALD ISLE, Seamus Kinneally's vessel, which was near double the size of my father's boat and served three times as many generations.

Seamus was old when I was young, back when I knew without anyone telling me that Seamus was Santa Claus in disguise, masquerading as a fisherman in the off-season, his white beard full and bushy and looking so much like snow even on days when the sun was strong enough to bake me on the inside. His beard wasn't alone on a wharf crowded with bearded men, but Seamus had a beard that held gifts. Quarters some days, Lego figures on others. More than once, a wrapped lollipop. He would extract presents from his fluffy facial hair and hold his treasures to me with his sea-thickened fingers, a nod of permission in his widened eyes. He was Santa Claus and no one could convince me differently.

On more than one night, when adults didn't think kids could hear through summer's open windows, I'd heard Dad talk about Seamus losing his daughters young. I spent my early childhood looking for his girls under rocks, in the spaces around puppies and new kittens, and in my reflection in tide pools. I'd been too young then to comprehend what loss meant, and in my young mind, I believed Seamus simply hadn't found his children yet. They were still here on the peninsula with us, holding up their committed end of a hide-and-seek game. He just had to find them.

Dad saw things differently, I know now, though he never said then. Not with words. Instead, he made sure Seamus had someone to see him off from the docks each day, just like Maia welcomes me home from every journey. Dad had known all about the loneliness that survives on the other side of loss, and he'd tried to fill that space for Seamus.

Now, Seamus is on the cove again, his smile beaming under his full beard and a full sun in the *In Memoriam* post, a snapshot that chokes me with a kind of sadness that softens my bones, melting me toward my early years, making me wonder why growing up and growing out of childhood doesn't hurt more than it does because for most of us, it's our first loss.

My thumb goes to the screen, ghosting over the hand-stenciled letters of *EMERALD ISLE* across his boat's stern, green in my memory but mist gray on my computer. Seamus would tell tales of the thousands of shades of green that sprang to life in Ireland, the color singing in the trees and the grasses and fields and mosses. Bursting at the edges of cliffs and within bouquets of shamrocks, the color's only limitation found in language, in how few words we had to name all the variations of fertile growth and new beginnings.

Seamus, being the all-knowing Father Christmas he was, saw how I lived with blue in this same way. Watching its hues play as they shifted across the sky and the sea, or along the back of a whale in the twilight underwater deep. Growing as a skin around a tart berry in the brambles. In iridescent muscle shells. The armor of my blue lobster. The faint bloodlines traveling like channels on the underside of my forearms that connect my life to my father's.

Seeing Seamus with his thumbs tucked behind the straps of his overalls, his chin thrown up in a high laugh, reminds me how there are so many kinds of joy in the world and too few words to name them. For a long time, I read the comments, on the page dedicated to Seamus and his legacy. No one writes about gifts from his beard—or floats a Father Christmas theory—and I latch onto this omission realizing that I was special to him, only registering now how much hurt and hope I must have brought this old man in my little girl-ness after he'd lost his young girls. Still, he didn't give me his heartbreak; he only gave me gifts.

I like the post with a click, something I've never done before because I'm a firm believer that liking happens in real time and in real experiences. But seeing Seamus on my screen fills my heart beyond its capacity for love. I need to put the overflow somewhere, so I give his post this fake heart even though Seamus deserves a real one, complicated as it is with all its flaws and goodness and mistakes.

And then, there's another gift, as if Seamus is still here, surprising me: in the front corner of the photo's frame, there's the edge of a boat. It's tied to the neighboring dock and almost indistinguishable from the sea of boats in the working harbor, except for the unmistakable *CH* of the *CHARLOTTE ANNE*. I'd know the lettering anywhere, just as I know the slooped shape of the stern, hand-carved and sanded by my father when he built our boat in the years between being a kid and becoming an adult, long before I knew him, back when the boat had worked under a different name, before he had a baby and my christening happened in the shallow tide on the same day Dad re-christened the boat.

I enlarge the photo, squint and veer closer, reaching for the unknowable corners of life that were cropped out of the shot, lost to me, no different than my dad.

When my DM notification dings, I jump. Not from surprise this time, but eagerness.

> @toothpicks3478
> Are you here?

> > @BirdieBlueBug
> > I am. Are you?

> @toothpicks3478
> Let me check.

I smile.

> > @BirdieBlueBug
> > Is that your post on
> > Seamus Kinneally?

> @toothpicks3478
> Yes, if you love it.

> @toothpicks3478
> No if you don't.

> @toothpicks3478
> But still a yes because I'm
> not good with lies.

> > @BirdieBlueBug
> > I really like it.

In fact, I love it. I love it so much I want someone to tell how much I love it. Someone who isn't Dad or Maia or even Mem. Someone like Logan who's a version of Logan that's not married. Someone who wants to hear all the reasons why a remembrance post like this is special—no, sacred—to me, and who won't be surprised by what I share because we've already trusted our histories and memories and imaginings to each other.

@toothpicks3478
I found the photo in the
archives. Judging from the
comments, Seamus seemed
like an exceptional human.

@BirdieBlueBug
I have no doubt.

Suddenly, I'm feeling shy about my connection to Seamus in the
presence of InstaMan, or maybe it's guilt for how fixated I am on the
tiny sliver of Dad's boat before it became my boat. I know my
undivided attention should settle squarely on Seamus, a man who
lived a full life and made mine fuller in the process. A man Dad
protected because at the end of the day, the family of a fisherman
aren't only the people we come home to, but the ones who keep us
safe when we can't be at home.

@BirdieBlueBug
Black-and-white photos
always gut me.

@toothpicks3478
In a good way?

@BirdieBlueBug
In a slowing down, summer
days from childhood were real
kind of way.

@BirdieBlueBug
Like our past matters.

@toothpicks3478
Heavy.

@toothpicks3478
And I agree. My past has kicked
my ass yet makes me respect
how I wouldn't be here without
it. For me, black-and-white
photos remind me that a full
color life only exists if we make it.

@BirdieBlueBug
Now who's heavy?

@BirdieBlueBug
Isn't this a safe space to talk
about favorite ice cream and
superior fruits?

@toothpicks3478
Buddha's Hand. It's a thing.
I looked it up. Technically a citrus
fruit, if you're a details person, and
definitely shaped like a hand. Since
I imagine Buddha's hand was a very
special hand, I assume it tastes as
good as it looks. Anyway, it smokes
Golden Delicious in the fancy
department. *Yawn*

@BirdieBlueBug
You're telling me about Buddha's
Hand but all I can hear is that you're
studying up for our DM sessions.

@toothpicks3478
Probably because I am.

@BirdieBlueBug
Why?

@toothpicks3478
Because they matter.

The three words hold me in a trance for a long while as I study their implications. He's saying that *I* matter, right? Or at least, time in this space with *me* matters. It's not social media that matters. It's me.

@toothpicks3478
In light of our recent exchanges
on all the ways we fail at
communication as a species,
I'd like to openly reveal that I'm
scared of scaring you off if it's
not already obvious I'm scared
of scaring you off.

@BirdieBlueBug
Not scared.

But is that true? Fear might be the weighty thing hanging in my chest, holding me back, slowing me up, making me reread his words two and even three times. Because I don't know this person. I mean, not really. And yet I do. At least, I recognize him more than I'm comfortable admitting. And maybe it's the memory of Seamus that makes me feel young again, searching for lost girls in tidal pools and finding my own reflection instead.

Maybe I still don't truly know the girl staring back at me, the one living her life from the surface, brave enough to be on the water, but never exploring its depths, or mine.

> @BirdieBlueBug
> What else did you research in preparation for our impromptu chats?

@toothpicks3478
I have a shameful google history of: How not to scare off strangers in DM rooms.

> @BirdieBlueBug
> Wait. Are DM spaces called rooms?

@toothpicks3478
They are not. Which probably explains my disturbing search results.

@toothpicks3478
I'm taking comfort in the fact that you had no idea either, proving we both really are new to this.

> @BirdieBlueBug
> I bet you write that in all your DMs.

@toothpicks3478
You're funny. You've been told that, right?

> @BirdieBlueBug
> I think I'm hilarious, though my humor is more biting sarcasm than laugh-out-loud hysterics, which isn't always a crowd favorite.

@toothpicks3478
I don't hate it.

@BirdieBlueBug
High praise.

@toothpicks3478
I'm trying to appear
confident and cool.

@BirdieBlueBug
What kind of cool?

@toothpicks3478
Danny Zuko in Grease cool.

@BirdieBlueBug
When he dances for Sandy
or disses her?

@toothpicks3478
Dances, definitely. I'm
a romantic all the way.

@BirdieBlueBug
That's the right answer.

@BirdieBlueBug
About Danny Zuko.

@toothpicks3478
Are we ignoring the
other bit?

@BirdieBlueBug
Not ignoring, but I'd have to do
a pretty deep dive on romance
research if it's your topic of choice
today.

@toothpicks3478
So...not a fan of Sandy
and Danny?

@BirdieBlueBug
Huge fan. I mean: Sandy and Danny.
But I'm the kind of person who thinks
about what happens after the perfect
couple jets off into the sunset in their
flying car.
You know, after the honeymoon, when
the kids and the bills come and Sandy
can't even look at Danny because he's
been wearing that hair gel for way too

long and couldn't he skip his grooming regimen just once to take out the trash or gift her with an uninterrupted hour to take a bath, maybe even dry her hair fully before she's asked to feed the kids, clean the house, report to work, schedule all the things and then slap a smile on her face because isn't she lucky?

@toothpicks3478
Okay. Now I'm a little scared of you.

@BirdieBlueBug
Now *that* I've been told before!

I don't tell InstaMan about how I've spent way too much time dissecting Danny's behaviors trying to determine if he really deserved Sandy in the end considering his fairly epic commitment to lying and cheating. No one needs that much Real Me.

Outside, a vehicle rumbles up the drive, and when I pop to the kitchen window, Haggard and Jimmy McFarland lumber out of Haggard's giant pick-up, his latest contraption hiding under a tarp in the bed.

@BirdieBlueBug
I need to go. Company.

@toothpicks3478
Jealous.

@toothpicks3478
And now I've made this awkward.

I smile, and close my laptop, meeting Haggard and Jimmy as they step inside the kitchen while knocking—letting themselves in the way people do in these parts—before pulling off orange hunting hats and wiping their boots.

"Wanna go sledding?" Haggard's cheeks shine red with cold, his smile as big as when we were kids and he'd stop by asking this exact question, or the seasonally modified: "Wanna ride bikes?"

"Yes." I don't expect the word to come as quickly as it does, but I'm so eager to get out of the house and out of my head and fully off my side of the peninsula that counting grains of rice seems like an attractive option for my attention at this point.

"Grab a helmet." Jimmy says. "Or you can borrow mine."

"Wait. I'm gonna need a helmet?"

"Oh, yeah." Haggard's mischief sparks a flame in his hazel eyes as his full smile tempts me out the door. "You're gonna need all the protection you can get."

As I grab my snowpants, gloves, and thrust on my boots, I think that crushes should come with this same warning. Maybe then we'd stand a chance of surviving them.

17

The Coast

I'd been tucked away so safely in the barn with the protection of Dad's Walkman and his ancient—yet surprisingly still relevant—eighties cassette tapes, I hadn't noticed the entire village of Christmas Cove moving plowed snow onto the common. Tractors work in a snaking line, hauling piles of early winter snow from front lawns and municipal parking lots. The mound they create is a mini ski hill. For super beginners, but still.

In Haggard's truck, my excitement builds. "Are we skiing?"

"Nope." Jimmy's enthusiasm is uncontainable. "It's gonna be a luge track for the festival."

"We were inspired by your mem," Haggard says. "She was telling us stories about how she and her kin used to slide all the way onto the frozen edges of the harbor in her day."

"My mem?" It's usually impossible to picture Mem as a kid, but an image comes to me as if a snapshot of her as a little girl with easy limbs and big ideas and endless energy, like she was a whole person with a whole existence before I slipped into her life.

Haggard throws his arm behind me in the middle of his bench front seat. "Memma Pinkham's spearheaded the entire project, Charles. There's no stopping her. I swear, she's like a kid again."

"Except bossier," Jimmy says.

"Don't know about that," Haggard says. "I'd bet on Memma Pinkham being born as bossy as they come, and I mean that with the utmost respect."

Haggard doesn't have to tell me he respects Mem. I can hear it in his voice. And he showed me while helping me when she was sick, making his way down to the hospital in Portland twice each week, alternating days with Maia and Hermon. He brough hot meals, lasting hugs, and news from the midcoast. He looked after the house while I couldn't be here, repaired the shingles when the big storm blew off a portion of the roof, and he never said a thing. Just made the repairs, kept the driveway plowed and the pipes from freezing all so I could focus my worry on my most important person.

Worry is the last thing on my mind now as I watch Mem waving her arms at Kermit's crane like she's guiding in an aircraft. Kermit dumps another impressive pile of snow onto a growing heap. A raised runway of snow leads away from the massive pile, the pathway pressed into the shape of a narrow, snaking road hugging the north side of the common, an area shaded by the protection of the evergreen tree line so a stray warm winter day won't have a chance to melt the snow back to water.

The luge track starts at its high summit. Actual snow stairs are carved into the side of the hill to access the starting point, the seam of each step spraypainted with a red line melting to pink in the snow, the marker warding off depth-blindness amid a sea of blazing white.

Mem acknowledges my arrival with a wave that sends Kermit the wrong message so his crane jerks and stutters. Haggard holds up the Time Out signal and ushers me off to the luge's finish circle, tasking me with the design of a landing area where sledders can end their ride in safety. The Farrin family donated dozens of hay bales from their inland farm up the coast, their sheep and goats and bunnies already drafted for the petting zoo portion of the Curmudgeons and Caviar festivities.

I join Kate Farrin in her half-hearted attempt to cordon off a safe landing space for lugers. Kate's the oldest of five girls and devotes all her energy to leaving the Cove after graduation next year—a life goal she can't help reiterating as her repeated eyerolls question my plan to create a horseshoe with the bales, a shape that mirrors the cove, because who isn't a fan of symmetry?

Kate, apparently. She responds to my design brilliance with a lazy but firm *"Whatever."*

When our first layer is in place, we form a second by stacking the bales across the seam of the pair below and skip every other bale, making the finished product look like a horizontal Jenga maze that kids are already burrowing up and through and over. Stacking bales is hard work and warms me. The bales feel so much like traps pulled from the deep, the way their boxy shape gets lifted across my pelvis as I haul them high, steadying each one against gravity.

When Haggard whistles for me to join him at the other side of the common, Kate sits cross-legged on a stray bale and pulls out her phone with such intensity I suspect the device might self-destruct if she doesn't check its notifications at regular intervals. Her thumb flicks up her screen and her eyes glaze, unlocking a zombie level stare.

I bend backward, sending a stretch through my shoulders. "You on Instagram?"

"Instagram's for boomers."

"Whatever that means," I say with a laugh.

She doesn't lift her eyes from her screen. "If you don't know what a boomer is, you might be a boomer."

A part of me wants to horrify her by following her account when I'm online next, commenting enthusiastically and awkwardly about what a great hay maze builder she is, but it's probably a good thing she doesn't use the platform because the prospect of locating her presence in a sea of social media makes my brain feel as if it's being pressed by an actual vice.

Haggard brings solace when I ask him what being a boomer means, his response confirming I should remain offended on many levels just before he reminds me how my seventeen-year-old attitude was sharp enough to cut glass so maybe I could also just shelve my judgement.

"Judgement shelved."

"Good. Take this helmet."

I pull on the hockey helmet, secure the strap under my chin. "Should I be scared?"

"Yes. We're the test runners."

"Explain."

"See that?" He points to the stand built at the top of the luge, a crude starting gate that looks less Olympian and more lumber pallet. "That's where we start. I'll go first. Then you. If we get flung off one of the bends, the crew will heighten the wall."

"Um...."

"There's no doubting in luging," he says.

"Luging cannot be a word."

"It is a word, and your new favorite sport. Strap in." He pats me on the head and scoops me under his arm like I'm a plank of wood, my hips locked under his grip until he delivers me to the start.

At the top, he gives me a salute and a plastic disk sled. "Don't die, Charles."

"Comforting."

Despite his helmet and face shield, I can see Haggard's smile, the way his joy inflates his shoulders wider, relaxing his neck so that it tips backwards.

"Charlie!" My name reaches me from the outskirts of the crowd.

I squint from behind my borrowed ski goggles to see Maia next to Sam in the throng, her magnificent hair like a mane and wrap all at once, her gloved hands cupped around her mouth.

"Blink twice if you're okay!" she yells, and I do, even if we both know she can't see me.

Sam leaves Maia's side to use a megaphone, which makes me question how and where Sam obtained a megaphone. I marvel over all the small and large preparations that have been made to ensure our first festival maintains the rich character of our peninsula.

Sam instructs the crowd to count down from ten. They do. In unison, slow and loud and determined, each number moving everyone closer to a shared outcome until the gathering yells "One!" and Haggard dives belly-first onto an inflated inner tube and sails down the luge track, his outstretched arms hitting the turns before his body.

The common practically sways with *oohs!* and *ahhhs!* And there's a collective *woah!* as he comes close—but just shy of catastrophically close—to flying over the snow bumper that acts as a rail along the riskiest bend. Haggard is flat and fast and fearless and I drop to my sled to catch up with him, not waiting for a countdown or directions or anything as I push onto the ice track and follow him to the bottom, my body twisting around the soft corners, picking up speed along the steep descent. When I get hung up on a section that isn't quite angled enough to maintain momentum, I scoot my disk over the high parts and push on because jamming down this track is the best thing I've done since I was in grade school and would pump my legs so hard on the swings that for a split second—at the highest height of my swing—my body would suspend in the air, as if I were made of wind and flight and freedom. Like now.

When the luge ends, I slide across frozen ground until my feet hit a hay bale like a bullseye. In one motion, I pull off my helmet, raise my arms, get hugged and victory-scooped by Haggard before I race him up the snow stairs to the starting line where we do it again, this time with Jimmy on our heels. In between our runs, Clyde Simmons sprays water along the track, making the unbroken ice slicker and treacherously wonderous.

No one can see me peek out from behind my ski goggles to search the crowd for Logan and Hannah as the day wears on and more brave souls run the luge after me, Haggard, and Jimmy complete enough trials to prove its safety and satisfy our fun quota.

The tree lights blink on just as dusk settles. A line forms from neighbors wanting their turn, makeshift sleds arriving as laundry baskets, large plastic storage bins, cardboard, and outdoor furniture cushions. Bets are placed on which improvised toboggin will be fastest. Amidst all the joy, the luge run sparkles, crystalized with ice and the fresh snow that confetti falls over the latest and greatest addition to our humble festival preparations on Christmas Cove.

My muscles are sore in a new way as we limp to Earl's Eats for the baked haddock and cornbread spread Hermon's set out for the town, diners throwing money into a bait bucket at the pick-up window so we're all pitching in, already giving to the Lobstermen's Fund, Hermon, and each other.

Maia crowds me as I shove a swiftly-constructed haddock sandwich into my mouth. I ache to regain enough energy to luge again. And again. In the cramped space, heat climbs across my skin, and my scalp feels damp with flattened hair, sweat collecting at my forehead, underarms and behind my knees. I peel off my sweater and hope the body odor isn't coming from me even as Maia's scrunched up nose assures me the stink is entirely mine.

"That looked...well, amazing."

"It was...." I swallow my mouthful of cornbread to avoid crumb spray. "It was the best thing I've ever done, hands down."

She rolls her eyes, feigning exasperation. "It cannot be *the best* unless it's been so long since you've had sex that you've forgotten all your pleasure centers."

"Can you please not say pleasure centers while I'm eating? Or ever? And when you're not preggers, I'm challenging you to a race. Or we're tandem tobogganing. I'll get you out there on a cafeteria tray like we did in little school if I have to." My smile's so contagious it jumps to Maia's face. She rubs her stomach and I put my hand over hers atop her baby bump. "I can say without reservation that I've never been overly interested in your internal pregnancy ecosystems, but the idea that your kid gets to basically luge in and around your belly everyday makes me more jealous than a normal, functioning adult should be."

Maia's smile deepens, as if my words connect her to today's events in a way she couldn't feel in her own body as she sat on the sidelines. I grab a second piece of cornbread as we head to the outside bench, me needing to cool down, Maia needing to protect her baby bump from the bumping crowd. I remain amazed by the heat emanating from the seat.

"So, I'm dying to know," Maia says. "Have you met her, Logan's wife? What's she like? She's awful, right? Wait. No, she's perfect, isn't she? Don't tell me. I've just entered my seventh month and the last thing I need is competition from some flawless human."

I shake my head. "You're still the fanciest person on the peninsula." I'd almost forgotten about Hannah and Logan and my inappropriate crush. Almost. My spine shakes off the cold climbing my back. "Haven't seen her."

"No one's seen the mystery woman, apparently. I've had my spies out all day. I don't think Logan or Hannah have left the lighthouse."

Hearing his name with hers physically hurts in a way I know it shouldn't. So, I ignore the feelings. Suppress the confusion. You know, all the normal, healthy coping techniques. "What spies exactly?"

"We live in a town of three hundred and fifty-two and a half people. Literally everyone is a spy. Besides we're all interested. For different reasons, obviously, but still curious."

"I'm not curious."

"That might be the most fantastic lie I've ever heard you tell, Charlotte Pinkham, and we choreographed some doozies trying to dodge curfews junior year, but if you believe this lie you're trying to sell me now then I'll let you have it, even if we both know you're only lying to yourself."

"Harsh. And who says doozies?"

"I'm an influencer. I'm bringing it back."

"From 1940? Also, can we please talk about anything else? It's been such a good day and I think the subject of my lighthouse guests has reached its natural end."

"I disagree. Plus, I bring intel." Her body proudly straightens to deliver gossip. "I'll warn you my information is spotty at best, but also top notch."

"Go."

"I turned my sleuthing genius to your InstaMan and I unearthed his name, if you want to know it. Wait. Do you know his name already?"

"I do not." The thought of InstaMan having a name—being a real person in the real world—makes me uneasy and I brush away a lone flake of snow that falls to my thigh.

"Okay, good. You know how I live to be the one to break news."

"I'm aware."

She ignores my snark but doesn't miss how I lean in. "His name is Ellis. He's been volunteering as the social media guru for the last few months. I don't have a last name because of pesky privacy laws and all, but I did start following the fishing account—which you know is entirely against my religion—just to see if he'd strike up random DMs with me or invite me to his private account like he did for your sexy online time."

"And?" I hate how my heart is in my throat, all anticipation and skepticism because if I can't have Logan, I want whatever this is with InstaMan to be mine and only mine.

"Nothing. Nada."

It's a relief to discover @toothpicks3478 isn't cruising followers indiscriminately, but I'm not sure I'm comfortable having my DM space overlap with real life. If I'd wanted to know more about him, I knew how to find him. I could have asked him, but I didn't. And there are reasons for that. As if in agreement, the cold descends on us, the air turning dry as the dusting of snow commits to being a storm with flakes growing fatter and bolder, their intensity promising a thick layer of white by morning.

"He's some hotshot architect or builder or something, though like I said, the details are admittedly spotty. I do know the front office lady is majorly crushing on him."

"Huh." I try to picture Instahuman as Ellis, a man who might spend his days creating blueprints for neighborhoods and community centers, law offices and sprawling waterfront mansions like the ones dotting the coast of Maine, looking as out of place here as the seasonal people who own them.

"He started volunteering to help out a friend, maybe even someone we know." She elbows me and lifts her eyebrows with intrigue. "He sounds selfless and nice. Maybe the kind of person you could meet in person. Would you do that? Meet up in real life?"

"Well, I don't know. Did you grab his mom's maiden name while you were at it? His Social Security number? It feels a bit amateur you're not delivering the goods on the name of the first school he attended when you're asking me to commit to the enormous step of meeting this stranger."

"Hilarious. And I'm ignoring the amateur remark." She hurries me back to her question with a wave.

"No, Maia. I wouldn't meet him in person."

"Why not?" she says, unsatisfied. "We'd choose a public place. Somewhere safe. And I'd go with, lurking at a neighboring table, obviously."

"I love that my DMing with a stranger has now become a *we*."

"It's always been a *we*. And you're getting off topic. If you present a solid argument for why you don't want to invite this person into the realm of your real life, I'll stop sleuthing."

"Because he's a stranger."

"Everyone is a stranger until you meet, and technically you've already met so your response doesn't remotely qualify as a solid reason for me to stop nudging you."

"I feel like there are some fairly significant facts you're choosing to overlook in your reasoning. Like, first, we haven't met—not even a little bit—which is clear from us having this conversation in which *you* told me Ellis's name instead of Ellis himself."

She dismisses my logic with a practiced flick of her wrist.

"More importantly, I actually like chatting with him, and it's the anonymous part that makes it so satisfying. He's funny in an understatedly hilarious kind of way, and I like what we have."

"This is the second time you've told me he's funny, third if you count your unnecessary addition of *hilarious*, which I'd like to ignore but can't because now I'm jealous of this boy with his *oh so dreamy* sense of humor considering how I'm the funny in your life."

"Wow, that took a quick turn."

"Again, welcome to my pregnancy."

I shiver. "You should be happy for me. Instaman puts my brain in a good headspace."

"Ellis," she corrects.

"Instaman. He makes me not hate the internet."

"Miracle man," she says under her breath.

"Exactly. Whatever weird thing we have is working." I feel Maia's smile growing, and when I turn it's Cheshire wide—cheeks full with a thought she's trying not blurt. "Go ahead...say it. You know you want to."

"Ellis could be your lobster." She hooks my arm with hers while her knee-high leather boots tiptoe a jig in the gathering snow. "You could *looooove* him."

"You could not be more immature."

"Oh, you know I can." She reaches for my hand. "I want you to find your lobster, Charlie."

"Lobsters don't have happily ever afters."

"Blah, blah...I know, but it's romantic to think they do. And even more fantastically dreamy to think my best friend with her heart of granite might actually be starting to thaw, which I'm aware is a mixed metaphor but go with me here." She gives my arm a shake. "Admit you're not the same person you were when you wrote that first blog post, and the change is either because of Logan or InstaEllis or the karmic placement of two beautiful boy souls in your orbit simultaneously. Oh my god!" she screams. "You are in a love triangle, Charlie Pinkham." Her mitten flies to cover her mouth in mock shock. "Words the universe never thought could be uttered."

"You're pretty proud of yourself over there, aren't you?"

She nods, biting the Ruby Woo red of her bottom lip.

"I admit I've begun to tolerate the concept of romance, but a love triangle is a stretch, even for you."

I'm happy to sit outside under the simplicity of fresh snowfall, but Maia's already fitting me in a wedding dress next to a guy whose decidedly indistinguishable face isn't the least bit of an obstacle in her party planning.

"I need to go at my own pace—"

"But you're going," she interrupts. "Is that what you're telling me? Because that's what I'm hearing. Even my readers feel it, this shift in you, a newly-sprouted willingness to dip your toe into the love pool."

"Okay, you are never allowed to say love pool again and I'm not dipping any toes. I'm wearing sensible boots as I take a vigorously healthy stroll around the edges with my hands in my pockets, rubbernecking a bit."

"I'll take rubbernecking all day—"

"Do not make that perverted!" I scold.

"I'll behave. As long as you're taking steps. I've honestly never been prouder, not even when my kids took their actual first steps. Oh, god. I might be a crap mom."

"You are not a crap mom, not even on your worst day. Trust me. Crap moms are my area of expertise."

18

The Cars

We stay on our beloved bench for a long time and when Haggard spills out of the diner with a hearty hello, he drags enough heat outside to brush our faces.

"Well, ladies, I'm off!" Haggard says. "Climb aboard, Charles, and I'll deliver you back from whence you came." He backs close to me, bending forward slightly, his arms at his sides, palms flicking upward like eager stirrups.

"Go on," Maia says. "Get on up there. No day is a bad day when it ends on the back of a handsome man. I'll tell Mem you hitched a ride home with Haggard. If Hermon can't take her to the cottage, Sam can."

"Yeah?" I ask Maia.

"'Course. Now mount up, sistah."

Haggard twists to pat his shoulder. "Just like old times. Remember when you broke your leg freshman year and I motored you between classes?"

Maia stands, elbows me with a snicker. "Motored you."

"You are Beavis and Butthead," I tell her, stepping onto the bench and throwing my arms around Haggard's neck, tightening my legs at his middle as he cradles the underside of my thighs. He jumps once, hoisting me to a snug position across his back. "You should head inside, Mai." He nods to the diner. "Sam's lost without his bride."

"That man is amazing." Maia shoves her fist to the side of her rear hip and bends backwards. "He's got a sixth sense for when Mama needs sleep. And a foot rub. And ice cream."

"Aren't you perpetually in need of pampering?"

"I'd take offense if it weren't true."

We exchange goodnights and Haggard piggybacks me to the common as we talk about the sheer awesomeness of the lobster trap tree that lends a sparkly glow to the luge track behind it.

"Whaddya say we shake things up for tomorrow, Charles? Sled down the track on those cafeteria trays we were always getting in trouble for in elementary school?"

"I was just talking about that with Maia!"

"No way."

"Way."

"Good times," Haggard says, and they were. "So, whaddya say? Race ya."

"I'm hauling tomorrow, but my renegade elementary school self will be there in spirit." I tighten my arms at his neck and rest my head to watch the white glow of our artificial lights bending and blurring against the night so their gleam looks less like color and more like comfort.

Which is exactly why I don't see a figure approach until Haggard calls a cheery *Good Evening!* and my face lifts past Haggard's shoulder to see Logan. Unearthed from his love lighthouse. Away from all the sheets and the sex. If I could burrow inside Haggard and hide out the next ten minutes of my existence, I would.

"You here to join the fun?" Haggard bellows. "There's a happy mob inside if their noise wasn't what tempted you over."

Logan smiles at Haggard, but doesn't make eye contact with me. In fact, his eyes do everything but look at me. They roam around me. Study my body pieces. My arms wrapped at Haggard's neck, hands clasped at his front. My legs at his sides, his arms balancing my weight. Logan throws a short cough. "I'm grabbing take-out tonight, actually."

Of course he is. He'd need sustenance for All the Sex. Just as I think it, Logan's eyes jump to mine like a reprimand. My skin fires with a heat that makes my stomach lurch.

"How are you, Charlie?" Logan asks.

"Good," I manage, hands-down achieving the World's Most Awkward one-syllable response.

Logan takes a step back as if my presence physically pushes him away. He makes small talk with Haggard about the luge, the day, the celebrations he heard from the lighthouse, all while managing to expertly avoid me, which is no easy feat considering I'm attached to Haggard. Whatever. He can ignore me all he wants, and while I'm here being awkward, I search the dark for perfect Hannah, queen of the four-million thread count sheets.

The shadows give up nothing. Nada. No Hannah. Against my will, my crush studies Logan's face for signs of fatigue from a day of indoor physical exertion. And I really do try my hardest not to notice how he's sporting a new-to-me wool cap and jeans that hang loose at his hips under his trademark puffy jacket, which shouldn't look good on him but absolutely does now that I know the cut of him underneath.

Honestly, I blame his abs for my inability to corral my imagination.

"You need to join us tomorrow!" Haggard claps a hand to Logan's shoulder so my calf brushes Logan's hard chest. Great. My skin fires with heat even as a gust of wind blasts us from the north. I hold Haggard tighter, afraid of the light feeling in my head. "We need all hands on deck for festival prep, if you're up for it."

Logan's eyes flash to mine as he takes a bigger step back from me and my leg and my cooties, apparently. My foot twitches with a need to be near him again, even as he retreats another small step, turning his careful body to the harbor and the wind.

What is even happening? How can I remember every minute detail of our letter-destroying caper and the always-easy chatter between us on the boat, while he's departed to some far-off place where I don't exist? He casts his eyes to the sky as if checking the status of the storm even as snowfall coats our hats and shoulders. Okay, fine. I had— have—an inappropriate crush. I own that. But I wasn't alone in my flirtation, was I? Sharing that apple was hot and he knew it. *And* it was *his* idea. Trusting each other with our past was risky and we both showed up for that. And now that his wife's here, he's ignoring me?

"I'll be away tomorrow," Logan says. "But another day for sure." He could not sound more non-committal.

I nudge Haggard with my heels like he's a pony and I need to mosey on out of this one-horse situation. He boosts me higher on his back as goodbyes are mumbled. As Haggard walks me to his truck, I allow my attention to twist once to catch sight of Logan as he nears the diner. He's watching the harbor and the sea, the lighthouse—as if he misses them, as if he misses *her*.

My frustration is exhausting and my breathing has devolved into exasperated huffs by the time Haggard drives slowly down my long driveway, his giant headlights splashing a pearly glow across the side of our tiny cottage, Dad's barn, and the lighthouse.

"Cove Light looks pretty all lit up," Haggard says as we draw closer. "Shame her beacon's never worked."

I think of Hannah inside. Every light on. Her, waiting. Alone. As Logan retrieves their take-out. How she can't be bothered to join him or the town. Suddenly, it feels right that she's pretentious and highly unlikeable because that would make Logan less attractive by association and I need Logan to be less attractive because I didn't imagine his changed behavior, did I? How easy it was for him to ignore me? It's possible my irritation toward Hannah is displaced, but frustration needs to go somewhere.

"Do you think it's weird Logan's wife hasn't come outside all day?" The question is out before I'd fully committed to asking it.

"Logan's married?" Haggard puts the truck in park, but doesn't cut the engine or the lights. "Huh."

"*Huh*, what? *Huh*, funny. *Huh*, interesting or *huh*, that doesn't align with things you know?"

His face twists, trying to translate my investigatory vigor. "Dunno. Doesn't seem like the married type."

"What's a married type?"

"Not someone who's renting a lighthouse alone." He props his elbow to the door and lazily taps his thumb against the steering wheel.

"Tell you the truth, I thought it was his girlfriend visiting the way they were wrapped in each other this morning."

My stomach curdles. "Wait." I reach for the key, turn off the engine so the cab lights shine too brightly, making Haggard squint and wince all at once as I force him to make eye contact. "You saw her? Like actually set eyes on her?"

His smile lifts the corner of his mouth and his interest. "Course I saw her. What's with all the intrigue? Is she Bigfoot's sister or something?"

This is no time for jokes. This sighting calls for Maia's next-level inquisition but all I can manage is: "What was she like?"

"She looked cold, or cold before I saw her, anyway."

"Oh my god, Haggard! You need to do better at communicating. This is important." My words are harsher than Haggard deserves, but apologies can come later. "When did you see her? Where? What did she say? Does she seem nice? Was she funny? Serious? Is she staying on until Christmas? Did she seem happy to be here?"

Was she competent, beautiful, sexy, devoted...exhausted from bed aerobics?

"I can confidently say I can maybe answer half of one of those questions."

"How is that possible?"

"Well, one, I'm not a reporter. Two, I'm a dude. Three, I didn't actually meet her."

"Say more things about that last bit so you don't succumb to the wrath of my knuckle punch."

He rubs his upper arm at the mock threat. "I didn't talk to her. She was on the rocks with Logan when Frankie and I took the runabout out of the cove to see if we could get a flounder or two to rise."

"And?"

"We didn't catch anything."

"Haggard!"

"Oh, them." He shrugs. "They looked close. Which is why I didn't think he was married, you know?"

177

"No. I don't."

"Aw, come on. Ask me about fishing or how to swap out a carburetor and I can deliver the play-by-play you're looking for. Otherwise, all I can say is they were on the breakwater, close enough to have a blanket pulled around their shoulders."

A blanket. Shared. I fall back against the plush seat, defeated.

"What's this all about, Charles?"

"Nothing, just curious who I'm renting to."

"It sounds to me like you're more interested in him than her."

I begin my fervent protest, which he doesn't even pretend to entertain as he flicks his high beams toward Cove Light and points without lifting his hand from the steering wheel. "That car that arrived yesterday?"

I move to his side of the cab, lean against him for a clearer view. "That car's got Maine plates. Maybe the answers to some of your real questions—the ones you aren't asking—are in that plate."

"How so?"

"The two license plates are from different states, Charles."

I twist to press into Haggard with a full body hug. When I pull away, I smack a big, loud kiss on the side of his bushy beard. He rubs at his facial hair. "Now if you'd kissed me like that in Mrs. Harkin's class, you'd have made me the happiest third grader in history."

When I hug Haggard again, I could not be more grateful for him in this moment, because there's a story in the cars' plates. Okay, sure. She could have driven a rental and there's probably an easy reason they'd have cars with plates belonging to states that sit five hours from each other but I don't see the logic; I see possibility. Maybe the mystery of the cars can explain all Logan's behaviors, before and after Hannah's arrival.

Because what if being wrapped in a hug means they're honoring their break up? Setting aside time to be kind to one another as they uncouple? Whatever the case, it gives me the drop of hope I need. I kiss Haggard at his cheek, this time in rapid fire succession so that I'm perfectly positioned to see Logan turn to us at the window, his take-out boxes tucked under one arm. He waves to Haggard, and me practically in Haggard's lap.

Haggard lowers his window as I drop back to my side of the cab. "I'm counting on you day after tomorrow!"

Logan raises an arm over his head in a full wave but doesn't turn to us as he heads into the lighthouse where the opening door offers a glimpse of Hannah at the table, a computer screen glowing sliver against her face. I can't make her out fully even if her perfect posture and elegantly crossed legs are details I'll never be able to unsee. Just like I'll never forget the way Logan keeps his head down as he slips inside, twisting his body and raising a look our way just before he disappears behind the door.

"Cars never lie," Haggard is saying and I'm only half listening as I search for signs of movement in the small, high windows of the tapered lighthouse, its sealed ecosystem as unexplorable as the ocean bottom. "Keep your head on, Charles," Haggard tells me as I muscle open the door and nearly fall out of his elevated rig. "And be safe out there tomorrow."

"Always," I tell him, even if walking into my home and crashing onto my bed doesn't feel like safety at all. In fact, I've never felt more confused or vulnerable, and I have no one to blame but myself.

~ Love & Lobsters ~

Lobsters are widely known as rigid creatures with hard shells, and this isn't untrue. Lobsters come equipped with armor, an exterior shield against the harshness of predators and any unexpected attack on their quiet, solitary lives.

Tough as they may seem, though, a lobster's body is gelatinous and yielding underneath their armored exterior, their skin delicate and soft. Fragile. Vulnerable. These conflicting traits thrust a lobster into lifelong battle with its own self, a reality that exposes them to considerable, repeating risk, particularly when they molt.

In simplest terms, the hard, protective outer shell of the lobster is almost constantly at odds with the interior needs of the lobster.

This is the boring science bit, how basic biology tells us the inside body of a lobster must continually grow and develop, always changing and evolving, even as its shell remains fixed in shape and size. The hard exterior is incapable of adapting to growth so the lobster must shed the confines of its outer protective armor as it makes room for its inner expansion, a process that leaves even the toughest lobsters susceptible and defenseless during the time it takes to grow a new shell.

A lobster uses the tools available to her in her environment to help with the molting process. To shed her confining armor, she'll pump salt water through her body to increase pressure underneath the shell to pop it free, essentially splitting herself at the seams. The lobster shell is cast off, leaving the lobster helpless and powerless, laying on her side until she can recover enough to gather the strength needed to wriggle out of her hard claws, then her legs, her stomach, and even her teeth. Yes, her teeth. She will rip out parts of her own body and diet to half her size before a molt. If she doesn't manage these tasks successfully, she risks dying from the effort it takes to free herself from the restraints of her old shell.

Many lobsters don't survive the transition.

When enough strength returns, and she can again stand, the weakened lobster's first restorative task is to consume her old shell. She devours the vitamins and minerals packed into the hard lining, ensuring her new shell will thicken quickly and her exposed time on the seabed will not be in vain.

When I learned about the lobster molting process, I was a teenager and spoke fluent frustration. I was at war with my own body daily. My boobs hadn't come in fast enough. When they did arrive, there were days I wanted to press them back inside of me, tuck them behind my ribs and be a kid again, curling in my grandmother's lap—sometimes on the same days I was screaming in protest for a curfew extension.

The push and pull were real.

And all the while, I grew. Longer, fuller, bigger, leaner, stronger. And it hurt. Some days I felt the pain in my bones, some days in my heart. My body was literally making room for my adulthood, my change, my growth. I sympathized with the molting lobster then, and I do now. Because lately I've been forced to examine my own rigidity and vulnerability when it comes to love. If a lobster can risk death to expand her body by fifty percent to accommodate growth, how much am I willing to risk? Am I strong enough to admit a desire to love and be loved sometimes threatens to split my seams?

Because love is about opening yourself up, even though the risk is massive and trusting in change will leave you vulnerable and unprotected. You will, in all likelihood, need to expose the weakest parts of your being. Still, love is the ultimate. Sometimes it's self-love and sometimes is platonic love or familial love, but it's all love.

One type of love isn't necessarily safer than the next; it's all a risk. Each genre of love requires a shedding of our protective layers, an exposure of our true selves. In any loving relationship, we need to open ourselves up, split the seams to make room for growth, creating space for a new person. A person we can trust with our heart. If we are careful with theirs.

So, if you find yourself asking what you're willing to risk for love, look to the lobsters—male and female—who risk everything to make room for growth.

Maybe casting off our hardened shells will involve peril and pain and leave us feeling helpless with the spinal strength of ice cream, but we aren't lobsters. Maybe we shouldn't let our hardened shells restrict us.

19

The Complication

In bed, I pile pillows into a secondary headboard and lean back, folding my legs to a shelf so I can type:

> @BirdieBlueBug
> Where's your head at tonight?

It's projection or transference—whatever the clinical term is for asking someone else about a problem you're wrestling with in hopes their answer will solve your conundrum. It's lazy psychology, or wishful thinking, definitely the coward's way out—or in—because I should start this chat with InstaEllis by revealing Maia's intel. How knowing @toothpicks3478's name has made this DM room murky somehow, the way sand and muck get churned up on the seabed in response to jarring activity, turning the water cloudy within the disrupted ecosystem.

> @toothpicks3478
> Wrestling with a reoccurring nightmare that all other adults received the memo on how to be a functioning human and I missed it.

> @toothpicks3478
> Except it's not a nightmare; it's my reality.

> @BirdieBlueBug
> I'm intrigued by your confident use of the semi-colon. I could never pull that off.

@BirdieBlueBug
In my limited experience, anyone
who can throw down advanced
punctuation with such unabashed
authority is highly in-tune to the
adulting game.

@toothpicks3478
You realize you're proving
my point.

@BirdieBlueBug
Explain.

@toothpicks3478
What I lack in communication
skills in the real world, I make
up for in my stunning display
of punctuation.

@BirdieBlueBug
Have you tried hand gestures?
I've heard they're remarkably
effective when communicating
complex ideas.

@toothpicks3478
Sky writing might be more
effective at this point.

@BirdieBlueBug
Okay, walk me through it. What
exactly are you trying to tell who?
Or is it whom? Asking for a friend.

@toothpicks3478
It may be illegal to use
'whom' in DM rooms.

@BirdieBlueBug
Is it possible we're not actually
addressing your nightmare?

@toothpicks3478
No, it's good.

@BirdieBlueBug
He types and then waits too
long to expand....

@toothpicks3478
Ha! Sorry.

@toothpicks3478
I'm preoccupied by self-doubt.

@BirdieBlueBug
About?

@toothpicks3478
Past failings, mostly.

@BirdieBlueBug
Define.

@toothpicks3478
My fiancé left me after
we'd been together
for almost ten years.

@BirdieBlueBug
Ten years!?

@toothpicks3478
Well, sure. When you
write it like that.

@BirdieBlueBug
And you're trying to
get her back?

I wait, wanting his response to be no even as I have no right to
want anything from him.

@toothpicks3478
No.

@toothpicks3478
More like trying to determine
if I can trust again, and if I'm
still a terrible communicator.

@BirdieBlueBug
Ah, so. Small issues.

@toothpicks3478
Maybe. I mean, what if love
isn't anything more than
logistics? Right time, right
place; chemical attraction;
willingness to trust; shared
interests, and availability.

@BirdieBlueBug
Now your semi-colon is
just showing off.

@toothpicks3478
My punctuation
impresses you?

@BirdieBlueBug
Absolutely. I'm definingly rethinking my
decision to sit-up sleep during Mrs.
Fayette's sixth grade grammar lessons.

@toothpicks3478
Are we getting off topic?

@BirdieBlueBug
Likely; I mean; if I knew what the topic
was to begin with; but I don't; not
really; since you're very vague; which
I appreciate; as I've generally found that
avoidance has been my key survival
strategy for navigating interpersonal stuff
and I'm trying to model this approach for
you; you know; so you feel like you have a
life guide at your side as you venture;
out into; the real;world.

@toothpicks3478
Nailed it.

@BirdieBlueBug
Knew it.

@BirdieBlueBug
Also, in the spirt of fully acknowledging
trust and interpersonal communication is
messy, can I share something unexpected?

@toothpicks3478
Yes, but the proper form for
an interrogative statement
is: Can? I tell you something;
unexpected.

@BirdieBlueBug
Aren't all questions interrogative
statements? English grammar might
be a little too pompous for its own good.

@BirdieBlueBug
Also, my question's a serious one.

@toothpicks3478
I'm all eyes.

@BirdieBlueBug
My friend stalked you. I didn't ask
her to; in fact, I asked her not to.

@toothpicks3478
And, BOOM! The student
becomes the teacher.

> @BirdieBlueBug
> My supremely placed semi-colon is
> a ploy to lull you into a place of trust
> before the reveal.

@toothpicks3478
Reveal? Stalked me how?

> @BirdieBlueBug
> She contacted the Midcoast Maine
> Lobstermen's Association, and they
> said you were a volunteer. But I
> promise her stalking was only because
> she wanted to protect me, make sure
> you were legitimate or nice or
> legitimately nice.

> @BirdieBlueBug
> I'm sorry.

> @BirdieBlueBug
> Are you still here?

> @BirdieBlueBug
> Are you mad?

> @BirdieBlueBug
> Should I go?

@toothpicks3478
What's my name?

> @BirdieBlueBug
> Ellis.

@toothpicks3478
Right.

> @BirdieBlueBug
> So why does nothing about this
> bit of our exchange feel right?

@toothpicks3478
It's fine, really. I just didn't know
you wanted to know my name.
You could have asked. I would
have preferred you asked.

> @BirdieBlueBug
> This wasn't me. I've been
> Happy with things as they are.

@toothpicks3478
Same.

@toothpicks3478
Can I request we table this
topic for another time?

> @BirdieBlueBug
> Tabled. Totally tabled.

> @BirdieBlueBug
> Again, I'm sorry.

> @BirdieBlueBug
> It felt dishonest not to tell you.

@toothpicks3478
I'm glad you did, but also,
I should go.

> @BirdieBlueBug
> Why do I simultaneously respect
> your request and hate it? If you're
> leaving because of your complicated
> interpersonal nightmare stuff, then
> that's great (except for the complicated
> interpersonal nightmare stuff, obviously),
> but if you're leaving because of this reveal,
> then I kind of wish I could take it back.

@toothpicks3478
I think I just need to be
alone with my complicated
interpersonal nightmare
stuff for a beat.

> @BirdieBlueBug
> Totally fair.

Except his silence doesn't feel fair. It feels terrible. Like I've hurt a person I had no intention of hurting, a person who didn't deserve to be hurt.

Not for the first time in my life, I'd give anything for that wizard-behind-the-curtain to explain to me all the ways that honesty is always the best way to go, except when it isn't. And how can a mere mortal possibly know the difference?

20

The Consequence

The next morning, I head to Instagram before I dress for work, checking for a message from Ellis. There's nothing. I try not to notice the way my stomach drops with disappointment, realizing there's so much I wanted to ask him. Like, will he ever trust in our exchanges enough to explain *toothpicks*? And why did he choose to follow me from his personal account? Did he take comfort in our chats the way I had?

Would I have worked up the nerve to ask the questions I can't stop asking myself? Like, is it possible to crush on a person you've never met in person? Was he something more than a diversion and now it's too late to explore that possibility? I'm unprepared for the lack of opportunity to get answers, and it feels like a loss.

I can't think of anything to write InstaEllis except I'm sorry. I consider revealing my name, or some other detail to make us even. But I already feel my defense mechanisms kicking in, forging that armor I depend on to keep me from feeling exposed and at-risk. My hard shell tightening around me in an ongoing, enduring effort to avoid. getting. hurt.

Some refer to this protective mechanism as a wall. Mine is a fortress.

Or has been.

> @BirdieBlueBug
> Would it help if you could ask me
> any one question? You decide what
> that is. My name or some other detail.
> Then we'll be even and this DM room
> will stop being awkward.
> Eager; to hear;your thoughts.

Managing my DM relationship makes me late to my boat so I arrive at the dock closer to three a.m., although no one but me would categorize DMing with InstaEllis as a relationship. Except it was, for me—a safe one. But while I was so busy focusing on keeping my armor thick to shield myself, I hadn't fully realized how another person's hardened shell could hurt me, too. Even in all my efforts to protect myself, I'm unprotected.

When I arrive on the boat, I'm efficient about storing my bag in the hold and running my usual safety checks, breaking only for a sip of drink that's still too hot in my stainless mug, because of course hot chocolate must also betray me. I'm clearly crap at all my relationships, even the ones I have with hot beverages.

I turn my focus to a day of hard work, the outlet that's consistently been my ultimate distraction, a way of exhausting my body so my mind is too tired to spiral. I lean in. Turn the key and flick on my running lights before scraping the ice off my windshield, my fingers already numbing in the predawn cold. Still, this is where they belong, not in a DM room typing with a stranger I'm barely on a first-name basis with. I just need a day of hauling traps, getting my head straight, doing the thing that brings me solace and sustenance and a sense of purpose. A day at sea where there's no room for interpersonal hiccups.

Over the rumble of the warming engine at the dock, I hear my name and jerk my head high for Mem, even as my entire body wants it to be Logan, calling for me, telling me he's left Hannah, that a calendar-perfect life with a female lobster fisherman was what he's always wanted. It's ridiculous, of course. Still, hope fires through my chest, a quick, lighted thing.

In my imagination, his arms will be stretched wide as he runs across the rocks that morph into a blooming wildflower field on a clear summer day. His smile will be lifted by the sun. And I will be his full and determined destination. When he meets me, lifts me—and yes, twirls me—with so much wild abandon my legs kick up, my head will swing back, my hair cascading, all of me giving over to the joy of his arms around me while—

My name sounds again from beyond the breakwater, reaching through low-lying sea smoke. That's when I see the singular, friendly arc of Logan's wave, and it is fully, wholly enough. His attention trained on me feels like the sun. A gift and inspiration all at once. Okay, sure. He's sporting more clothing that my fantasies prefer, but the reality of him is better than anything I could dream up.

Begrudgingly, I return to earth. Where he's my guest and I'm his host. He'll be needing more wood for the fireplace, or maybe they lost sleep to an incessantly dripping faucet I'll have to fix before I fish. Defeated, I manage a short wave from low at my hip because something catastrophic had to happen at the lighthouse to bring him outside at three in the morning. In short sleeves. My name on his lips.

When he meets me on the dock, I've cut my engine. My mouth is dry as I fight a sinking feeling that confirms I don't want him to have a wife or an emergency at Cove Light.

"Everything okay?" I ask.

"Yeah, course." He extends a plain paper lunch bag, his fingers curled over the top fold. "For your trip. I had some fruit in need of an adventure."

He remembered.

Logan listened to my stories and understood their importance, enough to offer me this gift—a token that pulls my past to the present. I accept the bag with two hands. It feels too brittle, its paper skin barely thicker than a leaf turning brown on a cold limb.

"No bananas, I promise." He rubs his bare forearms, which are all beautiful wrists and modest muscle.

"Thank you." My gratitude is feeble repayment for this gesture that shows me Logan already knows me too well, too intimately.

I press the bag to my heart. I want to ask him what I mean to him, what our time has meant for him, why he's giving me this sendoff when he ignored me last night—just as the shape of a woman appears in the high window of the lighthouse kitchen. Logan sees my attention stray and follows my sightline.

"Hannah," he says.

"Yes," I say, barely a whisper.

He gives me a shorter wave now, one resigned to the space at his beautiful hip. "See ya, Charlie."

I nod. My throat clogged with the one question that's impossible to ask: Why does *see ya, Charlie* sound like a good-bye?

As he jogs back to the lighthouse, I can't make sense of how a good guy can be this mysterious. When I navigate away from the dock, I don't look back, grateful the lighthouse beacon is dark. If Cove Light had been capable of shining light toward the horizon, I couldn't have outrun the temptation for it to guide me home, returning to shore and the lure of Logan who somehow manages to feel like home and a place I need to run from.

A hundred pots are hauled, emptied, and lashed to the deck by the time my boat's ready to turn back. Only then do I allow myself to open the simple paper bag. All morning, I've hoped there was a note inside, something to explain Logan's unreadable behavior, some guidebook to understanding him. Maybe a list of emotions appropriate for me to feel. But there's no handbook or rules, only the fruit. A small container of pineapple and one apple.

I keep the exotic fruit in the container to bring home, and devour the yellow flesh of the golden apple, obsessing over the fact that the apple could be a message. Some secret way to tell me he remembered sharing an apple and that it was more than just a snack. It was intimacy and trust and sustenance. But even as I consider this, I don't want it to be true. I don't want Logan thinking any of these things when he's with Hannah because that's not fair to me or her or him.

When I set my course east, toward land, the wind has changed, tossing waves to crest over the bow of my boat, destabilizing my craft even though, like me, the Maine lobster boat is designed to carve through strong seas with its efficient construction. The displacement hull is sharp at the front so that the boat slices through water, pushing swells to either side, unlike pleasure crafts that ride atop waves. No, a Maine lobster boat is built to be sturdy. Dependable. Unwavering. Still, she takes a wave that's so violent it sends all my gear barreling to one side of the boat, my whole world nearly capsized.

By the time I'm done resetting the stacked traps, my knuckles are white from rough seas. My shoulders weigh too much, my brain can't stop spinning through endless attempts to make sense of the significance of a yellow apple and pineapple.

It's a relief when Maia raises me on the VHF as I pass Cove Light, the lobster trap tree guiding me home to a village that doesn't feel like home for the first time I can remember.

The harbor at Christmas Cove has always served as a safe haven for my heart. Even after loss, adolescence, betrayal, and illness, the horseshoe cove pulled around me, gathering me in its sustained embrace. Now, it's as if the rocky shoreline has changed, the rocks rearranged, sharper now, the depth of the water unreadable, the tides confused. Not because summer tourists descended on our village and changed the rhythm of our lives, but because one tourist—one person—has changed me.

"A few of us are gathering down at Earl's. Come. Mem's here," Maia tells me over the static on a private channel.

I push the side button on the receiver. "No way. I'm beat."

"What's wrong?"

"Tired. Like I said."

"I'm hearing you refuse a hot meal after being at sea all day so I'll ask again. What's wrong?"

"Hard seas. Harder hauls. I just want my bed."

"It's your call, but you'll be missed. By me. I'll miss you. Just in case that isn't clear."

Ahead, the tree lends its glow to the high luge run. Piles of oversized boxes, big as refrigerators, are wrapped in green and red holiday paper and arranged in stacks dotting the waterway like festive fence posts. Day-by-day Christmas Cove transforms with all the magic of Santa's workshop.

"Listen," Maia says. "This is the first time in my entire sea-adjacent life that I've been able to tolerate being around seafood without wanting to puke. I think my baby is gonna be a sea lover, and he's going to need a lot of his auntie Charlie."

"*He?*" I press the receiver to my lips, my grip tight.

"Yup. We had the sonogram today and the little monster is all boy. I got pee-pee proof and everything."

Joy springs inside of me. "Maia! Congratulations! Sam must be thrilled."

"You know Sam. Pragmatist to the core. He wants a healthy baby and healthy mama over anything else."

"Well, I'm thrilled for you both."

"Listen, I need to sit. My feet are swollen and Mama needs to elevate. Sam's got a chair and pillows for me at the diner. Come. Let Hermon make you a burger before you crash."

"I do need to unload my catch."

"Spoken like you really love me."

"I do, it's just—"

"I know." Her voice is low and soft over the speaker. "Come over. Get a kiss and pretend you already love my little martian in the sonogram I shove in your face then I'll let you get your rest."

"Deal."

After my catch is set to the holding tanks on the dockside of Earl's Eats, I head inside the diner where a half dozen volunteers hover over stock pots of clam chowder simmering on Hermon's twelve-burner grill. The chowder recipe is his father's, passed down from his grandfather before that. Hermon sells bags of frozen clam chowder to tourists who drive the length of our isolated peninsula to get a taste of the authentic Downeast home cooking. Some because Maia's blog has made it famous, others because it's just that good.

The idea around tonight's mass production is simple. Serve hot chowder during the fast-approaching festival and overstock the freezer shelves so when winter tourists fall in love with the hardy soup-that's-a-meal, they'll want to buy a bag or five for their holiday dinner table, and the considerable mark-up will go straight to the Lobstermen's Fund. The plan was hatched during our trip home from Adventure Day and it feels satisfying to see it come to fruition.

Haggard folds me inside his strong hug. "You here to cook or chat?"

My face scrunches at the choice. "Maybe neither? I came to see Maia then head home."

"Rough out there today?"

I nod, exhausted by the tumult of the sea and the more confusing turmoil inside of me. "I got a great haul, though. It's in the tanks."

"Everybody doing their part," Haggard says, his chest swelling with pride as he tugs me closer.

Maia waves a small black-and-white ultrasound photo at me from where she's seated at a table with Hermon and Mem, each wearing bibs, gloves and shower caps that Maia singularly manages to make look stylish.

"I'm gonna go say hi," I tell Haggard.

"No can do, Charles. Not unless you scrub up to scrub in." With his arm slung over my shoulders, he turns me to the Food Preparation & Hygiene notice hung on the wall, just next to stacks of spare aprons, caps, and gloves at the prep sink. "We can't go contaminating tourists, much as you'd like that." He jostles me closer and the door chimes behind us, announcing new visitors.

Logan and Hannah.

My heart lurches because she is here and next to him, a paired couple connected by the link at their elbows, so close I smell the soft vanilla of her perfume. Logan makes introductions I only half hear because I'm obsessing on the soft peach glow of her skin, the lines at her eyes that deepen when she smiles, her minimal makeup and pilates-straight posture. My manners are on autopilot as I accept the gentle hand she offers me after peeling off her gloves, finger by finger, in the way of old school movie actresses. It gives me time to study her—okay, obsess on her.

"I've heard so much about you, Charlie. It's good to finally be here to meet you in person." She puts her free hand over our hands locked together, her touch tender and comforting all at once. "I'm fascinated by your work. I have so many questions."

"Hopefully I have answers," I say. "Are you finding everything's comfortable at the lighthouse?"

"Oh, yes! Delightful. Isn't it Logan?"

The two of them coupled makes my body slip its fatigue and I am fully present as I stand in Hannah's orbit. The woman clutching my hand is all kindness. She's older than me, but not old. Her hair is blonde, with silver streaks. She's practically luminescent next to Logan, her dark eyes inquisitive as she looks around the coordinated chaos of the diner, asking, "Now, what's all this?"

Haggard starts to explain but Maia's at the partition, smoothly interrupting. "Hi. I'm Maia, resident busy body." She nods a curt hello to Logan. "Normally, I'd shake your hand," she tells Hannah, "but we've been decontaminated." Maia raises her gloves hands like a surgeon after scrubbing in. "We're making chowder. Want to join?"

"Ah, Maia." Hannah says, soft as a secret. "You're exactly as beautiful as I pictured you. You're absolutely radiant."

"I told Hannah about everyone on the cove," Logan offers, almost as an apology.

Maia's eyebrows flick to me before she and Haggard explain the great chowder cook-in and its purpose. Logan doesn't look at me. He steps back in the tight space just as Hannah reaches for his arm.

"I'd like to stay, Lo." Hannah places her hand to the chest of his pufferjacket. "That is," she says to Haggard and Maia, "if you'll let strangers lend a hand for a good cause."

"More the merrier!" Haggard says.

"Agreed," Maia says. "I'll show you where to wash up."

Hannah puts a finger to her lip. "One thing, though. Lo told me about the fundraiser and he'd had an idea about the lighthouse." She turns to Logan. "Is Charlie the one I tell?"

"What's the idea?" I ask before he can answer, relieved to have somewhere to focus other than Logan's unyielding avoidance, which has pushed me back a half-step.

"You should tell them, Lo. It was your vision." Hannah glows as she encourages Logan to the limelight.

"We thought you could give tours of the lighthouse, if that's something that you'd be okay with. Charge tickets. And you..."—Logan's gaze flicks so quickly from me to Haggard I'm unsure he sees me at all—"or Haggard could be the friendly tour guide."

Haggard claps me on the shoulder. "Charles has harbored a lifelong dream to be a friendly tour guide."

"No," I say, too sharply. "We couldn't interrupt your vacation. It's such a kind offer, but we really can't accept it."

"I think you can." Hannah leans toward me then. "Lo and I will even disappear to a hotel to free up the space for tours. Consider it part of our donation to a wonderful cause."

"I'm kind of loving this idea," Maia says. "We could draw people to the other side of the peninsula, expand the reach of the experience. What do you think, Charlie?"

"I think...." It's likely I won't survive two consecutive weeks of Hannah's presence on the peninsula, her abbreviated nickname for Logan, or him avoiding me. A stint in a hotel seems like a break I can get behind. "We can work out the details tomorrow but for now, I desperately need a shower."

Hannah smiles as if she doesn't notice my filthy jacket or my sea-stained overalls or the stench of me. "It was really good to meet you, Charlie. Now"—she looks to Maia—"show me how I can be useful."

"Hannah." Logan throws her name like a lasso, drawing her attention back. "Are you sure?"

"After today, I need to be around people," she tells him. "Go ahead home with the groceries. I'll catch up soon enough. A little fine company and a good, brisk walk will be just the ticket for me tonight." She ducks to the other side of the rope to join Maia where Hannah's easy-going laugh fills the air, making me jealous of Logan, how he gets to be near her, be both the source of her laughter and its landing place.

Logan pays for his take-out order and mumbles a good-bye to me and Haggard as he steps outside, the high-chiming bell announcing his departure.

Maia shoots me a look from the wash station that I don't even try to decode. Instead, I dash outside without a plan. My steps are hard and hurried and I wish I were wearing revenge lipstick and a killer skirt, or at least clothes that don't smell like the sea bottom. Because I want Logan to see me as more than a fisherman or a landlord. I'm a person. Someone he's connected to, and someone he's hurt. Because who is he to join me on the boat and bring me fruit and share parts of his past and then act as if he doesn't know me the minute Hannah arrives? Not only do I not deserve to be ignored, but being ignored makes me convinced he deserves to be yelled at.

"Logan! Hold up!" I sprint to him, stopping too close to his body, his heat.

"Charlie." He leans toward me. "Everything okay?"

"No." Nothing's okay and he knows it or else why would he ask? I'm more winded than I should be after the short sprint, but every emotion I've ever had seems to have risen in me, ready to tell Logan just how *not okay* I am. In fact, I'm furious. "You need to stop."

Under the holiday lights, he searches my eyes as if memorizing them, which is infuriating and proving my point in real time. "Stop what?"

"Um, all of it. You can't be kind and generous and generally amazing to me and my family and friends. You can't fish with me. Or offer access to the lighthouse for our fundraiser. You can't give me fruit before the sun comes up and then act as if I don't even exist when your wife arrives."

I half-raise my arms, then let them drop in frustration. If I were a lobster, my brain would be in my throat. Instead, it's my heart in my throat—all of me a tangled mess.

"Because I don't think I imagined you flirting, or maybe I did and that's on me but you're my renter, and you and your wife are my guests. I'm glad for that but our interactions need to stop there. I want you to enjoy your stay and make the most of your visit to Maine but I need boundaries so my head stops spinning."

Logan combs his fingers through his waterfall of blonde hair that falls back into stupid, perfect place. "Charlie."

"I'm serious, Logan." It physically hurts to say his name, to sever myself from him while he's on the peninsula, but the alternative is far more painful.

"Charlie." His two fingers jump to catch the cuff of my jacket, light as a whisper before dropping away. His body motions as if he wants to take a full step toward me but stops. "Charlie." Both hands are in his hair again, as if massaging thoughts to the surface. "Do you think Hannah is my wife?"

"Yes, of course. Why wouldn't I think Hannah is your wife? Everybody thinks Hannah is your wife."

His brow knits as he looks off into the distance beyond the sea. Then he stares down at me, deliberate and intense. "Why would anybody think Hannah is my wife?"

All at once I can't think of one reason, but remember all the reasons.

"Charlie, Hannah is my mother's wife. She's been married to my mother for nearly as long as I've been alive."

"Your mother's wife? Like, your stepmother?"

"No. Hannah isn't my mom, but she's not a step removed either. She showed up for me like a mom. Still does. She's my Hannah."

I hear the way Hannah inhabits a space that is mother, family, trusted person—no different than Mem. And I feel myself leaning toward his words that are confessions and explanations and permission, even as I chastise myself for my own bias, how it never occurred to me Logan's mother had a wife, or that Logan had someone dear to mourn with.

Had I clung to the idea of his marriage for me? So he could be unavailable? So I could protect myself? Now it's my turn to step back.

"I'm not married, Charlie." Logan's eyes draw dark as they search mine. "I've never been married."

"I had no idea. I mean, I just assumed."

"Why didn't you ask?" He inches closer, his breath slowing, the space between us tightening.

My heart races, my head dizzy. "I don't know how to ask about things that aren't my business. And you talked about Hannah like you were a couple."

"Did I? That feels disturbing." A slow smile forms. "So, just so I'm clear, you're saying this misunderstanding is my fault?"

"No. Of course not. It's no one's fault…" I trail off because this is very likely all my fault. But right here, right now, my brain crams with the rush of Logan's closeness, his confessions, the possibility he presents.

Because Logan is not married.

"Charlie?" he says, reeling me back.

I look to him and his eyes are pond blue, smoky with depth. He pins me with his stare.

"I'm here," I say.

"Can I haul with you tomorrow?"

His question overwhelms me with its simplicity, and it draws up the one word I've wanted to say to him since he loaded traps into my truck, his steady, unassuming kindness as dependable as a lighthouse:

"Yes."

~ Love & Lobsters ~

Lobsters are wild and brilliant, a species that's managed to survive one hundred and forty million years due to the richness of the ocean floor. That's one hundred and thirty-four million years longer than humans.

It's a lot of time to be on the planet.

A lot of time to hone survival skills, understand physical limitations, and perfect communication. By comparison, humans are children. So young as a species we're almost hardwired to make mistakes, get tripped up in currents of apprehension, swells of assumption, tidal waves of confusion.

Maybe it would be easier to be a lobster. To know our bodies and boundaries so intuitively we'd rarely need companionship.

But we are not lobsters.

We are young.

Limitless.

And wild at heart.

21

The Cards

When I email my post to Maia after cursing her for all my unanswered texts, there's a message waiting:

@toothpicks3478
I have my one question.

> @BirdieBlueBug
> I'm ready.

@toothpicks3478
I'll need some time to properly
prepare for asking said question.
And more time to spiral with
self-doubt, questioning if it's the
right question.

> @BirdieBlueBug
> Now I'm scared.
> Should I brace myself?

@toothpicks3478
Not at all. My conundrum is
more about how I ask this
question and not what I'm asking.

@toothpicks3478
Or not asking.

@toothpicks3478
I'm not sure.

@toothpicks3478
See? I need a little time.

> @BirdieBlueBug
> I'm proud of you for not shying
> away from asking.

> @BirdieBlueBug
> And I'm glad I didn't scare you off.

I feel guilt for overlooking InstaEllis in favor of obsessing over Logan's single status, and frustration for how a normal human might walk over to the lighthouse door and say something normal like *hi*.

Instead, I head to the woodpile behind the barn to chop wood by lamplight. I split. Stack. Repeat. My mind is singularly focused on my task, a chore specifically chosen for its ability to force concentration and physical exertion. I let my arms rest only when Mem and Hermon return.

It's more than a little stalkery the way I lean against the barn to spy on Hermon as he walks around his truck to open Mem's door, extending his hand as if she's a princess stepping out of a high carriage. Together, they welcome Hannah out of the backseat, and I'm captivated by the effortless way they work in tandem, decades of friendship creating a wordless fluidity between them.

How am I only now noticing this partnership, this trust that sits between them? How did I not see her love for Hermon? His love for her? And why does their chance at love taste like jealousy in my mouth?

"Would you like to come in for tea?" Mem asks.

"I'm eager to be back with Logan, but thank you," Hannah says, flaunting her ability to *so easily* pop over to the lighthouse when the same small journey would feel like crossing an entire ocean for me. "Tonight has been lovely. I'm so grateful you allowed me to be part of your festival efforts. I haven't laughed that much in a long time."

"Well now, don't be a stranger," Mem tells her.

"*Ayuh,*" Hermon agrees.

When Hermon and Mem are alone in the driveway, he invites her into the pocket of his chest, a space he creates that buoys her rather than swallows. My heart aches when Hermon drives away because his absence must stretch like hollowness within Mem, a void in the exact shape of another person. Her person. A connection I never imagined she needed because I'd spent my life thinking I was everything she needed. Me. The center of her universe and mine.

"You can stop gawking now, Charlie girl," Mem calls, using the eyes in the back of her head like when I was a teenager and snuck in and out of the house, operating under the misapprehension that I was smarter than her.

"Come inside before your nosing about gets you into trouble. I've got something I need to tell you."

Oh, god.

My nerves fire.

The wind seems to change its course in an instant.

What if Hermon's embrace conveyed something other than love? A gesture made of condolences? For Mem's leukemia returning. Or worse. The barn door fights me as I jam it shut, my fingertips fumbling with the sudden cold that gets trapped under my skin, my body shifting into survival mode like with the first stages of hypothermia, my blood instinctively rushing to save my heart, the place where Mem lives.

"What's going on?" I storm into the house, breathless, my palm thrust to the wall just below Dad's picture.

"Get your boots off and join me for a cuppa." Mem sets the kettle to boil like everything is normal as my heart beats too fast and too high in my chest.

I strip quickly out of my snow gear, never taking my eyes from Mem straining water over loose tea leaves, her hands accommodating their slight tremor, the shake that took root in her nerves and became normal when I wasn't looking, all while the 1950's Bakelite Kit-Cat Clock animates time on the wall behind her, the rolling googly eyes and metronomically swinging tail reminding me how time gets stolen in seconds before it's gone entirely.

"Did you have a good night?" Mem places steaming mugs in front of each of us as we sit.

"My night isn't important. What do you need to tell me?" My fingers grip the table's edge, bracing for the disclosure that Mem's sick. Hasn't been feeling well. Needs more tests.

Mem's face is so serious, almost impossible to read. "I have news."

Her eyes wash past me, then to Dad's picture.

"Tell me. What's going on?" My voice is tender, already applying care as treatment.

She kneads one palm, then the next.

"Mem?" My prompt is a whisper, a plea.

"Earlier tonight." She meets my rapt interest with an expression I've never seen before. "Hermon asked me to marry him, Charlie."

A noise escapes me as I collapse against the back of my chair, the antique legs protesting from their joints. "Okay." It's the only word I can manage as I struggle for a deep inhale.

"I said yes, Charlie girl." She worries her teacup with a spin. "And that's the part I need to talk to you about—"

"You said yes?" My repetition is faint as distant fog.

"I did. And I know I should have come to you first to have a conversation about whether I should say yes or no or maybe. And maybe I should have had a conversation or two with myself to discuss a thing like marriage, but Hermon Benner was kneeling in front of me despite his bad knees, asking for my hand and expecting an answer with his whole body and I'm not getting any younger and I wanted to say yes, so I said yes." She shifts the coaster under her mug with a small twist before meeting my eyes.

"Is that everything you wanted to tell me?"

"That's my whole truth the way I lived it."

My smile grows, soft but deep. "I'm happy for you, Mem. And Hermon."

"You're no fan of change, Charlie girl, and this union is gonna mean change."

I stand to hug her and it's not the squeeze she gives my shoulder multiple times in the course of our busy days; it's a full embrace. "Bring on the change."

"It does my heart good to have your blessing, Charlie girl."

I drape my arms around Mem, pulling her close the way she tugged me tight after my parents left us in each other's care. She's shorter than me now, her bones thin and shrinking beneath my hold, but she's here. Right now. The only moment that matters.

The Kit-Cat clock watches, keeping time.

When I'm at sea, I watch for rogue waves. When any mariner sees one coming, luck and knowledge provide her with the opportunity to raise her hull, meeting the unruly wave head on. Or she risks capsizing. I hadn't been looking for a rogue wave on land, but that's what the relationship between Mem and Hermon has felt like. A powerfully unstoppable surge, their two lives joining, mounting into a beautiful crest, a current of committed connection I've never been brave enough to explore for myself.

Maia bursts through the door. "Logan's not married!"

I dart my eyebrows across the table. "Mem's gonna be."

"Ohhhh!" Maia says in wondrous amazement as she unwraps her scarf, pooling it to the table in a curl. "Tell me everything."

"Hermon Benner asked me to be his wife and I told him yes."

Maia shakes her head. "Nope. Sorry. I need details of the proposal. You're not getting off that easy."

"Hermon gave me a card or two. It wasn't fancy." Mem taps her coaster, her face softening with a wry smile.

"Liar!" Maia scoffs. "You and Charlie are both terrible liars. Spill."

Mem shoots Maia an artful lift of her eyebrow. "In my day, a girl didn't give up all her secrets."

"Secrets and details are different things. Out with it," Maia demands.

Mem grabs her bag and returns to her seat. "He gave me a card, as I said—"

"Must have been one hell of a card." Maia's practically drooling.

I lean back, watching youth resurface in my grandmother, introducing me to a version of her I'd arrived too late to meet.

"Well, yes. Hermon made a series of cards." Mem's smile lifts.

"So romantic." Maia swoons.

"He drew Snoopy dancing on the front. He did a good job making that character. He used to draw a bit when we were back in school but I hadn't—" She trails off, as if guarding some part of this memory for herself.

When she slides a handmade card across the table, she opens it for us, reading the words scrawled in careful cursive: *"I have loved you since math class."* Within the fold of the card is a photo of Mem and Hermon in the one-room peninsula schoolhouse of the fifties, their heads pressed together as they sit on a bench seat, their computation books opened flat in front of them, a shared ruler guiding their work. The image steals my breath, reshapes my understanding of my grandmother. The photograph isn't black-and-white, but brown with age. Old with years and yet, Mem and Hermon are somehow fully formed in their young, serious faces, their collective attention determined to solve the problem presented to their budding minds.

The second card—numbered for order—is another sketch of Snoopy, this time with Woodstock, again drawn in Hermon's shaky hand. Inside are the words: *I have loved you since Homecoming.* The included photo is of Hermon in an Army uniform, Mem in a tulle gown, the two of them looking away from the camera, toward each other, as if trying to keep the world outside, their adolescent love fierce and untouchable.

In the third card: *I have loved you since you were reborn as a mother.* The picture of Mem holding Dad as a newborn is a photo I've seen before, but never from Hermon's perspective. Tears get locked in my chest, emotion building behind my eyes because my dad's arrival pushed Hermon away, kept him at a distance.

I have loved you through wellness. Mem's perched on the rock in a daring two-piece bikini of the seventies, her lips painted in a brave dark shade.

I have loved you through sickness. Hermon's hand holds Mem's, the artful photo a close-up of their fingers intertwined, the unmistakable thin cotton material of her hospital nightgown behind their clasp.

Hermon had visited Mem every few days, giving me the opportunity to step away, take a shower, get something to eat, and it never occurred to me that Hermon was visiting *his person*, showing up as her forever person.

Expansive, enduring love sat right next to me so many times and I'd been blind to its presence.

I have loved you through discovery. This photo is of me at six, along with Dad and Birdie Blue, my beautiful exotic catch in my small hands aboard the *CHARLOTTE ANNE.* This snapshot captures my brightest day, yet my memory can't say who took the picture, who was on the passing boat to commemorate this moment, or why I've never seen this photo until now. My fingers reach out, holding the image straight at its white Polaroid edges, as if trying to hold onto a moment that's mine and yet reframed, treasured by another person for different reasons entirely. I can't help think of Seamus, the way it would make sense he'd be on the water that day, the way it feels right that he'd leave me the gift of new perspective.

I have loved you from up close. Mem and Hermon are sitting on the Christmas Cove common, the grass thick with summer, the horizon stretched out before them. Mem and Hermon have their backs to the camera, their heads tilting toward one another, not quite touching like in their math lesson, but no one could look at this photo and not see the way they wanted to bend toward each other, find rest and balance there.

My insides hiccup with hurt for how long Mem has had to wait. Because of life, circumstances, choices, fate. Because of me.

I have loved you from afar. A photo of Mem as a pre-teen stopped on her bike with two other girls behind her, the lighthouse behind them, a wiry dog waiting faithfully at her front wheel.

I will love you into forever. With this last card, there is no photo. Only a ring. One single, thin band. Taped to the card. Under the ring: *You are my eternity.*

There wasn't a day when I ever imagined falling in love with Hermon Benner, but here I am. Me and Maia and Mem, all smitten kittens.

"Why aren't you wearing the ring?" I ask.

"I want it to be my wedding ring. I only need one ring and I want Hermon to put it on my finger."

"This is the greatest love story ever told," Maia says, full tears streaming her face.

"Charlie, I'd like you to marry us."

"I'd be honored."

"On the night before the Solstice," Mem tell us. "We're not wasting any more time."

"That's just over a week away," I say.

"And totally doable," Maia interjects. "I'll plan your wedding and three honeymoons, if you'll let me."

"Nonsense. You've got enough on your plate."

Maia gives a sorry-not-sorry shake of her head. "You're stuck with me and my party planning prowess."

"Well, all right, but the ceremony will be in the village with no fancier decorations than what the festival has planned or we'll head to the town hall. We don't want any fuss and no waste. If we don't already have it, we don't need it. No one should be spending their hard-earned money to celebrate my love for Hermon. Love is the only thing we get in life that's free. It shouldn't cost anyone a dime to celebrate it."

"This is very romantic," Maia says. "We'll treat it like an extension of the festival, approach the whole *understated* event like community-supported agriculture, participants pitching in to bring in a wedding no different than a harvest."

"That sounds just about perfect," Mem says. "No fuss. And nothing dies for the ceremony. No cut flowers. We take only what we need from the sea and we keep that balance. No more."

"Easy peasy," Maia says.

"Then I have two additional requests," Mem says.

"Anything," Maia and I say in unison.

"We want the ceremony to be outside."

I hear the words Mem doesn't say, the current of logic running like drift through so many of her recent decisions, how Mem's time in the sterile confines of a hospital has pushed her to the outside more than ever this past year, as if her lungs and cells and spirit are still trying to slake their thirst for the blue dome of the outdoors she was deprived of for months.

"Done," Maia says. "No concerns about your guests freezing?"

"If they're not hardy enough to stand a little chill, they're probably not friends or family to either of us. Our day together only matters because I get to stand beside a man I've loved nearly all my life, a man who waited for me and doesn't blame me for the time we lost together and the kids we didn't make together. Promising him I'll stay by his side for all the remaining steps I've got in me is something that needs to be done next to nature. If anyone's interested in being part of that promise, better tell them to bundle up."

"Noted," Maia says.

"What was the second thing, Mem?"

"I think four honeymoons will be better than three." A mischievous smile curls up the side of Mem's face and she throws me a wink before giving the table a hard knock and grabbing her mug of tea, telling us she's tucking in for bed.

Mem leaves the proposal photos spread across our family table like a museum exhibit, the thoughtful romance a wash of love that's nearly impossible to digest all at once.

"Your mem's getting married and Logan isn't married. This is all feeling very serendipitous."

"Those two realities are separate things entirely."

"How can you say that? Your love story is here, too, Charlie." Maia rearranges the photos so the picture of me holding up Birdie Blue is at the center. "Not just then, but now. Can't you feel it pulsing? How the past is reminding you to trust in love? You might not know it but you're smack dab in the middle of a classic romcom conundrum.

Because that big question InstaEllis is going to ask? He's gonna want to meet for coffee or zoom. You know that, don't you? And Logan will profess his undying love for you any second now and then you'll have to choose. Do you pick the nice boy who is so painfully mysterious you can't easily know him? Or do you choose the dark-eyed bad boy with tasteful tattoos who slipped into your DMs and bears his soul in your tasteful online banter, all while managing to be *so funny* it's kind of hard for me to fully like him?

"InstaEllis has dark eyes and ink, huh?"

"Of course. Classic romcom dichotomy. But the important take away here is that this is the part of the movie when the boy gets the girl and the girl gets the boy. It's my favorite part! Even as I know it's coming, the girl-getting-the-boy climax can never come fast enough for me."

"You're missing so many perv jokes here it's unsettling."

"Get your head in the game, Pinkham. Which one do you choose? Logan, right? Or InstaEllis. Shit, this is hard. Is this hard?"

"Again, perv opportunities. I think it's you who needs to get her head in the game."

"Focus, Pinkham."

"I am." I neatly collect the photos, placing each one in its rightful card. "This isn't about me." I stack the cards to an orderly pile. "It's taken Mem a lifetime to get her boy, and that feels like the only important thing right now."

"Charlie...."

"Can we focus on getting my officiant license? I need your help, since you do the internet with less hate than I do."

"Fine." Maia huffs before helping me submit my application to the state. We sit in the kitchen, steeped in Hermon's romantic gestures and our plans for the wedding until Mem returns to suggest Maia scoots home, no different than when Mem shood us off the phone when we were pre-teens, telling Maia I needed my sleep no matter what school-based drama was developing that needed to be dissected and analyzed.

"Charlie's hauling tomorrow," Mem tells Maia like I'm not right here. "She needs her rest."

"Charlie needs a little love of her own," Maia snarks.

"If there's a person on this earth who knows what they need, it's Charlie."

Mem hurries me off to my room, her footsteps nipping at my heels. When she tucks me in, it's like no time has passed since she became my early and only caregiver. She kisses me on the forehead and brushes her thumb over the spot, making sure her tenderness never leaves my skin. When she turns off my overhead light, she stops at the door and I'm a kid again, fabricating nightmares I'd always carry to Mem's bed once the house went dark, just so she'd let me sleep next to her because she was my everything.

Now I want to tell her how I'm made of her blood and bone and wouldn't know how to breathe without her.

She rests her palm on the doorjamb. "You'll be my best person at the ceremony, Charlie."

"Of course."

"I mean it. There are no labels for you, Charlie girl. You're not my maid of honor or my bridesmaid or even our minister. You're my deepest love."

Like always, Mem has the perfect words.

"You're my mem." My voice hitches over the name I'd invented so long ago to join the words Mom and Gram, creating a new word entirely, just as Mem has made space for me to be her granddaughter and daughter and everything in between.

~ Love & Lobsters ~

In lobster love, females have all the power.

Female lobsters initiate mating, and many can take or leave the mating rituals altogether. In fact, if there are no males in the vicinity, nearly three quarters of female lobsters won't mate at all because, why bother? It's all an enormous hassle.

Female lobsters will only make themselves vulnerable for the right male lobster because their commitment is a big one. Unlike their male counterparts, female lobsters need to shed their shell to mate, becoming so fully defenseless that they're wise to interrogate their options in the sea. If the men aren't bringing it, the females wait.

And wait.

Now, sure. They're waiting for things that might seem shallow to us, like a male lobster with the finest home: an enclave mansion of hardscrabble rock on the seabed floor, his dwelling covered in fine sediment and organisms and perhaps some ornamental shells scattered for decoration. His den excites the female because his fine digs are evidence of his alpha status, that he's fought hard and overcome his rivals to keep the keys to his swank, spacious mancave under the sea. The female lobster isn't playing coy when she cruises in front of the male's patch of rocky ocean bottom, hanging around, being her beautiful female self, wearing her irresistible lobster perfume made of pheromones and promises. She's deciding.

The male needs to wait for the female to be ready.

He must hole up during her rousing drive-bys until she's prepared to commit.

If she likes what she sees, she'll pee in his general direction. From her face. Don't judge. You can google the details, but that's the gist. And this is the lobster's dance.

If and when the female enters the male lobster's shelter, she holds out her claws with the tips pointed downward as if waiting for the male to put a ring on it.

He doesn't.

Instead of a gemstone presented in a collection box, the male and female actually box.

The male jabs to determine where the female's shell has become hollow, estimating how long it will take her to molt, as if assessing how much effort he'll need to commit to foreplay. He is, after all, a male.

The female jabs to loosen her shell.

To humans, it might look like a violent form of undressing, but the lobster couple is building trust, the consenting pair displaying what looks like aggression all while kicking up sand and water, stirring movement that aerates their shared den and broadcasts their love.

He's hers.

She's his.

For now.

Because no female lobster has ever redecorated her cozy little nest on the sandy bottom to make room for a long-term partner, just as no male lobster will give up his sea bottom mantuary to let a lady love move in permanently.

Don't get me wrong, lobsters can be found together, just not *together* together. Female lobsters entertain males for sexy time then leave to carry around thousands of eggs (ten thousand for every pound of their weight, if you're counting) until they feel safe enough to release the fruits of their coupling to the wild. The female chooses her timing for mating and her time to bring forth the next generation. She is in control.

A female will only enter a male's den if it serves her.

The behaviors of a female lobster can help us to ask questions of our own choices, like: What are our needs for a mate? A partner? What are the spaces in which we build trust? And how long should our courtships run?

Recently, I've had a front row seat to watching someone dear to me surrender to romantic love. My grandmother had identified her male decades ago, but couldn't initiate coupling because of a number of factors, like having to unexpectedly care for me. Life events prevented her from entering her male's den, but still, she was there, inviting him into romantic trust. She kept her respectable distance from a man she loved because she prioritized the den she'd made with me, a singular ecosystem that couldn't make space for a love interest.

Now, long after any reproductive imperative has expired for this couple, they've made room for their love, surrendering to its magnetic pull. They've agreed to shed their hardened skins for each other, becoming more vulnerable in their journey to become closer. Through this process, they've emerged stronger. She has dipped her claw to him and he will put a ring on her finger.

Their future den is unknown.

I'm certain their cohabitation will kick up lots of gritty, lonesome feelings within me, fine as grains of sand, but her likely move to a new den makes room in my den, and I am a female.

I have all the power.

I can stay here alone, or break with tradition and let someone inside. A partner to box with, trust with, explore. Because time is a constant. Days and years and decades will move past us and our needs and wants and insecurities at breakneck speed, spitting us out on the other side of our prime, forcing us to look around our den to consider if we made the right choices along the way.

Did we take the risks that may not have been risks at all? Grab hold of the opportunities to grow into our best selves? With someone else?

And have those choices made all the difference?

22

The Companion

At the dock the next morning, I prep the boat trying not to notice how Logan is late, conceivably, but not forgivably, oversleeping on the one day of fishing when I'm actually prepared for him to join me on the *CHARLOTTE ANNE.*

I flick on my running lights as short harbor waves roil my boat and insecurities. Because I know Logan. He's steady, dependable. He has a history of pre-punctuality, and stepping back from me. He's not here for a reason. And that reason would be me, right? I mean, I am out here solo. My stomach turns over because there's no room for vulnerability at sea.

"*MerSea* to *BlueBug*," Maia says quietly over the VHF, her voice a life raft. "Find me on 11."

I switch to the private channel. "Morning, Sunshine."

"Hardly. Casey's got the stomach bug and she's been throwing up since last night and I can't sleep because you know what I was thinking the whole time she was throwing up?"

I lean against the back of my captain's chair, grateful to have Maia's voice with me. "Please, tell me. In graphic, precise detail. Set the scene. Really commit to the play-by-play. You know how I love me a vomit story."

"Well then, buckle up because while my beautiful, fragile daughter was heaving her little belly contents out, I was stroking her hair and rubbing her back and telling her she was doing great, that it all had to come up, the body knows what it needs."

"So, this is, what? An update on your super mom status?"

"No. That's just it. While I was being all great and supportive on the outside, I was thinking how glad I was *she* was the one getting sick for once, instead of me, considering how I had morning sickness every day I was cooking her in my belly. I. Am. Awful. Right? That's an awful thing to think. Good moms don't think those thoughts. And now I have a little boy on the way who's gonna pee all over the bathroom walls even though there's a toilet right in front of him, and who I'll never be able to stop from developing into a full-grown hairy man so he'll have mommy issues and smelly teen socks that will be crusty hard on his filthy floor with what I can only hope will be dried mud and athletic grime."

"Wow. That's a lot."

"Welcome to 2:30 a.m. me."

"First, I love the face off 2:30 a.m. you. Your voice is all low and groggy and a little sexy. And I can only imagine how great you smell from all the puke."

"Says the woman dressed in fish guts."

I look down at the legs and bib of my orange overalls, the slippery stains dark and sloppy, each smudge a badge. "Whatever. Look, you're honest. The only bad parents are the ones who keep their shit bottled up so tight it explodes later and hurts people. You're good, Maia. This is just you in your third trimester. Remember it was the same with Casey and Lillie? When you were pregnant with Lillie, you freaked out because you loved Casey's perfect, unblemished two-year-old cheeks so much you were afraid you had vampiric tendencies. All because you had the fleeting desire to suck her baby youth dry to get back your own."

"God. Do not ever tell anyone that."

"No need. It's all in the book I'm writing."

"Ignoring your sassiness to say you *should* write a book. Or write more. You're a really good writer, Charlie. I don't even think it's the hormones that make me teary when I read your posts."

"It's the hormones. There's no crying in lobstering."

"But you're not writing about lobster fishing, Charlie. You're writing about love."

"Um, no. I'm writing about what lobsters can teach us about the complicated, messy bits—"

"Of love. Do you ever read the comments on your blog posts?"

"Have you met me?"

"Hands down the overwhelming questions are: *who is this female lobster fisherman* and *who is the person stealing her heart?*"

"Why do I feel like you're editorializing?"

"Fine. Don't believe me. Read for yourself. My followers are watching you fall open to the idea of love, even if you can't see it for yourself."

"All I see is that Logan was supposed to meet me here but has decided I should fish alone. Seems like a pretty heavy indicator of not-love."

"You think?"

"You don't?"

"I think you should look behind you."

I jerk around so fast my neck gives a twinge of protest. And there's Logan, approaching the dock with his day bag slung over his shoulder. Hannah is next to him, a cashmere wrap pulled across her middle as the wind plucks at its free-floating hem.

"Gotta go." I hang up on Maia and my breathing is jumpy, restless. Because Logan's here. And somehow that feels way more complicated than him being late, or even rejecting me.

"Charlie. I'm sorry to be late. Hannah wanted to see us off."

Hannah looks from bow to stern, taking in the length of the boat, its size and scope, appearing as fresh as if she arrived here from a spa, her skin glowing, her smile bright, her blond silver hair brushed back into a tight, efficient bun. "Logan's mom would have loved this."

"Would you like to join? There's plenty of room."

"Oh, no. Three's a crowd. You kids have fun, but I want to hear all about it when you get back. I delight in listening to Logan talk about you and his time at sea with you."

As she takes a step back to hug Logan and exchange goodbyes, my brain is capable of processing one singular takeaway: Logan doesn't just talk about me to Hannah; he tells her stories about me. Me. The not-married Logan talks to his not-wife Hannah about me, Charlotte Anne Pinkham, fourth generation female lobster fisherman whose internal blush is at critical risk of catching fire as I try to play it cool.

Onboard, Logan stows his bag. I exit the pilothouse to pull in the fenders and untie our lines. Hannah waves from the dock as I return to the wheel where muscle memory kicks in and I fix my focus on the outstretched ocean beyond the harbor. Still, I feel the heat pressing between me and Logan in the wheelhouse like it's a third passenger, a magnetic pull I no longer have to deny noticing or liking. The freedom to think my fantasy calendar thoughts sends a swell of excitement down the length of my body. The spruce smell of Logan wafts exhilaration under and over my skin, around my ears and yes, between my toes. It's annoying and satisfying.

And allowed.

"Thanks for waiting." Color rises to Logan's cheeks. "You don't strike me as the type to tolerate tardy arrivals."

Tardy arrivals. Who says that? His dorkiness makes me smirk. And also? He hasn't just been sharing stories about me to Hannah. Nope. He's been pondering things about my personality traits—like my stand on punctuality and my tolerance levels. Not the sexiest stuff, sure. But he's been reading me, puzzling me out—an endeavor that feels sexy-adjacent.

"It worked out perfectly." I go for breezy. It's a stretch. "Maia was having a mini crisis."

"Everything okay?" He looks at me, his eyes squinted, his brow lines so serious it makes him almost too beautiful to look at so of course I turn away.

"Maia is a perfect human. She just has a hard time seeing it sometimes."

"And you reminded her?"

"It's sort of my job when she's in her third trimester."

He lets out a short laugh. "I can see that."

Stupid interrupting sea. I join Logan at the trap.

"A lumpfish! Very cool." Not nearly as captivating as my imagination, but I push my fantasies aside after a quick glance at Logan's capable thighs. "Do you want to free her?"

"Will she eat me?"

"She will not." I laugh. "Her mouth is a suction cup, totally safe."

"Okay, because I really am very fond of my fingers."

As am I.

"You're good." I say. "Support her front and under her belly."

"Yeah?"

My nod invites him to the task. "Go for it."

Logan reaches in, his approach slow and kind as he removes the fish that earned its name from its lumped shape.

I pat the high curve of her pink, rounded back. "She's small enough you might be able to suction her to a surface."

"I'm not doing that."

"You won't hurt her. Attaching is how she sticks to rocky ledges and algae, blending in with the color of her skin, leaping out to surprise attack her prey. Suction is her superpower. Let her shine."

"Only if you'll do it with me."

I place my gloved hands gently over Logan's and guide the plump fish to the fiberglass wall behind the sorting table where we press her gently against the surface to let her decide. Our hands steady each other's and we exchange a long look that makes my insides leap before the fish suckles onto the boat, all of her weight shifting toward purchase.

"We can let her go," I say. "She can hold her body weight. Ready? Keep your hands underneath, just in case."

Together, we release our coordinated hold on the juvenile fish and she suspends herself from the wall, looking like a magnet or a decoration, impossibly skilled and beautiful, filled with grace. An acrobat from the deep.

"That might be the coolest thing I've ever seen."

"She's a beauty," I agree, mesmerized by the soft pastel blush of her underbelly. "I've only caught green ones before, maybe one brown." I cup my hands around her like a nest and she releases her suction so I turn her over to study her fleshy pink underside, this miraculously soft color surviving by camouflage in the deep. I take her to the edge of the boat and hold her up, letting her underbelly glow in the sun, imprinting her to my memory.

"Does she get a snack?"

"She does. Something small."

And a nickname. Pinky, I think as Logan slips a slice of herring into her mouth and I hold the fish at eye-level so she faces us, her high eyes and grumpy expression studying us as we study her. The slice of herring hangs in a halfmoon out of her jaws and she gives a short wag of her dorsal fin.

"I think she's ready." I release her overboard, low to the water, and wish I could follow her all the way down to the places where she hides and hunts. I watch the surface for a long time, hoping she'll come back, even as I know I'll never see her again. I feel the same kind of deep loss as when I released Birdie Blue after catching a glimpse of her remarkable existence as she journeyed topside, under the sun, into my heart.

23

The Question

Logan's watches me say my silent goodbye to Pinky Fishcadero and doesn't question my time spent at the rail, watching the unsettled sea until my stomach growls. "Hungry?" I ask.

"Very."

I cut the engine and Logan gathers our bags from stowage.

He holds my father's lunchbox across his very fine thighs, tapping his thumb against the pail. "Okay, this is awkward."

"My lunch?"

"No." He clears his throat. "You know the reason I was late?"

"Hannah."

"Yes, but specifically…." He hugs the lunchbox closer, his shoulders rigid. "Hannah and I had a disagreement. Well, a difference of opinion."

I toss a nod at my lunchpail as I swivel in the captain's chair. "On whether or not I should have my lunch?"

"Kind of?"

"I'm lost."

"Well, if there's any chance of this going well you should know Hannah and I never argue. Like, ever. She was the peacekeeper in my family when I was younger and, as I've mentioned, horribly unforgivable toward my mom, always thinking I knew best about rules and helmets and my body's physical tolerance for skateboard stunts."

"You were a skateboarder?"

"Still am."

"Huh."

"Huh good? Or huh bad?"

"Huh interesting." But I'm more interested in how he's not exactly holding my father's metal pail lunchbox, but using it as a shield. "So, this morning's disagreement?"

"Right. So. After thinking on this as we fished, I'm convinced Hannah was right and I shouldn't have tucked a note into your lunchbox. Except I did. And now I want to remove it out without you seeing it or asking me what it is so that I can confidently appear as a person who makes better decisions."

"You put a note in my lunch?" I twist my gaze, confused.

"I did, when I boarded this morning, and I regret it. It's just a piece of paper, but it also has the potential to ruin this perfect day."

My shoulder blades push together for posturing and strength because I've had my share of ruinous papers. Mem's Do Not Resuscitate order from her physician; Power of Attorney; Health Proxy; her Last Will and Testament; bills that mounted too quickly; dozens of get-well cards, and journaled notes for her obituary, the hardest think I've ever written.

"The paper is in there?" I point to my lunch container, a slight tremble appearing in my hand.

"Yes. And now that I see the look on your face and how your brain's running its scenarios the way it does, I stand by my choice to slip it into your lunch pail because ultimately, I believe in honesty and full transparency. Just remember that when you read it, okay?"

He passes me my lunch pail, his look so vulnerable and raw, it dares me to move to him, hold his head against my chest, steady him the way he did for me when panic visited me off the dark shores of Christmas Cove. I want to comfort him, but I'm human. I want to read the paper more.

I'm careful with the fold, like the seam is fragile as I peel one half of the note away from itself, but my process is slow because I'm the fragile one, not truly prepared to read a note that has the potential to destroy a day Logan has called perfect. But here, on faint blue lines, in small, careful block letters, one question appears in thin black ink:

Are you @BirdieBlueBug?

Check box: Yes □ or No □

His meticulous square boxes look drawn by a steady hand, the lines as tight and true as the grid lines on graph paper and nautical maps. These are the details my mind chooses to latch onto because it can't make sense of this question, twenty miles from shore and my laptop.

"What is this? Do you know Ellis?"

He smiles fully, then pulls it back. "It is you." His voice is a whisper.

I look to the note, then back to him. "How do you know about me and...bluebug?"

"I didn't. Not until right now. It is you, right?"

"Yeah." The word forms from a deep breathlessness because I'm unable to sync my two worlds.

"I'm toothpicks3478," Logan says, his palm raising to his chest. "Which now that I say it out loud, I realize is a terrible username."

"No." I shake my head, clinging tight to the lunchpail on my lap. "His name is Ellis. Ellis," I repeat, my mind bending to our DM exchanges where I revealed so much. "Yes, Ellis. Maia found out his name is Ellis."

I say the name enough times to make it real, to force this revelation to make sense, even as I take a quick scan around the boat to where a camera could be hiding for Karma for Christmas because this is a twist I didn't see coming.

"My middle name is Ellis," he offers eagerly. "I have a story about how my name is Ellis at the association and if you ever want to hear it some—"

"A story?" I say, baffled. "How can you have a story for your name being something other than Logan?"

"It's not a particularly fascinating story, Charlie, but it holds up, I promise. Still, the fact remains: I'm him and he's me and Logan Ellis West is crap at interpersonal communication and I don't want to be with you." He presses his palms to his eyes. "No. That absolutely came out wrong. I *do* want to be *with* you. So much. Which is why I'm here, being a fool. I just don't want to be crap at communication with you, something I'm failing spectacularly at even now." He shifts in his seat, leaning forward. "Last night, when you thought I was married I couldn't even think what I'd done to make you form that assumption."

"You wear a ring."

He strips off his gloves and his hammered silver band flashes in the sunlight. He wiggles his fingers. "Wrong hand. When I told you I didn't know anything about weddings, I wasn't lying, but I know the wedding ring finger and this ring is not on that finger. There's a story here, too, and I'd be happy to tell it to you if you ever talk to me again, which I hope you do." He tilts his head as if trying to see around my eyes and into my thoughts.

My head shakes. No, rattles. "How did you know it was me?"

"I didn't. Not right away. Then I thought it might be you. I hoped it was you."

The sincerity in this admission overwhelms me, making me squirm in my seat, ready to run but we're at sea and there's nowhere to go.

"Then I posted the tribute to Seamus Kinneally and you didn't say anything. I had overwhelming confidence that you'd comment on the post if you were bluebug, because I knew you'd see the stern of the *CHARLOTTE ANNE* in the background the way I had. I'd been selecting photos at random from our archives and then I saw your boat. It was like you were there, or it was meant to be. I thought you'd say something in our exchanges about your relationship but then you didn't and I knew you'd have your reasons but—"

I hold up my hand. "Are you saying you used Seamus to lure me out?"

He pulls off his cap and rakes his hands through his thick hair. "When you say it like that it sounds shady, though my discovery was random. Did I prioritize this photo over another? Okay, yes. But I'm not a stalker, Charlie. Just a total, incurable nerd."

Something like mischief flashes across his eyes so quickly I almost don't catch it except for the dimple it imprints beside his bottom lip, an indent so small and sweet and signature it pulls at something inside of me, wakening that freedom I have when I'm Anonymous Me.

"I have so many questions."

I want to know about when he suspected it was me and why.

I want to hear him say again how he wants to be with me.

"I'll answer all your questions, whatever you ask. I figured I was wrong, you know, when you didn't say anything about your connection to Seamus, or your boat in that picture. Then, oh, god. I shouldn't admit this."

The waves roll us and I find I want him to say all the things, my body inclining toward his revelations because I can't make sense of how this can be, how I didn't see it, how I've always wanted to escape to Logan, even when I needed escape from him.

"I poured over the timestamps of our exchanges, trying to figure out if you were home when they were sent because I've seen your sad cell phone."

My hand pushes against the middle pocket of my overalls to protect my phone from ridicule.

"I know that sounds really stalkery. I do. I hear my words and I'm completely aware of why Hannah advised me not to tell you...at least not now...or not out here. But all of this boils down to one thing." He dips his head to pull up my unblinking stare. He holds my gaze, his eyes darkening with an intensity I've only associated with the deepest ocean until now. "I wanted it to be you, Charlie."

The way he says my name and then bites his bottom lip sends a whole-body tremor through me.

"I've come to really love the freedom and honesty of our DM space because I'm hopelessly awkward around you in person. You're so confident on the boat and in your community, it's intimidating. But your confidence is your best feature. It's why I'm drawn to you. Like a moth to a flame." He takes a deep breath while I try to gather my thoughts. "But the fact that you haven't said anything has me rethinking this reveal. No. I take that back. More than anything moving forward, I don't want misunderstandings to come between us. I want you to fully know who I am, and I want to know you. Really know you. If you want that, too."

I need Maia. Because I don't know what I want now that my pseudo love triangle has compressed into parallel lines. Me, alongside this other person. The one who makes me laugh in our chats. Fantasize when he's close. Is a moth to my flame. Oh, god. Breath stutters in me as the last weeks rush back: the desire, the unencumbered trust in our DMs. The miscalculations of his marriage. My heart discovering its terrifying, vulnerable nooks.

"I think I know what will make this less awkward," Logan offers after I'm quiet for too long.

I throw a suspicious laugh. "What could possibly make this less awkward?"

"A tutorial in the use of the semi-colon." He throws up his hands in defense of the idea. "I know...I know," he says playfully yet guardedly, as if testing the waters. "You're too proud to ask for a private grammar lesson. I get it. I do. That complicated bit of disjointed punctuation is intimidating." A slow grin slips up the side of his face, bringing shine to his eyes. "But I've done the math. The semi-colon will reduce the awkwardness of this conversation by at least 78.24 percent."

"That's a very specific number."

"My hope is that data points impress you because this is me, Charlie. I'm a nerd. I love machines and gears and motors and math, and being on the ocean with you."

Warmth floods from my heart to my head, swaying me, stealing my words because I don't want to say anything for fear I'll miss out on anything he's saying, especially my name. If he only said my name for the rest of time, I think I'd be okay with that.

"And you don't have to speak to me after today but I hope you will, Charlie. It's why I'm willing to risk disclosing my nerdom all while sounding like a stalker, split personality, and overall mess of a person because I think you're worth every risk."

My pulse rushes, rising as if to meet the fullness of Logan—two people in one—a combination I never expected but wished for all the same.

"Since I'm obviously killing it, I just—" He fishes another slip of paper out of the back pocket of his jeans so that his overalls dip down, exposing the tight flesh where his hip hollows against his low stomach. "I know I'm breaking all sorts of DM room etiquette by asking two questions, but while I'm out on this ledge." He hands me a second note, one I practically snatch from his fingers, which reads:

Is Haggard your boyfriend?

Check box: Yes □ or No □

I bark out a laugh even as I appreciate the precision of his hand-drawn squares, the care he took to sketch the boxes. The flawlessly straight edges of the paper he cut into strips.

"No. Haggard is definitely not my boyfriend." Just saying the words makes a full laugh rise.

"This is good intel. And it's good to hear your laugh." A smile creeps up the side of his face, carving his dimple, his eyes flashing at me and disrupting my once reliable equilibrium.

"What would ever make you think Haggard was my boyfriend?" I only half listen for the answer because the person I met in the DM chats who was baffled by communicating with others was Logan. And now he's here in front of me, trying to get to know me better, fumbling through complicated interpersonal communication no different than I am, each of us getting it wrong as we try to get it right.

Logan's cheeks redden. "I wasn't sure, and maybe I shouldn't say."

My eyebrows rise in a challenge. "*Now* you're going to hold back?"

"Okay." He swipes one hand through his hair. "There was one time we were online and you said you had company. This sounds *soooo* creepy, but I looked outside the window and Haggard had just arrived at your place."

"Ha!" I remember the day, and my need to get as far from Logan as our short peninsula would allow. "I only left with Haggard because I had to get away from married Logan because the thoughts I was having about married Logan were not thoughts I should've been having about a married man." The words fall out of me easily, without pretense, as if I'm talking to Maia and my defenses are non-existent.

He leans forward with no sign of shyness. "Is it wrong to be intrigued by your improper thoughts? This seems like an important topic worthy of our time."

"No way." I jostle the slip. "One visit from Haggard cannot be the reason you wrote this."

"I'd like to reserve the right to carve out time to circle back to your inappropriate thoughts later, and will say that Haggard is…well, he's quite handsy."

"Handsy?" My smile is full now, daring.

"I don't know many people who lift others off the ground, and you didn't seem to hate it."

"Haggard is all love. He's handsy"—I make air quotes—"with everybody. I thought I saw him feel you up when you were building that tree."

"I did feel a little violated." He places a dramatic palm to his chest. "But, seriously. Weren't you two making out in his truck?"

"Making out in his truck?" I snort. Then. "Oh…."

"See? You were, weren't you?"

"Um, no. Hard no. I kissed Haggard on his very platonic face because he helped me see a way through all the questions I had about you and your married status. And also? Why didn't you just ask? If you thought I was dating Haggard, how come you never asked me?"

"How does a person even do that?" He smiles as he parrots my words, a move that makes my own smile deepen. "Look, I'm not a guy who can find words or confidence easily and asking you anything too personal when we were together felt like too big a risk. Maybe I didn't want to scare you off. Or lose my connection to you. I don't know how to explain my rationale, but it felt safe to keep to myself at the time."

"But I see you as confident. The way you took over architecting the trap tree and everything you've done for the festival—"

"I'm a confident engineer. Math, I know. Numbers can be trusted."

"Like time and tides."

"Exactly."

It's the first time I see Logan in me, and me in Logan, two people trying to calculate the distance between like and love while measuring how much we'll risk to bridge that gap. For the rest of the day, conversation swirls easily between us. When the harbor comes into view, Maia raises me on the radio.

"You two kids have fun out there?" I hear her grin through the receiver, as Logan blushes.

Me? All I can think about is Logan saying he wants to be with me.

24

The Confidence

"A moth to the flame of your confidence? He actually said that?" Maia asks.

"He did. Why? Is that weird?" I climb to my bed and pull my knees to my chest, the phone closer to my ear.

"That's your call, but it's totally working for me. Mama got a little excited, if you know what I mean."

I know exactly what she means.

"And he said he wanted you to be the person he was talking to on Insta? Those exact words?"

"And that he hoped it would be me."

"Then what? I hope you shoved your tongue down his throat."

"Says the romance expert. No. No making out. No hand holding. Just talking. And working. Then you radioed, and he helped me stack the traps into storage."

"Stop it."

"I'm serious. Mem came home when we were done so there wasn't really a chance to do or say anything but goodbye."

"But you have your computer open right now, don't you? Hoping he'll message you in your dirty little DM space."

"Maybe."

"That's my girl!"

"But I'm also trying to think of the right thing to type because I should make the next move, right? I mean, he did most of the talking and...ugh. All of this is so stressful."

"The words will come. Also, I'm really proud of you. I think you handled this like a mature, big girl adult because in Karma for Christmas the heroine would be shocked and offended by this character reveal to the point where the misunderstanding would thrust the two main characters apart in a forced fight so the audience would be unsure if the girl would get the boy and the boy would get the girl."

"What you're describing is mind games. You know that, right?"

"Listen, romcoms aren't perfect. Except they kind of are."

"Good thing this is my actual life and not your latest binge."

"You're my perpetual binge, Charlotte Pinkham. Give me some spoilers: what happens next?"

"No plans. And I'm trying a new thing where I don't overthink or overreact or generally try to control the situation. Hence the hovering over the DM room."

"You're adorable," Maia says.

"I feel like I'm twelve."

"Intoxicating, isn't it?"

"More like exhausting. It's a miracle teenagers don't get ulcers instead of zits."

"Zits are the perfect segue to discuss your mem's wedding."

"Gross."

"Yes, well, I need your attention. I have updates." Maia updates me on the progress of the cake, seating, and ceremony with logistical precision as I brave a sip of steaming elderberry tea, grateful for the woodstove warmth stealing the chill from my room. "I thought we could have some evergreens do double duty." She snickers. "I said duty."

"Happy with yourself?"

"Always. What do you think about trees lining the road to the common on both sides as you come into Christmas Cove from Earl's Eats? All lit up with white lights so the corridor between the restaurant and the cove is essentially an aisle."

"Sounds beautiful."

"Good. I've got a delivery coming from Glidden Landshapers."

"Of course you do."

"They're lending us forty live spruce trees, root balls and all. Their crew will crane them into place if you're there to tell them where."

"I'm on it. When?"

"Tomorrow."

"Good thing I didn't make plans. Also, Mem will love the living trees. You're kind of phenomenal at event planning."

"Yes, *and!* I have thoughts on the dress. Still formulating, and I want your input. In the meantime, what's the status on the curmudgeon side of things? Besides all the flannel and beards?"

"How dare you. Curmudgeons are my people. And I'll have you know our low rent portion of the festival will have a fairly epic ice cutting arena with Bristol's premier ice sculptor."

She gasps an inhale. "Wow! Impressive."

"Don't sound so shocked."

"Shocked and impressed are different inflections and you know it."

"What do you think about using some of those trees to make a ceremony circle for Mem and Hermon? Then that protected area can be used for adults-only festival activities."

"Perv."

"I meant ice sculpting."

"Sure you did. Wait!" Maia says. "What was that? Did I hear a ding?"

"I cannot even with your bionic hearing. And, yes." I bite at the corner of my thumbnail as I read:

> @toothpicks3478
> Hi.

"Put me on speaker and tell me everything."

"Too much pressure. I'll fill you in later."

"Illegal!"

"I'm sorry. I love you, but I gotta leave you."

"Your love interest is already tearing us apart!" Maia yells.

"Not a love interest. A love investigation. I'm hanging up now."

"Nooooo—"

> @toothpicks3478
> So, full disclosure, I've been
> watching my phone to see if
> you'd show up here and you
> haven't and now I'm insecure.

My fingers are quick to the keys:

> @BirdieBlueBug
> I have no idea what you mean.
> I'm so busy and emotionally
> secure I almost forgot DM rooms
> were a thing.

@toothpicks3478
They're a thing.

The decisiveness in his response makes the base of my stomach flutter, driving a dull, delicious ache just below my middle.

@toothpicks3478
I'm unclear on the decorum
for how many days a person
should wait before dropping
into a DM room after disclosing
they've been the person in the
DM room all along.

> @BirdieBlueBug
> The etiquette on this
> subject is fuzzy.

@toothpicks3478
It definitely deserves its
own chapter
in our handbook.

> @BirdieBlueBug
> You may want to find another
> co-author. It's generally safe to
> assume I'm unfamiliar with most
> decorum. Decorums? Can that
> even be plural? Why do I think
> you're an English tutor?

@toothpicks3478
Not an English tutor.

> @BirdieBlueBug
> Actual facts about you don't have a
> chance of surviving our rumor mill.

@toothpicks3478
There are rumors about me?

> @BirdieBlueBug
> Many.

@BirdieBlueBug
I started all of them.

@BirdieBlueBug
You're welcome.

@toothpicks3478
I'm glad you're back, Charlie.

And there it is. My name in our DM room.

@BirdieBlueBug
I'm glad to be back, Logan.

@toothpicks3478
Huh.

@toothpicks3478
Seeing my name here is
an unexpected thrill.

@toothpicks3478
And I'm an engineer, if you
care to right my profession
in the rumor mill.

@BirdieBlueBug
Depends on the kind of
engineering you do.

@toothpicks3478
I re-engineer old cars
to make them electric.

@BirdieBlueBug
Woah.

@toothpicks3478
I like to think so.

@toothpicks3478
I've loved classic cars since
I was a kid so it feels like
cheating that this is my job.

@BirdieBlueBug
I love that you love
your job!

@toothpicks3478
This does not surprise me.

@BirdieBlueBug
I mean, I feel like that tracks.
I'm known for losing my surprise
factor fairly quickly.

@toothpicks3478
You are surprise personified.

The dip in my core becomes a heated, low pulsing rush that spreads as it ignites. I swallow hard.

@toothpicks3478
*"Personify: represent or
embody (a quality, concept,
etc.) in a physical form."*

@toothpicks3478
In case you sit-up slept
during the sixth grade
figure of speech unit, too.

@BirdieBlueBug
I'm paying attention now.

@toothpicks3478
Is it okay to say this
pleases me?

@BirdieBlueBug
Yes.

@toothpicks3478
It pleases me I have
your attention.

@toothpicks3478
And stresses me out.

@toothpicks3478
I want to be careful with it.

@toothpicks3478
Your attention.

@BirdieBlueBug
Is it okay to say you're
killing it so far?

@BirdieBlueBug
And that my attention
thanks you.

@toothpicks3478
My smile is very big.

> @BirdieBlueBug
> You have a very nice smile.

@toothpicks3478
Okay now my smile
just hurts.

> @BirdieBlueBug
> Is your smile flirting
> with my attention?

@toothpicks3478
Depends.

@toothpicks3478
Is it working?

> @BirdieBlueBug
> Yes. My attention asked
> for your smile's number.

@toothpicks3478
Can I tell you something?

@toothpicks3478
Or have I reached my cap
for reveals today?

> @BirdieBlueBug
> Tell me.

@toothpicks3478
I'm happy you're
BirdieBlueBug.

@toothpicks3478
And that you're right
next door.

> @BirdieBlueBug
> What would you have done
> if the account didn't belong
> to me?

@toothpicks3478
I'd apologize to her for always
thinking of someone else.

@toothpicks3478
Honestly, Charlie, I never even
let myself think BirdieBlueBug
could be anyone but you.

@toothpicks3478
That's how badly I wanted
you to be you.

@BirdieBlueBug
But you didn't know?

@toothpicks3478
When I met you, I thought
maybe but then you wrote
to me about your dad, but
didn't say he'd passed.

@BirdieBlueBug
I'm a pretty private person
with strangers.

@toothpicks3478
I know.

@toothpicks3478
Or knew.

@toothpicks3478
That's me using the past
tense of a verb, showing
off a little in case you
needed a grammatically
sound reason to be here.

@BirdieBlueBug
No dramatic displays of
grammar needed. I don't
want to be anywhere else.

@toothpicks3478
Oof.

@toothpicks3478
Okay. I felt that one.

@toothpicks3478
In my toes.

@toothpicks3478
You might be a romantic,
Charlie BlueBug.

@BirdieBlueBug
Not a romantic, but I do
play one on the ocean.

@toothpicks3478
I've gotten used to typing
in this DM room picturing
your face, hearing your voice.
Even when I wasn't sure it was
you, I told myself it was you.
I told myself a lot of things just
to make the dream of you a
reality because I was falling for
you in two places.

> @BirdieBlueBug
> Oof. My toes.

> @BirdieBlueBug
> To be clear, you were thinking
> of me when you wrote about
> having the perfect day?

@toothpicks3478
Thinking about you and
writing about you because
we'd just spent the day
together on the ocean.

> @BirdieBlueBug
> And the extensive
> fruit research?

@toothpicks3478
I was trying to find a way to
crowbar my stellar fruit
research into one of our lunch
breaks but chickened out.

> @BirdieBlueBug
> What made you brave?

@toothpicks3478
You.

@toothpicks3478
When I was writing my
clever note, I thought, well,
if she can be so wrong about
her assumptions, isn't there a
chance I'm right about mine?

> @BirdieBlueBug
> Ah! So, me thinking you were
> married was actually a good thing?

@toothpicks3478
I feel like we lost too much
time to that misconception.

        @BirdieBlueBug
        Or did it make space for us here?

        @BirdieBlueBug
        Bright side and all.

        @BirdieBlueBug
        Because I like you here.

@toothpicks3478
I like you everywhere.

Want rises in me, fierce as a current.

        @BirdieBlueBug
        Hold on. What was your
        complicated interpersonal stuff?

@toothpicks3478
You are my complicated
interpersonal stuff.

        @BirdieBlueBug
        Still?

@toothpicks3478
Yes and no.

        @BirdieBlueBug
        Say more.

@toothpicks3478
Well. I want to ask you on a
date but you're my host and
my neighbor and my fishing
guide so I don't know how to
do that exactly, a conundrum
which lands me firmly back in
the complicated interpersonal
arena.

        @BirdieBlueBug
        Tomorrow.

@toothpicks3478
Cryptic.

        @BirdieBlueBug
        I'm not fishing.

@toothpicks3478
I can't believe I'm writing
this, but I'm not free
tomorrow. Sam left a note
at the lighthouse, asking
me to help with a tree
delivery or something.

@BirdieBlueBug
Of course he did.

@BirdieBlueBug
How do you eyeroll in a DM?

@toothpicks3478
Why are we eyerolling Sam?

@BirdieBlueBug
Not Sam. It's his wife Maia and
her love of meet-cutes. Sam asked
you to help him because I'm the one
in charge of setting trees tomorrow.

@BirdieBlueBug
But are we a *we* now?
Eyerolling in unison?

@toothpicks3478
We are.

@toothpicks3478
That's a declarative phrase.

25

The Courtyard

I'm all nerves as I knock on the lighthouse door just after nine the next morning to pick up Logan as planned. Hannah welcomes me inside with a polished smile and a graceful swing of her arm. "Come in, come in. It's so nice to see you again."

"Thank you." A twitch hikes my spine because it always feels strange to enter the lighthouse when other people are living in it, the space taking on their smell, their small piles of belongings.

Hannah settles easily onto a casual seat upon the stone in front of the fireplace just beyond the tight kitchen. "Can I interest you in a warm croissant? Some blackberries?"

"That sounds delicious, but no." I raise my steel mug. "I'm all set."

Something about Hannah's formality unsettles me. Boarding school vibes live in her crisp articulation and exceptional posture, reminding me she's from away. Like Logan. Both of them leaving next month.

"Has Logan left already?"

"He's upstairs," she says.

I steal a look toward the staircase.

"The lighthouse is really charming. Truly delightful."

"I'm so glad." Flame cracks its way through a wet log in the fireplace, the loud spark making me flinch even as Hannah sits inches from the explosive snap, unfazed, her composure stitched tight.

"Logan tells me your great-great-grandmother built Cove Light, is that right?"

"Yes." My palms sweat.

It's fairly surreal to be casually chatting with a woman I've been curious about for so long, like all the scenarios I'd created about her are having a hard time synching with the reality of her. And the stakes seem even higher somehow now that I know she's Logan's second mom with an instinct to protect him.

Hannah looks at me sideways, her smile softening her cheeks, lighting her eyes. "I like that you descend from a long line of strong women. Your grandmother's something special indeed."

"She's one of a kind."

"I can see the love you have for her in the way your face changes when she's the subject."

"She's my everything."

"Yes," Hannah says, assessing. She slaps at her top knee as if to break the awkwardness of the moment. "Now, Charlie. I must ask you how you thought Logan and I were married, and you're not allowed to spare any detail." She wags her finger. "Because the thing I love more than all other joys in life is a good story. And I want to know yours." She pats the hearth across from her. "Sit."

So much for avoiding awkwardness. I try to sound easy going as I recount her reservation, the shared address, my general respect for people's personal lives, Logan's ring, my speculation and confusion and careful misreading of the situation.

Hannah watches me, spellbound. "Fascinating."

"Is it?" I ask with a nervous laugh.

"Of course. Beginnings are always captivating." She stands. "Dolly would have gotten a kick out of how she was the impetus for you and Logan to cross paths. It was her dream to stay in this lighthouse after all."

She pivots for the steep staircase, the skin on the back of her hand age-spotted as it reaches for the rail—her lone indicator of age as she climbs nimbly up the narrow, twisting steps until only the chunky black heels of her Scandinavian clogs show.

"Lo," she says in a near whisper. "Lo, honey. Charlie's downstairs."

Muffled movement covers a hushed word or two and I move to the door to give them privacy, a near impossible achievement in the cramped keeper's quarters of a lighthouse.

Hannah descends slowly, while Logan rushes behind her, his body appearing in stages, emerging first as feet in rumpled woolen socks, then long, lean legs in worn-in jeans that fall comfortably about his knees. And hips. His navy cotton T-shirt slack just above the leather belt except where a pinch of fabric is caught at the waist. When his shoulders arrive and he ducks below the rise to see me, I pull in a breath.

His smile opens for me. "Charlie. Is it nine o'clock already?"

"I can come back if you're not ready."

"No. I'm glad you're here. I'm ready. More than ready." He turns to Hannah and she plucks a fat pencil from where it's tucked into his white blonde hair, the movement so gentle and maternal, it wakes a sleeping need inside me. "I was in the middle of a design." He removes his earbuds to his back pocket.

"Where are you off to? Landscaping, was it?" Hannah asks.

"Yup. A tree delivery." Logan's words pop quick and high, so much like a younger boy readying for an adventure.

"Sounds delightful," Hannah says.

I set my hand to the door as they crowd the breezeway, Logan pulling his jacket over his shoulders, one arm then the next, his crisp muscles disappearing under the coat's puffiness.

Hannah strokes the thick coat at Logan's forearm, brushing free invisible debris. "Do you like this jacket, Charlie?"

"It's the first thing I noticed."

She nods. "I was concerned about him up here in the Maine cold. Though I think I bought the coat more to calm my worry than to keep him warm."

"The jacket's perfect." My chest swells with embarrassment for how I'd judged Pufferman and his puffy coat.

Logan is a nice guy, the kind of nice guy who commits to wearing a questionable jacket because it was purchased by someone who loves him. And Hannah is a nurturer, trying to protect him when she can't be close. So much love is threaded through his silly parka and I'd missed it, all because my stubborn attention was focused on all the wrong things.

They exchange kisses on the cheek and he pulls on his hat just as we step outside, the crisp mid-morning air rushing to our faces.

"So, tell me about the trees," he says, all enthusiasm. "What's our purpose today?"

"Transforming the cove. Nothing too taxing."

"It's a natural talent the way you make enormous undertakings sound achievable with a day's work."

"Yankee pragmatism, I guess." I give a short laugh as we walk past the cottage and I let myself think about what life could look like if Logan lived next store and wasn't simply visiting.

Would every morning start like this? Morning cocoa with a splash of banter? A cozy pre-dawn visit before we got on with the work of the day? Or could nights end like this, too? Me making room for Logan on the couch. Me, making room for Logan in my life.

A sharp breeze cuts across the harbor, as if to remind me Logan's stay has an expiration date, just like every story has an ending.

"Hey, where'd you go?" Logan stops walking, draws up my gaze.

"I'm here," I lie. In truth, my unrest is multiplying, every instinct telling me to run before he leaves.

"Good. There's no pressure. We're both figuring this out. And our walk doesn't have to be more than a stroll to the common. One step at a time."

Logan reaches for my hand, his eyes asking for permission as my fingers grant it, our gloves finding the grooves and hollows of one another. "Baby steps?" He gives my hand a light squeeze.

I nod. "Okay." Even as I'm next to Logan, I crave the way the DM room felt timeless and limitless, unbound by proximity or a rental contract. And I miss the way InstaEllis was a distraction from Logan, a neutral place to process my feelings and failings. "Tell me about toothpicks?"

"Ah." We resume our walk and he inhales the deep cold before letting out a long, beautiful exhale that seems to transport him through time. "I grabbed a box of toothpicks from my mom's purse. I was four, maybe five. I'd spilled them on the rug and she was annoyed until she saw me lining them up, building them into log houses and towns, fences and tents. She let me play for hours. And the next day, more hours."

"A budding engineer."

"That's what my mom saw. She started bringing home a box of toothpicks every time she went out to eat. Rinse and repeat."

I can almost feel the thick, relaxed rug under my feet, and the murmur of his mother encouraging his creativity. "I like picturing you as a little kid."

He gives my hand a squeeze and as we walk, a delicate layer of ice crunches under our footsteps, the road ahead white and untouched with its thin veil of fresh snowfall. "The thing is, Charlie...." He waits a beat and I find I want to be inside his head, searching for the words with him because that's how stories get set down, right? By the words we choose and those we don't use? "That four-year-old could get really, *really* caught up in a task."

"I have no problem believing this after seeing you help build the trap tree."

"Well, yes. Exactly. I get fixated on things and hyper-focus. I've been known to disappear for hours when I'm working on a project, sometimes days. I shut everything else out, and it's cost me."

I cross an arm against my chest to keep the wind out, maybe protect my heart. "Your fiancé?"

"And more, but yes."

"What happened?" I suddenly want to know everything about their relationship even as its proof that all good things end.

"We met in high school and dated through college. A few years after graduation, we got engaged and I think she expected me to change and I didn't and then she moved on."

We reach the center point of the turn in the road so the harbor spreads like a rolling saltwater meadow at our side. "That sounds like a very condensed synopsis of a complicated relationship."

"Maybe but the pattern feels more important than the details. I shut out my fiancé and my mom a lot. I regret it more than I could ever say, of course." He takes a stuttered breath, slows his steps. "Now I'm trying to keep my obsessive focus in check and let the world in, try new things."

"I think maybe I'm the same."

"You also have a huge, fanatical crush on math?"

"Ha, no. But math and lobstering…maybe it's all the same armor."

"Okay, fair. And highly astute."

"It's protection, you know."

"I do. Except I also know I'm Toothpicks and you're Bluebug— and we're also Charlie and Logan. Statistically speaking, that doubles our chances of being good together. And, I mean, if you really want to nerd out, some statisticians might say it quadruples our chances. So maybe we don't need all the armor."

I stop to face him, and he doesn't let go of my hand. "I think I'm generationally—or maybe genetically—ill-equipped for commitment and romance. All of it. So, when you say our chances are doubled or quadrupled, all I can think is: our chances for what?"

He looks at me, his eyes soft and sure. "For a really nice walk. That's all this is. Just a walk. Is that something you want?"

I exhale, and it's pure relief. "I can do a walk."

"See?" He gives my hand a tender squeeze. "We're already slaying it." He sweeps his free arm toward the common spread out before us. "So, trees. What's our tree day look like? Walk me through it. Who are the players?"

"Mason Glidden. Kind of a town legend."

"I'm fascinated already."

It's impossible not to be carried away on Logan's lightness, meet him there. "Mason runs an architectural landscaping company down in Damariscotta. Apparently, some uber wealthy family from away is building a house and ordered nearly a hundred full grown blue spruces for the property. The permits weren't approved at the build site before the first frost hit so Mason's loaning us the trees from inventory to use for the festival."

"That's a massive undertaking. Delivering full-grown blue spruces is no joke."

"Well, there's a story there."

"I would expect nothing less." His elbow nudges mine playfully. "Tell me."

"The cliff notes? Mem's mom helped out Mason's grandmother during the Great Depression."

"*The* Great Depression. As in, a hundred years ago?"

"Memory is a precious resource here on the cove. It can be used for good or evil."

"Riveting. Continue."

"Mem's mom took in Mason's grandmother and her six kids to live at the lighthouse when they lost their house to the bank. They borrowed our simple rowboat to fish, and Mem's mother even fixed it so the state paid Mrs. Glidden a stipend for her lighthouse keeping services, which probably helped save both families."

"I could live for a very long time and never get tired of your family's stories."

"That's the thing about this place people from away have a hard time understanding," I tell him. "In most parts of Maine, it's nearly impossible to know a person without knowing how you're connected to the last three generations of their people. We've cultivated this unique interdependence with fierce independence at its core."

"Seems straightforward enough. People remember debts of kindness and pay them back when they can. The way life should be. And I don't just mean Maine's state motto. I mean, the way people *should* treat each other. With kindness and respect for those who came before. If you ask me, Mainers are doing it right."

"I like to think so."

He pumps my palm twice, but keeps his gaze trained toward the common as we talk about Mem's wedding and festival preparations. He brainstorms the placement of spruces, an activity that requires light math with just enough computations to make his bottom lip get tucked into a delicious bite.

We hear the landscape trucks before we see them, and Logan tosses out his final suggestion: "If we stagger the trees on either side of the road the lights will appear in one unbroken row as you look from the harbor. On land, you'll be walking or driving the tree-lined lane, a spruce on one side or the other. And, of course that will help the span of the line be longer."

"Of course." I bite my own lip.

Logan smiles, his attention so intense it makes me miss him ten minutes later as he gives directions to the delivery drivers and I fill Kermit Hodge in on the plan.

Regrettably, I didn't bring ear plugs. The jerking crane, crashing tailgates and creaky engines are deafening, our proximity to them making talk impossible, but Logan and I exchange smiles across the distance between us. The guys at Glidden Landshapers unload one forty-foot blue spruce, then another. With each root ball wrapped in burlap, the trees sit off kilter so Haggard and Logan wedge firewood to straighten each trunk before Haggard gives the signal for Kermit's crane to let go. When the ornamental conifers are in place in an alternating line, Logan joins me as we take a step back to witness the scope of the cove's transformation. Full, fat trees line the one-lane road, their branches as welcoming as outstretched arms, their hard, silver-blue needles stirring up the fresh scent of forest.

The smell makes me think of my father, the way he'd tell me how the sea and trees worked in unison to keep our air clean, our oceans pure. He's with me as I tell Haggard about my design for a private ceremony circle for Mem and her vows.

"If we place these last eight trees in a ring, we'll cut the wind from the harbor but also create an intimate setting in the middle of all this big nature," I tell him.

"I like it." Haggard strokes his beard. "And we could even flood the circle after the ceremony. Make an ice-skating rink for the littles at the festival. Small, but it'll do."

"Or a courtyard for rest," Logan offers. "Or one of those photobooths. People love those."

The care and attention Logan shows the cove feels like he's doing a drive-by outside my lobster den, lending his skill to those I love as an offering. When straightening the ceremony circle of trees becomes warm work and his jacket is tossed to the side of the road so that it's just him and a Henley hugging his muscles, I want to invite him inside. Because his shirt is just loose enough that my hand could easily travel up the channel of his spine to explore his muscular back in a way that tenses my body into a building storm.

"You okay?" Logan pinches my jacket at the elbow, stirring my mind to the present.

"Yeah, good."

He nods, his eyes growing dark and heated. "Where do you go when you disappear like that?"

"I don't know what you mean. I've never been more present."

He holds a half smile. "So you heard all about my lighting technique?"

"'Course. I was intrigued."

"You sure about that? You seemed a million miles away."

I shake off the proximity of him, and all the ways my imagination wants to close the short gap between us.

"I'm here," I say, my voice unsteady. All day, people have been sorting string lights donated from the families at Christmas Cove, meticulously repairing sets and coiling them for use. "Maximum wattage." I'm feeling a bit smug about my ability to pull up the last thing I remember about his firm back—I mean, plan.

"I either need to be in charge or sit this part out," Logan says. "My approach to stringing lights is high maintenance, which I acknowledge is not for everyone."

"I'm willing to bet no one else has a light stringing technique to ensure maximum wattage so I think you're the leading expert by a wide margin."

"Okay. You asked for it. We'll start by wrapping the lights close to the trunk of the tree on the first pass."

"There's more than one pass?"

"Oh, Charlie." He chuckles. "You have much to learn. There are three."

"Three! I'm not sure I can stay awake for a tutorial on three layers of lights."

"Not layers." He raises a finger. "That's important to keep in mind. Think dimensions, as in taking up space."

I smile, my cheeks cold, my heart pounding for this man and all his quirks.

"The second string should run across the mid-section of each bow."

"Mid bow. Got it."

"You're mocking me."

"I'm enjoying you."

His spine straightens, his look softens. "Huh." He takes me in, his eyes scanning mine, looking happy with what they find. "The third and final dimension of lighting is draped on the outer needles of each branch creating what some notable reviewers have termed a perfected masterpiece of luminescent artistry."

"I'm very excited for this perfected masterpiece of luminescent artistry."

~ ~ ~

@BirdieBlueBug
I like that you're a confident decision maker.

@toothpicks3478
In general?

@BirdieBlueBug
Yes. But specifically, your directions for light stringing.

@toothpicks3478
Ha! I knew you'd call me out for my persnickety technique.

> @BirdieBlueBug
> I thought it was a turn on.

@toothpicks3478
Huh. That DM is a turn on.

@toothpicks3478
Hang on while I grab a
screenshot.

> @BirdieBlueBug
> Haul with me tomorrow?

@toothpicks3478
Ugh. Okay, I'm *really* not
free tomorrow. Hannah
and I have a commitment.

> @BirdieBlueBug
> You're effortlessly vague
> about your general
> plans, do you know that?

@toothpicks3478
Does that make me
seem more mysterious?

> @BirdieBlueBug
> A thousand percent.

I'm ending the day at Maia's where Logan walked me after hours of tree placement and decoration, little Casey pulling me inside and away from any opportunity for me to kiss Logan goodnight.

She might be my niece, but I'm still sort of not thrilled with her.

I was able to sneak into the DM room using Maia's computer while she bathed her minions, and I'm still floating from our exchange. When Maia joins me at her dining room table that's heaped with simultaneous projects, she brings tea. "Sam's putting the girls down so I'm officially on adult time, which is perfect since I need to hear all the details of your sordid little story. Leave out nothing."

I bore her with the tree update, which she tolerates if I agree to call it choreographing.

"Snore. At this rate, I'll have this baby before you and Logan touch tongues." She unearths a taupe-striped gift box and pops its lid. Photos of our youth drive my fingers inside. "Choose your favorites. And why the long wait for the first kiss? And why am I in a position where I have to ask after these details? I feel like you should spill more than you're spilling."

"There's nothing to spill. We're still figuring all this out." I set aside a photo of me and Maia on our matching new banana yellow bikes. Age ten. Mem's handwritten date scrawled on the upper back corner.

"What's there to figure out? Your lips want to make out with his lips. His lips are begging for yours. Seems pretty simple to me."

"I did really want to kiss him."

"Listen, if I know anything, it's that kissing rules. Get yourself some. My pregnancy hormones and I agree Logan would be an exceptional kisser."

"Female hormones getting a vote should be a thing. In all matters." I pluck a photo from when we were six, our legs all skinned knobby knees as we sat at the base of an apple tree in the late day shade, our noses pink and just beginning to freckle. "Remember this?"

Maia grabs for the picture. "Oh my god, look how young we were!"

"And so fashionable." We twinned out in tie-dye shorts and blue shirts with red sneakers, our hair in ponytails of the same length, nailing the rainbows and unicorns vibe.

"Remember you chose those turquoise studs when you got your ears pierced because they matched your shirt?" Maia says.

"Aw, I loved that shirt. It was my first true love."

"Yeah," she laughs. "We were so young and dumb that neither of us even considered you'd actually have to change your shirt at some point during the eight weeks it took for our ear holes to heal."

"I stand by my choice." Though I regretted the turquoise in later years, I'd love the stone then because my mother wore it in an oversized drop around her neck. It's strange to see a photo of me, pre-betrayal, my features unhardened.

She sets the photo flat on the table. "You asked your dad for five dollars for those earrings, remember?"

"Five dollars with one zero after the five."

"Ha! Yup. Fifty bucks. It was a brilliant negotiating strategy."

My heart surges with memory. "My dad fell for it every time."

"He didn't fall for it, Charlie. He fed it. Whenever we'd want anything expensive, he'd wait for you to ask: *Dad, we only need a dollar for the fair. With two zeros after it, please.* Then his smile would brighten like it had actual wattage. You were his whole world, Charlie. I didn't see it then because we were little and clueless, but now I can tell you without reservation that your father loved you more than the breath in his body."

Emotion chokes my chest and she stands to hug me for a long time because I wasn't the only one who lost my dad. "I miss little kid us."

"There's a lot to miss," Maia says.

As we prep for Mem's celebration, surrounded by memories, my dad is present in our hearts and in sepia Polaroids from when he was impossibly young. Mem, too, stares back at us from when she was a baby. Then, Mem as a pre-teen ballerina posed at the lighthouse rocks, where a lifetime awaits her on the horizon.

26

The Coq au Vin

After hauling all day, I head to the shower, only cruising by my computer casually to check my empty DMs. There weren't any cars in front of Cove Light when I offloaded my traps then my catch before tying up, which makes me pout more than might be considered appropriate for an adult as I scrub the day from my skin. I drop a note after taming my hair into a sloppy braid:

@BirdieBlueBug
How was your vague day?

@toothpicks3478
Come over.

@BirdieBlueBug
Where?

@toothpicks3478
I know this quaint little lighthouse. It's a bit out of the way. I'll ping you directions.

@BirdieBlueBug
But you're not home.
There's no car.

@BirdieBlueBug
Was checking for a friend.

@BirdieBlueBug
As part of my official host duties.

@toothpicks3478
No car. No Hannah.

@toothpicks3478
Come over.

"Shy my ass!" Maia says when I call her in a panic. "His assertiveness is sexy as fuck."

"Right? That's a bossy DM. I didn't know nice boys bossed like that."

"Nice boys have a surprising way of surprising."

"I need boots. Stat. Probably a beret or two. And if you can show me how to twist myself into one of those fashionable wrap skirts of yours, I won't say no. I'm in critical need of all the guidance."

"Stop. You're spiraling."

"Is that what this is?" I fan my face with my hand.

"You calling me for fashion advice? Yeah, that's spiraling. Take a deep breath."

"Breathing is impossible at a time like this."

"You need to break your planning down to the two simplest, most basic components of date preparation."

"No, *you* need to break down my planning into the basic components of date preparation because until this moment I had no idea there were only two."

"It's common knowledge, passed down by mothers around the globe." Maia's speaking so slow and calm I want to catapult through the phone line and shake her.

"Is stalling a key part of date preparation? Because we don't really have the time to revisit the fact that my mother never really carved out time to bestow life advice."

"Right. Sorry. I mean, about your mom, obviously but—"

"Maia!"

"Wear clean underwear and be yourself."

"That's it? *That's* your no-fail wisdom?"

"It's solid. I stand by it."

"You live for romance and happily ever afters and you're giving me *clean underwear* and *be my authentic self*?"

"He wants to see *you*, Charlie. Not some costume you borrow from me. Just be you, looking like you."

"And the clean underwear?"

"Well, that's just leaving the house 101."

"But don't I need—"

"Go!"

With whirlwind efficiency, I choose my favorite black leggings and chunky socks and Dad's Live Aid T-shirt. The worn cotton is soft now, rubbed thinner at the shoulders and hems, and feels like a second skin under the upmarket sky-blue hoodie Maia hoped would inspire me toward yoga and an increased color palette in my wardrobe.

When I've yanked the kitchen door fully closed behind me, my feet sting as a reprimand for forgetting footwear. Ugh. I race back inside, changing my socks and tugging on boots to properly prepare for winter and my walk to the lighthouse as Logan's two-word demand thumps inside of me with the same rhythm as my heartbeat: *come over.*

He opens the door before I knock. Inside, the air is fogged thick with the promise of creamy comfort food simmering in a pot dwarfing the small, two-burner stove. He's wearing jeans, a long-sleeved tee pushed up at his forearms, a delicious smile, and Mem's pie-baking apron.

"Hey," I say.

Logan takes a half step toward me. "Hey." His stare is so intense I feel its weight on my skin, the pulse it wakens low in my core. "Let me take your coat."

He motions for me to turn around. I do. His hands tuck under the fabric at my neckline, his knuckles grazing my flesh along the edges of my collarbone as he floats my jacket off my shoulders, tugging my arms straight and back against my sides. He holds the gathered fabric at my wrists for a beat, his warm breath climbing the bare skin at my neck. A shiver races through me. When he fully removes my coat to hang it on a wall peg behind the door, he brushes my side with his and gooseflesh races over my flesh. I rub at my forearms.

"You doing okay?" he asks, his eyes searching.

"Think so."

"This can just be dinner. No need to overthink it." His smile coaxes mine to rise.

"Just dinner," I repeat, calmed by his calm.

"It must be strange to be a guest in your own lighthouse, no?"

"It's a first."

"Excellent. Let's toast to firsts." He offers two glasses of wine: one red, one white. My attention toggles between glasses when all I can see are his beautiful fingers wrapped around the stems, his ring that isn't a wedding ring. "We're making Coq Au Vin, if that helps you decide."

I dart a look into the living room where the fire in the hearth sparks and snaps.

"What are you looking for?"

"Hannah?"

His smile grows. "Why would Hannah be here?"

"You said *we*. *We're* making Coq Au Vin."

"You and me." A small laugh escapes his lips. "Is that not obvious?"

"It is now." I reach for wine.

"Ah, you're a purist. Burgundy pairs best with our dish."

"You should be disillusioned of any expectation that I can cook, help you cook, or generally not be a disaster in the kitchen." I take a sip of the wine, which is warm and makes me thirsty for more even as I'm swallowing. "If we were in the DM room, I'd disclose how I have no idea what wine pairing even means."

He nods, his smile flirty. "Okay, first. Cooking is way easier than lobster fishing so I'm certain you'll pick it up quickly."

"Ah, okay. So, Coq Au Vin is a *beginner* dish? And I shouldn't be intimidated by my inability to spell it?"

"Like everything, cooking is about slow steps and timing."

Oof.

He lowers the flame on the back burner so a lid stops jumping. "What do you typically make for dinner?"

"Is this your way of gauging how tragic I am?"

"It is."

"Well played." I take a short sip of the thick wine, the alcohol slowing my mind, cozying my pulse.

"Are we talking cold cereal? Warm pop tarts?" He cracks the oven door and a blast of sweet, lemony steam escapes. "Or are you more of a frozen meal girl?"

"Most days I'm an eat-whatever-Mem-brings-home-from-the-diner-girl. But other nights I get a little wild and warm up leftovers from the diner."

He turns his back to the counter, crosses his arms against his silly apron. "Good to know what I'm working with." He eyes a bowl of vegetables. "Can you chop?"

I nod with confidence. "I can."

He offers me an apron from the drawer so I set down my wine. The thumb holes of my yoga top seem counterintuitive to food preparation and the fabric is too tight to roll up so I pull off my top layer and feel instantly more comfortable. Until I see the way Logan's jaw has tensed. His stare, darkened.

"So, where is Hannah exactly?" There's no way Logan doesn't notice the tremor in my voice or the way I forget about the apron completely.

"She's out." His stare on me is intense as he traces the rim of his glass. He gives his head a quick shake before sipping his wine. "I believe she's showing Hermon how to make lobster bisque."

"Really? It's not a formal policy or anything, but we generally don't expect labor from our guests."

"Work expectations could definitely impact your Yelp reviews." His soft smile creeps over his infuriatingly gorgeous face. "This was all Hannah, though. She had an inspiration for the 'caviar'"—he makes one-fingered air quotes while holding his glass—"side of the festivities, and offered to bake lobster tails to be served in a shallow bed of lobster bisque."

"Oh my god, that sounds good! I mean…,"—I pretend clear my throat—"she really shouldn't be helping with the festival."

He trades his wine for a plump tomato, rolls the orb in his palm then down his forearm until he pops it free to catch it underhanded.

"Party trick?"

"I'm trying to impress you with my fourth-grade baseball prowess." He blows on the skin of the fruit like he's the cool kid but all I feel is the heat of him, the oven, and the fire in the next room. "Is it working?"

Oh, it's working. Because Logan isn't just setting the tomato to the counter. He's in a late-autumn garden, shirtless, harvesting vegetables, the sheen of sweat on his—

"Charlie."

"I'm here."

The wine makes it impossible to keep my head straight so I take stock of what I know. The tiny lightkeeper's cottage. The stone fireplace and its mini sitting area. The sister room at the back, the only bedroom with a queen bed that fills most of the space. The lantern room I can't see from the kitchen.

"I've been sleeping upstairs since Hannah arrived," he says, as if tracking my attention.

"Stop it. In the light room? There's no space."

"Not true." He arranges three tomatoes next to a bouquet of rinsed kale. "Space is nothing more than creativity and a committed willingness to spoon an enormous light."

"Sounds romantic."

"I like to think so."

Huh.

He looks past me, past the stairs. "There's something spectacular about being up that high, overlooking the sea and the harbor, having a three-sixty view of your surroundings."

"It bodes well for me as your host that you enjoy being stuffed into small spaces that lack all privacy and a proper bed."

"Probably best that's not the description you settled on for your listing."

"Under-promise and over-deliver."

"I'd say your lighthouse and your listing are perfect, Charlie."

God. He should not be allowed to say my name.

He taps the side of a knife to a cutting board. "Hannah booked a hotel for the festival so you can charge tickets for a lighthouse dining experience, complete with tour, baked lobster around an outdoor fire, wine, and good storytelling. She'll host, of course."

"I really can't ask you two to leave your rental. Or cook. Or host. Or clean up."

His one eyebrow raises. "You didn't ask. We offered." He tosses an unpeeled onion from one hand to the other, its crispy skin ruffling. "She's been brainstorming a name for the experience. Something like *LáTaste* at *La Light*." He laughs. "So, yeah, there's no turning back now. That's why Hannah's trading recipes over at Earl's while your grandmother's at Maia's hashing out wedding plans."

"How is it you know more about what's happening on this peninsula than I do?"

"I don't know more. I was just particularly interested in everyone's whereabouts tonight." His eyes darken, color replaced with intent. "Come here."

Oh, god.

At the sink, he flicks on the faucet with his wrist, nudging the nozzle toward hot. He guides me to the basin so that he's behind me. He lifts one of my hands, then the other, raising my palms upward. His thumbs skate over the heels of my hands while he applies the slightest pressure and my breath hitches.

"Good hygiene is a priority in my kitchen," he says.

His heartbeat presses against my back as he squirts a dime of soap to the hollow of each of my palms, the skin there throbbing with anticipation. The suds build. His fingers slip between mine as a shiver floats through me. I lean my head back, let it rest on his chest. He turns off the water, hands me a towel. It's a struggle to keep the room in focus.

His dishtowel gets flung over his shoulder in a practiced flip before he passes me the onion, his fingers rolling over mine. He positions the cutting board and knife in front of me. "Thin disks," he instructs.

"With the skin on or off?"

He laughs. "Okay. Step one. Remove the skin." He moves behind me again, his hips steady. His mouth inches from my ear. "Removing an onion skin is a tricky maneuver that puts the art in culinary art." My neck bends to the side, making room for him, begging him to come closer.

"Art, huh?" My voice swims in the wine.

His arms reach around my sides so my back is against his chest. His body expands with our closeness, and I feel him inhaling my scent, drinking me in. Somehow, he's able to train his focus on the dumb onion and the knife that I have no interest in. Until his hand covers mine and he tutors me in how to cut through slippery layers. His muscles control my movements as they press close, the two of us working as one, his heart thudding against my back.

We peel the first layer free together so the thick skin drops away and the sweet, bright inside glows with pearlescent flesh. "You're a natural." He releases my hands, stepping back and making my balance uneasy. He searches my eyes. "No tears?"

I shake my head. "No tears."

"Then carrots are next. If you can master the onion solo."

"No pressure, though, right?" Something about his proximity now makes me viscerally aware of how much it will hurt to lose Logan when he leaves, after his presence has transformed my home and my life out here. Like the memory of him is already imprinted onto my dock, my boat, this kitchen, the light.

We prep, his expert movements knowledgeable, his hands stopping only to slip across the small of my back as he passes behind me, no different than the way his body oriented against mine on the boat, warning me he was close. My stomach tightens.

When he's behind me again, his arm rounds my shoulder to offer a shallow ladle to my lips. Onion and cream and gentle spices flood my senses. I take a deep inhale, too pragmatic to be fooled by homecooked meals and soft lighting and wine selections that don't have staying power. Still. It's all intoxicating. His methodical cooking. The way he rolls me into the art of his process. The precision he offers, and demands. The trust he invites.

I spin to face him, the light sauce still warm on my lips. My back steadies against the counter as breath suspends between us, our lips close and quivering.

"Can this be just a kiss?" I ask him. Me.

He nods, leaning in as if to bite my bottom lip, but holds my gaze. Somewhere far away, the ladle clanks to the sink. The room disappears as his hands cinch around my hips before he hoists me to the counter and nothing matters beyond Logan's fingers owning the curve of my thighs.

My lips hover near his, my eyes trained on his mouth. I lean in and hesitate, our breath so close it mixes. He collapses his forehead softly to mine and I study him. The hitch in his breathing. The want rippling off his body. The restraint we both try to master. My whole world reduces to the closeness of his mouth and my hunger for him. I move slowly, my lips brushing his as his breath skips. I wait a beat and then can't any longer. I press my lips to his and our kiss is soft, unhurried, tasting of salt and the sea, my home.

Our lips meet and linger. Pull back. Breathe. We sample the nearness of each other long enough for time to slip away. We are all hesitation and tenderness until our want builds and he thrusts my hips to his just as I wrap my legs and cinch my ankles around his back. I pull him closer, giving permission, my greedy fingers grabbing fistfuls of his hair, wanting more of him, all of him. He moans into my mouth. Heaves me against his hips. Onto his hips. Turning his mouth away from mine only to shut off the stove and burners as he balances me across his center, his one arm tucked under my bottom, his free hand arriving at my neck with an appetite.

He carries me to the loveseat where I straddle him. With the fireplace at my back, Logan's lips explore my neck that reclines away from his kisses to give him more canvas, more skin to cover and claim.

"This is so much better than a DM room," he murmurs, his breath under my ear before his tongue meets mine again, all want and hunger.

My back arches as his palms probe under my tee and across my lower back. The room sways as we kiss and hold on. We are floating, grabbing for one another, riding on a cresting wave building from the current swirling between flesh and desire. I move his arms lower, toward my legs, the muscles in my thighs taut with greed and need.

"You feel amazing, Charlie." His lips curl into mine before his mouth skates to my collarbone, asking permission and laying claim all at once.

The heat is too much. I cast off my shirt, throw it to the floor and Logan stops. With his hands on my back, he leans away to stare at me in the glow of the fire, my flesh made of light and shadows.

"God, you're beautiful." His jaw tenses and a gray storm darkens his eyes. I'm afloat in his hard stare, the whole of me wanting to be anchored and pulled down by him. I tug his shoulders forward, strip off his shirt to see the cut of his chest, my own outline casting shadows onto the hard ridges of his muscles, his taught stomach, the ripple of hair above his beltline and... the apron bunched at his waist.

I tug at the knot of fabric just below his navel. "This is sexy stuff," I say with a half laugh.

"When it comes to seduction, aprons are an overlooked contributor to the—"

I push my finger to his mouth. "It's my grandmother's apron. You need to take it off." Laughter is gone from my voice, replaced with dark determination.

"Gone. Totally gone." He strips the apron away and pulls me to him, his arm balancing me across his lap before he bends to the floor, kneeling as he lowers my back to the braided rug so that I lay in front of the fire. He hovers above me, his chest catching the orange glow of firelight, the flecks of light glistening off his skin as if he's wet, liquid. I take him in, the expanse of him. His tapered stomach dipping into his low hips, his jeans slipping at his hipbones. I raise my fingers to the ridge there and trace the tight skin, the valleys and peaks of him. When my finger travels the line under his belt, he moans and falls closer toward me, his arms bracing his weight just before our bodies meet, air passing through the crevice between us, skipping over our skin like a promise.

"I want you so badly."

"I'm here," I tell him, my voice gravel and heat as my body begs for the tide of his movements, my blood rushing, my insides pooling with a need for him to be inside of me, for me to be lost in him.

He drops his head with a hard push of breath and collapses to his side, his face propped by his elbow. "You are perfect, Charlie." Two fingers trace my shoulder, soft as a wink as they travel down my side to the curve of my hip. "I've wanted you since the day I first saw you."

"In your puffy jacket and wingtips." I try not to feel vulnerable or exposed by his move to my side. Still, I roll onto my hip, raise my arm to cover my chest, make my legs close over themselves.

"I couldn't believe how beautiful you were when I first checked in. I acted all interested in the ocean but you took my breath away."

"Impossible." I throw a small laugh. "I was grimy from fishing."

His shrug lifts against my body. "What can I say? It worked for me."

"I want to say the same about your wingtips."

"Don't hate the wingtips. They give me confidence." His finger explores the spill of my collarbone that rises to his touch. "Like you."

His caress skirts the edge of my bra, a tease that begs for him to uncover and explore, his fingers feathering along my side, over my hip. My breath and need expand as my back arches.

"Do that always." His voice is dark with ache.

I open my eyes to his stare. "Do what?"

"Breathe." He caresses the rise of one breast, then another, my deep inhale making them full. "I'd be happy just to watch you breathe. To *feel* you breathe, Charlie."

I pull his lips to mine. When we meet, he devours me, his tongue exploring my mouth, my neck, my breast where he teases my flesh taught with his flicking tongue. He pulls me under him and thrusts one thigh between my legs. He straddles me, his back straight as his stare fixes down on me, his fingers clasping around my ankle, lifting it to the shelf of his shoulder. His hand finds my foot, cupping the bowl of my arch as his gaze pins me, his eyes inky with resolve. His probing fingers explore my calf, then circle the bony knot of my knee as if it's clay, his hands molding it, shaping it, memorizing it before traveling the highway of my inner thigh. I reach for his waist where I tug at the loops of his jeans to heave him so close, his low, breathy moan gets muffled in the valley of my chest.

Then his hand is on mine at his hip, his fingers clamping around me, his body hardening, sharpening, pulling away.

"Charlie." He twists to his side again, lowering my leg. His head propped away from mine. "Can we...?" He lets out a ragged breath. "Can we take a break?"

"What's wrong?" My insides curl with need, even as my body unspools from his.

"Nothing. There is absolutely nothing wrong. You"—his eyes glide along my flesh, his thumb tracing the rise of my cheek, my jawline, the side of my neck that pushes into his touch—"are perfection." He pulls his hand back, rubs at his hair. "I just. I want to slow down."

"Okay." My eyes scramble to find my shirt.

"I want you, Charlie. I do. So much you can't know."

"Okay," I say, breathier now.

"I just don't want to go too fast and ruin what we have." He rests on his back, his two hands raking his hair.

My searching fingers find the corner of my shirt and I tug the soft cotton over my chest. My brain spirals, my body trying to return from exhilaration.

"Can we slow down? Is that okay?" he asks.

"Of course." I want to want what he wants, but I've been all-in tonight, wanting him and only him.

"Stay with me. Right here. Just like this." He nestles his head into the bowl between my breast and shoulder. "I never want to be anywhere else."

But is that true? Because isn't slowing down just another way of stopping? Of recognizing something wasn't working. Like maybe our connection didn't feel as good for him.

His leg blankets mine, his fingers twisting my messy braid into a soft knot in his palm as my head is cradled by his hand. For a long time, he traces the landscape of my stomach, roaming the hills and valleys of me, my body trying not to stutter with every aching pass. The fire dies back as Logan's petting slows, his breath steadying, his body falling limp with sleep beside me.

While I watch calm soften his features, I find I want to be here when he wakes up. And not just tomorrow or later tonight. No. I want to watch him wake up for all the days to come. I want to be next to him as his tender blue eyes adjust from a dream haze, his mind caught in a liminal space between weightlessness and reality, his face losing the serenity of sleep as it tightens toward the demands of each day.

But I can't help the way he's made me feel vulnerable. And how wanting a future with him throws me off balance. Can I even trust his desire when he pulled away? My body becomes rigid with the answer.

"Logan." I press at his shoulder and he stirs. "I can't do this. It's not...not something I should have started. I have to go."

"No. Don't leave." His attention is sleepy. "Stay," he begs.

"I can't."

~ ~ ~

My head crams with a lifetime of loss and betrayal as I head to the cottage, the harbor's darkness drawing around me like a cloak, my breathing so fast and panicked it's hard to inhale fully. But I don't turn back to the lighthouse or even let myself think about how I let my guard down.

When I duck into my bedroom, I send an unanswered S.O.S. to Maia from my window. She doesn't respond to my texts or repeated calls. And the one person I've been turning to lately for distraction is the same person who asked me to take it slow right before he stopped completely.

27

The Catch

After a sleepless night, I'm running on adrenaline and sugar as I set the fishing coordinates on my dash, the empty seat beside me seeming to pitch the boat off kilter as if to remind me fishing is better with Logan.

Behind the wheel, I settle in, throttling out of the harbor, around the bend of the cove as I look for his silhouette on the rocks, listen for his voice calling my name. All the things I shouldn't be doing because I need Christmas Cove to return a normal place where I'm not searching for him or thinking about him under me on the loveseat or feeling the fire of him on my skin.

At some point, I might even forget the sinking sensation of him pulling away.

My first trap is heavy and awkward even as it only carries one lobster—a specimen so enormous it seems impossible he fit inside the kitchen. Water cascades off his broad back as I place him onto the sorting table. I've only heard legend of lobsters this large, fishermen elongating their animated arms, the creature growing bigger during each retelling of the story. But this catch doesn't need embellishment. His crusher claw alone is the size of a regulation lobster. He is a grandfather, a survivor. A magnificent monster.

On the table, his tail curls in protest as he tries to scurry across the metal but can't get purchase. His crusher claw snaps at the air. He is out of his ecosystem, posturing to defend himself, protect himself. Maybe he's been topside before and his defenses are honed. Or maybe it's his first time above the surface. Either way, he knows he's far from his natural element when my grip wraps around his abdomen and I raise him to the sky.

"Welcome to the above, old man. What do you think?" The waking sun is an amber compass on the horizon, the brightness of it bleeding over the sea and this creature that is brown and barnacled with deep sea life. "That's the sun." I squint past him. "Have you felt it on your belly before?"

I find I want the massive lobster to answer me, tell me of the detailed routes and discoveries of his travels, how many journeys he's made onto boats, how many times he's inspired awe in fishermen. Then he'll dive back to the sea bottom, returning to his underwater mancave to brush off human oils and settle into his rocky lounger, grateful to be home, exhausted by the expedition. He could have hundreds of stories, no different than humans.

"Whaddaya think, Dad? Met this guy before in your travels?"

I'm hungry to see some evidence of this lobster's life above ground, a story notched into his shell. But this marvel of a lobster is free of human markings. He is a warrior. Unscathed. He is enviable and beautiful.

When tears build behind my eyes, one escapes down my cheek, a silent, solitary acknowledgement of how much I want Logan here to share this moment with me, even as I have to let him go. Exhaustion builds in my muscles as I set the beautiful creature down. Mindfully, I select the largest mackerel from the bait bin before offering it to his crusher claw.

"Whatever you've done to protect yourself all this time is admirable," I tell him. "I'm so glad you're on the planet so we could meet."

I set him to the sea and he slides beneath the waves, the two of us left to our separate worlds where we belong. I lash the emptied trap to my boat and follow my lines through my harvest, pulling pots from the water to store for winter. When I eat lunch, I try not to think about Logan offering me pineapple and a smile, his orange overalls pulling down at his hip, his energy halving the labor.

When nearly all of my pots are pulled and I turn toward home, it's Logan I thank first. Then Dad. As I near the harbor, the line of spruce trees looks like a glorious runway of light, the tree trap a centerpiece. Logan's lighting technique gives the glow depth, each tree looking like something you could enter, explore. A hideaway worthy of children's books and dreams. My smile is more sadness than joy as I remember his detailed instructions for stringing lights, his commitment to making the cove shine, and more. So much more.

My radio wakes with static. "*MerSea* to *BlueBug*," Maia says. "Is that you creeping beyond the cove? Find me on 11."

I flick my search light twice before switching to the private channel and picking up the handle. "I wish you were with me to see how beautiful the harbor looks."

"Smelly boats are kryptonite for the blowout."

"Maybe, but I think you'd dig seeing our little hamlet from a distance. The ceremony circle is glorious and the row of lighted spruces makes Christmas Cove look worthy of having you as a resident."

"Okay, now you're speaking my love language."

"Flattery?"

"Exactly."

"So, you'll come out?"

"Unlikely. And why are we talking about your smelly boat when I'm overdue for the deets from last night? Sorry about missing your call and your"—she counts under her breath—"eleven texts."

"I'm not proud of my behavior."

"With him or my phone?"

"Both, maybe."

"Excellent. This means Mama's in for some juicy details. Come over. But just you, no smell."

The current pushes my boat closer to the harbor and Cove Light where I'm peeling an onion with Logan standing behind me. On the loveseat with my legs wrapped around him, the skin of my bare back teased by his fingers, the ridges of my collarbone starved for his lips.

"I need to unload my catch and traps. Then shower, apparently. So, it'll be a minute."

"Chop chop, woman. Sam took Thing One and Thing Two to visit with his mom so it's a girl's night."

"Will there be food? I'm starving."

I follow the rocky line of the shore to enter the mouth of the harbor, the holiday lights flickering onto the slack water, their shine jumping like hot oil across the surface of a pan. Then I see the safari jeep parked in front of the lighthouse, one of those short, boxy all-terrain vehicles British people can't seem to get enough of.

"What's with the truck at the light?"

"Out of Africa? No idea. Possibly a squatter."

"Explain."

"The truck showed up this afternoon with a delivery, maybe? There was a large box involved, but that's all I could see. Then, when the driver didn't exit, I devolved into hypothesizing vacation murders."

"Sounds like your third trimester paranoia is right on time."

"Well, considering you're the human renting to Logan, while also being the human boning said renter, maybe you could just ask who the arriving party is and why they're visiting."

"Not boning Logan."

"Okay. Get over here faster. I'll warm Thai take-out."

"On my way."

It's a comfort Logan's car isn't home as I ferry my traps to the dock one by one, even if I do feel him watching me, this sense that he's never far away yet always out of reach.

I shouldn't care who's visiting Cove Light, but I do. Is his guest in front of the fire now, inches from where my T-shirt was abandoned to the floor while I sat on top of Logan? I almost expect Hermon to give me the play-by-play of activity at the lighthouse as he meets me at the wharf to help me unload my catch.

"Still trapping?" Hermon moves a pair of lobsters to the deep tanks that constantly churn saltwater through the hold so our part of the world can stay true to its claim of *Fresh Seafood!*

"One more haul of the season tomorrow then I'm in for the year."

He nods knowingly.

We work hard in near silence as cold Mainers do until my boat's empty and I rest my hip against the dock rail. "You ready to make an honest woman out of my grandmother?"

"*Ayuh*. Been ready longer than ya've been alive."

I smile. "Sounds like true love."

"One life, one love. That's how it's been for me." He shucks off his gloves, flattens their knife-proof palms against one another. "I'm the luckiest man now she's finally said yes to me."

My head cocks. "Finally?"

"I've been asking yer grandmother to marry me every year since I returned home from the service, Charlie. Five decades now. Never missed a year."

"I had no idea."

"Well, ya know yer grandmother. Always fixin' to keep her words close."

I laugh. "You two might be the perfect pair."

"I've been telling her that same thing comin' on fifty-two years now." He tilts his trucker hat upward, scratching his impressive head of enduring silver hair. "And I need ya to know this ceremony isn't a marriage for me, Charlie. It's my life. Yer mem's been my better half since long before she agreed to be my better half."

Hermon's sincerity stings, both with the fullness of love and its absence. I envy Hermon's conviction that's spanned decades, his unfaltering belief that Mem has always been his once in a lifetime, all while I'm unable to navigate the commitment of a short-term hook-up.

"I got something to ask ya, if that suits."

"Yes, anything." I'm expecting some request for the ceremony that's mere days away: a poem, a reading, a decoration to enhance their union.

"I want yer mem to live with me. Here." He motions toward his apartment above the restaurant. "And I'm gonna ask her. Every bit of me is hoping she'll say yes to me a second time, but I need ya to know I'm asking before I ask. This love includes ya, too, Charlie." He scratches at his scruffy beard. "I might be an old man, but I'm not foolish enough to think yer mem'll make any decision that doesn't suit her. Thing is, I want her here. Close to me. Not across the harbor. And I want ya to want that for us. If she wants that for us." He nods at the cottage. "And we'll both be right here. Closer than close. Just across the way for ya—no different than I've stayed close to yer mem my entire life."

It's hard to fight back the tears for Hermon loving Mem the way he does, and for the way he's nesting. Hermon's making space in his heart and home for Mem, digging through his hardscrabble abode to invite his female inside.

"There's only one thing about your request that matters to me," I say.

"What's that now?"

"That you're the kind of man who'll let Mem decide what's best for her."

"Ya got a good heart, Charlie Pinkham."

"Mem's been a good teacher. For me, and my heart." It's a hard truth that gets lodged in my throat.

I cast a look over to the lighthouse and the cottage, our little slip of land perched against the sea. Is this how Mem will see our home in the days ahead? Will we say goodnight across the lapping water using Morse code? Or will she and Hermon move into the cottage and I'll be at Cove Light, unable to be free of my memory of Logan?

When I reach Maia's house, I set my boots to her tidy mudroom and run to the kids' bathroom, yelling, "I'm here but I stink so give me five! And have food on the table before I eat your face!"

In the shower, I let the hot water pulse over me, rinsing the sea and salt from my skin. My grandfather lobster makes an appearance when I close my eyes, joined by Dad at the rail, the two of us marveling over the mighty creature as we talk about Mem and Hermon and love and what change looks like for me and our family and our peninsula.

Like always, Dad's visits are too short. I dry off, dressing in my underwear and bra but keep the unicorn hoodie towel twisted around my hair, and a yellow dinosaur towel cloaked around my middle. I join Maia in her spotless mid-century modern kitchen, dropping to a wooden butterfly chair to be served.

"You look ridiculous and also fairly amazing," she says.

I rub water from one eye with a hot pink unicorn hoof. "I'm getting one of these. Adult towels are so boring."

"Adulting is largely a bore fest. Its baffling to me why teenagers are dying to get to the other side of puberty so fast." She passes a steaming plate of twice-fried Thai noodles my way and I hurry a pile onto my fork and into my mouth.

"Your manners are impeccable."

"Sorry. Do I have to perform for you?" I open my mouth half full of chewed food, too tired and hungry to ask if she likes seafood before she gets to see my food.

"You should get animal-themed towels. You're a child." She stands behind me, plucking the unicorn off my head by its horn before scrubbing my hair and scalp dry with the terrycloth, inviting my head to recline onto her full middle like it's a spa sink. "Now, tell me everything."

I eat and download her on the food prep tutorial that involved Logan's body sliding against mine as he guided my hands under soap and around a knife and the slippery flesh of an onion.

"Oof." She balls the towel to her lap, fans her face. "Steamy."

"Yup. Then I kissed him."

"You didn't!" She sits quickly.

"I did." I set my fork to my empty plate.

"He's a good kisser, isn't he? He looks like he'd be next level."

"He is a next level good kisser."

"Swoon. And?"

"And then we fooled around and it was perfect until it wasn't."

"What? That's impossible. What happened?"

"I have no idea. It just all went…wrong. He pulled away, said something about taking things slow—"

"Jesus. No two people have ever taken things slower."

"Thank you. It all felt like an excuse to not be with me and I freaked out and then I left."

"You left?" She scoots me from my chair when I nod, tucking her arm into mine as she leads me to her bedroom at the back of the house. "I feel like you're blowing past good stuff. Somehow you skipped from first kiss and hot petting to you running away. Why do I feel like lots of details are being conveniently left out of this narrative?"

"It's not a new story." In her room, I collapse onto her bed, my limbs sinking into the doughy middle of her mattress topped with a luxurious comforter. "Oh my god, your bed is a cloud!" I squish at a pillow so filled with downy goodness it feels fuller and thicker than any pillow has a right to be.

"Merino cashmere," Maia says. "Woven by a goat farmer up in Blue Hill. Her products just came under the *Mer*/Sea brand and I'm not sorry."

"No wonder you and Sam keep having babies. This bedding is epic."

"You're deflecting. How did sexy time skip to a panic attack?" Maia positions a sewing pin between her lips. "Stand up. I need to measure you."

"Did I say panic attack?"

"Did you split without saying a proper goodbye? Without fully articulating your line of thinking or emotions? All while barely breathing?" She unrolls a paper tape measure across my bra and hips.

"It's like you were there."

"I don't get it. You said the kissing was good and I assume the petting was good because…, well, look at him."

"Yes. It was all great. Amazing great. Until he fell asleep."

She spins me to face her. "He didn't!"

"No, of course he didn't. Mostly because I'm way too alluring. In fact, we're still having tantric sex right now."

"That's a lot of sarcasm for one sentence." Maia measures my neck. "He really fell asleep?"

"He did."

"Ouch."

"Exactly."

She skillfully detaches the fluffy, white hem from a child's holiday dress, cutting it to size and fastening it around my neck with a brooch backing.

My fingers float to the soft choker. "How are you this talented?"

"It's fabric and a pin, Charlie. It's not rocket science."

"Says you."

"So where did you leave it?" She drops her hands to her sides, tilting her head to assess her progress.

"I poked him, I think—to wake him up."

"Oof."

"I told him I was leaving and left." The whole scene feels too sharp, too painful to recount.

"Did you leave a note?"

"No."

"Write a DM later?"

"No."

"Leave onion slices in a smiley face on the counter?"

"I was sort of in the middle of a freakout, though it's becoming clear why I've never had a functional relationship."

"You're in a functional relationship with me." Maia lifts my arms, drapes a long sheet of red velvet around my frame.

"You don't count." The fabric is supple between my fingers, an extravagance that's impossible to ignore. "You just had velvet lying around, did you?"

"Don't judge. I bought this bolt when I was feeling crafty and inspired to make holiday dresses for the girls, but then Sam put this third baby inside me so now I'm using it to make a very special officiant dress for you."

"Magician."

"Hardly," she says.

"It's honestly difficult to believe you're my friend. I mean, you're immensely talented and I'm kind of intimidated by how you so casually conquer the shit out of your perfect universe."

"Take a look in the mirror, Charlie." She pins the fabric at the top ridge of my side ribs, pulling it snug around my hips and butt so it already looks like a strapless, empire-waist dress. She holds my shoulders. "Our universes may be different, but I'd say you're the intimidating one. I mean, look at you. You're a goddess and you're brilliant and kind and the only reason you're not with Logan or some other boy is because you can't see yourself as a goddess who is brilliant and kind and worthy." She lets the fabric slack at my hips. "God, I hope you wore sexy underwear with Logan and not these granny panties."

"Don't shame the fishing panties. They're sensible. Non-slip and non-wedgie. A girl's best friend on a boat."

"They're an abomination."

I tug at the lush velvet at my chest. "Don't forget to leave room for long underwear."

"You're not wearing long underwear beneath this dress."

"Okay then I'm wearing my coat over this dress and no one will see your masterpiece. And you should start preparing now for me to wear my boots."

"Uh-uh. No lobstering gear allowed!"

"Not my fishing boots. My good muck boots."

"Please let me loan you footwear."

"Nope. My sensible, rugged boots are just big enough to insert warmers. When my feet are warm and dry, I'm happy in whatever weather Maine throws at us."

"What I'm hearing is that there's still time for negotiations." She de-burritos the red velvet from my skin and hands me a sweatshirt and leggings, which I pull on, inhaling the renewing spring scent of Maia's laundry. "You might not know this but fancy underwear can feel very empowering. You know, like that last post you wrote, about females having all the power. That's the way you describe the lobster universe, so why the duck-and-run with Logan? What happened to all that emboldening she-power?"

"For one, I'm not a lobster."

We settle onto her bed, me cross-legged, Maia on her side where she props her belly with a pillow long enough to reach the space between her knees. "What if I floated a couple of theories?" she says.

"Float away."

"Maybe you're more like a lobster than you think."

"This should be good."

"I'm serious. Maybe the hurt, human side of you is trying to sabotage anything with Logan before it starts. Is this you keeping your protective shell thick to prevent your heart from getting pummeled?"

"My heart felt pretty pummeled when he pulled away and then fell asleep."

"Right, but...." She hesitates.

"Say it." I drop back against her ocean of plush pillows. "You're not exactly known for holding back."

"Who cares if Logan lives somewhere else or wants to take things slower than two people have ever taken a relationship or hook-up or whatever this is? Like, really—who cares? He's here now and you clearly dig him, and you don't know he's going to hurt you just because other people have hurt you. Why not just have fun? Don't overthink things. If you're honest with him about where you're at, maybe it will be okay to meet him where he's at."

~ ~ ~

But it's Logan who meets me when I dock at the cottage after returning from Maia's, his hands thrust to his puffy pockets, his shoulders lifted against the shrill wind. "You left." He reaches for my lines, helps me tie up.

"You fell asleep on me."

His hand reaches for mine, but I pretend not to see it and walk the path to the cottage, Logan following. He runs in front, stopping me as he turns to get my full attention.

"Charlie, I fell asleep because I was next to you and I'd never been any place better than next to you. The heat and the fire and your body. Jesus. It was all so overwhelming. I think I succumbed to sensory overload or something. I'm sorry if that hurt you. I was just…in new territory." The sea beats against the shore making the wood dock moan.

"I get it. It's fine."

"It doesn't sound fine."

"Last night was…," I start. "I mean, being with you is…." I want to finish the sentences, but I can't give over the truth of them and make myself more vulnerable. "It's amazing you're here now saying that being with me is the best, but you've been stepping back from me for weeks, keeping your distance, making sure you never got too close. Then I got too close last night and I got hurt and I left."

"I didn't mean to hurt you."

"I didn't mean to run. But it wasn't really a choice. More like survival instinct kicking into high gear. Waking me up, you know?"

Logan holds my gaze under the stars that pierce the blanket of night. "Charlie, I thought you were in a relationship. That's why I kept my distance. Don't you get it?" He stares through me, all the way past my defenses, beyond the hard shell to my soft bits he makes softer. "You would brush against me on the boat and your touch wouldn't leave my skin for days, like you'd marked me."

He lifts my chin toward him, rushing heat through my body. "And I didn't fall asleep on you, Charlie. I fell asleep *with* you. I forgot about the dinner cooking and all the ways I wanted to impress you because my arms were around you. My body wrapped in yours. The taste of you on my lips. I never want to be anywhere else."

Every inch of me wants to kiss him, pull him close and be sloppy and ravenous and unrelenting with the way we reach for each other and explore one other. But I can't risk the hurt that lives on the other side of all this want.

"I can't, Logan. Really. You said you didn't want any more misunderstandings between us so this is me, all me. I'm truly not built for love or romance or whatever this is. I'm not who you want me to be. I can never be that person."

The light flicks on in the cottage kitchen.

"I need to go," I tell him. "And I need you to let me go. I promise you'll thank me."

I hear him call my name as I walk toward the cottage, but I don't turn around. Instead, I walk the length of the cove and return to Maia, where she lets me cry in her arms, holding me the way she did when my mom left, when my dad died, when Mem got sick, and when Mem went into remission.

"I'm so tired," I sob.

"I'm here," she says, stroking my hair and letting me grieve. "I'll always be here."

28

The Comments

I wake in Maia's bed, a gourmet hot chocolate steaming on the side table.

"Good afternoon, sleepy." She rubs my shin under the decadent covers.

My eyes find the alarm clock that reads 1:17 and I bolt upright.

"Relax. I called Mem last night and she knows you're safe with me. We both agreed you needed sleep." She pats my leg. "Take your time getting up, and we'll head to the common. Sam's there with the kids waiting on us. There's a ton to do." When she stands, she hands me an envelope. "Also, this came for you." She drops it to the covers. "It's beyond adorable. If you don't run to this man, I might."

"You opened it?"

"'Course."

The note is folded in two. I peel it open to see a cartoon line drawing of a large lobster kicking back in a rock lounger. A book is cracked open at an angle on his lap, the title printed across the front cover, and abbreviated on the spine: Birdie Bluebug and Toothpicks: The Greatest Love Story Never Told. Above the door to the lobster's den is a sign that reads: DM Room. A bowl of Buddha's hand fruit is on the table next to the reading lobster, an arrow and callout identifying the variety. Three other books line the simple shelf: Handbook for Adulting, Grammar Made Easy, and A Lobster's Guide to Australia.

"Did Logan give you this?"

"He came by early this morning. I made muffins and tried to convince him you weren't as tragic as you are."

"And?"

"He said you're perfect. Baggage and all."

"He didn't."

"Not exactly, but close enough for it to count." She peels the liner from a blueberry muffin she plucks from my breakfast tray. "He said he wasn't giving up on you, which made me swoon."

"Don't encourage him."

"Me? Never. I'm just a bystander here to support you. Even if I think you're making a huge mistake."

"How so?" I fold the drawing in half, then half again.

"He's your lobster, Charlie, and you're too stubborn and proud to see it. He could love you. Like *love*, love you. And you can't get out of your own way enough to entertain the possibility?"

"That's not fair. And lobsters don't—"

"Yeah. I get it. They don't mate for life." She sets down the muffin, slapping her hands free of crumbs. "This is your perfectly-timed third act in Karma for Christmas, Charlie. When the viewer thinks all is lost between the love interests."

"Again. This is my actual life. Not some dumb movie."

"Right, yeah. I know. You're an expert in shutting down possibilities." Her fists land on her hips. "But that cartoon he made for you? That was *for you*, Charlie. The person he knew from the cove and the person he met online. You. And you're all he wants. You've been mooning over him since he got here but now that he's available you decide to pull away. It's sort of classic Charlie, isn't it?"

"First of all, I don't moon over people. And second, is this you being on my side? Because it kind of feels like you being an asshole."

"Maybe that's what you need. Loving you unconditionally hasn't been enough to make you believe you're worthy of love—or that love is worth taking every risk—so, yeah. I'll be an asshole if it wakes you up."

I stand. Grab my clothes. "Happily ever afters aren't actually realistic for most people. You get that, right? What you and Sam have isn't for everyone, and we don't all need to find our one true love to feel whole."

"Careful," Maia warns.

"Sorry, but we can't all be you, Maia."

"I don't want you to be me. I want you to see there's a man right here, right now, who wants to give you his time and trust while all you can think about are ways to shut him down. Tough Charlie, never vulnerable."

Maia crosses her arms at her chest and raises her chin as if asking gravity to hold back her tears.

"Does love mean getting hurt?" she says. "Hell, yeah. But I don't want to live in a world that doesn't have messy, complicated, beautiful, boundless love at its center. I don't want to raise my kids in a world where love doesn't come first. So, I get it, you've been hurt. Big love brings big loss, but that's not a news flash, Charlie, and you're not special—"

"Harsh."

"And true."

"I'm gonna go."

"Sounds about right," Maia says sharply, opening the door for me. "When you're at home listening to your poor-me soundtrack, take a look at the comments on your posts. Not only are you capable of love, Charlie, you inspire it."

Nausea stirs in my stomach as I hate walk home, passing small clusters of people preparing the common. Jimmy and Jace McFarland offload brightly-painted ice fishing shacks from a trailer, the tiny houses arranged to look like a miniature Nordic village. Haggard waves a delivery of portable bathrooms into place. Kermit uses his crane to plant green metal stakes into the frozen ground along the road. Hannah and Kate decorate and connect the metal posts with garland made from colorful braided fishing rope. Kate's invested in hanging a red lobster buoy on each metal stake, her phone nowhere to be seen. And even though it feels like everyone's eyes are on me, Mem doesn't even see me from where she and Hermon erect wooden sandwich board signs that point to food & refreshments, games, lighthouse tours, and more.

Everywhere I look, my community is showing up for each other, showing up for me. Again. Tears sting my skin, turning cold against my cheeks as I walk into the wind, but I don't brush them away. Because Maia's right. I'm not special. And I was wrong last year—all those months in the hospital with Mem when I thought I was the one doing all the care. It was our village that kept us going. Maia stewarding Cove Light, Haggard safeguarding the cottage, Herman buoying Mem's spirit. I've never been alone. Not even when I've been out at sea alone.

My whole life, I've been trusting in the love from my community so why does it feel impossible to trust the kind of connection Logan's offering?

By the time I reach the cottage, my vision is so blurred by tears I almost miss the small notecard tied to the door with twine. Logan's precise, handwritten words feel both familiar and something I already miss:

> Maine has a desert. In total, it's twenty acres
> of barren glacial sand. I think this desert exists
> between Maine's coast and forests just to prove
> that unexpected terrain is beautiful.

I curl the small card in my tight fist and dive onto my bed, kicking my legs hard against the mattress while letting go of a deep, crazed scream that feels so good I do it again. When I sit up, I notice the backside of the card. Logan has written words:

> Forgive me?
> Check box: Yes □ or No □

I pop open my screen, needing the protection of the DM room to respond. But there's an email from the State of Maine. I click to find my officiant's license for Mem's Solstice wedding ceremony that's only two days away. I want to share the news with Mem and Maia, but I've pushed Maia away and Mem's already moving on toward her great love.

Online, I try to be confident or capable enough to give Logan the perfect response that would simultaneously heal my heart and allow me to trust. But the alphabet is only twenty-six letters. Not nearly enough to say all the things I need to say to explain all the ways I'm broken.

I print the license and ache over the distance I've wedged between me and Maia. Maybe it's an invisible olive branch, but without her here, I do the thing that makes me feel closer to her: I follow her advice to visit my posts on her *Mer*/Sea site.

A pop-up box fills my screen when I reach her page. It's an invitation to the Curmudgeons & Caviar Festival. The graphic sends me to a separate site dedicated to the festival, with a link to purchase tickets. She's created a scrolling photo feed of the trap tree on the common at dusk. The Polar Luge Run. Cove Light at sunrise. Hermon and Mem making soup in the diner's kitchen. Haggard standing at the helm of Bobby Pelletier's lobster boat wearing a full red Santa suit, his own bushy beard stuffed with cotton balls, one arm waving a high arc of sincere welcome. I scroll through the photo feed again and love is everywhere. Every preparation is for love, made with love. Love of community. Our way of life on the cove. Our ancestors and our communal future.

And there's risk, too. No one knows if the festival will be a success and net us more than we're collectively contributing. But risk isn't the thing I see when I look at the glorious event this village created from nothing more than giant hearts and hard work.

Even as I head to my posts to read the comments, I know I'm doing it just so I can return to Maia and tell her I followed her advice, and that I'm sorry. I'm not prepared for the hundreds of people responding to my words, as if my posts have welcomed strangers to Christmas Cove without them ever arriving on our shores.

I read my first post in full, cringing at how I disclosed lobsters don't mate for life, which feels awkwardly aggressive now, but maybe I wanted to burst everyone's romantic bubble. If I couldn't believe in love and happily ever after then no one should. I can practically feel my hard shell tightening around me as I read words that seem written by another person entirely. Then, the comments:

☀ *Hi. I'd like to be a badass, take-no-shit lobster please. These creatures know what is up.*

☀ **Changes career to female lobster fisherman**

☀ *Why did no one teach me this in schooool? I would have liked teen me so much more.*

☀ *Were talkin about lobsters tho right?*

☀ *ive spent my life stuck with the wrong person and i. am. being. consumed.*

☀ *#LifeGoals. A dream to live on Christmas Cove.*

I nudge my screen closer, all of me wanting to meet the people who were engaged enough to comment on my life, my vocation, my thoughts. When I scroll to my second post, I'm returned to thinking all the inappropriate thoughts about married Logan. It's captivating to see how people connected, applying my lobster logic to their own circumstances.

☀ *my new favorite everything: "the planet is mostly ocean and oceans are mostly undiscovered worlds"*

☀ *She's writing to you, cheaters.*

☀ *Taken means Taken. Boo ya.*

☀ *I need this column always. Please make this a thing.*

☀ *who are you and what have you done with my low expectations?!*

My post on the optimism and resolve of lobstermen "never pulling an empty pot" has so many comments it's almost impossible to believe how invested readers had already become with my simple life at sea:

☀ *I'm officially obsessed with this column and all things lobstering. Please let me live on your boat.*

☀ *Achievement unlocked: whole new level of optimism*

☀ *Is it wrong I want a Sea Raven for a pet?*

☀ *Hang on. Is C.P. telling us to wait for our one in one million, or is she writing about a one in a million in her life? Any True Love podcasters out there?*

☀ *There are different colored lobsters!???!*

☀ *"Hold out for the 1 in 100 million." Pah-reach.*

☀ *where have lobsters been all my life?*

☆ *how are lobsters and lobstermen this amazing?*

I bark laugh at the troll comments telling readers how we can make four thousand dollars a week by just doing THIS ONE THING. And how we should all be watching episode five of a show I've never heard of. Still, there's the fervent readers who not only relate to my words, but have been inspired toward bravery:

☆ *A NEW MAN IN HER KITCHEN!!!!!!!!!! MEOW!*
☆ *This post gave me the courage to invite someone new to my kitchen! Hoping she stays!*

And:

☆ *Face pee is nasty. And I'm kind of down for this advice.*
☆ *Solid relationship guidance: don't pee in people's faces.*

I'm humbled by:

☆ *we literally don't deserve how wise this is:*
   "Not every lobster is a keeper.
   Not every person a good fit.
   Timing and care matter."
☆ *Sus. Were lobsters created solely to serve as the perfect analogy for lessons in love?*

And grateful for:

☆ *Rigid creatures. Hard shells. Solitary life. Sounds super sad. Girl, you need a date!*
☆ *females!!! all the power!*
☆ *I cannot unread that lobsters have to wriggle out of their own teeth!!!*
☆ *Anyone else think our author might have a love interest she's softening her shell for?*
☆ *you had me at: FEMALES HAVE ALL THE POWER*
☆ *bro sees her creepin outside his den*
☆ *Shedding all my armor for a work friend—ready to risk it all, friend!*
☆ *#dietgoals #half my size*
☆ *Females having all the power should be a thing.*

Even here, love is everywhere.

Maia's words revisit, reminding me I'm not special. All love is risk worth taking.

I toggle over to the DM room wishing I were better at apologies and communication and all of it. But I'm not. I'm me. Singularly me in a messy package that Logan sees and wants.

> @BirdieBlueBug
> Will you fish with me tomorrow?

I wait for a response that doesn't come.

> @BirdieBlueBug
> It'll just be a fishing trip.

> @BirdieBlueBug
> Baby steps.

When I chew my thumbnail so low it stings, I slam my laptop closed and go to my window that faces Maia's to flash F-O-R-G-I-V-E? with the light in my shadeless lamp. It's the same request Logan made of me, the same request I want to make of everyone I've hurt.

A-L-W-A-Y-S! arrives in a series of long and short signals of light. I'm hugging the dumb lamp close to my chest when Maia calls. "I'm coming over. And I'm bringing cake," she says.

We fall heavily onto my bed after gorging on sugar and apologies. Our limbs twist together like when we painted each other's faces with make-up the summer we prepared for middle school, or when we tried to keep the room from spinning after too much stolen vodka in high school. She holds my palm at the side of her belly, over the place where her baby kicks.

"It is literally incredible that women grow humans." A punch rockets against her flesh and I feel the push on my palm, Baby's first high five. "I feel like this power is all anyone should ever be talking about."

"How women are goddesses?"

"Yes, exactly. I mean, you are making a human body *inside* your body."

"I'm aware." She laughs.

"I know, but it's badass. Women should be worshipped for this power on the regular."

"Why do you think I keep Sam around?"

"Ha!" I'm so happy to be in my own kind of womb with Maia at my side that I almost don't hear the knock, the kitchen door opening, a voice throwing a searching *hello?* into the house.

Maia and I meet Logan at the kitchen entrance, the door shut behind him, an unreadable look on his face. "Is it okay I came inside?"

"God, yes." Maia kisses me on the cheek. "I'll disappear and give you two a beat."

"Hey," he says.

"Hi."

"How are you?"

"A mess, obviously." I wave at the table, my movements gawky. "Do you want to sit? Have coffee?"

He laughs.

"What's funny?" Why must self-doubt creep in so quickly?

"I guess I expected you to offer me hot chocolate."

I smile. "It really is the only thing I can cook."

"I didn't come here for you to wait on me. I came here to say yes to your offer to fish."

"Oh! Good, great."

He takes one step closer, the table a hard ocean between us. "And to tell you I'm sorry."

I move closer, my hands grabbing for purchase on the chair's high finials. "I'm the one that needs to apologize. I shouldn't have pushed you away like I did. You deserve better."

"I don't want anything better or different. I just want a chance with you. It kills me that I might have hurt you. And maybe I don't deserve another chance but I'm asking for one."

Logan is all risk right now. Doing the hard thing: putting his feelings out there, knowing my response could crush him.

"I think I want to give you all the chances," I say, "if you'll let me."

He moves across the kitchen so quickly it steals my breath. His body is so close, his stare on top of mine.

"Good. Because I don't want to take it slow with you, Charlie."

He lifts me onto the table and my legs instinctively wrap around his hips. He leans in to kiss me but hovers his lips to mine as we watch one another, our breath rising and quickening, my chest filling with anticipation. When he kisses me, I can't get enough of his mouth, the sweet taste of him, the way he pins down my thighs with his palms. When he stops, my head spins.

"I'm all in, Charlie," he whispers in my ear. "Meet me here."

"Yeah." I'm breathless as he leaves, letting himself out as a blast of cold air shakes me from my stupor.

"You two make up?" Maia asks, returning at the sound of the door closing.

I nod. "How much did you hear?"

"I heard him basically apologize for your feelings so he seems like a keeper."

"Is that a lobster fishing reference?"

"If you need it to be."

I don't know what I need, except I do.

"I need you to never be mad at me again," I tell her. "My life is shit without you."

"Same. Just promise to be kinder to yourself. Romantic love isn't the enemy, Charlotte Pinkham."

She grabs a gallon of locally crafted mint chip ice cream from the freezer, and pops the top as she takes a seat at the table. After her first bite, she points her spoon at me. "You know, you might actually like giving over control. Especially to a hot slice of man like Logan."

"Maybe," I say, knowing Maia hasn't been wrong yet.

29

The Control

Logan meets me at the boat the next morning with a hardy "Hey."

"Good morning," I say to his face curled into a smile that floats all the way to his eyes as if he's got a secret, even if he gets right to work, untying my lines, and setting the boat free from the dock.

From his seat in the wheelhouse, he studies me and I do my best to focus on the horizon and my instrument panel but it's hard when his sly smile is everywhere. When Cove Light is far behind us, he nudges forward in his seat, then stands so close I feel his breath on my cheek.

"Cut the engine," he whispers into my ear, and I do.

He turns me to him, my legs on either side of his. "I want a redo."

I laugh, even as my thighs sense this is no laughing matter.

He threads one finger under each suspender of my overalls, his controlled touch humming over my breasts as he peels the straps down.

"I know the boat is your territory, but I'd like to show you how the other night should have gone down." He kisses my neck softly just below my ear. I twist into him. "Would that be okay?"

"Mm hmm," I manage.

"Excellent. Because you deserve my full attention." He kisses my jaw, stopping only to let his teeth tug at my bottom lip. "I shouldn't have asked you to slow down."

"No?"

"No." His grip tightens to a fist around my suspenders, and he uses the tautness to pull me to him. Hard and with purpose, pinning my arms at my sides. "I was trying to protect myself, protect us." He leaves a kiss at the arch of one eyebrow, then the other. "But the thing is, Charlie, we can keep trying to protect ourselves or we can jump in." His hand comes to my neck, and he turns my mouth up for him. "Because I want you," he says. "All of you. No more waiting. No more headiness and fear getting in the way."

I nod, breathless, the boat rocking us even as he's steady against me.

"What if we put all our hesitations to the side and trusted our attraction?" A fleeting kiss lands on my lips before fluttering away.

My body aches to connect with his, for his hands to touch me, for me to be bold enough to touch him.

"Female lobsters make the first move when coupling," I tell him.

He kisses my neck, nudging my fleece to find my collarbone with his soft lips. "Then make it now. As long as your first move is to give me permission."

"Yes," I breathe.

Time seems to slow and stand still, our bodies hovering in a promise that is all risk and intoxication. When his one finger finds my side, his touch traces a line over my arm, along my ribs, dipping into the hollow of my side stomach before it reaches into my overalls where he lifts me off my seat, gripping my bottom with the full plate of his hand.

"God you're beautiful." He tugs me closer. "Just in case there was any doubt about my attraction to you or my ability to stay awake in your presence."

My hips push against his, my body giving permission for his hands to slide along my stomach and lower back, bracing me, anchoring me, yanking me to him so that his mouth gets lost in my neck for so long I'm sure I'll die from an overdose of ecstasy and the thrill of giving over control.

He twists me onto his lap so my legs straddle him the way they did on the loveseat, my arms wrapped at his neck, my fingers exploring the hard lines of his upper back. He jerks my hips toward his, a rush of heat surging inside me as he twists the strap of my overalls before sliding it slowly over the heel of my shoulder that rounds for him, drawing inward to make space for the strap to fall away, for more of my body to be exposed, for his mouth to find all of me.

"Is this okay?" he whispers onto my neck.

I nod, a breathy *yes* escaping my lips.

"Good." He meets my eyes. "Because it's just a boat ride."

"Baby steps," I say, my body melting toward his.

Logan trains his eyes on mine as he gathers my shirt at the waist, pooling the fabric into itself before he inches the material slowly over my quaking stomach...then the rise of my breasts...until the roll of cotton covers my head, obscuring my vision. He holds me in blindness and arousal and surrender for a feast of moments before he frees my shirt and my breath. Cold washes into the cabin through the seams of the door, its chilling intrusion prickling my flesh, forcing tiny bumps to rise on my skin as if its Logan's breath making my flesh rise everywhere and all at once.

He scans my exposed skin for an eternity as if mapping me, committing my curves to memory. When his eyes meet mine again, a hard wave of want pulses beneath my skin, tightening my pelvis, slicking the softest parts of me as I push myself against him. Logan is quick to remove my sports bra and it's a thrill to be half naked in full nature, my bare chest meeting the waking dawn.

"I have a theory," he whispers from the space between my breasts, his voice low and dark and filled with want. He hikes my hips tight with his. "If we keep our bodies this close there won't be any room for misunderstandings to find their way between us again."

"This feels like a solid theory."

"I'll have to test it, of course. Data points are my specialty."

I feel his expertise in his unyielding exploration of my body with his fingers, his tongue, the way he spreads me back along the seat with the skate of his open palm, pushing me into place as he brands me with the scent of him. I can barely breathe because he is reaching all my points, gathering my data as his tongue and his fingers drive me to the edge, taunting me as the sea moves beneath us, its waves rising and falling, churning and pushing, his touch filling me with a wave of heat that builds inside of me until there is no more room for it and everything I am crashes out of me with a cry that drowns out all other noise, his voice steadying over the whispered word *yes* as he pulls a long, slick *sssss* across length of my orgasm.

After, he gathers my spent body onto the hammock of his lap and kisses my face, my neck—his lips finding the fold behind my ear, his tongue caressing the fleshy part of my lobe where his teeth come together in a playful bite.

"Best start to the day ever," he says at my ear.

The breath in me rebuilds as I gather strength. "Maybe for me more than you."

"Don't count on it."

I bury my face against his neck. "I've had fantasies about you on this boat, but nothing like that."

"Huh."

"Yeah." The word is a push of breath, the full giving over of control. "Real Logan is way hotter than fantasy Logan, if you're wondering."

"That's a relief. I've heard it's usually the other way around. Not for me, specifically," he rushes to clarify. "But in general. I mean, right? Isn't it widely held knowledge that the fantasy of someone is always better than the reality? I'm talking too much, aren't I?"

"Yes."

"Did I talk in your fantasies?"

"No."

"Excellent." He kisses my shoulder. "So, wait. What was I doing if I wasn't talking?"

I love how his vulnerability's returning after such a beautiful show of strength.

"You prefer to be shirtless in my daydreams that often morph into calendar photos where you're mostly bending over things. Hauling traps. Wearing your Grundens."

"Orange waterproof coveralls?"

"Yup." My p pops. "Once, you made an appearance as a very studious professor at an ivy league desk doing professorly things while wearing nothing but wire-rimmed glasses."

"And that worked for you?"

"It all worked."

"Huh."

I pinch the material at his hip. "My fantasies like you in these overalls."

"These are all very, very excellent data points."

~ ~ ~

When I gather my senses enough to meet our first string, we pull the pots in our practiced way and strap them to the deck. He tells me he's sad not to fish anymore, and I tell him it's always best to end the season on a high note.

"Was today a high note?" he asks at the rail.

"The highest."

Over lunch he explains there were four Logans working at Maine's Midcoast Lobstermen Association when he started volunteering.

"It felt easier to go by my middle name. Reduce confusion. See? Not the most riveting story."

But it is. Like everything he shares, this is one more piece of Logan falling into place, the fullness of this man's life filling out like a puzzle taking shape, one fragment at a time.

"And the dog in your Instagram pictures?"

A smile lights his face as a high wave curls against the side of the boat. "Scooby."

"Scooby?"

"Scoobs is the best. Man, I miss him. He's been on a dog party bender with my friend's dogs for the month. I'll be lucky if he even recognizes me when I get back."

Back. To his normal life. A life without me. And I try to make that okay because he's here now and that's enough.

"I don't want any more confusion with you, Charlie. If you have a question, ask it. I mean it."

"I do have one question. A pondering, really."

"Excellent callback." He reaches for my hand, caresses the ridges of my knuckles with his thumb. "What's your pondering?"

"That thing you did this morning. Is that legal to do twice a day? Asking for a friend."

Logan's eyes turn dark and he releases my hand, putting one finger to my chest, pushing me inside the pilot house until my back reaches the console where I pull him closer. We kiss hungrily and surrender to the floor in the cramped space between the two seats, Logan securing softness around us with emergency blankets as he strips layers off of me hungrily, studying my fully bare skin in the full winter sunlight. He sits back, grabs my foot, kissing the arch, the mound of my calf, the hill of my knee, climbing up my thigh until his mouth lands in the pulsing middle of me, my hips rising to meet him, his touch, his tenderness, his hunger.

By the time we see land, my body's floating somewhere between spent and ravenous, a dreamy state I can't hide from Maia when she welcomes me on the VHF, tells me to meet her and Mem at Earl's solo so we can review eleventh hour wedding plans. I drop Logan and my traps at the dock and unload my final catch to the holding tanks.

When I arrive inside the diner, Maia's quick smile rises with a knowing laugh. "Good day at sea?"

"Don't go jinxing a good day at sea." Mem's hand rubs at my shoulder.

"Yeah, Maia," I tease.

Maia shakes her head at me, her side eye smirk endless as we tie up final logistics for Mem's wedding that's arriving in less than twenty-four hours: the potluck food, Casey and Lillie as pine cone girls, the pacing of the ceremony, guest list and more.

When Mem's had enough of our fussing, she retreats to a booth at the back to snuggle with Hermon where he's organizing receipts from the day.

Maia slides close to me on the booth. "You did it today, didn't you? You've got sex face."

"Not sex face."

"Liar."

"Not lying."

Maia eyes me.

My smile curls. "We did lots and lots and lots of other stuff."

"Hell, yeah." She leans back, crossing her arms onto her belly. "Charlotte Pinkham, sex kitten of the high seas. Would it be wrong of me to want to capitalize on this moment to ask you for one final blog post before Christmas?"

"Sure." There's an easy shrug in my shoulders. "Whatever you need."

"*Damn,* girl."

"You have no idea." I gather my coat and deliver my goodbye to Mem, asking Hermon: "Isn't it bad luck to see the bride before the wedding night?"

"Only thing bad between us was staying apart for too long," Memma tells me.

When I get home, I go straight to my laptop, where Logan is waiting for me.

> @toothpicks3478
> I can still taste you.

> @BirdieBlueBug
> I can still feel you on me.

> @BirdieBlueBug
> Come over.

Logan is at my door within seconds, his hair ruffled, one sneaker untied, the laces wet with slush. "I waited as long as I could," he says, and I laugh, inviting him inside. "I'd let you take my coat, but as you can see, I was unable to manage basic self-maintenance after your offer arrived."

"Your disheveledness pleases me."

He kisses me and his nose is frozen from the short commute. I take his hand and walk him to my room where I invite him out of his fleece, then his Henley, my fingers exploring the ridges of him, investigating the band of flesh under his belt before I loosen his buckle, popping one, two and then three buttons open from his jeans, allowing them to drop to the floor. I sit him to the bed, peal his pants free. I pull the covers over us and his arm wraps around me.

"Stay for a sleepover?" I ask.

"I wouldn't want to be anywhere else." His legs link into mine and my head rests at his chest where his heartbeat drums.

"Would it be weird if I worked on something on my computer during our sleepover?" I ask.

"Are you going to DM me?"

I laugh, fetching my laptop from the side table before returning my body to Logan's. "I want to read over my speech for Mem's wedding one more time, and I owe Maia my last blog post."

Logan sits straighter, eyeing my laptop. "Is that how you get to our DM room?"

"It is." My palm smooth over my computer's cover as I settle it onto my thighs.

"Were you in bed when you wrote me?"

I look around, remembering. "Almost always."

"This is another very good data point, Charlie. Though I'm having a hard time picturing you as a blogger."

"Definitely not a blogger. I wrote a few posts for Maia—"

"Ah! This is what you were talking about in our DMs? Your sophomore slump?"

"How could you possibly piece that together?"

"Anyone paying attention would make the connection."

Huh.

He pulls my hand to his mouth, kisses my open palm. "What do you write about?"

"Lobsters."

"Ah."

"And love."

"Well. Now I have to read these posts. For research, of course."

"Not happening." I snuggle deeper against Logan, opening my reading for Mem. Logan scrolls through his phone and its blue light shines onto his chin and chest in a way I try very hard to ignore.

When I've edited my words for Maia so many times, I end up exactly where I started, I close my laptop with a soft snap.

"Time for sleep?" Logan asks, clicking off his phone.

"For some reason, I'm exhausted." I fake a yawn that is only half-fake, and turn out the light.

"Charlie," Logan whispers, folding me into his arms, his body wrapping mine, his lips brushing hair from my neck to make space for his words to reach my ear. Softly. Gently. "If I'd known about your love and lobsters column, I would have consumed your writing long before tonight."

I burrow deeper against his neckline, suddenly bashful. "You read my posts?"

"All while sitting in bed next to the fierce, phenomenal author." His finger caresses the round of my bare shoulder.

"And?" My eyes squeeze shut.

"And I wish I'd known about your writing sooner." Then I would've had three places to fall for you." He turns me on my side, so the length of him is behind me, his breath at my hairline. "Here." He pulls me against the shape of him. "In our DM rooms." He bites softly at my neck. "And in your column." He raises his knee behind my knees, jackknifing us closer. "I've been hungry for you since the day I met you. I'm here with you and still need a thousand years to satisfy my appetite for you."

"Maybe *you* should write a romance column."

"Maybe you could read me your posts someday. I want to see your face and hear your voice while you read about love."

"And lobsters."

"Of course."

Maybe it's the dark making me bold, telling me it's okay to want him to watch me read. But who can give all that to another person?

"Never."

"Then at least tell me what the next post will say."

I bite my lip. "Don't know," I lie. "It's a work in progress."

30

The Commitment

The smell of hot chocolate meets me the next morning as Logan sets a mug to my bedside table trying hard not to complain about his toes nearly freezing off from his walk to the kitchen and back. He warms the soles of his feet against the heat of my inner thigh. While we're slow and waking, I think I could get used to this. His closeness. The beat of his heart against my ear. The ease of comfort that has always pulsed around us, neither of us needing to fill the air with sound. Logan, as mine. It's a dangerous fantasy to fall into so I steady my expectations. Already steeling for check-out day.

We watch each other's bodies as we dress in the morning light, and when he kisses me goodbye his hand sweeps my hair into a low ponytail. "Is it corny to say I miss you already?"

"Yes."

"Then I'll apologize now for being cliché because I miss you already."

"Same."

~ ~ ~

Mem's already at Maia's when I arrive for my shower and blowout. She's fidgeting, eager to get on with the ceremony already. Some small part of me wonders if there's a small part of her that worries Hermon won't show up. Can a person ever truly trust another person? Because another person is always their own person, capable of independent decisions and plans and thoughts that could open another to hurt. I shake off the thought.

Maia sets out a deep tray of water to soak Mem's feet and my grandmother relaxes deeper into the chair, her shoulders softening. Maia washes my hair first, over the sink, her fingers massaging the ridges of my scalp as she applies pressure in circles that grow larger as they repeat. When I sit up, I'm fully relaxed for my blowout that seems to leave me with twice as much hair.

Sam covertly delivers mini-cubes of cantaloupe and watermelon to the hallway like he's room service and we're hotel guests, but his cultivated deference provides space for me, Mem, and Maia to exist in a world all our own, a calm before the storm of ceremony and change.

Maia styles Mem's hair with a string of pine needle garland placed like a crown, a small sprig of elderberries gathered at the back. Mem gushes in the mirror at her natural tiara, her fingers lifting carefully to Maia's art. Together, we slip Mem into her simple white sweater and Maia helps Mem step into a white eyelet skirt, full as a sail.

Mem gasps, her hand flying to her mouth. My steadying grip arrives at her elbow as we see the squares of fabric Maia's added to the skirt's folds, into which Maia has sewn Mem's life.

"Charlie's christening cap," Maia tells us, rubbing at the lace at Mem's hip.

"A cloth napkin from when Earl's Eats opened in 1937." The small red lobster of the logo is soft pink now, the color faded to time.

"And here." Maia's fingers trace a block of faded navy yarn, the tight moss stitch so much like Mem's favorite knitting pattern. "This was provided by Mason Glidden, a piece of the blanket your mother stitched for his great-grandmother during the lean years of the Depression. Not that his family will call it that, even now, thanks to how much the women in your family helped his."

Mem's eyes fill with tears and I pass her tissues, grabbing a few for myself. "Oh, Maia." Mem's voice is choked with gratitude as my own tears spill over, a tide of love washing over us, through us.

"And here," Maia says. "Is a picture my children drew for their great-grandmother. You might not be ours by blood, Mem, but you're family." Scratches of reds and pinks cover a swatch. "It's a stick figure dog. And a tree, I think. I have no idea why."

"Maia." My word is a whisper. Mem is speechless.

"This one's my contribution." Maia pinches a square of fabric at Mem's knee, a swatch of silk embroidered with Mem's birth date, my father's birth date, my birth date. Today's date.

My chest hiccups with the hard push of pure love and I hug Maia from behind, careful with the soft middle of her, the way she's always been so careful with my heart.

"Get all your crying out now, ladies," Maia says, hiccupping over a sob. "Makeup is next. Oh! I made one last thing." She extracts an azure blue garter belt from a box on her dresser, stretching the silky fabric across her fingers so I see the canary yellow in it, our family's fishing colors. The material is old, weather beaten but still bright. "I made it from the buoy flags your dad used," Maia tells me. She hands the garter to Mem. "Something old, something new, something blue, something borrowed—all in one fell swoop so you don't worry anyone's making a fuss over you."

Mem places the fabric to her cheek, drawing Dad close. "If this is a fuss, then I'm not convinced I want it to stop."

"Luckily you've picked a fine man who'll fuss over you for as long as you let him," Maia tells her.

My eyes are so full when I answer the door to Sam's knock that he's blurry as he passes me a tray of mimosas and finger sandwiches.

"Keep it together, Charlie," he whispers. "It's not your wedding."

Sam winks, just as Maia yells, "Not yet, anyway!" from across the room, and a laugh pops from deep inside me for this family's ridiculous hearing.

Sam leans in to deposit a kiss on my cheek and squeezes my elbow with a quick pump. "I'm proud of you." His whisper lowers. "Letting go of a woman like your mem isn't easy. I've got two decades to prepare for this day with my girls and it still won't be enough time."

And I don't doubt it. As much as Sam is present for every minute of his children's youth, he must worry about the horizon, the world we're leaving for them, the people they'll choose to walk beside in their journeys. It's a lot. And I feel it, too. Like my whole human experience is too big for its shell sometimes.

Maia is next level at applying our make-up as we eat and laugh with such ease that we're all surprised when Sam knocks with our two o'clock warning. "Can Lil and Casey visit?"

The girls don't wait for Maia's invitation. They peel inside, Casey's mouth falling open. "Aunt Chawlie! You wook like Misses Cwaus."

Gathering the red velvet fabric at my thighs, I do my best curtsy to Casey and her compliment. Underneath my strapless, empire waist dress is the long-sleeved white yoga top Maia lent me, along with white leggings, as snug as a second skin. At my neck is a white choker, my brown hair blown so thick and full it rivals Maia's mane. Mem wears the same white choker, her brooch in the front, her simple silver drop earrings dangling to meet her proud shoulders.

Maia's girls gather to her thighs, one on either side.

"You all look beautiful," Sam tells us.

"Are you ready to become little fashionistas in your dresses?" Maia asks her daughters.

"Yes, Mommy!" and "Oh, goodie!" serenade Maia as she leads them back to Sam, planting kisses to their eager lips. "Daddy's got a surprise if you follow him."

"Is it a unicorn?" Casey shouts as she leaves.

"Almost time," Mem tells me after Maia quickly pins the hem on Mem's skirt. "Come closer, Charlie." Mem holds my forearms. "You are a beautiful person, Charlie. My favorite person. And I can honestly say that you have never looked more stunning than in this moment. Your dad would mistake today as your wedding, and he'd be boasting about the quality of his kin, because you, Charlie, are the finest person I've known in my long life and you've made an old woman proud to live to be an old woman. Watching you and Maia grow has been my biggest accomplishment. My greatest joy. Now help me get into a coat and over to that common so you can marry me off already."

"Done," I say, my chuckle mostly made of tears.

Sam escorts us into the car and Casey and Lillie wriggle with the anticipation of Christmas arriving early. When we unload at the common, Haggard has four fires burning in the ceremony circle made sacred by the ring of spruce trees.

"One in every cardinal direction, the rocks carried here by families from the peninsula," Haggard tells us. He points toward a short red rug. "Here's a ceremonial place for you to stand, Charles. I thought it was fitting for the couple to face true north." He twists, boxing out a space with his arms unstretched. "And here's where your mem and Hermon would be when they say their vows, but you can adjust if you want. It's not centered on the harbor exactly."

It's not. The harbor will be on one side, the town on the other. True north faces the middle bend of the harbor, the place where the earth gives way to water, mating to form a coastline.

"It's perfect, Haggard."

He rolls out a pastel quilt to serve as a rug where Mem and Hermon will stand to exchange their forevers.

"Do you need a stand?" Haggard asks. "For papers or anything? I borrowed one from the music room at the high school."

"I'm good. It's all up here." I point to my head, even though my words were born in my heart.

While I wait for Mem, I'm surrounded by spruce trees strung with white lights and berry garland, protected by the harbor and warmed by the fires built by neighbors. It's hard to make sense of all the moments that brought us here but I can smell change in the dry, winter air, like a new season arriving. Not the promise of spring or the dying back of fall or even the fertility of summer. This new season feels wholly different and deserved, like love and romance. A timeless and timely shift.

When Hermon joins me, he's looking handsome and not the least bit nervous in his long, black overcoat and top hat from another century. A wide red scarf sits snug at his neck.

"Ready?" I ask.

"*Ayuh.*"

I smile, and catch a glimpse of Logan's face above the gathered, standing crowd. He stares in my direction as if the trees and decorations and warming fires are nothing compared to me, in front of him, on display. I shiver from the memory of him in my bed, still fresh in my mind. He throws a half smile that turns dark and bold and makes me shift in my clunky boots, my toes pointing toward him.

From somewhere beyond the trees, a guitar's song rises, and Maia's daughters appear dressed in thick red coats, their faces concentrated on the task of tossing cedar wood chips, red berries, and loose pine needles to the snow aisle from their swinging baskets until they see their dad and run into his arms. Maia appears next, Mem beside her. My breath stutters.

Mem is cloud-like and ethereal in her white jacket and her white eyelet skirt that glides over the snowy ground. Her gaze fixes on Hermon as she takes one step, then another, walking to me even as her life detours from mine, the love and loss twisting my heart. But when it's only me and Mem and Hermon in a triangle in front of our community—surrounded by the sea and our cottage and the common and Earl's Eats, the species of tree my father loved above all forest trees, the waves lapping at the shore as fire warms us—the union feels right.

Hermon takes Mem's hand. "Get on with it, Charlie. I'm not waitin' another minute for this fine woman."

I laugh, and settle easily into my speech because saying what I want to say is as instinctive and necessary as breathing.

Straightening my shoulders, I'm buoyed by the ocean behind me, Mem in front of me.

"When tourists visit our part of the world, they're quickly mesmerized by Maine's coastal waters. It's easy to see why, because the sea is ever-changing and responsive, engaged always in a delicate dance with the moon. But for those of us who live here, we honor and respect the granite ledge along our shores just the same. The granite in these parts is lined. Grooved. Because it has endured. It serves to hold up islands and act as the foundation for our homes. Granite is strong. Always unique. Ever-present.

"This is how I think of my grandmother, my mem. A woman I've seen withstand storms with grace, anchor others when currents raged, provide shelter for those who needed rest, and offer care after the squalls receded. I'm not certain how I got to be the soft thing at the center of this elegant rock's world, but I've always been sure I didn't want to give her away. After all, granite is fixed. Forever.

"That changes today. Today, I share her with Hermon, a sturdy rock of a Maine-built man, born of the same enduring grit, a man who loves my mem with infinite intensity, and a heart that's big enough to welcome us both.

"Mem, do you take Hermon Benner to be your rock? To stand beside you, endure alongside you, cherish your beauty and uniqueness?"

"*Ayuh,*" she says, and those gathered close let out a collective laugh as pride swells in me for the sense of humor my mem gifted me, no different than my capable shoulders, wide eyes, and careful heart.

"And Hermon. Do you take an oath today to cherish my mem, Anne Alice Pinkham, for how she is both granite and ocean? Are you committed to honoring all her undiscovered depths and the bounty she brings forth?"

"With all my heart," Hermon says, and my own heart skips for him, toward him.

"Then I feel privileged to be the first to call you wife and husband, Mrs. and Mr. Pinkham Benner, Queen and King of Earl's Eats, the luckiest people this planet has protected."

Hermon bends Mem in an old-fashioned dip and plants a dramatic kiss on her lips to the delight of the cheering crowd. Music rolls in, and clapping joins, the attendees sweeping in movement behind the married couple as they head into Earl's for a toast and the joy that awaits.

Mem's love feels like a Happily Ever After and a Happily Ever Now and a Happily Ever Yesterday as she joins Hermon in their happily ever forever, their bodies leaning toward one another as if by magnetic attraction. And as the crowd moves and morphs, synchronized as a school of fish, one person stands alone for me.

Logan.

He's wearing his cable knit fishing sweater and a new set of orange overalls, a black bow tie secured at his neck. His wingtips are here, too. His gaze hangs on me, committed and unchanged as he makes his way toward me, gathering my hands in his. "Hi," he says.

"Nice uniform."

His smile curls. "I've heard it works for you."

"The rumors are not wrong."

Logan spreads my arms like wings, taking in the long expanse of my limbs he's seen at work on the ocean so many times. The toes of my sensible boots. Then, my middle, wrapped in the velvet strapless dress cinched simply with a white ribbon. "This color on you, Charlie." He twirls me once, slowly, taking me in. "The way the light shifts over your skin and dress. You're magnificent. Like one in one hundred million."

31

The Coitus

We spend the hours after the ceremony in the night and the light, moving in and out of Earl's Eats as games and conversation and laughter spill us into all corners of the common, toasts coming quickly and often, an entire village delighting in the idea of love.

Logan watches me from across the common where he's chatting with Sam and Haggard, each of the men holding one of Maia's daughters.

"Time to get the minions home," Maia tells me. "Mama's exhausted."

"You pulled off the extraordinary and deserve all the rest," I tell her.

"I might be the only one to get any." She nods at Logan with his dark stare trained on me, his gaze unshifting as he walks toward us. Maia takes Lillie onto her side and we exchange kisses and goodnights.

Logan places his two fingers to my hip and leans in close to my ear, whispering, "Take me home."

Maia hugs me goodbye. "I heard that," she says.

"Stop it. You did not."

She raises her eyebrows and Logan takes up the space she makes when she leaves, his hand arriving at the small of my back.

"I'm going to say goodnight to your grandmother and Hermon," he tells me. "Suddenly, I'm really, very tired." The energy in his voice is the opposite of tired.

We make our goodbyes that feel too big and too quick so I don't say goodbye to Mem, only: "I'll see you tomorrow. And tomorrow's tomorrow."

"Goodnight, Charlie girl," she says, as if she's in the doorway to my room, her hand on the light.

~ ~ ~

The cottage is cold when we arrive home, and Logan makes a fire as he tells me Hannah didn't feel comfortable attending the intimate wedding, but she'll be with the village tomorrow, celebrating the solstice, helping with lighthouse tours as needed.

"Is it okay I'm here?" Logan comes to me, his hands at my waist.

I nod. In truth, I'd be anywhere with him right now. The pilot house of my boat, the back of a car, the aisle of a grocery store, in line at the registry of motor vehicles. Just to be near him. Nothing more needs to happen than his hands at my hips and the intentness of his gaze right here, right now.

But I'm not sad when he dips down to find my mouth, his kiss tender and searching, his lips playing with mine, drawing them up and close and connected to the push of his breath. Restraint ripples in his shoulders and I'm ravenous to know the feel of him ripped open, unanchored, free to let his body know mine in a language new to us both. He takes my hand, leads me to the fire where the heat laps at my side. His finger runs along the top of my dress, skirting over the one-piece and under the velvet. My chest rises for him.

"Can we sit?" he asks.

"Here?"

"Right here."

"Of course. Let me get a blanket."

"No." He puts his lips to mine. "Stay right here." His finger trails the length of my spine from between my shoulders to my bottom and I don't move. Not one inch.

Logan returns with the comforter from my bed, the pillows, too. He makes a lumpy picnic blanket and stands to survey his work, his hands on his hips just before they pull off his sweater because the fire is hot now. His crisp white T-shirt and bow tie are like a garnish for his orange overalls, which secure his place in November.

"We don't allow fishing gear in the house, although this"—I tug at his bowtie—"is all working as a very, very sexy calendar photo. I slip the straps from his shoulders, one by one, his breath stuttering when my hands meet his waist and smooth onto his bottom, guiding the fishing overalls to the floor where he steps free, kicking them to the side.

"No fishing gear in the house is a very good rule," he tells me while watching me stare at his body, my breath shallow. He inches closer. "I want this off." He flicks at the collar of the yoga top.

I squirm and pull the sides of the shirt up from underneath my velvet dress. He tugs the fabric over my head. His attention glides over my exposed collarbone, his fingers following. He bends before me and hikes up my dress. Slowly. The wave of soft fabric brushes over my ankles, my knees, my bottom. He finds the waist of my leggings and tugs them lower, waking fire on my skin, under my skin.

He stands back to see me in the dress, naked underneath except for my underwear. I am flesh and velvet and wrapped for him. He comes to me so his fists can gather the material of my skirt until my dress is bunched at my waist. He lifts me to his middle, balancing me across his thighs. My legs lock around him as my arms explore the tight, round bulge of his triceps, his whole body taut for me. He lays me down on the makeshift bed of pillows.

His knee pushes between mine, nudging my legs open, my body making space for him as his leg inches higher. He props himself over me, his fingers exploring the places of my body that don't care if he's staying or leaving because I have never been so present as I am right now, my whole being awake, alive, ready.

"Do you want this, Charlie? Tell me."

"I want this."

"That's a declarative sentence." His half-smile lifts to his eyes.

"Really? A grammar lesson?" I'm breathless and hot as I push at his chest so that he rolls off of me and I straddle him. "Actually, I feel like that's the right call."

He sits up so that our bodies meet, our hands hammocked at the small of each other's backs. "I want you to know I'm rocked by you. Here, now. In the DM room. The feel of you on me. The idea of you. The reality of you." His thumb caresses my bottom lip.

"Then be with me."

He gives a soft shake of his head. "I have one condition."

"Anything." I am built of breath and desire.

He trails kisses up the length of my neck. "Read me your last blog post." His voice soft, hovering at my ear.

"What?" I push his chest away. "You're ridiculous."

His smile grows, playful and wide until his stare morphs into something dark and wanting. "Please."

The one word is enough for me to do anything. Almost.

"I can't."

"You're doing that thing you do when you withdraw to think things through. Tell me what you're thinking."

"It's too much. If we are together…you know."

"If we have sex."

"Yes," I say.

"It will be incredible."

"Yes, but reading to you before that will make me too vulnerable."

"More vulnerable than sex?"

"Not more. But yeah, more. Then you'll have my body and my words and *my voice* reading my words to you. That feels like too much to give when you're leaving."

"Am I going somewhere?"

"Not now, but you will."

"Why?"

"Because you live in Rhode Island."

He holds my gaze. "Why would you think I live in Rhode Island?" His palms curl around my lower back as I sit up straighter.

"You and Hannah live in Rhode Island. You have the same address."

"Technically, but only because I'm the executor to my mother's will. I grew up there, but I live in Maine, Charlie. Inland Maine, but still. My business is in Portland and I just sold my place to be closer to the city." His fingers draw a line down my spine. "So technically my belongings live in storage while I live in your lighthouse."

"That's impossible."

He lets out a laugh. "Not impossible. I told you this."

"Um, no. You didn't."

"I did. Back when I had to go to Augusta for some legal work."

"I figured it was…I don't know, a local office to help you with whatever you'd started in Rhode Island."

He leans back on his elbows now. He clocks me with his dark eyes, a grin forming in that beautiful bottom lip. "But what about the fact that I handle social media for Maine's Midcoast Lobstermen Association?"

"I guess I didn't actually think about that." My head spins. Because maybe on some level I did know. I saw the clues and ignored them. Telling myself he'd leave so I didn't risk becoming vulnerable.

"My Insta handle is 3478, Charlie. The number of miles in Maine's coastline. It was our first conversation."

"You remember that?"

"I remember everything."

"So, you're not leaving the state?"

"Not leaving," he says, drawing his body up against mine. "I have Maine plates on my car. That must have been a clue."

"Wait. Out of Africa is your car?"

He laughs. "Out of Africa?"

"The safari mobile. Maia saw it arrive, but thought it was a delivery."

"Geez. A guy can't get away with anything on this peninsula."

"It's a problem."

"Not for me." He kisses my collarbone, a place I never knew needed to be kissed until now. "I drove Hannah's car here from Rhode Island and she flew into Augusta, getting a rental car."

"With Maine plates."

"Exactly. I returned the rental and drove back with one of my conversions."

"Wait. The safari mobile is electric?"

"Technically, it's an electric Land Rover, but yes."

Rebuilding a car? Making something new from something old? It feels impossible to be more impressed by him and yet I'm hungry with curiosity to know everything about him. Then, a seal bark laugh leaps out of me and I drop my head to his chest.

"What's so funny?" He pulls up my chin so I meet his eyes.

"Haggard told me the answers to my questions about you could be found in your license plates and he wasn't wrong."

"You had questions about me?" His eyes flicker in the firelight.

"I had…, like one question."

"And you asked Haggard?"

"I might have mentioned you offhandedly."

"All while I thought you were dating Haggard?"

"Still not dating Haggard."

"This is a good thing." He flicks a look over the length of my body. "Do you have any more questions about where I live or where I'm from?"

"If I did, I wouldn't ask them."

"Why not?"

"Because that smirk on your face is out of control."

"Yeah, well." His smile deepens. "You asked Haggard about me."

"Barely. It was a half question at best."

His eyes search mine. "How does it feel like I know so much about you, yet there's so much more to learn?"

"Same. And it freaks me out so maybe we don't talk too much about that right now."

"Excellent." He sweeps his hand under my hair and gathers it around his loose fist. "We were getting off the topic of complete nakedness anyway. And reading to me, of course."

"Not reading."

"It's just one reading, Charlie," he says. "That's what we do, right? One daring thing at a time."

"It's so much more than a reading."

He strokes the line of my jaw with his knuckle, the fire lighting his eyes as they search me, see me. I tighten my legs around the spill of Logan below me as he rests his head upon the cradle of his hands. And as vulnerable as the idea of him being an audience to my words makes me, I'm also safe. In my cottage, next to a fire, with a person I trust. Who isn't going anywhere. Something about our staggered path to arrive at this moment feels right. So filled with trust there isn't room for doubt.

I pull my laptop toward me and open the document.

"Love & Lobsters," I begin, my screen my only armor. By the flicker of firelight, I read to Logan.

"For a female lobster to mate, she must make herself vulnerable, slipping her defensive exterior and exposing her inner softness. In this state of pre-mating, she is pliable, exposed, defenseless. Preparing. The male lobster senses the female is vulnerable and he is tender with her. The water in the surrounding ocean swirls with her pheromones and he approaches gently, his antennules sniffing at her as he draws close, announcing his intent, preparing himself and his mate as if asking for consent, participation, permission. He lowers his claws, those hard defensive parts of him that allow him to brave the wild. He gives over to the female's scent, her exposed body.

"With claws closed and lowered, he will circle her, slowly, repeatedly, stroking her tender, delicate flesh with the compassionate caress of his large antennae. He is patient and committed in his dance of courtship, seducing her nakedness until the female rises for him, using all her spent strength to thrust her body into a standing posture, signaling to her mate that her body is ready—that her new shell has hardened just enough to give her agency and enough stamina to be a partner in the mating process.

"The male knows this signal and responds to her movement by traveling nearer to her, securing his large claws to the sea bottom for support so that his small legs are free to rotate her body into an embrace, turning her onto her back so they lay face-to-face with one another, the male on top, the female fully underneath his weight, his control, his kindness. The lobsters remain connected as they fan their swimmerets along their partner's bodies, stroking each other in anticipation as they explore, excite, tantalize one other while engaging in bottomless trust. After a long time, the male thrusts against the female before he dismounts, and the female rallies enough strength in her tail to reset herself, regaining the ability to walk to a protected nook to rest.

"After coitus, the male also seeks respite. The male and female lobsters do this separately, in opposite corners of the den where the female will remain until she and her shell are strong enough to return to the open ocean with her eggs and armor and dignity firmly intact. The male will move on to another female to repeat the tender process, neither of them willing to commit to coupling beyond sex.

"To my knowledge, no one has seen lobsters mate in the open ocean. There is speculation about the sexy time of lobsters in the wild because of scientific observation and study, where humans try to simulate the environment that would stimulate lobsters. But there is still so much we don't know. Except for one thing.

"Lobsters take their time with one another and they are careful, giving partners. They respond to tenderness with tenderness. The male explores the female's body as he stimulates her, the pre-mating ritual of lobster foreplay lasting far longer than actual mating. For a species built for fighting, their time spent mating is a slow, elaborate, exotic dance. Lobsters are unhurried when intimate, carefully signaling their desires, their needs, and their readiness.

"Our human world can learn a lot from lobster courtship behaviors. They teach us that risking our most vulnerable self to another person isn't a risk at all if both participants risk their vulnerability.

"When all things are equal, mating can occur in a bed of shared commitment, a sea of trust."

I look to Logan, our eyes locking. "The end," I say.

"Not the end," he tells me. "Not even close." He grabs hold of my bottom, raising himself as a seat under my weight. "You, Charlie, are infinite. Now, would it be okay if I stopped trying to control myself around you?"

"Yes."

He pulls me fully on top of him before rolling me to my back until I'm quivering and vulnerable as he takes his time with me, arousing me, stimulating me, making me rise to meet him and his tenderness. Again. And again.

And again.

32

The Commercialization

Logan is stoking embers in the morning fireplace, and when he sees me stir, he dives under the covers to meet my body that's still thrumming from his touch. He kisses me softly on the forehead, the movements of a kind, reliable, mysterious nice boy. He brushes hair from my face and I climb on top of him, his hands steadying me as my hips link with his. My rocking motion is slow to begin, tentative, as if our body parts are meeting for the first time. We don't break eye contact. The fire pops next to us as my rhythm quickens. I drop my hands to his chest and become a wave breaking over him, crashing back and forth, a rushing, churning tide. His palms push at my shoulders, leaving my hips weightless, suspended, all of me floating on top of him as I reach the edge of him, the rhythm of us swirling together until we crash into the pool of our mutual satisfaction.

We both take time to catch our breath, luxuriate in the power of our own bodies and the symphony of us together.

"I could get used to this," Logan says before dashing to the kitchen, returning quickly with a plate-sized omelet, the shredded cheese melted into rigid curls on top. "I kept the lid on the pan. I think it's still warm." We eat with our fingers. Pieces of egg and broccoli and scallion and tomato shoveled to our mouths to regain our strength, fuel our growth. We shower together as if by habit, the two of us sharing water and exchanging pleasure.

When we dry off, I extend my arm rigid. "This is three feet," I tell him. "That's the distance you need to stay away from me today if there's any possibility of me being productive."

"I don't like it." He grabs my arm, twists me to him in the sweep of a dance twirl before kissing me on the tip of my nose. "But I'll obey."

"My brain and body thank you."

When the house phone rings, I run to meet it, my hair still dripping. "Hello?"

"Get your shit together, Pinkham," Maia says. "You're late for festivus day."

"I'm on it. Out the door in five."

"Make it three. And wear that outfit you were sporting last night. I'll explain later."

"It's…a little wrinkled."

She laughs. "Of course it is. Well, get it ironed and get over here. Wait! When I say ironed, I mean smooth the velvet flat with your hands and sit on it strategically. Don't put actual heat on it."

"You're describing the only kind of ironing I know."

"Have you even looked beyond your shack o' sin yet this morning? Check out the common when you manage to climb off Three."

I smile, but don't correct her. Because Logan is Logan. Not Three. Not Pufferman. Just all mine.

"Stuck-up Camden woke up jealous of Christmas Cove today, girl. See for yourself."

Maia hangs up and I drift to the kitchen window that's etched in frost at the edges as if framing my view of the common that's already filling with dozens of people. Trees are lit, tables readied with food and drink. A line of pedestrians stream down the tree-lined road, candy cane signs welcoming people to Christmas Cove.

Logan joins me at the window, his steady chest behind me, his hands resting at my hips. We watch a six-masted schooner arrive from the river, its poles decorated with lights and strung with evergreen garland. A giant wreath drapes the captain's wheel.

"That's the Dodge family," I tell him. "Their people have been on this peninsula for ten generations, like mine."

These neighbors are showing up because showing up is what's important, and because Maine is a place where the past matters as much as our todays and tomorrows.

"Lots of families made their living building ships near here. Schooners, too. And barks, clippers, and steamers—all bound for Australia, California's gold rush, and trade in India and the Mediterranean."

"I love how you talk about this place like I'm from away."

"You are. If your family hasn't been in Maine for at least four generations, you're from away."

"Noted. Also, I'm taking you to Australia. Not on a schooner, but we're going."

I turn to Logan and his arms drape over my shoulders in a half hug that feels like full trust. "Okay."

"Okay?" His brow furrows. "Just like that? You're not worried about the crocodiles or the cone snails or deadly jellyfish?"

"Nope." I kiss the inner bend of his elbow. "You said traveling is only good when there's a place to return home to and I have that. So, yes. Australia. And all the unique deadly creatures protecting it. But before that, I'll need a passport. And before that, I need to get to the common."

"Then get your boogie on, Bluebug." He slaps at my bottom and we dress to join Maia collecting tickets, kids already darting in and out of the Caribbean-bright fishing huts, the luge line backing up as riders check their height and the fit of the safety gear at the start of the run, no different than a real-life theme park. And then there's the Maine craft breweries station. Frozen Whoopie Pie Toss. Santa arriving via helicopter. The chowdah cook-off. The polar plunge. Face painting and a bouncy house because sometimes basic is fabulous.

"I need Charlie to officiate some weddings," Maia tells Logan when we meet up, like I'm not standing right next to her, even as I have no idea what she's talking about. "First one's at ten o'clock."

"Got it," Logan says, as if my structured time is no surprise to him. "And you want me shuttling people back and forth to Cove Light still?"

"For sure. How many people does the safari mobile have room for?"

"I've got seating and seatbelts for five. Hannah texted that she's ready to receive tour groups. And the plan is for me and Hermon to deliver the baked lobster entrees starting at noon so she can serve them to anyone who bought the extended dining package."

My head spins at the details that got sorted while I wasn't looking.

"Perfect." Maia leads me away and Logan throws up his hands in mock defeat, a beautiful smile blooming on his face. So beautiful that I only see him for him in this moment. No calendar pose. No costume. I see Logan showing up. Standing in front of the harbor, Cove Light behind him, the beam of his artfully uneven smile trained on me.

"Charlie," Maia says, after she's dragged me to the ceremony circle. She motions me close to a couple I don't recognize. "This is Gillian Borling and her fiancé Stephanie Hill, here from Ohio. They would like the honor of being the first couple married by our local legend, the female lobsterman who found her happily ever after this season. Stephanie, Gillian, this is Charlotte. Charlie to her friends."

"Jill," the woman corrects, inviting informality. "It is such an honor to meet you. I'm fangirling a bit, if I'm honest. Your column was everything to us."

Stephanie nods, the two of them blushing.

It's only now I realize Jill's dressed in head-to-toe white and Stephanie's wearing a purple plaid suit that compliments the shit out of her and her fiery red hair.

I throw Maia a side-eye she ignores.

"We'd already planned to be married on the Solstice, but we couldn't resist the chance to get hitched in Christmas Cove after reading your posts," Stephanie says, gazing at her fiancé. "It was too romantic to pass up. Plus, she's all caviar and I've dedicated my life to curmudgeonry so there's that."

I laugh my ridiculous seal bark laugh because I like these people. These brides to be. These strangers who have come to support my people because we are all connected in the end.

"We're thrilled to have you," Maia says. She pulls me aside in a huddle. "The circle is exactly as it was last night." She doesn't make room for questions. "Haggard got the fires burning."

As if on command, Haggard, Mem, and Kermit arrive as witnesses, Mem giving my elbow a sturdy hug with her strong hands, her smile restful and full.

Maia explains the cardinal directions of the fire settings, how the couples will face the officiant at true north, just as she does with all seven ceremonies I perform, each engaged pair arriving with their story. How they fell in love. How they found and followed Maia's blog and my column all the way to today, each of them in love with one another and the mysticism Maine stirs within them.

And I find that love is everywhere.

Literally surrounding me.

Some couples are here because of my love: my fierce love for my ride-or-die, my undying love for my grandmother, and the unexpected love that allowed me to lower my defenses.

The couples I marry bring their love to the festival and thank me for the ways my growing love allowed them to trust deeper, communicate better. Throughout the day, there are face pee jokes and compliments. Promises and futures forged. Logan ferries guests in repeated trips around the bend of the harbor, his truck old and new all at once, electrically silent in its expeditions, the addition of him to our peninsula widening our reach, growing our capacity. No different than love itself.

I learn so much from the people I meet and the love they share, and I think this is the point, *this* is why we risk everything. Because we are all only stories in the end, and all our origins and characters and plot twists are forged of love.

33

The Christmas

The rush and intoxication and hard work of three straight days of hosting festivities and marriages, food and fun, have us exhausted by Christmas Eve when Logan and I crash in front of the fireplace, eating the last of our chowder, my lids heavy, my muscles spent.

"Do you have energy for a walk?" he asks. "Just a quick sprint to town?"

"I do not. I need bed and I need it now."

"What if I said I wanted to give you an early Christmas present?"

"I'll grab my coat."

His arm drapes across my shoulders on our walk, the night still with snowfall, the schooner gone from the harbor now, the festival lights off, Curmudgeons and Caviar a success in more ways than we could have imagined. The Maine's Midcoast Lobstermen's Association forges onward with a healthy new fund to support families in times of need. Haggard has already gathered a committee to invest the proceeds and another committee to plan for next year's festival. I've made my own plan for paying down Mem's medical debt, which involves the same simple philosophy Logan and I engage when things feel overwhelming: baby steps.

As we walk, I'm unsure how to tell Logan I didn't get him anything for Christmas, but I'm certain I'll tell him. Between us there are no more unasked questions. No more thoughts unshared. No more assumptions. No more getting it wrong.

"So, how great is this gift you got me?" I ask as we approach the common. "Because I didn't get you anything and if your present is dinner for two at Earl's, I'll only feel slightly bad, but if it's something bigger, my shame will increase incrementally and in proportion to the size of the gift."

"It's not the size of the gift that matters, Charlie."

I laugh. Pervy Maia in my ear.

He slows, setting his hands to my waist just at the lip of the common, the toes of our boots practically dipping into the harbor where the near full moon watches its full reflection.

"I wrote something. And I should preface this by saying I've never written anything for anyone before unless you count engineering manuals, but this piece of original writing falls into a category all its own. I hope you agree. It's called Love & Lobsters & Lighthouses."

"What?" I laugh.

He holds up his hand. "There will be allotted time for questions and laughter at the end."

I motion a zipper across my lips, but can't contain my smile.

"It's tough being a lobster eye." He reads from a small notebook he frees from his jacket pocket and I am drunk on this man. "See, the American Lobster has large claws, bright shells, and interesting mating behaviors that historically steal the limelight when humans observe lobsters and generally comment on lobster behavior. But a lobster's eye is fascinating. I think it deserves more of our attention. For one, a lobster's eye is made up of thousands of squares that operate like many tiny eyes. This, you may deduce, is in stark contrast to a human's neatly rounded eye.

"The lobster's eye reflects light, unlike the human eye that refracts light.

"What does this mean for a lobster?

"Well, for one, she can't see images the way humans do. She will rely on light and its reflection to judge her surroundings. She sees an image, even if she can't see it clearly. Her eye will reflect light so that all of the beams of her eye are replicated onto a particular focal point.

"She can detect motion in dim light.

"She is likely blind in bright light.

"The unique make-up of the lobster eye has been studied for decades by researchers and even helped in the development of x-ray scanners. This is cool if you're a nerd like me, but it's also important for non-nerds and anyone needing an x-ray. Because light is spectacular and surprising and necessary." He looks at me now, our eyes connecting.

"Lately I've been comparing the way a lobster's eye reflects light with the way a lighthouse's Fresnel lens is able to generate light using glass prisms. The lobster has nearly 10,000 squares within its eye so it can shift light in all directions, make sense of it, focus it. The Fresnel lens within a lighthouse was designed to change the direction light travels so all the light exits the lens in the same direction. The prisms in the lens accomplish this marvel by refracting light and reflecting it as well.

"Think human eye meets lobster eye.

"And what is the result?

"When you train all your light on one person, we call it love. When the person you love fixes all their light on you, you feel light. Love is light."

He clears his throat. "Now for the tricky bit." He shines his phone flashlight to the sea once. Then twice. Then a third time, as if Maia is across the harbor, receiving my Morse code.

We wait for a beat. Then another.

Logan's feet shift, his breath stuttering. I grab hold of his arm, ready to forgive him for whatever bit of technology has failed him because he is my gift and I don't need anything more than him. Here on the peninsula. Next to me in this moment.

I take a deep breath in the dark and move closer to Logan just as the high, searching beacon in the lighthouse beams on, training its reaching stretch of light out to the sea and the horizon and the deep beyond.

"Oh my god," I cry, the sight of the beacon pushing me back a step, then two, Logan there to steady me, my words a mix of shock and fullness and something I've never felt, a satisfaction I can't name.

Logan takes my hand but doesn't ask me to take my attention from the light.

Outdoor floodlights begin to flick on around people's homes, the rustling of neighbors on the peninsula noticing Cove Light's reanimated rays—some for the first time, some remembering its power and purpose from their youth. Before the muffled movements become decodable sounds, Logan links his fingers with mine.

Together, we stare at the beacon.

"You are light personified, Charlie Pinkham," he tells me. "People turn toward you, because you are the brave light that guides them home. It's what you do for me, Charlie. To me."

I'm stunned silent by this radiant beam that feels like something I've known my whole life even though I'm seeing it for the first time. I've missed this warning light while living in my safe harbor, but now the dark is transformed, all because of the light Logan brought with him to our peninsula, to me.

And this light, this addition, this new thing, feels like returning home.

As if I've belonged here always.

In awe of this light and the person beside me.

THE END.

Except not really...

Author's Note

The place we now call Maine is home to the sovereign people of the Wabanaki Confederacy: the Penobscot, Passamaquoddy, Maliseet, and Mi'kmaq peoples. This novel was created on—and inspired by— the unceded land and water of the Wabanaki people, the original stewards of the Wabanakik. Stories, like conversations, often serve as entry points for healing. To participate in this communal process, please visit Wabanaki REACH at mainewabanakireach.org.

This novel contains a fictionalized version of a fishermen's collective. In reality, the Maine Coast Fishermen's Association *"works to enhance the sustainability of Maine's fisheries by advocating for the needs of community-based fishermen and the environmental restoration of the Gulf of Maine."* Their tireless advocacy, research, and grit helps sustain vital nutrition and industry in Maine. Their timely initiatives protect working waterfront against the perils of gentrification, and the *Fishermen Feeding Mainers Program* provides seafood and dignity to hungry neighbors. The Maine way of life isn't an accident; it's a commitment. And it takes a village.

On-demand lobster traps are a new and controversial technology that comes with a hefty price tag for Maine lobstermen. I'm not a lobsterman, nor do I come from a fishing family. I've spent a lifetime inspired by New England's coastal waters and the brave women and men who care for the sea, its wellness, and its future—always looking for ways to maintain balance for family, industry, and nature. It's an honor to live at the periphery of their work and legacy. All errors depicting this way of life are entirely my own.

Maine is home to 65 lighthouses and 3,478 miles of tide coastline. We have quaint villages. Colorful buoys. Whoopie pies. Lobsters. Lakes. Blueberries and foliage. But our greatest resource is our people. Like Robert Ball, Round Pond's harbormaster for 31 years, who took a break from lobstering to answer my questions, share his honest laughter, and remind me that integrity and generosity are the richest ingredients in Maine's recipe for living *The Way Life Should Be.*

Also, pumpkin regattas. They're a thing: mainepumpkinfest.com

Also a thing? Maine lobstermen who give lobsters snacks: following Jacob Knowles' Insta or TikTok will be your next favorite everything.

Acknowledgements

It's impossible to list everyone who's supported this creative effort—an endeavor I always find infinitely harder than writing an actual book. My mom, of course. I mean, she's my mom. And for my dad—I miss your quick wit, sharp intelligence, and fierce pride every.single.day.

There's no THANK YOU big enough for my writer friends who show up for me. My lifelong friends who put up with me. My students who inspire me. My children and bonus children who challenge me.

This book wouldn't have been born if it weren't for a random mention of cannibalism in a chill text from a real-life Maia (Zewert). I'd never have survived edits if not for Alicia Johnson from the other Portland. Love and art wouldn't sit at the center of my universe without wild, beautiful hearts like the one found in Tilly Freeman. I'd have stopped storytelling long ago if it weren't for my agent and friend, Becca Podos. I could live on a steady diet of Jess Bahowick's gifs, and remain grateful to women like Lauren Cucci who are sunshine personified.

Special thanks to early readers and champions: Mom, Amber Smith, Elizabeth Ames, Kathleen Glasgow, Elisabeth McKetta, Deidre Mask, Keith Warren. And Kate Borsig, Lauren Palmer and Allyson Goodwin and the Boothbay book club that feeds my appetite for good book talk and good people. For Maine—I'm unsure what I did to deserve you. For Tivnan, because. To Phoebe Buffay for forever linking love and lobsters. For Sheila and Dave Hatch—for giving me a place to write, and a place to repair. Endless thanks to the women and men who fish the sea and gifted me their patience and knowledge.

Thank you to booksellers and librarians who maintain the river of storytelling for us all. And to everyone who has helped another person heal, grow, grieve, and dream—all by sharing a story. Thank you to each and every person who actively cultivates kindness…and love.

When I finished my first draft, a friend pointed out the resemblance between Logan and my husband. I'd missed it, but of course I'd base a love story around the kind, patient human who is still my 1 in 100 million. Thank you for thirty years. You are my true north, the only person I'd want to hike beside in this world.

To all humans—young and old—who do brave things. Thank you.

Love &
Lighthouses

Arriving 2025!